JACK AND THE GIANT KILLER

A DETECTIVE JACK STRATTON NOVEL

CHRISTOPHER GREYSON

GREYSON MEDIA

Novels featuring Jack Stratton in order:

AND THEN SHE WAS GONE
GIRL JACKED
JACK KNIFED
JACKS ARE WILD
JACK AND THE GIANT KILLER
DATA JACK
JACK OF HEARTS
JACK FROST

Also by Christopher Greyson:

PURE OF HEART

THE GIRL WHO LIVED

JACK AND THE GIANT KILLER
Copyright © Greyson Media October 3, 2014

Find out more about the author and upcoming books online at www.ChristopherGreyson.com.

ISBN: 1-68399-050-1
ISBN-13: 978-1-68399-050-5

CONTENTS

Chapter 1 - Lady 1
Chapter 2 - Delivery 5
Chapter 3 - Surprise 8
Chapter 4 - It's Awake 13
Chapter 5 - She's a Queen 16
Chapter 6 - Almost Doesn't Count 21
Chapter 7 - Replacement 27
Chapter 8 - I Wish I Knew Who 32
Chapter 9 - It's the Principle 33
Chapter 10 - The Snow Globe 37
Chapter 11 - Titus 42
Chapter 12 - I'm Going to Bring an Army 47
Chapter 13 - I Need a Favor 53
Chapter 14 - Nosykins 57
Chapter 15 - A Mini-Volcano 63
Chapter 16 - Three Points 69
Chapter 17 - Holly Road 74
Chapter 18 - A Walking Wrecking Ball 79
Chapter 19 - I Have a Plan for That 81
Chapter 20 - Mouthwash 83
Chapter 21 - The Poet 88
Chapter 22 - Grease-E 92
Chapter 23 - Little Z 97
Chapter 24 - Life's Not Fair 102
Chapter 25 - Welcome to Darrington 107
Chapter 26 - A KAWAH Bag 112
Chapter 27 - It's Evil 115
Chapter 28 - They're Not Safe 118
Chapter 29 - Learn Fast 121
Chapter 30 - As Seen on TV 125
Chapter 31 - Skunk Stink 128
Chapter 32 - Under the Bus 132
Chapter 33 - You Sound Like My Wife 136
Chapter 34 - Bill's Burger Hut 138
Chapter 35 - They Should Be Afraid 143
Chapter 36 - That's Big 146
Chapter 37 - Night Terrors 149
Chapter 38 - Your Car's Moving 152
Chapter 39 - Keep Me on Speed Dial 156
Chapter 40 - Don't Do It 160
Chapter 41 - Something Worse 165
Chapter 42 - My Mom Told Me 167
Chapter 43 - Do You Think I'm Tall? 173
Chapter 44 - Trust Me, I Know 175
Chapter 45 - Bonded 179
Chapter 46 - I Want Them Unbribed 187

Chapter 47 - If She's Lady.. 190
Chapter 48 - I Never Promised.. 192
The Detective Jack Stratton Mystery-Thriller Series.................... 195
Acknowledgments 199
About the Author.. 200

1

LADY

Through the tall, thick bushes, she saw her favorite place up ahead—the dog park. She strained against the leash, but Daniel's strong arm restrained her. Lady wanted her freedom, and she loved to run around the old converted baseball field surrounded by a chain-link fence. When the town built the new high school, they changed the area into a place where dogs like her could run free.

As soon as they reached the gravel parking lot, Daniel bent low to unhook the snap on her collar. Lady raised her head and lifted her chin. Daniel was like her—a giant. He towered above other humans as she did among other dogs. He scratched behind her ears and put his hand on her collar.

As she sensed her approaching freedom, her paws raked the ground. She knew he didn't see the little terrier with the long-haired woman inside the park. If he saw her, he'd never let her off the leash.

Lady's whole body quivered as Daniel's large thumb fumbled with the latch. To her, the sound of the clasp as it disconnected was like the firing of a starter's pistol.

Click.

She bolted free. Her huge muscles pushed her paws into the ground, and she sprang over the tall fence.

Freedom.

She let out a happy roar, grateful to run. She'd been cooped up in a small apartment all day, and for a hundred-and-ten-pound dog, that was far too confining. Lady lowered her head and sped toward the opposite corner of the field. Her muscles stretched, flexed, and felt wonderful as the ground raced by underneath her.

As she sprinted along the edge of the field, she looked back. Daniel casually strolled in through the gate, but as soon as he saw the red-haired woman, he froze. The woman looked from Daniel to the enormous dog that was now charging toward her own little dog. She protectively scooped her dog up into her arms.

Daniel came running over. He shouted at Lady, "Lady, stop!"

Darn. Always obedient, Lady skidded to a halt.

Daniel caught up to her, leaned down, and patted her head. Lady pressed against his massive legs and wagged her tail.

"She's a big baby," Daniel tried to reassure the woman.

"She's beautiful." The woman smiled with some trepidation as she held her own squirming animal tighter in her arms. "How old is she?"

"Two. She's a king shepherd."

"She certainly is. And look, she even has a spot on her chest that looks like a shield."

Lady's chest swelled at the compliment.

Daniel lowered his head. He was shy; Lady rarely saw him talk to other people.

The woman tilted her head and smiled at him.

His head rose. "What kind of dog is yours?"

"A terrier. Her name is Juliet."

"I love Shakespeare." Daniel's huge hand reached out and patted the little dog. It yapped and wiggled in response.

"I'm Lisa."

"Daniel."

"I've seen you two on the walking path before," she said. "Do you come here often?"

He nodded. "Mostly after work."

"I usually come in the afternoon. I work the night shift at the hospital, but today's my day off."

"That's great." Daniel rubbed the back of his neck. "I mean… great you have the night off."

Lisa glanced at her watch and frowned. "I'd love to talk more, but I have to get going. I'm meeting a friend for dinner."

Daniel's eyes searched her face. "A friend?"

"Girlfriend," she added quickly, with a little smile. "It was nice meeting you. Perhaps we'll see you here… tomorrow?"

Daniel started to speak, but instead just nodded.

Lisa waved as she walked through the gate and to her car.

As Daniel waved back, Lady bolted across the field. She charged around the outfield with delight. The wind against her face made her eyes water, but she pushed herself even harder. As she ran, she watched Lisa's car pull onto the deserted side street and then disappear around the corner. The ground became a blur. She whizzed by Daniel, dug down even deeper, and picked up more speed.

Run. Run faster.

Daniel clapped and cheered for her. She gulped in huge breaths and felt power course through her. The grass flicked up in the air as her paws sank into the turf and ripped out little tufts.

She headed back toward Daniel when she saw him pull the ball out of his pocket. She pranced sideways, fighting her momentum to change direction.

"You want it, girl?" Daniel drew back his arm and heaved the ball to the far side of the field.

She flew straight for it. The ball bounced high and to the left. Her weight shifted, and so did her trajectory. The ball bounced again, and she bounded forward and caught it in her jaws.

"Good job, Lady."

As she pranced back, she saw a vehicle stop at the end of the parking lot, behind the bushes. Its rear lights flashed.

"Lady, come," Daniel called, and she obeyed.

She moved to his side, and he clicked the leash onto her thick collar.

"I think they're having car trouble." Daniel rubbed her head. "Let me talk to them, then we'll come right back and play ball."

They went out the gate and walked along the fence toward the vehicle. As they got closer, Daniel stopped and knelt down. He looked into Lady's eyes and smiled. "Just wait here a second, girl. We don't want to scare them." He scratched behind her ears with both hands, and she licked his face. Laughing, he stood up and hooked the leash over the fence post.

Lady sat down and watched him walk over to the vehicle. He disappeared from view as he went around the bushes. She heard Daniel say hello, but the driver's voice was too quiet to make out the words.

And the longer Daniel spoke with the driver, the more Lady didn't like it. She sensed something was wrong. She let out a loud whine.

"It's okay, Lady," Daniel called out. "I'll be right back."

She jerked her head, and the leash tightened on the fence.

After another minute, she heard a commotion, followed by a loud thud. Lady jumped to her feet. The lights on the vehicle shook.

She barked. *Daniel?*

He didn't answer.

She barked again, even louder. Nothing.

Lady raised her chin and sniffed. A new scent hung in the air—blood.

She charged forward. The leash strained around her neck and snapped her back close to the fence. She growled, barked, and then lunged forward again. The entire fence shook, but it held her in place.

She heard someone step out onto the gravel, and she saw shoes, but they weren't Daniel's. She sniffed, but she couldn't pick up the person's scent—the air was heavy with the odor of blood now and that was all she could smell.

Lady roared. *Daniel?* She was worried someone was hurting her friend. She burst forward again, and the collar bit into her throat. Her front claws raked the gravel as she strained against the leash.

The driver walked toward her. Lady barked as the footsteps approached.

Suddenly, headlights from another car appeared at the end of the road. The feet stopped and turned in that direction. Lady gulped in a huge breath and barked louder than ever before. The driver hurried back to the vehicle. She saw the feet disappear inside, followed by the sound of the vehicle's door shutting.

Over and over again, Lady barked. The headlights from the other car disappeared as it turned down a side street.

As the driver's vehicle started, Lady scanned the area, desperately seeking any sign of Daniel, but there was none.

She shot forward with all her strength. The leash went taut. Her body twisted in the air, and she crashed onto the gravel, landing on her side. She whimpered in pain as the rocks dug through her thick fur and cut her.

The vehicle drove away.

Daniel.

Lady scrambled to her feet and then backed up against the fence. She ignored the taste of blood in her mouth and took a deep breath. She took one long stride, and she jumped. Her eyes watered and she gagged. The collar moved down her throat toward her broad chest. Leather stretched. The fence bent forward—and the clasp on the leash broke.

The vehicle picked up speed.

Blood surged into Lady's muscles, and her sharp canine teeth flashed as the need to protect her owner drove her forward. The trees next to the road flew by as she lowered her head and concentrated on one thing—speed. With each stride, dirt flew behind her as she charged along the road.

The vehicle reached the end of the street and stopped. Finding new hope, Lady laid her ears flat back against her head and dug in harder. Just as she narrowed the gap, the vehicle moved forward and took a right onto the main road.

Lady's weight shifted, and she cut into the woods to try to cut off the fleeing vehicle. Branches scraped at her face as she hurtled through the underbrush. She bounded over a log. The lights from the vehicle shone through the trees.

I can make it.

A briar patch stood in her way, but she didn't slow. The thorns tore at her flesh and she ignored the pain. She burst free onto the road just behind the vehicle. She let out a roar that echoed across the road.

The vehicle sped up.

Lady ran as fast as she could, but it wasn't fast enough to catch the car on the open road. The taillights became fainter as the vehicle moved ahead into the darkness. Spit and foam covered her mouth, but she continued to run. It wasn't until the lights disappeared completely from sight that she stopped and sniffed the air.

Nothing.

A car blew its horn. It narrowly missed her as it whizzed by. Lady shook. She took two steps forward and staggered sideways. *Daniel.* She gulped for air, her throat burning. On trembling legs, she stumbled over to the side of the road and collapsed in the grass.

2

DELIVERY

WHERE ARE YOU? Replacement texted.

Jack read it and cringed. He debated what to say, then replied: LOOKING FOR A JOB.

DO YOU NEED HELP?

NO THANKS.

She texted back: LET ME KNOW BEFORE YOU HEAD HOME. I HAVE A SURPRISE FOR YOU.

He tossed the phone down on the passenger seat of the Charger, picked up the piece of paper, and checked the number again: 76 Winslow. One look at the neglected duplex with five cars haphazardly parked outside caused Jack's shoulders to stiffen.

I never thought I'd end up doing this for a living.

He got out of the car and walked around to the trunk. The shadows lengthened as the sun started to set. As he scanned up and down the streets of the rundown neighborhood, he instinctively straightened. A group of men stood on the porch of the house next door, watching him.

Even the police travel in pairs in this neighborhood. I look like an easy mark.

Jack opened the trunk and took out three pizza boxes. Out of the corner of his eye, he saw the men return to talking among themselves. He made his way up the broken concrete walkway, shifted the boxes to his left hand, and knocked on the door.

"Hold on a minute," a woman's shrill voice called out from inside. The dark-green door creaked open, and a thirty-something-year-old woman stared at him. She was dressed in a loose brown blouse and six-inch heels, and her blue jeans were so painted on Jack was tempted to look for brushstrokes. She leaned her dyed blond hair against the doorjamb and looked Jack up and down. A lusty smile spread across her face. "Please tell me you're a stripper-gram."

Jack felt the color rise to his cheeks. After having been dismissed from the Darrington police force, his current struggle to pay the bills made that idea tempt him more than he cared to admit. He pulled the Pisa Pizza red-and-black baseball cap down further over his thick dark-brown hair and tried to push the thought of how far he'd fallen out of his head.

"I have three specials for you." At six foot one, handsome, fit, toned, and dressed in a black shirt with a giant pizza slice on the back, Jack could've been the pizza delivery poster boy. He handed the woman the boxes, and her smile widened as she opened the door wider.

Jack scanned the living room. *Two guys on the couch watching TV. Blondie here, but no Ramon.*

"Who's at the door?" someone called from down the hallway.

"It's the pizza man," Blondie barked back.

"I have a cheese, a pepperoni, and," Jack opened the box to give her a good look, "a bacon and egg pizza."

"It's your favorite," Blondie called over her shoulder. She took the boxes and set them on a table beside the door.

"I didn't order any pizza." A pudgy guy in a T-shirt and jeans stomped down the hallway. Jack recognized him right away from the wanted poster in his pocket—Ramon Jenkins.

"This isn't 67 Winslow?" Jack looked down at the fake pizza order in his hand.

"No, jackass." Ramon laughed. "This is 76."

"Crud. My mistake." Jack shrugged as he reached behind his back and grabbed his handcuffs.

"Thanks for the pizza," Ramon scoffed as he reached for a slice.

For Jack, everything slowed down. He lunged forward. One handcuff clicked on Ramon's outstretched right wrist. Jack pushed Ramon against the doorframe and then yanked backward and up on Ramon's arm. Ramon gasped. Jack pulled higher. Ramon's left arm involuntarily rose. Jack snagged it and snapped the cuff shut in one fluid motion.

Jack jammed Ramon's face against the wall, then turned to look at the two men on the couch who sat there, shocked.

"Titus sent me," he growled. The men froze. The name Titus affected people in this neighborhood that way. They knew if they ever wanted bail—never cross Titus.

"You can't just come in," Ramon whined.

"Yeah, I can. You skipped bond. Now shut up," Jack snarled. He jerked Ramon away from the wall and faced him out the door. "Walk," he ordered.

Jack kept an eye on the two guys and Blondie. None of them moved. He yanked the door closed behind him, then pushed Ramon down the walkway toward the car.

"Come on," Ramon begged. "I was gonna go talk to Titus after the game."

"Shut up." Jack kept an eye on the men next door. They walked to the edge of the porch as they watched him, but they didn't come down the steps.

Jack pushed Ramon against the Charger and patted him down. Finding nothing, he opened the back door. "Get in." He held on to Ramon's shirt collar as he sat him down in the back seat, then he hurried around the front and climbed into the driver's seat.

Jack dropped the Charger into drive and checked the rearview. The men had stayed on the porch, and no one had exited Ramon's house.

"Come on," Ramon pleaded. "Take me to Titus and I'll explain."

"Save it. You skipped court twice."

Ramon squirmed in the back seat. "How'd you find me?"

Jack wanted to brag and tell Ramon that his ex-girlfriend had let slip a trivial detail when he'd interviewed her—that Ramon loved bacon and egg pizza. Jack wanted to boast about getting the assistant manager at the Pisa Pizza to look up anyone around here who had ordered those weird toppings. But Jack kept his mouth shut. He wouldn't say anything that might let Ramon know who'd helped put him back in prison.

Charging me fifty bucks for the hat and shirt was a little steep, though.

"Where are you taking me?" Ramon asked.

"The Bay."

Ramon hung his head. No one wanted to go behind bars—but especially not to Long Bay.

Cool air rushed into the car as Jack put down the windows. He rolled his shoulders and checked the rearview mirror. *Don't let your guard down.*

As he turned onto the highway, Ramon called out, "Can you at least play some music?"

Jack settled back into the seat, and a wiseass grin crossed his face. "Sure."

He turned on the radio and selected song eleven. Johnny Cash's ballad "God's Gonna Cut You Down" echoed as the jet-black Charger flew down the road toward the jail.

3

SURPRISE

Jack walked through the door of the apartment. His side ached, and he wanted to take a shower to get rid of the smell of the jail that clung faintly to his clothes. Like a paperboy tossing newspapers, he flung the contents of his pockets onto the kitchen counter and hurried toward his bedroom door. As he started to turn the door handle, behind him the door to the apartment flew open.

"Hey, kid."

Replacement looked up, and a flash of surprise lit her face. "You're home."

"Yeah." He turned the knob.

"Jack, wait!" She rushed toward him, but he'd already started to open the bedroom door.

Fur and fangs flew as a snarling, barking beast leapt at his face. Jack jumped back and yanked the door shut so hard his hand slipped off the doorknob. He fell backward and landed hard on his butt.

"Jack."

Jack stared openmouthed at the closed door. The animal on the other side was howling and scratching at the wood.

"Oh, shoot." Replacement put her hands over her mouth.

Jack thrust out a hand. "What the hell is in my bedroom?"

Her shoulders scrunched up. "I did ask you to tell me before you came home."

"Wait. Me getting almost eaten right now is somehow *my* fault?"

"No. Not at all." Replacement shook her head and then stopped. "Well, kinda."

"It's *kinda* my fault for walking into my own apartment?"

"I told you I had a surprise." Replacement gave him a smile that showed all her teeth. "Surprise."

"Not funny. What's wrong with the monster trapped in my bedroom?"

"She's just scared."

"You call that scared?" Jack's lip curled. "What the hell is it?"

"She's a dog, silly." Replacement dropped a bag of dog food on the floor and helped Jack up.

"That's no dog—it's a horse with fangs." Jack grabbed her hand. "Why's it in my bedroom?"

"She's my new case." Replacement straightened up and put her shoulders back.

Jack shook his head as if he had water in his ears. "What?"

"She's lost."

"A lost dog?" Jack looked at the closed bedroom door. The animal continued to scratch on the other side. "Well, congratulations. You found it. Now take it back."

"She's not an it, she's a *her*. And I didn't find her." Her brunette ponytail bounced. "She's my client. I need to find her owner."

Jack's mouth opened and closed a few times before the words tumbled out. "Your client? I know you're still new to the whole private investigator thing, but I think your clients need to be human."

"Well, the dog's not *technically* my client. Mrs. Sawyer is."

"The sweet little old lady? Why'd she hire you?"

"The dog followed her cat home." Replacement picked up the dog food bag and walked into the kitchen.

"You mean the General?"

"Yeah." She hip-checked the giant dog food bag, trying to shove it into the small pantry cupboard. "The dog came into her yard, so she called the Darrington animal shelter." She glared down at the bag.

Jack shook his head and came over to help. With one easy shove, he pushed the bag in and then shut the pantry door. "And?"

"But then she asked them what would happen to the dog if they didn't find the owner. They said that after thirty days…" Replacement shuddered. "They'd put the dog to sleep. So Mrs. Sawyer hired me to find the dog's owner."

"Why isn't the dog staying with Mrs. Sawyer?"

"I guess the General and the dog weren't getting along."

"What about a kennel?"

"Well, you know, she's on a fixed income, so I thought the dog could stay here."

"No. No way. And why did you put the dog in *my* bedroom instead of yours, anyway?"

"I let her choose. She seemed to like it in there. I guess it's 'cause you smell so good." She blushed.

Jack just glared.

"Please, Jack? Mrs. Sawyer is so nice." Replacement rocked back on her heels. "She offered fifty dollars. I know it's not much, but—"

"Not much?" Jack looked up at the ceiling. "Do you have any idea how much it's going to cost you to board that horse? Or how much food it'll eat?"

"Yeah, dog food *is* pretty expensive." Replacement looked at the cupboard. "But I got a deal on that."

"I think that entire bag's going to be its breakfast."

Replacement grinned sheepishly. "Please? It'll only be a day or two, tops."

"Absolutely not. Look, I can't believe that Mrs. Stevens isn't knocking at the door with an eviction notice already."

Replacement pouted, and as her green eyes widened, Jack could feel his resolve starting to melt.

"If Mrs. Stevens says it's okay, can I keep her here for just a few days?" Replacement pleaded. "I'll keep her in my room from now on."

Jack rubbed the back of his neck. He knew the building had a strict no-pet policy. "If Mrs. Stevens allows it, you can keep it here."

Replacement's face lit up. "Sweet. She already said yes."

Jack's mouth fell open. "What? She never allows pets." Jack pointed an accusatory finger. "And you knew she'd said yes already. You tricked that out of me."

Replacement grinned and then hopped over to the bedroom door. "Baby?" Her voice rose higher than usual as she reached for the door handle.

"Don't open—"

She turned the handle.

The dog sprang out of the door and landed in front of Replacement. She bared her teeth and barked so loudly that Jack would have covered his ears if his hands weren't ready to try to fend off an attack.

Replacement grabbed the dog's huge collar with both hands and planted her feet. If the animal wasn't snarling at him, Jack would have laughed at the ridiculousness of this small woman trying to restrain such a powerful dog. She might as well have grabbed a truck by the bumper.

Jack had seen a lot of big German shepherds in the Army and on the police force, so he knew this dog had to be a mixed breed. A huge shepherd weighed around ninety pounds and stood two feet tall at the shoulders. This dog was twenty pounds heavier than that and at least six inches taller.

"Easy, Princess. Easy. Jack's our friend." Replacement spoke to it as if she were talking to a toddler.

"Princess?" Jack snapped, and the dog barked at him again.

"Shh, that's her name," Replacement scolded. "Use a soft baby voice."

"What?" Jack barked loudly.

So did the dog.

Jack took a step back.

"Talk to her like you're talking to a baby," Replacement cautioned.

Jack exhaled and spoke through gritted teeth. "Get the werewolf under control before I get my gun."

"Jack!" Replacement gasped.

The dog growled low and moved forward again.

"Princess, sit," Replacement commanded, and the dog obeyed. "Don't even joke like that."

"Seriously." Jack forced himself to keep his voice low and even. "Put it in your bedroom."

Replacement rubbed the dog's thick neck and kissed its head. "Come on, Cookie."

"Cookie?"

"Doesn't she look like a big cookie?" Replacement hugged the dog.

"I thought its name was Princess."

Replacement rolled her eyes as she walked over to her bedroom. "I don't know her real name. I'm seeing what works best. Right now I think she looks like a big chocolate chip cookie."

Jack angled his head and appraised the dog. Her fur was a mix of black and golden brown. Her nose and lips were a solid black. Her eyes were a deep honey brown. Her back was broad and muscular, and her full chest had a patch of golden brown in the shape of a shield.

"If you're looking for name suggestions, I'd go with something like Hellhound," Jack joked.

Replacement scowled.

"What kind of dog is it?" Jack asked.

She shrugged. "German shepherd?"

"No. It's way too big. It looks like a shepherd, but it's more like a sumo shepherd."

"Jack." Replacement put her hands over the dog's ears. "Don't call her fat."

"I didn't call her fat, but she's huge. Look at her. She's as big as you."

Replacement's eyes narrowed. "As big as me?"

Damn. "That's not what I meant. You're tiny." He waved his hands. "I mean the dog's not fat, just thick. Not that you're thick. It was a bad joke."

Replacement put her hand on her hip.

"Beep, beep… Do you hear that sound?" Jack put his hand to his ear. "That's me backing out of this conversation."

Replacement led the dog into her bedroom and shut the door.

Jack rubbed his temples. "How do I get myself into these situations? You bring the King Kong of dogs home and I end up in the doghouse?" he called out as he kicked off his shoes, reached up to the ceiling, and stretched out.

He spent a few minutes bending and twisting before Replacement's bedroom door opened and she zipped out. She hurried over and watched him with all the intensity of a scientist conducting an experiment.

"Take off your shirt," she ordered.

Jack groaned but obeyed. He inhaled as her fingers traced the outline of the scar on his side. "It looks great. It's faded a lot. Get on the floor."

Jack was used to this; after twelve weeks it had become their evening routine. He lay down on the circular carpet on his stomach and let his arms go loose at his sides.

"How's it feel inside?" she asked.

"Fine. You spoke to the doctor last week. He gave me a clean bill of health."

She straddled his thighs. "For light exercise. He was impressed with your progress but said the muscles and tissues will take months to fully recover. I wish you'd wait a little longer to find a job."

She'd go crazy if she knew I already took one as a bounty hunter. But what was I supposed to do? The hospital bills were piling up.

"I've been coding for a few websites," she continued, "and I've gotten a few PI gigs. Nothing big, but we have some money coming in."

Jack moaned as she rubbed his back. "We're doing great, kid. Besides, you know me— I'll go out of my mind if I just sit around."

She rubbed deeper, and Jack's back cracked. "Thank you for letting Cookie stay here."

He lay there and enjoyed the massage. "I just thought of something. Don't some dogs have those chips now?"

"Oh, yeah. I read about them once." Her hands traveled up to his shoulders. "It holds all the dog's and owner's information."

"We'll take it over to the animal shelter tomorrow. If she has one, they should have a way to read it or something."

"Another case solved." Replacement put her hands over her head.

Jack laughed, and Replacement slid off his back and sat on the floor. Jack rolled over and sat up so they faced each other.

"We should celebrate," Jack said.

She smiled. "How?"

"I was wondering if you wanted to go out to dinner tomorrow night?"

Replacement's eyes lit up. "Really?"

"I can make reservations at Antonelli's."

Replacement wiggled in place and squealed. "I love Italian."

Jack exhaled and stretched his back. His side throbbed, but he ignored it. He looked into her large green eyes, and the corner of his mouth ticked up. *She's beautiful.* Jack's eyes traveled over her petite, five-foot-four frame. She'd been doing all the physical therapy along with him, so she was in incredible shape. His eyes drifted back up to hers. He grinned, but when he tried to press his lips back together, they quickly parted, and he found himself smiling once more.

"What?" Replacement's eyes darted away before returning to his.

"I'm feeling almost a hundred percent. And you wanted to wait until I was better before our relationship... progressed."

Replacement's broad grin faded into a shy smile. Her chin dipped down and she nodded.

Jack leaned in and tilted his head. "Thank you for taking care of me," he whispered before kissing her softly.

Their lips pressed together. Her lips were soft, warm, wet. He inhaled her scent, and his chest swelled. Her hand slid up his arm.

Replacement purred, and her little kisses intensified. Their heads shifted sides, and as they rubbed noses, she smiled. His hands traveled to her waist. His fingers caressed her sides, and she leaned closer.

Her tongue darted in and then out of his mouth, and his chased after it. He pulled her close, and her hands slid through his thick hair. She leaned back, panting.

"Slow," she said softly as her hands pressed against his chest and she breathed deeply.

"Sure." Jack smiled crookedly.

She bit her bottom lip, and Jack leaned forward. "Do you—" The dog barked and scratched at the door.

Damn.

Replacement hopped up so fast that she was already backing away for the bedroom before Jack could stop her.

"I'd better..." She stopped and looked him up and down. "... get in there and calm down." She flushed. "Calm Cookie down." She giggled.

When she opened the door, the dog stood there with Replacement's Raggedy Ann doll in her mouth. Jack expected Replacement to get upset, but she switched to her baby talk voice. "You want a dolly? You can have it. There's a good girl."

"You're just going to give your doll to the beast? I thought that was your doll when you were little or something."

Replacement shook her head. "No. I saw it at the Salvation Army and thought it looked retro. Besides, she likes it." She smiled back at him. "'Night."

Before Jack could protest, Replacement zipped into the room and closed the door. He rubbed his face and felt his day-old stubble.

I should've shaved.

4

IT'S AWAKE

Jack woke up early and stumbled for the kitchen and a cup of coffee. Rubbing his eyes, he took down his favorite coffee mug and Replacement's flowered cup. While he made the coffee, he heard the click of thick nails on wood.

It's awake.

Jack leaned over the kitchen counter and watched as the enormous dog trotted out of Replacement's bedroom. The dog turned to face him. Her ears lay back on her head and her eyes narrowed. She carried something between her massive jaws that dripped with saliva, but Jack couldn't make out what it was.

The dog seemed to relax, and then her ears went back up and she opened her mouth. The object tumbled out and landed on the floor with a wet smack. Jack examined the pile of cloth and rubber and realized it was one of his sneakers.

The dog's tongue rolled from her mouth, and she shook her head.

"Seriously?"

She turned and trotted back into Replacement's bedroom.

"Get back here." Jack rushed after her but stopped in the doorway when the dog barked.

Replacement sat up in her bed, trying to cover her ears while she pulled the blanket around herself. "Cookie, quiet. What's going on?"

"That mutant mutt ate my sneaker."

Replacement slipped out of bed. The dog pressed against her and nearly knocked her back onto the mattress. "Shh. It's okay, Cookie. Stop yelling, Jack. You're upsetting her."

"I'm upsetting *her*?"

"You have another pair." Replacement rubbed her eyes with the palms of her hands. "She probably smelled something on them."

"Yeah—my scent. That thing hates me." The dog growled. "See?" Jack thrust both hands toward the dog.

"You're freaking her out by yelling. You're freaking me out, too. I just woke up."

Jack stomped back into the living room and kicked the dripping shoe toward the door. "I'm taking a shower and then we're leaving."

***

When he emerged from the bedroom, Replacement was waiting for him, a cup of coffee and an English muffin topped with peanut butter in hand.

"Eat, and then we'll head for the car."

Jack's head snapped around to look at the dog. "There's no way I'm going to let the clawed monster into the Charger."

"I was going to take her in the Bug."

"It won't fit."

"Of course she will. How do you think I got her here?" Replacement turned her hands up.

Jack rolled his eyes. "I figured you rode the beast home."

She laughed, grabbed his hand, and bowed her head. "Thank you, God, for this food and for Jack. Please help us find Cookie's owner. In Jesus' name, Amen."

She wrapped her arms around his waist. He fought to keep the scowl on his face, but as she squeezed him tighter, it faded.

Replacement leaned back and smiled. "You're going to help me, right?"

He nodded. She pulled him down and kissed his cheek. He restrained himself from drawing her back in before she bounded off for the closet. Jack munched on his breakfast as she rooted around before triumphantly holding up a length of rope. She danced over to the dog and tied the rope onto her collar.

"That'll hold." She stood up and beamed.

Jack's eyes traveled over her athletic figure. Her T-shirt wasn't tight, but the cut of the faded pink fabric made his mind drift to other things.

"Ready?"

Her question broke him out of his daydream. Jack took another swig of coffee and headed for the door. Replacement led with the dog, and Jack followed at a safe distance.

When they reached the Bug, Jack stopped and laughed. "Are you sure it fits?" He opened the passenger door, put down the front seat, and moved out of the way.

"Come on, Cookie." Replacement clapped her hand to her thigh and tugged the leash, but the dog wouldn't budge.

"I don't think she'll fit."

"That's not helping, Jack." She frowned, then handed Jack the rope. "Here. You try."

Jack took a step toward the car and pulled on the rope. The dog planted her feet and her ears lay back on her head. She barked.

"Are you trying to get me eaten?" Jack asked. "How'd you get the beast into the car at Mrs. Sawyer's?"

Replacement's eyes lit up, and then she sprinted back toward the apartment building. "I have to go get something."

Jack leaned up against the car. "Sit," Jack growled at the dog, who growled back. *Just get the information off the chip and the dog off my hands. Happy Replacement, happy me.*

A minute later, Replacement dashed back and put her hands on her legs while she caught her breath.

"While you were gone, I taught the beast a trick," Jack announced with a grin. "Watch. Ready? Stand there." He thrust both hands out at the dog, who didn't move. "Ta-da!"

Replacement laughed.

"Wait, there's more." He theatrically put a hand above his head. "Growl." He gave a little tug on the rope, and the dog growled. "Speak." Jack took a step forward, and she barked.

"Stop it." Replacement hopped over to the car. "Come on, girl." She held up a biscuit and tossed it into the car.

The dog shot past Jack as she scrambled into the back seat after the treat. The whole car rocked back and forth on its chassis as she grabbed the biscuit and turned around three times before lying down.

"Good thinking." Jack put the front seat up.

Replacement sighed. "I'd like to take credit, but it was Mrs. Sawyer's idea. She's so sweet."

Jack looked into the back seat. "I'll follow you in the Charger."

"What? Why?"

"I'm not going to sit in front of the furry gargoyle in that tiny car. Haven't you seen that show *Animals Gone Crazy*?"

"Don't be such a scaredy-cat. She won't bite you."

Jack eyed the dog in the back, but hesitantly slid into the passenger seat.

I'm an idiot. I'd rather risk getting my face chewed off than have her think I'm a chicken.

"Ready?" Replacement started the car.

"Drive fast."

Replacement rolled down the windows and zipped out of the parking lot.

"Did Mrs. Sawyer see which way the dog came from?" Jack asked. "There aren't that many homes in her area, but there's also Pine Creek Golf Club." He turned sideways and leaned against the door so he could keep an eye on the dog.

Replacement shook her head. "No. All she said was she found the dog wedged into the General's cat door."

Jack smirked as he pictured that.

"When I got there, Cookie was waiting on the porch."

The golf course is enormous. If the dog wandered onto it, it could have come from anywhere.

Replacement chuckled and bit her lip.

"What?" Jack asked.

"Mrs. Sawyer told me to say hi."

Jack eyed her suspiciously. "That's it? Hi? Did she say anything else?"

Replacement nodded. "She told me to hang on to you. She said you're a keeper." Replacement grinned and gave Jack a big wink.

5

SHE'S A QUEEN

The little blue Bug turned onto the dead-end road.

"I hope it's open." Replacement pointed to the long one-story building set back on a little hill.

"Someone's here." Jack tapped his fingers on the window and pointed to a car parked outside.

Replacement parked in front of the animal shelter. Jack nearly dove out of the car the second it came to a stop.

"Hey, wait a minute…" Replacement's face scrunched up as she got out. "You *are* scared of her."

"Scared?" Jack scoffed. "No. But do I like Franken-wolf breathing down my neck the whole ride while it's plotting to eat me? No."

The dog jumped out of the car, and the little Bug rocked back and forth. The dog shook as if she had just gotten out of a bath.

Replacement patted her back. "Good girl. You were such a good baby on the ride," she cooed.

Jack headed up the ramp to the shelter. The dog yanked Replacement forward, so she stumbled up next to Jack. Replacement started to loop the rope around her wrist, but Jack grabbed the rope and stopped her.

"Seriously, kid. Don't do that. You won't be able to let go if the beast takes off. Chewbacca here could pull your arm off."

"Chewie!" Replacement hopped up and down. "That's perfect." She leaned over and hugged the dog.

Jack rubbed between his eyes and chuckled. He opened the door and held it for Replacement and the dog.

They walked into an empty waiting room with two rows of attached chairs in the middle. A counter was against the far wall next to a double door. Replacement headed straight to the reception window behind the counter.

A young woman was typing on a computer. A prominent, dyed-pink streak ran down the middle of her jet-black hair, and a silver nose ring and a short-sleeved shirt revealing arms covered in tattoos completed her ensemble. Although she appeared fierce, she smiled nervously.

"Are you looking to adopt?" She looked hopeful.

Jack shook his head but returned her smile. "Not today. We actually found a lost dog."

"You're dropping off?" Her shoulders sagged.

"No," Replacement replied. "We're here to get her checked for a chip. We hope to locate the owner, but we're *not* leaving her."

The woman's smile returned. "Have you checked the board?"

Replacement shook her head. The woman hopped off her stool, came out the big doors, and strode over to an old chalkboard on rollers. One side was covered with pictures of lost pets. "Missing," "beloved family dog," "like our own child"—the words hit Jack hard as he searched for a picture of the dog that sat next to him.

"If someone's lost a dog, we help them create a flyer. Do you see her here?" the woman asked.

Jack scanned the posters and frowned.

Replacement shook her head. "I don't see her."

"I'll let Ryan know you'd like him to check for a chip. I'd really recommend you have the dog examined, too. If she was lost, you want to make sure nothing happened to her."

"They can do that here?"

"Sure. It's not too busy. I think he can do it after he checks the chip. There's a small fee."

Of course there's a fee. Maybe I can talk Replacement into charging the dog's owner to cover some of these expenses.

"Do you get a lot of missing animals?" Replacement asked.

The woman nodded. "Too many. Sometimes they have a chip, but there're a lot that don't. The guys here do what they can to place them, but it's hard." She made a face. "Too many dogs—not enough homes."

Replacement's lip curled. "I heard. That blows."

The woman held out her hand. "I'm Lacie."

"I'm Alice. That's Jack, and this is Chewie."

Lacie rubbed behind the dog's ears. "She's so fluffy."

Replacement grinned and joined in patting the dog.

"Let me go see if they can squeeze you in." Lacie headed back through the doors.

Jack scanned the board again, and his eyes narrowed.

"What?" Replacement asked.

"There's no flyer for the dog. That means the owner hasn't been here."

"Do you think they aren't looking?"

"They haven't looked *here*, anyway. I'm just thinking it through. Dog food is expensive. The dog's huge. She seems young, so maybe they got her as a puppy. The dog keeps growing, and it keeps getting more expensive to keep it."

"You think they don't want her?" Replacement pulled the dog closer to herself.

Jack held up a hand. "It's just a thought. It's a possibility, though."

"But she looks taken care of."

The doors opened and Lacie said, "They're ready."

As they followed her down a linoleum-tiled hallway, the dog whined and pushed against Replacement, who almost fell into Jack. Lacie led them to a room with a metal table, three plastic chairs, and a couple of cabinets.

"We'll just get Chewie up on the table and take a look at her."

Replacement eyed the waist-high table and then asked Jack, "Can you pick her up?"

Jack scoffed. "Why don't I just put barbecue sauce on my nose and ask her to bite my face off?"

Lacie laughed. "I've got it." She reached under the table with her foot and pressed a pedal. The table lowered almost to the floor.

"Thanks." Replacement smiled. "Have you worked here long?"

"Only a few months. I'm technically the assistant office manager."

Lacie attached the leash to a pole on the table, and she and Replacement managed to coax the dog onto it. They then stood on either side of the table trying to comfort the giant animal, who was now trembling and whining. Lacie felt around with her foot, located the pedal, and raised the table to waist height.

The door swung open and a man entered. Medium height and thin build—Jack pegged him as being in his early thirties. He had round glasses and a wavy brown ponytail, and he wore khaki shorts and a blue T-shirt. "Wow," he exclaimed. "You're a big girl." He walked over to the table. "Look at you." He held his hand out in a fist for the dog to sniff, and then patted her head. "She's a king." He turned back to Jack. "Ryan Warner."

"Jack Stratton. Alice Campbell. We found this lost dog, and we're hoping you can help us find the owner."

"She's beautiful." Ryan nodded to Alice and patted the dog's back. "She's a king shepherd."

Replacement's eyes widened. "I've heard of a German shepherd."

Ryan felt around the dog's neck. "Regular shepherds aren't this big, especially females. She's a mix of Shiloh, German, and long-haired shepherd. It's a giant breed. A king shepherd."

Replacement beamed. "She's a girl. That makes her a queen shepherd."

Jack started to open his mouth, but closed it when she shot him a look.

Ryan pulled out a penlight and looked at the dog's eyes. "My, what beautiful eyes you have," he said.

"I'd be careful," Jack joked. "Little Red Riding Hood said that to the big bad wolf, and I think this dog's bigger and badder."

Ryan laughed. "It ended okay for Riding Hood, if I remember correctly."

"It didn't end too well for the grandmother," Jack muttered. Replacement's eyes narrowed. Jack cleared his throat. "When a dog's lost, how do people find the owners?"

"Usually it's the owner who finds the dog." Ryan spoke as his hands moved over the dog's chest and throat. "Is this her regular collar?"

"It's the collar she had on when we found her," Replacement said.

"Why do you ask?" Jack asked.

"She has some bruising around her throat." Ryan lifted up the fur, but a rumble in the dog's chest made him lower it back down. "Let's just take my word for it. She's a little sensitive around her neck, so I wondered if you were using a choke collar. Sometimes those aren't the best."

Replacement rubbed Chewie's back.

The door swung open, and a man in a wheelchair rolled in. "Sorry to interrupt," he said. "Lacie, Mrs. Thornton's trying to pay her bill, and I think I charged her twice."

Lacie grinned mischievously. "Just say it's a donation."

"Lacie." Ryan peered over the rim of his glasses.

"I'll go fix it." She headed around the table. The man in the wheelchair held the door for her.

"Carl, can you get me a scanner?" Ryan asked. "Hopefully Chewie here has a chip that'll let us know exactly where she lives."

"Chewie? Cool name." Carl wheeled around and pulled a scanner from a cabinet.

Jack tried not to stare at Carl's legs. He wondered if the man was a wounded veteran. He looked to be in his late twenties and had his black hair buzzed military short. "Jack Stratton." He held out his hand.

"Carl Harris."

"This is Alice."

"Pleased to meet you." Alice stepped forward, and her small hand disappeared into Carl's large grip.

Ryan took the scanner from Carl. "Can you give me a hand with the leash?"

Carl wheeled over to where Lacie had stood and took hold of the leash.

"I'm just going to check for a chip." Ryan gently patted the dog's head. While he stroked her fur, he moved the scanner down her back.

The dog trembled and whimpered loudly. Her nails clicked on the metal table.

"It's okay, girl." Replacement rubbed her neck. "I think she's been to the vet before."

"Seems like it. She's acting like a kid remembering the shot they got at their last trip to the doctor's office. Almost done." Ryan spoke softly.

"Easy, baby." Replacement rubbed the dog's head.

Ryan moved the scanner closer to her fur, then he shook his head. "Sorry, but she doesn't have a chip."

Replacement frowned and rubbed the dog's neck. "It's okay," she whispered in her ear.

"Let me give her a quick once-over." Ryan handed Carl the scanner. "It looks like she got into a briar patch. I see some scratches and would like to check her for thorns."

"You're a brave man." Jack took a step back.

Carl spoke softly to the dog while Ryan examined her. After a few minutes, Ryan stepped back. "She's a king shepherd all right. Beautiful dog, and she looks as healthy as a horse."

"She's as big as one," Jack mumbled, receiving three sideways looks in response.

All three held on to the dog while Ryan stepped on the pedal and lowered the table.

"Sorry about the chip," Ryan said as Carl undid the leash.

"Thank you for checking," Replacement said.

"She looks very well cared for." Ryan pushed his glasses higher on his nose. "I'd bet someone is looking for her."

"Can you tell how long she's been gone?" Replacement asked.

"I can't even tell that she's been gone at all. She's well brushed. No matting. It couldn't be more than a few days."

"Would you call me if you hear anything?" Replacement handed a card to Ryan.

She had her own business cards printed? Good thinking. Jack gave her a wink, and she stood a little straighter.

"Sure, of course," Ryan said.

"We do offer dog boarding," Carl said.

"No, thank you," Replacement responded quickly.

"Before we go," Jack said, "is there anything else you suggest we can do to find the owner?"

Ryan exchanged a look with Carl. "You could check the dog park. It's right over on Honeycutt."

"People post flyers on the board there." Carl held the door open with his wheelchair.

"Well, thank you very much," Replacement said. She shook Ryan's hand, and so did Jack.

Jack and Replacement made their way to the front. As Replacement brought the dog outside, Jack walked over to Lacie at the counter.

"Did she have a chip?" Lacie asked.

Jack shook his head. "How much do I owe you?" He cringed when she showed him the bill for forty dollars, but put it on the credit card. "Please give us a call if anyone comes in."

The dog's probably eaten fifty dollars in food and sneakers already, and now another forty bucks. I'd better find the owner of this money pit soon.

6

ALMOST DOESN'T COUNT

As they pulled into the dog park on Honeycutt, the dog's head shot up. A blond-haired woman was in the fenced area throwing a ball to a little collie.

"One second." Replacement turned fully around in her seat to reach back toward the dog. She loosened the big knot on the dog's collar. "This looks uncomfortable."

"The rope *should* be tight." Jack leaned away as the dog turned her snout toward him.

"Don't you see how cute she is?" Replacement's voice went up. "I want to pick her up and give her a big hug." She held both sides of the dog's face and got nose to nose with her.

"Three things I'm going to say. One, you'd need a forklift to pick her up. Two, I wouldn't keep putting your face near that lion's mouth. I've seen enough videos on the Internet—it never ends well. And three, loosening that knot is not a good idea."

Replacement looked at him and mashed her lips together. Then her face lit up and she fluffed the dog's head. "Jack's just jealous," she said in baby talk. "Yes he is."

The dog wagged her tail, and Jack was almost sure she smirked at him.

"I wouldn't do that. You're running with scissors." Jack opened the door.

When Replacement got out of the car, the dog leapt out of the back seat and surged forward. Replacement held tightly to the rope, but the rope didn't hold tightly to the dog. A half second later, Replacement was holding nothing but an untied rope, and the dog was galloping toward the fence. It effortlessly leapt over it.

Jack took off after her. He grabbed the fence with one hand and hurdled over it in a flash. Jack sprinted after the dog, but she lowered her head and sped up. Then she altered her course to intercept the little collie.

That beast is going to eat the other dog. "Dog! Stop!" he shouted.

The woman kept her back to Jack even as he screamed.

"Chewie!" Replacement called from behind him. She was struggling to climb over the fence.

The collie saw the huge dog thundering toward him, and froze.

Jack's feet were a blur, but the dog was much faster. Jack screamed, "Lady, pick your dog up! *Stop! Heel!* Pick your dog up! *Lady!*"

The dog suddenly stopped. Jack rushed up and grabbed her by the collar. Panting, he looked down at the little collie, which playfully trotted forward and sniffed the giant dog.

Replacement dashed up next to Jack and skidded to a stop with one sneaker on her foot and the other in her hand. She turned beet red as she grabbed Jack's arm and pulled on her shoe. "Sorry. I got stuck on the stupid fence."

The woman turned around and gasped. She smiled sheepishly as she took earbuds out of her ears. "Hi. Did you say something?"

Jack's mouth fell open. *Yeah. I was trying to warn you that a werewolf was going to eat you and your dog, but your music is so stinking loud you wouldn't have known if Godzilla was coming.*

"Hi. Do you know this dog?" Replacement asked.

"I've seen her before." The woman threw the tennis ball, and both dogs took off after it.

Replacement exhaled. "We're looking for the owner. You wouldn't happen to know his name?"

The woman fidgeted with the leash in her hands. "I'm sorry, no. I've seen the guy here a lot, but we mostly just wave at each other."

"Do you know where he lives?" Replacement reached for a business card. "Alice Campbell."

"I'm Stacy. Sorry, I don't know where he lives. When he comes, I think he's usually walking. I see him go down the path that leads to the pond." She pointed over to the trail that ran along the fence. "It circles around the pond. It doesn't take long to walk it, maybe twenty minutes."

Replacement nodded. "What does he look like?" She glanced at Jack. He reassured her with a little nod.

"He's a big guy. Brown hair. It's, like, medium length. It's a little wavy... I think. He's a T-shirt and jeans type of guy."

"You said 'big guy.' Overweight, you mean?"

"No, not fat. Really tall, with broad shoulders."

Replacement pointed a thumb at Jack. "Like compared to Jack here?"

"Taller."

Replacement's face scrunched up. "Jack's six one. Is this guy a giant?"

"Yeah. He's at least five or six inches taller." Stacy pointed up at a branch overhead. "I got a Frisbee stuck in that tree. He just walked right over, reached up, and took it down."

"Do you remember if he ever said anything about where he lives or works?" Replacement asked.

Stacy shook her head. "We rarely spoke, and when we did it was chitchat stuff. I think he's shy. I don't know very much, sorry."

"You're doing great," Jack said. "Does he come alone?"

"I've only seen him with the dog."

"Well, thank you for your time. If you remember anything, please give me a call," Replacement said.

Stacy nodded and then looked at the dogs, who were racing along the edge of the field. She cupped her hands to her mouth and called, "Trixie! Trixie!"

The dogs ignored her and kept on running.

Replacement stuck two fingers in her mouth and whistled so loudly Stacy covered her ears and Jack leaned away. The dogs spun around and raced back to them.

Jack wiggled a finger in his ear. "Did Chandler teach you to whistle like that?"

Replacement smiled as she started to tie the rope around Chewie's collar. "Nope. Aunt Haddie."

Jack laughed. He remembered how Aunt Haddie would walk out on the porch and whistle for them to come home for dinner.

Replacement held her hand underneath the dog's mouth. "Give me the ball, Chewie," she demanded.

The dog opened her mouth. A tennis ball covered in spit tumbled out onto Replacement's palm.

"Yuck," Jack said.

Replacement held the ball with two fingers and handed it to Stacy. "Sorry."

"It's okay." Stacy laughed. "Dogs will be dogs."

Once Replacement finished tying the rope onto the collar, Chewie jogged for the exit. Jack and Replacement ran behind her.

When they reached the gate, Jack started to open it, then stopped. "Wait. I have an idea. Let's follow the dog. Let her lead us to her home."

"Sweet. That's smart. Chewie can do it." She leaned over and rubbed behind the dog's ears. Chewie danced back and forth. Replacement spoke in a baby voice. "She's my good girl. She's a little princess. You need to find your way home, okay? Okay."

Jack held the gate open for them, and the dog trotted out, followed by Replacement. She went forward a few feet and then turned to look back at Replacement.

"Go, girl! Go," Replacement encouraged.

"Home! Go home!" Jack grinned. "That sounds good."

Replacement frowned. She jogged forward, and the dog followed.

"Don't lead her in a direction," Jack called out.

"She's following me. How do I not lead her in a direction?"

Jack leaned back against the fence and watched as Replacement kept up her pleading. Jack shook his head.

But as he looked away, he noticed a leash draped around a pole farther down the fence. While Replacement continued her coaxing, Jack walked down and took the thick red leather leash off the pole. "Look at this."

Replacement lifted her head, but the dog flew over to Jack so fast that Replacement could barely keep up. When they reached Jack, the dog sat down at his feet and barked. Jack handed the leash to Replacement.

"It's the same leather as Chewie's collar," Replacement said.

"Check this out." Jack pointed to the metal clasp. "It broke." He looked over at the place on the fence where he'd found the leash. "She's a powerful dog. If you left her tied to the fence and she wanted to go, this leash wouldn't hold her."

Replacement rubbed the dog's neck. "Poor baby. That must have been how you hurt your neck."

"I'm sure the beast's fine."

"She's not a beast. She's a beauty. Beauty! That name rocks. Do you like it?"

Jack rubbed the side of his face. "All these names may be getting the dog confused. Even I'm getting confused. Maybe you should stick to one?"

"I'm going to try it out." She tossed Jack the leash, and the dog pranced in a circle. "You're a good doggy, Beauty. Yes, you are."

"Wait. I want to see if this works." Jack undid the rope around the collar.

"Aren't we supposed to keep the leash on?" Replacement crossed her arms.

Jack's hands went out and he smiled awkwardly. "She follows you when the leash is on. Maybe if we let her go free she'll run home." He held the leash up. The dog barked and wagged her thick tail. "Ready?" Jack jogged in place, and she barked again. "Home? Let's go!"

Jack took a step forward, and the dog took off at a full sprint.

Wow.

"Wait!" Replacement yelled. Her legs sprang into action and she raced after the fleeing dog.

Jack ran after them. A broad grin spread across his face as he watched Replacement. She had the form of a sprinter. Jack's long legs stretched out and his arms cut through the air. He was fast, but in a sprint, she was faster.

The three of them sped along the side of the road. The dog slowed down, allowing them to catch up, and then she barked and took off again. Replacement glanced over her shoulder, and Jack saw her smile.

This might work.

As they rounded a corner, the sign for the Archstone apartment complex came into view. The dog raced down the sidewalk and headed up a walkway.

Replacement kicked it into high gear to keep up, but Jack's side began to throb, and the doctor's warning about overexerting himself echoed in his ear. He forced himself to slow down to a jog. "Hold up," he yelled, but they'd already disappeared behind a three-story apartment building.

Jack knew the area from having patrolled the neighborhood. The Archstone apartment complex was a mix of townhouses and apartments. On the whole, it was quiet, rarely getting any police calls, but he vividly recalled helping the EMTs take an unusually large gentleman out through the back door of one unit because they couldn't get the stretcher down the staircase.

The first-floor apartments have walkouts. If the owner lives here with a dog that big, I'll bet he lives on the first floor.

Jack trotted off the sidewalk and headed around the building. Replacement stood in front of the back door of the last apartment. She waved him over.

"Beauty's freaking out." She leaned down to rub the whimpering dog's neck.

The dog scratched at the door.

"I'd say this is her home." Jack looked into the darkened kitchen. "Of course you knocked?"

Replacement gave him a "duh" look, then peered through the door's glass panes. Jack didn't see that she'd pressed her face against the glass before he pounded on the bottom panel of the door. The vibration went up the door, and Replacement jumped back.

"Doofus," she snapped as she rubbed her forehead.

"Sorry."

"I said I knocked."

Jack shrugged. "You could've girl knocked."

"Girl knocked?" Replacement made a fist. "Do you want me to pound on it?"

"No."

The door to the apartment next door opened, and an older man stuck his head out. "Can I help you?" He stayed partly behind the door and eyed them suspiciously.

"Hi." Jack gave a little wave to put the older man at ease. "We're looking for this dog's owner."

The man looked toward the dog. "Yeah, I think it's the dog from next door. It looks big enough. Can you make it bark?"

"What?" Jack asked.

"I hear it mostly. I know its bark," the old man explained. He scratched the stubble on his chin.

Jack looked down at the dog. "Speak."

The dog sat there.

"Speak," Replacement urged. She rubbed the dog's neck.

The dog barked.

"Yeah, it lives there." The old man frowned and thumbed his hand toward the apartment. "Loudest dog I ever heard. You'd figure people would get a little dog for a small apartment, not a great big thing like that."

"What's your neighbor's name?" Jack asked.

The old man squinted, and his face wrinkled even more. He shook his head. "I don't get out much."

"Can you tell me the last time you saw him?" Jack asked.

"I mind my own business," the old man snapped. He waved a gnarled hand in the air. "He's a big guy. I know that. Real big. Friendly enough, but like I said, I keep to myself."

Jack turned to Replacement and held out a hand. "Can I have one of your cards?" Jack took it from her and turned back to the old man. "When he comes back, can you tell him we stopped by?"

The old man took the card and frowned. "Of course I will."

"What apartment number is his?" Jack asked.

"403," the old man muttered, then he backed inside and shut his door, hard.

"Do you have another card?"

"I only have a few. Do you like them?" Replacement handed him one and stood close.

"I'm proud of you. They look professional." Jack flipped the card over and wrote: WE FOUND YOUR DOG. PLEASE CALL ASAP. He wedged the card into the molding on the top glass plane, with the note facing inward.

"Now what?" Replacement asked.

"Let's go home. Now that we have his address, we can do a reverse phone lookup and give him a call." Jack winked.

"Sweet." Replacement grinned. "You're almost home, Beauty."

As Jack walked away, he heard Replacement groan. He turned around and saw the dog had planted her feet. Replacement was pulling on the leash, but the dog wasn't moving.

"Come on, Beauty," Replacement pleaded. "We'll come back. I promise."

The dog didn't budge.

"Start walking. She'll follow." Jack turned and moved away.

"You think so?" Replacement's face filled with concern as she caught up to him.

"Yeah. Don't look back. It's like dealing with a stubborn little kid."

"How do you know how to deal with a stubborn little kid?" Replacement asked. Jack smirked.

"Me? Ha ha, funny—not." Replacement rolled her eyes.

They went around the corner and waited. And waited. Replacement exhaled and glared at Jack.

"How's this my fault?" Jack grumbled under his breath as he walked back.

He found the dog lying outside the door with her head on her paws.

"Come on. Here. Let's go!" Jack clapped.

The dog shifted her legs but stayed put, her eyes glued to the door.

"Oh, baby." Replacement rushed forward and ran over to the dog. "Beauty's sad." She got down on her knees and rubbed the dog's head.

"Do you have another biscuit?" Jack asked.

"Back in the car."

"I'll run back and get it."

Replacement nodded and stroked the dog's fur. "Jack will be right back, and then we can find out the phone number and get you home." She looked up at Jack. "This sucks. She's almost home."

Jack jogged to the car, and the dog whined.

It does suck. Sometimes "almost" doesn't count.

7

REPLACEMENT

Replacement looked around the dimly lit restaurant and bit her lip. She leaned over the white tablecloth and whispered to Jack, "Do you think she's okay?" She was wearing the brown dress with white trim she'd bought in Hope Falls. She had on only the faintest makeup, but her eyes popped and her lips glistened.

Jack buttered a roll. "She's fine. You want one?" He offered it to her.

"I should have asked Mrs. Stevens to watch her." She looked toward the door.

"She'll be fine. Did you find out the guy's name?"

She nodded. "Daniel Branson. I ran his address and got his phone number. I called and left a message."

Jack froze. "You ran him?" He leaned in and whispered, "You're not accessing the police database again, *right?*"

"Me?" Replacement grinned. "I used my background checker programs. They're all available on the net." She waved her hand. "A reverse phone number lookup's nothing."

Jack leaned back and exhaled.

Replacement's hand shot out as Jack went to take a bite. "You didn't pray."

"It's a roll. Don't I pray before the food?" He put the roll back on his plate.

"A roll is food." Replacement closed her eyes and wiggled in her seat. One eye popped open as she reached out for Jack's hand.

Jack felt the color rise in his neck as he took her hand and bowed his head.

"Thank you, God, for all of this. Please lead us to Daniel and help Biscuit be okay tonight. Thank you for Jack. In Jesus' name, we pray."

"Amen. Biscuit?" Jack asked.

"Mrs. Sawyer was right—she loves biscuits. So I was thinking about calling her Biscuit."

"I'm glad Mrs. Sawyer didn't feed her donuts."

Replacement giggled, but then she stopped and her mouth fell open.

"You can't call her Donut," Jack protested.

Replacement laughed. "Gotcha!"

The waitress came over with two house salads.

"Look, Daniel's going to call you back, and I'm laying odds that dog's name isn't Biscuit." Jack put his napkin in his lap. "No guy would ever name his dog Biscuit."

Replacement pulled her salad closer. "I'm not trying to guess. I'm just thinking what I'd call her if she were mine."

"Don't get attached," Jack cautioned.

"Do you like dogs?"

He stopped mid-bite. She leaned forward, and her big green eyes seemed even larger as she gazed at him. *What the hell do I say? I'm not a dog fan?* He swallowed. *Damn. I'm such a sucker for her—if she asks me, I'll get her one.* "I don't know. I never had a dog." Jack took a big bite of salad.

Replacement still eyed him hopefully. "Really? I was wondering—I came up with a weird idea."

Jack slowly raised the fork to his mouth. "Okay?"

She perked up. "You'll do it? Great."

"Whoa. I haven't heard it yet. I just meant okay like you can tell me okay, not that I'll do it okay."

Replacement wrinkled her nose. "Okay, here goes. I thought we could get to know each other better if, like, one night a week we get to ask each other one question."

Jack waited for a second to see whether there was more to the idea, but Replacement just sat there on the edge of her seat and watched him. He swallowed. "Sure."

She leaned even further forward, and her words rushed out. "It has to be something you really want to know, and the other person *has* to answer. No dodging, weaving, or staying silent. Full disclosure. Total, one hundred percent honesty."

Jack reached for his water. *There's no way I can agree to one hundred percent full disclosure. I'd be out of my mind. I'm not even that honest with myself.*

"Please?" The light caught the gold flecks in her green eyes, and he saw her swallow. She looked down and smoothed out her dress, and then her eyes darted around the room. "Forget it. It was a weird thought."

"No." Jack leaned in. "It's a great idea."

"You hesitated." She looked up, and her expression hovered between hopefulness and embarrassment.

"I was just thinking about the first question. That's all."

"Oh, okay." She squeezed her hands together. "You go first."

If she'd pulled a gun and pointed it at Jack's head, he'd have been calm and cool. But by asking him to think of the one question he really wanted to know about her… he panicked.

I need to have my head examined. I didn't think this through. He decided to go with the first question that popped into his head. "Why don't you like to be called Alice?"

When he saw her swallow, his chest tightened. He saw the sorrow in her eyes, and he immediately regretted asking the question. "I'm sorry." He held up a hand. "I just wondered."

Her gaze flitted down to the table and she blinked rapidly. "No, I'm sorry. This was my idea."

"I can ask something else."

"Nope." She shook her head and grimaced. "Those are the rules, right? I have to answer, so here it goes." She set her fork down and lifted her chin. Her brows pulled together and she looked right into his eyes. "I guess, because it's my mother's name."

"But I thought you and your mother got along great."

"We did." Replacement's shoulders squeezed upward. "I loved her so much, but after my parents died, I couldn't bear to hear her name. Someone would say 'Alice,' and there was this echo in my head of my father's voice. I kept waiting to hear the after."

Jack leaned forward. "The after?"

Replacement exhaled in a little puff. "See, whenever my dad talked to my mom, he'd add an after." She waved her hands back and forth, searching for the words. "After he said her name, he'd always add something. Something like 'Alice, honey' or 'Alice, darling.' I loved it. But when they died… it just drove me crazy. Someone would say 'Alice,' and I'd hear this faint echo of my dad saying it, but it was like the echo was broken. There was no after. I'd listen for it, but it would never come." She sniffled.

"If it bothers you, I won't use it." Jack reached out and touched the tip of her fingers.

"It doesn't bother me when you say it." She smiled.

"Do you want me to call you Alice?"

"No. But I don't mind when you say it once in a while."

"So you're okay with Replacement?"

She let out a huge sigh. "I like Replacement. It's special to me."

Jack's eyebrow went up.

"Chandler named me." Replacement rocked in her seat and then put her elbows on the table. "After my family died, I had nowhere to go. I went to this big foster home, and it was like I was in some evil fairy tale. I mean, one minute my family and I were going out for pizza, discussing what kind to get… and the next thing I remember I was waking up in the hospital.

"I didn't get to go to a funeral. I never got to go home again. They shoved me around from one home to another. No one wanted anything to do with me. I didn't talk, so it was sorta my fault. Everyone said I was creeping them out. But what could I say?"

Jack gripped his fork and fought back the urge to scoop her up in his arms. *Let her talk. She needs to get it out.*

"The other kids were horrid. They wouldn't stop teasing me. All I did was cry." She ran her hands along the sides of her head. "They moved me to this other home. That was the bad place."

Her hand trembled as she took a sip of water. Jack reached out for her, but she softly shook her head.

"I got placed in Aunt Haddie's care after that, but… I was so freaked by then. People either hated me or hurt me, and I thought it would be the same there—or worse. I was eleven, and I… I just wanted to die. The first day, I hid in a closet and prayed for it to end. I begged God to let me go be with my family. But then there was this little knock on the door—just a tiny tap. I thought it was a little kid, so I opened the door. And there was Chandler."

Jack pictured his giant friend standing there, and how scary it would be to an eleven-year-old girl.

"Chandler was huge. But he sat down on the floor with me. He told me he didn't know what I was going through because he still had his sister, Michelle, but he'd lost his parents in a fire. He understood me. One minute he felt like he had everything, and the next… it was gone. Then these big tears showed up in his eyes. I cried, and he did too. We talked for, like, hours. It was so awesome."

She sniffed and wiped her eyes.

"By then it was time for dinner, and I freaked again. I didn't want to come out of the closet." She chuckled. "Chandler got this serious look on his face and scanned me up and down. 'I'm going in the Army,' he said, 'and I need someone to fill my shoes.'" She laughed. "I looked down at his feet and they were like four of mine."

"I think he was a size fifteen," Jack said.

She folded her hands and pressed them against her lips. "He said, 'This person needs to watch over my Aunt Haddie and keep an eye on Michelle until I get back. But while they're doing that, everyone's going to treat that person how they treat me. You'll be my replacement. Do you know what that means? No one will pick on you, because you're my replacement. It means all the kisses and hugs Aunt Haddie gives me, she'll give you. It means all the cool stuff my sister Michelle does with me, she'll do with you. Do you think you can fill these shoes? Would you like that?' I was looking up at him in awe. I said, 'Yeah. I can. I'll be your replacement.' And that's how he introduced me to everyone. The name stuck."

Jack took her hand. "Chandler was proud of that."

"I loved it. It made me belong, you know? It was like his way of saying I fit in. I was part of the family because I was taking his place until he came back."

The waitress brought over a T-bone steak for Jack and chicken Marsala for Replacement. Jack, grateful for the distraction, quickly wiped his eyes.

"Why did you order a T-bone?" Replacement asked as the waitress walked away.

"Is that your question? Sweet!" Jack said.

"No! That doesn't count." She wiggled her fork at him.

"A T-bone's a two-for-one cut. That way I get a piece of tenderloin and a piece of strip steak. Win-win." He grinned.

Replacement's lip curled up mischievously. "I don't have to ask my question right away."

"That's not part of the rules."

"Yes it is. I made them." She smiled and took a bite of her roll.

"It'd be nice if you asked now."

"Why?" She bit her bottom lip.

Jack felt his pulse quicken. He'd been trying to keep things between them from going beyond second gear, but the way she was looking at him now made him want to forget about everything, including the food, and carry her back to the apartment.

"Because it's like waiting outside the principal's office and not knowing what he caught you doing." He leaned back and tried to play it cool. "But I'll wait."

She stuck out the tip of her tongue. "Fine. I'll ask." The color rose in her neck until the tops of her ears turned red. "When's the first time you thought you could be in love with me?"

Jack's heart thumped in his chest, and he coughed. "The first time I thought about it?" He took a sip of water.

"I'm just curious." She smoothed her napkin on the table.

Jack sighed. "We didn't hit it off too well when you came back into my life. Sorry about that."

Replacement waved her hand. "Totally forgotten and forgiven." She smiled. "Take your time."

"I don't have to really think about it. It was when I was in the hospital after I got hit by the car."

"That doesn't count. You were on drugs. That's when you first kissed me."

Jack sighed. "It counts. I remember it perfectly. I remember waking up—the tubes and lights—and you were there. I could see the fear in your eyes. You were so freaked out, I wanted to jump out of the hospital bed and kill whatever had you that scared. But when I realized your concern was for me," he held up his water glass, "that's the first time I thought I could be in love with you."

Replacement wiggled in her seat. "Then you kissed me. You kissed me first."

Jack laughed and ate a crouton. "Is that a big deal?"

"For a girl, yes." She giggled.

"I'd like to kiss you right now."

Replacement blushed.

They spent the rest of dinner talking, laughing, and slowly moving even closer together. They spent so much time paying attention to each other that they barely touched their dinners.

8

I WISH I KNEW WHO

As the Charger zoomed down the street, Replacement pointed to the convenience store on the corner. "Can we stop? We need milk and bread for breakfast."

Jack parked at the far corner and rushed around to get Replacement's door. The brightly lit store was busy. Two teenage cashiers huddled over their registers and pressed buttons while a line of seven people all rolled their eyes.

Replacement immediately headed for the refrigerated area, saying to Jack, "I'll get the milk—will you grab the bread?"

Jack went down an aisle, looking for the bread. He hesitated when he passed the condoms. *Slow. Don't rush her.* With a faint groan, he kept going. He found the bread, and after a quick check of the sell-by date, picked up a loaf.

A bottle shattered in the back of the store. Heads spun around. Jack searched for Replacement as he rushed toward the sound.

He found her looking out the store's window toward the gas pumps, a broken bottle of orange juice at her feet. When he saw the look of sheer terror on her face, he rushed to her side. Her skin was white and her eyes were wide. She grabbed his shirt with a trembling hand, and he pulled her close.

Jack scanned for potential threats. *Silver Toyota leaving the parking lot. Thirty-year-old guy pumping gas. Two clerks. Fat forty-year-old at the snack counter. Barbell boy near the magazines. Small guy buying soda.*

As Jack's piercing stare ripped into each one of them, they looked away. "Who is it? Did someone say something to you?"

She quickly shook her head, but he saw her look back out into the darkness. "I'm sorry. I'm just… I'm not feeling well. Can we go to the car?"

Jack wrapped his arm around her shoulder while one of the cashiers came over with a mop and bucket. Replacement looked at the floor and mumbled, "Sorry."

The teenager waved her off. "It was probably expired anyway."

Jack led Replacement to the door. She squeezed his hand. "Really. It's nothing."

Jack's eyes narrowed. *She's lying. Somebody scared the hell out of her. I wish I knew who.*

9

IT'S THE PRINCIPLE

"Are you sure you're okay?" Jack's right arm was around Replacement's waist, and the doggie bag with their leftovers from dinner dangled from his left as he fumbled with the apartment key.

"I'm fine. Really. I'm sorry I spoiled everything."

"Pfft," Jack scoffed. "You didn't spoil anything. If you're up for it, I'll make a little private dinner for two." He leaned down and kissed her cheek as he let the apartment door swing open.

"That sounds good—" Replacement gasped. "Oh, crap!"

Jack's mouth fell open.

The dog trotted up to them, dropped what remained of the couch's armrest, and sat down panting. Cushion stuffing covered the floor. The shredded couch leaned at an odd angle.

The takeout bag slipped from Jack's hand. "It ate my couch."

"Oh, no." Replacement rushed over to the dog. "Do you think she swallowed any of it? Will she be okay?"

Jack scanned the tattered remnants. "It ate the whole damn couch."

"Now's not the time to think about yourself." Replacement's lip trembled as she held the dog's head with both hands and examined inside the dog's mouth. The dog licked her face and panted.

"The demon dog is fine," Jack growled. "But look at my couch!" He thrust both hands out as he stomped over to the ruins of the sofa.

Then he noticed that bits of paper were strewn about as well. He went around to the back of the couch, where he hid his important papers, and saw the dog had ripped that open too. He leaned over and picked up a scrap of what looked like his insurance policy.

"Damn it!" he screamed at the ceiling. "It ate all my papers!"

Replacement scooted over, picked up a cushion, and tried to stuff the batting back in. "You said you only keep copies of your papers in the couch. The originals are in the safe. It's not as bad as it looks." The hope in her words wasn't conveyed by the look on her face.

"Seriously? It's totally destroyed."

"Look on the bright side. We needed a new one."

"No we didn't." Jack shook his head. "I loved this couch."

Replacement picked up another cushion, and all of the stuffing fell out onto her feet. She stammered, "Well, we can get a new one just like it."

Stupid dog. He glared at the dog as she trotted off toward the front door.

Jack rubbed his eyes with the heels of his hands. "Let's just forget about it, and we'll enjoy the rest of the night."

Replacement picked up a pile of stuffing and dropped it on the couch. "I don't know why Beauty would do this."

"Why? It's simple. It's a beast, and it hates me."

"She does not." Replacement turned around and yelled, "Oh, no! Beauty!"

Jack spun around.

The dog was sitting on her haunches. The rest of the steak Jack had brought home from the restaurant was hanging out of her mouth.

"No," Jack growled, and so did the dog. "Drop my steak, Beast."

Jack lunged forward, and the dog jumped up on all fours.

"Beauty!" Replacement tried to move between the two.

Jack's hand flashed out and grabbed one side of the steak, but the dog clamped down on the other. She shook her head while Jack pulled. "I said drop it, dog!"

The dog planted her feet and yanked backward. Jack shook the steak up and down. Claws clicked on the floor as Jack tugged the dog forward. Snarling, she snapped her head to the side. Jack refused to let go, so he was slammed into the wall.

Replacement threw her hands up. "Let it go, Jack. You can't eat it now anyway."

"It's the principle of the thing," he grumbled. "I'm not going to let the beast have it."

Then the dog shook her head wildly, Jack's hand slipped off the steak, and the dog bolted into Replacement's bedroom with her prize. Jack raced after her, but stopped at the doorway when the dog barked ferociously.

"I hope you choke on it," he yelled before he slammed the door shut.

"Jack!" Replacement stamped her foot.

"What?" Jack walked back over and grabbed the dropped takeout bag. Replacement's foam container lay closed and untouched. "See?" Jack pointed. "It hates me. It went for mine and left yours alone."

Replacement scoffed. "It's not because she hates you. You got steak."

Jack looked down at her. "We could make something else and... talk?"

As Replacement's smile faded, so did Jack's.

Damn.

She shook her head. "I'm just not feeling that well. Can I get a rain check?"

Thanks, dog. "Sure. Do you want anything? Maybe eating something will help."

Replacement shook her head again. Then she reached up to kiss him—on the cheek.

Damn.

"Sorry," she whispered, and she moved toward her bedroom.

Jack headed for the kitchen. "Does the beast need to go out before—damn it."

"What?" Replacement hurried over.

Jack turned his head, wrinkled his nose, and tried not to swear. "I guess it already went." He thrust his hands down at the kitchen floor.

"She must be embarrassed," Replacement said.

Jack stood there, blinking at her. "Yeah, I'm sure she's mortified."

Replacement took a step forward and turned paler than before.

"I've got this." Jack took her by the hand and led her back to her bedroom.

"No. I brought Beauty here—"

"Seriously. You're not feeling well, and cleaning that up won't help."

"Really?" She lowered her head. "Thank you." She slipped into her room and closed the door.

She must really be sick if she's not helping to clean this up. This sucks.

Jack spent the next fifteen minutes cleaning the kitchen. Just as he finished, a scratching sounded on Replacement's door.

"How could it possibly need to go again?" Jack muttered as he grabbed the leash and headed to Replacement's door.

When he opened it, the dog trotted out, but Replacement lay in the bed and didn't move. Jack stood there until he saw the rise of her chest and heard her soft breathing.

She's already asleep. Maybe she really is sick.

Jack grabbed the trash bag and took the dog out. Ten minutes later, they stood in front of Replacement's bedroom. But the dog refused to go in.

Jack pulled the leash, and the dog growled. It wouldn't budge.

"Get in her room," Jack whispered fiercely.

The dog sat down.

Replacement moaned and rolled over.

Jack shut the door.

"What the hell's the matter with you, dog?" Jack snarled, and the dog growled. "Do you want to sleep out here?" He gestured to the living room.

The dog just stared at him.

It's got food. It's got water. It just ate my steak. What else can it want?

Jack ran his fingers through his hair, then stomped over to his bedroom. The dog got up and followed him to his door.

"No," Jack said. But when he cracked his door open, the dog rushed past him. "Stop!"

The dog jumped up on his bed.

"No way." Jack lunged at the dog, but it spun around and snapped. "Get the hell off my bed or I'm going to shoot you." Every time he reached out, the dog flattened her ears and bared her teeth. "Get off."

She barked.

Jack closed the bedroom door, then turned to glare at the dog. He wrestled one of the blankets from his bed and stormed over to the corner of the room. "Listen, mammoth mutt, I don't want you here. You don't want to be here. I get it. But you're not waking up my girl, so shut up. You can sleep in here, but there's no way you're sleeping on my bed." He laid the blanket in the corner of the room.

Jack marched back over to the bed and glared at the dog.

The dog bared her teeth.

Jack did too.

Suddenly, the dog hopped off the bed and trotted over to the blanket. She walked around in a circle a few times and lay down.

Jack exhaled. As he shook off his remaining blankets, he looked at the dog on his floor. She lay with her head on her paws and stared back at him. He slid under the blankets and stared at the ceiling.

Just as his eyes started to close, the dog's head shot up, and she frantically looked around. After a second, she lay her head back down and whined. Jack exhaled and looked over the edge of the bed at her. She gazed at him with huge brown eyes.

"Seriously?"

The dog whimpered and shut her eyes.

Jack tossed back the covers and stomped out to the living room. He rubbed his eyes and scanned the floor. He bent over to check under the couch, and found the Raggedy Anne doll. Snagging it, he trudged back to his bedroom. He dropped the doll by the dog, and she caught it in her mouth before it reached the floor.

Jack got into bed, but as he switched the light off, the dog whined again. He lay there in the dark for a few seconds and held his breath, but she didn't make any other noises.

"It's okay, dog," Jack said aloud. "Daniel will call soon, and you'll get to go back home."

Great. Now I'm talking to a dog.

10

THE SNOW GLOBE

J ack kept his eyes closed as he tried to force himself to fall asleep. He concentrated on slowing his breathing and listening to his heartbeat. He felt that wave of sleep pulling him under, and his head rolled to the side.

***

As the Humvee hit a pothole, Jack's helmet tapped against the metal doorframe. His eyes snapped open.

Jack sat in the back of the Humvee with five other soldiers. Chandler had somehow managed to cram his enormous frame into the back and sat across from Jack. Mac and Tech sat across from each other, with Mac on Jack's right. Butcher sat in the passenger seat, and Hank drove. The heat was stifling. The blazing hot sun cast sharp shadows inside the vehicle.

Jack read the words on the back of the laminated picture he held in his hands.

DON'T DIE.

He smirked. *I don't have that much choice in the matter.*

He flipped the photo over and stared down at the smiling, beautiful girl with the sky-blue eyes and blond hair. He remembered how she'd tearfully clung to him and whispered those same words in his ear right before he left. He closed his eyes and almost felt her warm breath on his neck.

A photographer had snapped the picture right when she'd kissed his cheek, and the photo had ended up in some national magazine. The teary-eyed girlfriend hugging the tall, handsome soldier made for a good intro to a piece about the war. Both of them looked the part: Jack, the ideal soldier—ruggedly handsome, six foot one, and one hundred ninety-five pounds of solid muscle—and her, the all-American beauty, promising to wait for her beau as she proudly saw him off to the battlefield.

Kelly.

She'd laminated the picture and sealed a lock of her hair inside. He played with the corner of the plastic. He wanted to open it and take her hair out and touch it. To feel its softness. To smell her scent. Like it was a fire extinguisher behind a glass case, he wanted to break it open and put out the ache of missing her that burned in his chest. He closed his eyes and felt the tires bouncing off the ruts as the Humvee raced down the dirt road.

"Got mine." Chandler's deep voice rumbled. He held up a picture. Sweat poured down his smiling face.

Thin, mousy, and in his late teens, Tech leaned over and pointed at the picture. "Who're they?" He wiped his glasses.

Chandler pointed at a large black woman with a huge smile. "That's my Aunt Haddie." His finger moved to hover over a tall, attractive black girl with long hair. "That's my sister Michelle."

Mac started to wolf-whistle, but he froze as Chandler's icy glare ripped into him. "Sorry. Who's she?" Mac pointed to a short, cute white girl with a ponytail on top of her head.

"That's my other sister, Replacement."

Tech's eyebrows went up. "Ah… she's white."

Chandler shrugged. "So?" He stuck his chin out toward Jack. "*He's* my brother, and he's *lily* white."

Jack grinned.

Mac scoffed.

Chandler leaned toward Mac, and his huge frame seemed to grow in the tight space. "You got a problem with that?"

Jack looked away to hide his smile. He knew Chandler was kidding with Mac, but he was also making a point. Chandler saw people, not color.

"I didn't," Mac stammered, "think the Army let brothers serve in the same unit."

Chandler leaned back and laughed. "I'm just messing with you. We're foster brothers."

Mac exhaled and looked relieved. "Oh. That explains your little sister." He pointed. "The white one."

"The white one?" Chandler's jaw tightened.

Mac's mouth opened and closed. "Sorry… I…"

Chandler laughed.

Mac scowled. "Stop doing that. I couldn't remember her name. What did you call her? Replacement?"

"Yeah." Chandler nodded. "She's watching over everybody until I get home."

Jack stared at his friend. *He's still sending half his pay home. I don't know how he's gonna pay for college doing that.*

Tech kicked Jack's boot. "You never answered me before. Why do their eyes stay open?"

Before Jack could answer, Mac interrupted, "It's a stupid question." Mac shook his head, and sweat flew off his face and his thick red hair like a dog after a bath. "They stay open because of muscles or something."

"Seriously." Tech pushed his glasses up. "You've all seen it. Almost everybody dies with their eyes open."

"Pansies die with their eyes open." Butcher looked back from the front passenger seat with a snide smile. "Guess that's how we'll find you."

Tech went a little paler. "Screw you," he halfheartedly fired back. "It's sorta freaky. I was just wondering why."

"Maybe it's because they see something beautiful." Chandler's words seemed to hang in the oppressive air in the back of the Humvee.

Butcher's eyes narrowed, but his mouth stayed shut. Everyone turned to stare at Chandler, but no one dared say anything to the big man—except Jack.

Jack burst out laughing. "That's sweet," he teased his best friend.

Tech leaned forward and put his elbows on his knees. "Seriously, is that what you think, Chandler? Like beautiful what? Heaven or something?"

"Yeah."

Mac's lip curled. "Like clouds and harps and wings?"

"It's not like that." Chandler chuckled.

"And how do you know?" Butcher glared back.

Jack looked from his big friend to the faces of the other soldiers. There was a hunger in their eyes for Chandler's answer. They wanted to know. For a soldier, death could happen at any moment; they rode through the valley of the shadow of death each day, with the Reaper a constant companion. And they all had lain awake wondering what happens after. Now these men looked at Chandler like starving refugees waiting for him to dish out a meal.

"If you think about it, God made Eden paradise, but it was still Earth. There were flowers and trees, animals and people. There was no death. It was perfect. Isn't that Heaven? I think it'll be like that again, not floating around on clouds."

They rode along in silence for several minutes, each man lost in his own thoughts. Jack watched the sweat fall from his brow and quickly vanish when it hit the hot metal floor.

Tech looked up and put his hands on his thighs. "Well, that clinches it. When they find me, I want them to say I died with my eyes open. How about you, Jack? What do you want them to say when they find you?"

Jack thought for a second, then his mouth ticked up in a crooked grin. "When they find me, I want them to say, 'Look, he's still breathing.'"

Chandler kicked Jack's foot, and Mac shoved his shoulder. The laughter that filled the Humvee slowly baked off in the roasting heat. The men settled into silence as the lead vehicle of the three-car convoy kicked and bounced down the road.

Jack looked down the long, straight dirt road and frowned. He hated this stretch. Two steep hills ran along either side. He knew Black Hawks swept the route prior to them arriving and weren't far away, but he still felt the sweat run down the tight muscles of his broad back.

The radio crackled on. "Do not answer," the voice commanded.

It took Jack a second to recognize Joy's voice. She'd spoken at the briefing this morning. The intel analyst was petite and timid, but she'd stuck her chin out when she got to the front of the room, and her tone was serious as she warned them about the lack of chatter recently. That fact bothered Jack, but the look on Joy's face had made the point more than her words and the stats did. She was scared, but her fear was for them.

Everyone looked at the radio. A "do not answer" call when you were riding through hell always got your attention. "All units in area ten-two-thirty—eyes on. Out."

The radio clicked off, and Butcher scoffed. "I'm so sick of these stupid intel spooks trying to freak us out, kissing their way up the ladder. The broad's a suck-up."

"Seems like I remember her predicting that attack when we were in Tal Afar pretty accurately," Jack said.

"Screw you, Stratton. We get that crap almost every time we go."

Jack leaned forward. "Why don't you keep your eyes ahead?"

Butcher glared at him for another few seconds before turning around.

The Humvee fell into an eerie silence. Jack rechecked his gun. Chandler tried his best to stretch out his legs.

After a few minutes, Jack slipped sideways and scanned the road ahead. "Hank, did we go by those guys with the cart?"

Hank leaned forward. "No, we didn't."

Jack saw Hank's knuckles turn white as he stared down the empty road. *We passed three guys with a little cart earlier. Now that we've turned around, we should've seen them by this point. They're gone.* "Punch it," Jack ordered.

Hank floored it.

Just as the Humvee surged forward, bullets pinged off the sides of the vehicle.

Butcher fumbled for the radio. "Taking fire! Taking fire!" he shrieked.

Chandler leaned forward and roared, "West side! West side!"

Jack saw the shell hit directly in front of them. The Humvee slammed into the cloud of rising dirt and stones. He grabbed for the handle as he felt the front end of the Humvee rise into the air.

Mac shouted and covered his head. Hank pulled the steering wheel hard to the right, but the Humvee still came through the cloud of dirt at a sharp angle.

"Hang—" Hank was cut off as the Humvee rolled.

Everything not strapped down went flying, and the ear-piercing sound of tearing metal filled the vehicle. It was as though someone had drained all the water out of a snow globe and then shaken it. The soldiers smashed around inside like the pieces.

The Humvee crashed into a huge rock and jolted to a stop. Something slammed into Jack's face and chest, and everything went out of focus. Like a fighter who had taken a hard punch, Jack hung on to the edge of consciousness. He shook his head, struggled to keep his eyes open, and looked around.

The Humvee's upright and still on its wheels.

Tech lay crumpled on the floor at Jack's feet, groaning.

It must have been Tech who smashed into me.

Jack lifted his head and turned to the back of the Humvee. Chandler hadn't budged, but he was breathing hard. "You good?" Jack asked.

Chandler nodded.

Mac held his nose, and blood streamed through his fingers. Hank and Butcher were trying to sit up straight. The Humvee had spun around two hundred seventy degrees and landed facing the ridge.

"Hank." Jack pulled himself forward and grabbed Hank's shoulder. "Get us going."

Hank nodded. The left half of his face was already so swollen his eye was closed. He turned the ignition, but besides a faint electric hum, the Humvee was silent.

Think.

Jack shook his head in an attempt to clear both his vision and his head. His ears rang, and he just wanted to close his eyes and fall into the darkness that pulled at his mind.

Bullets rained down on them. Jack saw the flashes as the fighters on the ridge fired automatic weapons.

They've got height and line of sight advantage. We get outside and we're dead. If we stay here, a direct RPG hit and we're dead.

Something big blew up outside the left side of the Humvee. The whole vehicle shook, and everyone instinctively covered their heads.

We're sitting ducks.

As Jack looked out the shattered windshield up the ridge, everything changed. Huge clouds of dust flew into the air and fire rained down from the sky. Chunks of rock and earth burst upward as shells pounded the hillside. Massive plumes of dirt rose into the air, swirled by the wind. From somewhere high above them, a gunship was unloading more firepower than Jack had ever seen.

"AC-130!" Mac's fists shook as he cheered.

When the shelling stopped, the dust cloud continued to hang over the hillside. They stayed there in silence until they heard the sound of Humvees racing toward them.

"Man," Hank shook his head, "if it wasn't for the 130, we'd all be dead."

"Looks like Joy got them to have one watch over us." Jack exhaled.

"Mac!" Chandler yelled.

Everyone turned around. Mac was shaking violently and his eyes rolled back in his head. His body went rigid and then began to jerk spastically. He fell to the floor as he thrashed.

"Watch his head," Jack ordered Chandler.

Mac suddenly stopped moving.

Chandler leaned down. "Mac?"

A bullet casing rolled across the floor. Jack's heart pounded in his ears. Sweat ran down the sides of his face. The casing came to a stop with a faint clink that echoed in the silence.

Mac gasped for air.

***

Jack's eyes flew open. Sweat soaked the sheets. He let his arms roll out to his sides and didn't even think about moving. The nightmares of war always left him like this. Drained. He felt as if he'd been doing sprints after a full workout. He listened to his breathing slowly even out.

Mac made it. Tech's dead. IED. Hank committed suicide. I don't know about Butcher. Chandler...

He stared up into the darkness because he didn't want to close his eyes. He didn't know whether your eyes stayed open when you died because you caught a glimpse of Heaven, but he knew that when he closed his, he remembered Hell.

11

TITUS

Jack's phone buzzed on the nightstand. He fumbled to grab it and read the text message from Titus's secretary, Shawna: GOOD MORNING, HONEY. GOT TWO FOR YOU. TITUS NEEDS THEM BROUGHT IN ASAP.

Jack took a quick shower, got dressed in a black T-shirt, jeans, and sneakers, and threw open the bedroom door. The snarling beast dashed across the living room, baring its teeth, and barked ferociously. Jack managed to slam the door shut just before the dog reached him.

Damn it. He let his head fall against the door as he worked to calm his breathing and his heartbeat.

He heard Replacement praising the dog. "Beauty. Sit. Shh. Good girl. Good girl."

"Good girl?" Jack yelled. "How about bad dog? Can you keep that thing—?" Jack ripped open the door.

The dog lunged forward, barking. Replacement held on to the dog's collar, but the dog dragged her across the floor.

"SHUT UP!" Jack roared, and the dog stopped.

The two glared at each other and Replacement rubbed her own ears. "Wow, you two are loud," she muttered.

"We reached a truce last night, Beast, and you'd better keep it," Jack grumbled as he stormed by and into the kitchen.

When she saw the dog had calmed down, Replacement hesitantly let go of the collar. The dog trotted down the hallway and into Replacement's bedroom.

"Do you want me to make you breakfast?" Replacement offered.

He searched her face. "Are you feeling better?"

"I am. Can I make you some eggs?"

"No. I'm good. I have to go meet someone."

"Who?"

"Just a friend. I'm going to give him a hand." He kept his head lowered. "He needs some help with a job."

Replacement smiled, but Jack thought it looked forced. "I got another website design job. That'll help with some money."

"We're good. I have some cash coming in, okay?"

Replacement nodded and went over to the cabinet. "Let me pour you a coffee at least."

"Thanks. Are you gonna call Daniel?"

"Yeah. I tried once already."

Replacement handed him a brand-new travel mug with a strange rectangular socket at its base. Jack held it up and peered at it.

"What's that hole?" Jack asked.

"It has a built-in USB charger. It's to keep your coffee warm. You can charge it in your Charger." She giggled. "I sat through a new web provider presentation and got it free."

"You're such a geek." Jack almost dropped the coffee cup when she hit him in the arm. "I'll call you later."

"Be safe. Love you."

Jack still marveled at the ease with which those words rolled off her tongue. More amazing still was how good they felt rolling off his own.

"I love you too."

***

A bell chimed over the door as Jack walked into Titus Bail Bonds, a tiny office sandwiched between a rundown nail salon and an old pizza parlor in the middle of a dangerous neighborhood in downtown Fairfield. Even though the office had just opened for the day, two people sat in the small waiting area. One was a young pregnant woman who watched Jack with red-rimmed eyes. The other was an older man who appeared ready to explode. Jack immediately processed the possibilities. *Father bailing out a kid, and it's not the first time. From how mad he is, it's probably the last time he'll do it, though. Young girl is helping a man she hopes will be there when the baby is born.*

The young woman gazed at the floor. Jack sighed as he approached the counter.

"You're looking fina' than a piece o' china, Jackie." Shawna's rich voice filled the room. She was a short, heavyset black woman a year or two older than Jack. She wore a wig that was more orange than red and her matching dress strained at the seams, about to burst open.

Shawna pressed the buzzer to let him into the back office. Before he could even get through the door, though, she scampered over on her five-inch heels and gave him a huge hug. "I can't tell you how glad I am you're back in town."

She kept a hand on his back, but he felt it quickly sliding down. He stopped it traveling any lower. "Good morning to you too."

Shawna wiggled her eyebrows. "Can't blame a gal for trying." She grinned. Jack had known her all his life, and ever since they were kids, she'd flirted with him.

"Is Titus in?"

"Oh, don't think I'm just gonna let you run off. You need to see me first." She hurried over to the desk and picked up two manila folders. "I've got all your paperwork here. Remember to keep the bailpiece and the bond with you. They're both certified."

She flipped open the first folder, labeled "Lawrence Green." Inside was a mug shot of a man around two years older than Jack. One look at his pudgy face and Jack relaxed a bit.

"Is one of his eyebrows gone?" Jack looked closer at the picture.

Shawna laughed. "Yeah. Stupid dumbass burned it off. That's why he got arrested. It was an insurance scam gone bad."

"What went wrong?"

"Him." Shawna laughed again. "Not only did he try to torch a Lexus, but the idiot hooked a trailer to it and said all that stuff got burned up too."

Jack shook his head. "How much is he worth?"

"You have to talk to Titus about the money." Her lips pressed together in a tight line. "His momma put up the bond and she's hell-bent ticked off. She calls about five times a day."

"Where does she live?" Jack pulled out his notebook.

"Put that away." Shawna clucked as she took another sheet from the folder. "I watch out for my boys." She wiggled her eyebrows as she held up the page. "I wrote it all down."

"You're the best."

"Why thank you. Yes I am." Shawna patted her fake orange curls. "I don't know if I'd start with the mother if I were you, but I guess you've got your methods and they seem to be working. After all, even though you just started you're ahead of everyone this month."

Top bounty hunter. Jack suppressed a grin. Something inside him liked that title.

"Next up," Shawna grabbed the other folder, "Eddie Porter."

Jack looked at the smug-looking guy with a neck tattoo. His slicked-back black hair was greasy, and he had small eyes.

"He goes by Little-E but everyone calls him Grease-E." Shawna laughed. "He was arrested twice for assault."

"What's he up for now?"

"Bad checks. Lots of bad checks."

"Who posted his bail?" Peering at the list of priors, Jack was amazed he was even granted bail.

"Him. No one else was going to stick their neck out for that weasel."

"Why did Titus?" Jack asked.

Shawna shook her head and pressed her lips together. "Uh-uh. Never say anything about your boss. You have to ask Titus."

Jack gave her a wink and picked up the folders. "I will. Is he in?"

"He's with Bobbie G. They should be out soon."

"Bobbie? He works here?" Jack asked.

"Bobbie does bail enforcement too."

Jack had known Bobbie since they were kids. They liked each other, but they were never close.

That was because of Chandler.

Bobbie and Chandler never got along. Why that was, Jack never figured out. They were alike in so many ways. They grew up in the same neighborhood. They went to the same schools. Same church. Same sports teams. They were both huge black men, but Chandler was an inch taller and twenty pounds lighter. They could've been brothers, but put them together and you felt the uneasiness grow. No one understood it. Not Aunt Haddie, nor her best friend—Bobbie's mother.

"Wow. So Bobbie's bounty hunting."

"Yeah, but don't you worry. Business is good. Titus uses three, sometimes four. There's plenty of work to go around." She angled her head to the waiting room, and Jack noticed that two more people had come in.

The door to Titus's office opened, and while Shawna zipped in, Bobbie Gibson walked out. Bobbie was six four and over three hundred pounds. He had rolled up the sleeves on his army-green T-shirt to show off his massive biceps. He stopped short when he saw Jack, looked him up and down, broke into a broad grin, and nodded.

That was sort of a tradition with Jack and Bobbie: they didn't shake hands. No knuckle bumps either. They just nodded. It seemed to sum up their whole relationship. Still, Jack would always have Bobbie's back—and had done so on a few occasions.

"Good to see you, Bobbie."

"Welcome back, Jack. How you been?"

"I'm good. You?"

Bobbie inhaled and seemed to get even taller. "Good, really? I read about you in the funny papers, except it ain't so funny. How's your side?"

"Better every day."

Titus's office door opened and Shawna leaned out. "Jack? Titus can see you now."

"Good seeing you, Bobbie." Jack turned to go.

"Hey, Jack. I've been meaning to call you." Bobbie handed Jack his card. "Let me know if you want to go for a game of eight ball at Hannigan's sometime."

Jack looked back at Bobbie. It had been years since he had seen him, and there was something different about his face now. The hard edge to his eyes was gone. "Sure." Jack held up the card. "I'll give you a call."

"Any time. I usually swing in on the way home. They've still got great wings."

Jack nodded and walked into Titus's office. Shawna stepped aside and Jack passed her.

Titus J. Martin was seated behind an immense oak desk. Titus was in his mid-forties with a medium build. Dressed in a pressed white shirt, steel-gray tie, matching pants, and black leather shoes, he looked as if he'd be more comfortable in a corner office on Wall Street than here. His fingers flew over the keyboard before he triumphantly reached over and clicked the mouse.

"I just had to finish an email." He stood up and thrust out a hand.

Jack shook it and sat down. "Thanks for the call, Titus."

"Don't thank me, Jack. I need these two back, and I need them back soon. You're fast. Real fast. But if you don't get them soon, I'll bring in Bobbie G."

"How fast are we talking?" Jack tilted his head.

"End of the week, but the faster, the better. Larry Green's mother keeps calling me. She put up a lot of cash *and* her house. I can't believe he ran—never thought he'd do that to her. Anyway, I'll consider it a favor."

"I'll get it done," Jack said. "Do you have any idea where he'd be?"

"None. He's got a girl and a kid, but they all live at his mother's."

"I'll start with her then."

"The other guy, Eddie, watch out for him. He's a three-strike loser, and he likes to carry a knife."

"I've got it. You got any angle on where he hangs?"

"Eddie likes the ladies, but the ladies don't like Eddie. Eddie pays for his company."

"L Street?" Everyone in Fairfield knew L Street. Located in the worst section of town, it was the last of the Alphabet streets. In the middle, two strip clubs faced each other, but the whole stretch was known for prostitution.

"You know it." Titus leaned back and eyed Jack. "You know, you really seem to be taking to this job. How are things looking from your side?"

Jack tapped the armrest. "Fine. Long hours, rough neighbors, but you pay well."

Titus flashed a grin. "The pay is good because you're fast. It's a ratio. But you're good?"

"Yeah. I like catching bad guys."

Titus chuckled. "Just don't try to go too fast. And watch out for Grease-E. Be careful, Jack."

12

I'M GOING TO BRING AN ARMY

Jack walked up the concrete walkway to a pale-green duplex. It looked well cared for, and it had a homey feel to it. Several cars were parked in the driveway.

Before Jack reached the door, a young woman came out carrying four balloons and a banner. She looked to be in her early twenties, and her modest pullover summer dress complemented her dark-brown skin and medium-length curly hair. Because of her tall, lithe build, almost anything she wore would showcase her figure.

"Hello," she said, grinning broadly.

Jack smiled back. "Hi. I'm looking for Mrs. Green."

"Which one?" she asked over her shoulder as she taped the balloons to the side of the house.

"Elizabeth."

"She's my aunt. My mom's Mrs. Green also, and there's another Mrs. Green inside, too." She held up a banner that read *BABY GIRL* and angled her head toward one corner of it. "Do you mind?"

Jack grabbed the top corner, and she handed him a piece of tape. Together they hung the banner.

"I appreciate your help."

From inside the house, someone called out, "Mia, is that your uncle?" A very short, hefty woman in her mid-fifties opened the door. She looked frazzled. When her eyes met Jack's, she gave a little hop and frowned even more.

"Aunt Beth, this is…" Mia turned, looked at Jack, and chuckled. "I'm sorry, but I didn't even ask your name."

"I'm Jack Stratton. I'm looking for Lawrence."

Something fell to the floor inside, and both women's eyes blazed.

"Are you a friend of that no-good buffoon?" Elizabeth wiggled her finger under Jack's nose as she stomped forward. "You'd better not be here to say he didn't do it. I don't care if he did or not—he's got to go to court and stop calling anyone who'll listen and telling them he didn't do it."

Jack took three steps back as four women who looked almost identical to Elizabeth poured out of the house and down the steps. He immediately classified them by the color of their dresses: yellow, orange, blue, and pink. As the rainbow of stout women surrounded him, they all talked at once.

"Do you know where he is?"

"You tell him that his momma's so upset."

"Where is he?"

"That no-good—"

This isn't good. Jack held up his hands. "Titus sent me."

They stopped talking, but they continued to glare.

Elizabeth asked, "Well, did Titus find him yet?" Her words were so crisp they snapped.

"No, but—"

All of them shouted questions and objections. Their hands shot out in all directions while they berated him for not finding Lawrence.

"Wait a second." Orange stepped forward, reached up, and grabbed Jack's chin. She twisted his face back and forth, examining him. "You're one of Aunt Haddie's foster babies."

"He is," Pink proclaimed.

"I remember when you were little." Blue's smile was so big and warm that Jack grinned.

"That's Chandler's friend," Yellow called out from the back.

At the mention of Chandler's name, they all went quiet.

"How's Haddie?" Elizabeth stepped forward. "I meant to get over there. I stopped by a month ago."

Now I've gotta *find this guy.* "She's doing okay. Titus said I need to find Lawrence quickly."

Elizabeth's eyes welled up, and Mia stepped forward to put her arm around her shoulders. The whole rainbow protectively moved closer like a group of chicks.

"You do." Mia's eyes rounded in concern as they locked on Jack's. "If not, my aunt's out all that money, and I don't know what she's going to do."

The women all started to talk again. Everyone offered suggestions as to where they thought Lawrence would be hiding. People, places, and street names were tossed out.

Crowd control, Jack. Jack dropped his voice and raised the volume. "Elizabeth." The group stopped talking, and Jack let the silence hang in the air for a second before he continued. "I need just Elizabeth to answer this next question." He spoke low and with authority. "If Lawrence got into a fight with his girlfriend, where would he go?"

Elizabeth pointed to the woman in orange. "He'd go to Ricky's."

Orange tossed her hands up. "I told you I already grilled Ricky. Lawrence isn't there. Ricky hasn't seen him."

"Ma'am." Jack leaned in, and his eyes connected with hers. "What did you ask him? Exactly."

She put her hand on her chest. "I came right out and asked, 'Is Lawrence over at your place?' and he looked me right in the eye. He didn't even blink and he said, 'No, Momma. I haven't even heard from him.'"

She's telling the truth and her kid's lying. Elizabeth said that Lawrence has been calling everyone who'll listen, but he doesn't call his best friend? He's at Ricky's.

"Do you have an address for Ricky?"

"I just told—" she began, but Mia cut her off.

"He lives at 754 Bellington. He, my brother, and two cousins rent my Uncle Bryan's house."

"Do any of them have any priors?"

"None of them have nothing." Yellow stamped her foot.

"They stay there and play video games all day." Pink held out her hands and wiggled her thumbs like she was holding a game controller.

"He's probably there with Farrell and Isaac," Mia said.

Orange continued to protest her son's innocence. "Ricky doesn't know where Lawrence is. You need to look over at the Parker House."

"The Parker House?" Elizabeth scoffed. "Why'd he be at that hotel? He can't afford a night, let alone stay there."

"He worked there," Ricky's mother snapped.

"When he was sixteen, and they fired his sorry butt," Pink pointed out.

The group dissolved into griping and finger-pointing, so Jack backed up.

I got what I needed anyway. "Thank you for your time." He waved.

Only Mia waved back. Everyone else was so busy trying to make their point that they didn't even turn around as Jack headed back to his car.

***

Jack pulled up in front of a small light-blue ranch house with three cars in the driveway. The grass was long, and a stack of unpainted shutters sat on top of sawhorses. He grabbed the white envelope Shawna had given him, took out the certified letters, and put them in his front pocket.

I need an angle. Jack flipped open one of the manila folders. He folded Lawrence's spec sheet and put it in the envelope. Then he got out of the car and cracked his neck.

Lawrence is facing all nonviolent charges and has no other arrests. This should be a cakewalk, but I don't know what's behind that door or how things could change. He shifted his bulletproof vest, looked down at his chest, and clenched his teeth. *No badge.*

Jack never looked down on anyone's job, and now wasn't any different. It didn't matter whether you were a security guard or a cop to him—you still took a chance—but it was still strange to not have a badge on his chest. Every time he looked down and didn't see it, it reminded him he wasn't a cop anymore.

Three cars. Odds are five or six guys.

As Jack walked up the brick walkway, he looked at the weeds that had popped up among the rusting paint cans and wondered for how long ago the painting job had been abandoned. Muffled music blared from inside the house. The volume was so loud the windows shook.

Jack went through his mental checklist as he approached the door: vest, gun, boot gun, Taser, mace, cuffs, and ties.

He kept to the edge of the two cement steps and stopped on the left side of the door. Through the partially open blind, he saw three men standing around a couch and two guys sitting, holding controllers. Lawrence wasn't among them. The guy closest to the door kept tipping his head back and shouting something to an open doorway.

At least one other person is in the other room.

The music suddenly stopped, and everyone jumped up. A wide-eyed man ran over, pulled the shade partway back, and looked Jack up and down. His eyes got even larger, and he mashed the blinds closed.

Jack couldn't make out the harsh whispering of the men inside. He rang the doorbell and stepped back and to the left.

The whispering increased. Someone started to pull the blinds open, but they were abruptly yanked closed again.

Jack rang the doorbell a second time. The voices got louder and moved to just behind the door. Now Jack could hear what they were saying.

"Don't open the door, Ricky," someone warned.

"I'll get rid of him."

"Don't say nothing."

The door opened with a scraping sound, and a medium-built guy in his early twenties glared at Jack.

"Yeah?" he snarled.

Jack saw the beads of sweat forming on his forehead.

"Hi, Ricky." Jack set an informal tone and smiled. He guessed the guy opening the door was Ricky, and judging by the stunned look on the guy's face, he'd guessed correctly. "I'm just dropping off this paperwork that Lawrence forgot to sign." He held out the envelope.

Ricky blinked a couple of times before his mouth ticked into a grin. He grabbed the envelope, and his head started to turn toward the living room before he froze.

"Wait. Ah... Lawrence isn't here," he stuttered.

Bingo. "Seriously, Ricky?" Jack caught the closing door. "I have no time for this. Tell Lawrence to get his butt out here or—"

"You can't come in." A short guy with a crew cut and two gold teeth hurried into the hallway and stopped. "You need a warrant."

"Ricky." Jack dropped his voice even lower. "Do you want to handle this the easy way?"

"Close the door. Don't talk to him, Ricky." Gold Teeth waved his hand. "Don't say nothing."

"Seriously, Ricky." Jack smiled. "We can be done with this in a minute or—"

"Or what? Huh?" Gold Teeth crossed his arms in front of himself. "You can't come in. No warrant, no entry."

"Yeah." Ricky pushed on the door. "You can't do anything."

A smirk formed on Jack's face as he easily kept the door open with one hand while Ricky struggled against it. "That's where you're wrong, Ricky. See, if you don't send Lawrence out, I'm going to bring an army here."

Ricky looked nervously at Gold Teeth, who just scoffed. "He ain't got no army. He's no cop. He's probably not even a real bounty hunter. There's only one of him. Bounty hunters always go in at least pairs. Solo? Close the door."

"This is your last chance, Ricky."

"He ain't here. Now get out of my house." Ricky started to press even harder against the door, and Jack let it slowly close.

Jack heard the deadbolt slide into place, followed by laughter and clapping hands. Reaching into his pocket, Jack grabbed his phone and walked back to the car.

After two rings, a woman answered. "Hello?"

"It's Jack. He's at Ricky's."

Click.

Jack smiled, leaned back against the Charger, and folded his arms.

Fifteen minutes.

Jack made a big show of waiting. The music turned back on and the windows vibrated once more. After a few minutes, the blinds partially opened and someone peeked out. The blinds closed and someone turned the music up even louder.

Down the block, a sedan blew through a stop sign and came barreling toward him. A big SUV followed right behind, and a minivan brought up the rear.

Jack smiled.

The sedan drove right up on the grass and slammed to a stop. The other two cars parked on the street. Ten peeved women poured out of the vehicles and formed a mob on the front lawn. Elizabeth stood with her feet planted wide apart, and Mia stayed by her side. The women in the rainbow colors—as well as a few new women Jack hadn't seen before—formed a half-circle behind them.

Elizabeth faced Jack. "Is he inside?" Her eyes looked ready to pop out of her head, and her whole body quivered.

Jack grinned. "Yep. Two of you should go around back to make sure he doesn't try to run out that way."

Three women hurriedly waddled around back while the others stormed the front door better than any SWAT team could. Elizabeth took point and pounded on the door. It opened, and the women barged inside.

The music shut off and screams and swears flew. Something broke. Four of the guys raced from the house. After a minute, Ricky flew out too, his mother screaming right behind him. Jack couldn't make out exactly what she was saying, but every couple of words she swatted him across the back of his head.

With a mixture of disbelief and humiliation, Ricky gawked at Jack while he tried to shield his head from her smacking. "You called my mother?"

"Don't you say anything to him! He was right to call me. You lied right to your momma's face. You looked me in the eye and lied!" Ricky's mother swatted the back of his head again. "What else have you been lying about? What else?"

The rest of the women appeared in the doorway, dragging Lawrence from the building. Yellow's hand tightly gripped his hair while Pink held him by the back of his shirt and pants like a bouncer tossing a drunk out of a bar. They screamed, slapped, and berated him.

"Don't leave marks," Jack yelled as he opened the back door of the Charger. "I'll have to explain them."

Lawrence strained to make it to the safety of the car as the women got in a few more shots and hurled more insults. When Jack shut the car door behind him, the mob continued to yell at Lawrence through the window.

Elizabeth turned to look at Jack. He could see the emotions racing across her face like a fast-moving storm. The anger quickly turned to relief that soured into dismay. *Her baby's going to jail. Here comes the rain.*

Her lip trembled once, and then she lost it. She flung her head back and wailed. Huge tears flew from her eyes as she spun around and reached out for comfort. The mob that had been so intent on capturing Lawrence now transformed into a support group as they encircled the crying woman. They rubbed her shoulders and their voices softened.

Jack made his way around to the driver's side while the group walked Elizabeth to her car. Suddenly, she whipped back around and raced over to him.

"Momma!" Lawrence yelled through the closed window. "Don't do this, Momma."

Elizabeth pushed forward to stand next to the car.

"Momma, please," Lawrence begged. "I didn't do it. It's not my fault, Momma."

"Wait. Wait." She grabbed hold of Jack's arm. "He'll be okay, right? You'll take care of him?" Her hands clasped together, and she held them up to her mouth.

Jack nodded. "I need to take him in. Once he gets processed, if Titus agrees, you can bond him back out, but… he's going to run again."

The woman's lip quivered. Mia came up and put her arm around her shoulder. Mia mouthed, "Thank you," and led Elizabeth back to the car.

Jack jumped into the Charger, started it up, and took off. In the rearview mirror, he saw Elizabeth turn and take a couple of steps after the car. She stretched her arms out and cried.

Lawrence shook his head in the back seat and put his hands up to his ears.

13

I NEED A FAVOR

Jack sat in his car on L Street and looked back and forth between the two strip clubs. Both the La Jolla on the left and the Bare Necessities on the right were old bars that had been converted in the '80s. Jack's vantage point allowed him to keep an eye on the entrance to the adult video store next to Bare Necessities, too.

He glanced at the clock: 10:53 p.m. After sitting here for over five hours, his side throbbed. And the guys he saw scurry into the clubs and then stumble drunkenly out afterward weren't helping his mood.

Jack had already talked to the doormen at all three places. None of them had seen Grease-E, and none were fans of him either. They grabbed Jack's business card all too eagerly at just the prospect of Grease-E getting carted off to prison.

A car pulled up beside Jack and a young girl got out. She was pretty, barely twenty-one, and wore a simple dress. Jack would never have guessed she was a stripper if it weren't for the cowgirl costume with Velcro straps she carried over her shoulder. She kissed the young guy driving and hurried inside. The guy pulled away the second she turned around, not even waiting until she got inside.

Jack's fingers drummed the dashboard. *Men don't feel comfortable walking in this neighborhood at night, and Scumbag drops her off here in the middle of the street. And that's the least of it. He knows where she's going. He knows she's going to go take her clothes off for a bunch of drunk guys. But he still brings her here to do it.*

Jack had seen the pattern too many times. Guys like that scumbag were vampires who leeched off girls. He'd take all her money and she'd give him everything she had, but it wouldn't be enough. One morning, she'd wake up and he'd be gone—and all the sweet goodness in her would have been sucked dry.

Apart from an occasional raid or a disturbance call, Jack had never gone into a strip club—even in the Army. He'd never looked at porn, either. After his streetwalker mother had abandoned him, he'd always had this fear that he'd open the magazine and she'd be in it. His stomach curled at the thought. Then, as he got older, he thought about the fact that those girls were someone's mother, sister, or daughter. That was enough to keep his eyes off any of that crap.

He knew that the girl who'd just run into La Jolla had a thousand possible reasons for stripping, but he wasn't going to go along with it.

His phone rang, and he smiled. "Hey, Dad."

"Hi, honey," his adopted mother said in a fake low voice.

"That's a pretty poor imitation of Dad, Mom." Jack laughed.

"I borrowed his phone," she confessed. "I was thinking about you and wanted to call and let you know how much we love you."

Her thinking about me means I haven't called enough and she was worried. "I love you too, Mom. How are you both?"

"We're doing great, but we miss you. You're not overdoing it, are you?"

"No, Mom. I'm following doctor's orders."

"You mean Alice?" His mother laughed. "How is she?"

"She's good. I'm thinking about taking her with me and coming down to see you."

"That'd be lovely. I'll have to get the guest room ready and—"

"Mom, stop. I don't want to put you out. We can get a hotel—"

"Nonsense. You'll do no such thing. Do you think you'll come soon?"

"I'll try. I…" Jack trailed off as he watched an older prostitute he hadn't seen before round the corner and slowly walk along the edge of the street.

"I don't want to bother you, honey," his mom said. "I can tell you're in the middle of something. I just wanted to tell you we love you."

"I love you too, Mom. Tell Dad I love him. Bye-bye."

Talk to one more and then I'll go home.

He tossed open his door and groaned as he got out of the car.

The woman's eyes narrowed as he approached. Jack gave a little nod and stopped a few feet away. When he spoke, he tried to soften his voice. "Hi. I was wondering if I could ask you a few questions?"

"You're a cop." Her eyes darted around, and she looked ready to bolt.

"No. I need a favor, though."

"You?" Her voice rose, along with her eyebrows. "You want to pay for it?"

"Not that kind of favor." Jack stammered and then coughed. "I'm looking for a guy."

Her neck lengthened, and her hands went to her hips. "I'm a girl," she snapped.

"No, no—I'm trying to find Eddie Porter."

"Eddie who?"

"Porter." Jack fumbled with the wanted poster in his pocket. "He goes by—"

"Grease-E! That good-for-nothing lowlife scum sucker. Are you friends? He stiffed me for a—"

"No. I'm trying to find him because he skipped bond."

Her hands flopped at her sides and she gave Jack a look that screamed *you should have just told me.* "If I knew where Grease-E was, I'd put a bow on his slimy head and give him to you."

"When's the last time you saw him?"

She tilted her head and squished up her face. "Five days ago?" She nodded. "Yeah, I gave him a—"

"I don't need details." Jack took a business card from his pocket and a twenty. "What's your name?"

"Debra. But everyone calls me Da Jewel." She grinned and did a mini-curtsy.

"That's nice. Is he a regular?"

"Unfortunately. None of the other girls wanna touch him, but a buck's a buck, right?" She shrugged.

"Is there a particular night he comes by, or is it random?"

"He's on assistance, so he comes every check day."

Jack tried not to make a disgusted face. *Good use of my tax dollars.* "When's the next check day?"

She scrunched up her face again. "Two days." She grinned.

"Debra, I need you to do me a favor, okay?"

"Yeah, sure."

"I'm going to give you twenty dollars now." As he handed her the card and money, her hand shot out and snagged the cash with lightning speed. "You call me if you see him and there will be more."

"How much?" She took two steps forward, and the cloud of perfume that followed her hit Jack square in the face.

He tried not to cough.

You need the money, Jack. She's not a charity case. Twenty bucks will do it. Say twenty bucks.

"Fifty." *Stupid softy.*

She smiled so warmly Jack felt his mouth tick up.

A man cleared his throat behind Jack. "What does she have to do for that fifty dollars?"

Because of the tone, Jack knew the man's profession before he looked back. He slowly turned around and gave a sideways smile to the older cop, who frowned at him. The cop looked over Jack's shoulder and waved Da Jewel forward.

"Come on, Debra. Go stand over at the wall while I call it in."

"Call it in?" Jack repeated before his eyes flew wide. "Wait a second—you don't think...? I wasn't—I—"

"Save it, pal." The cop reached for his shoulder radio. "I saw you solicit."

"*Solicit?* No." Jack held up both hands and quickly read his badge. "Reed, I'm working for Titus Bail Bonds."

"Sure," Reed scoffed, but his hand stayed off the radio.

"In my front pocket is the certificate. I'm looking for Eddie Porter."

"Grease-E?" Reed's eyes flashed. "They let him out again?"

Jack nodded and returned the look of frustration. "Sucks. We put them in, they get right out."

"We?" Reed inhaled. "You're not a cop, you're—sorry. That wasn't called for. You said you're a bail bondsman?"

"I work for Titus Bail Bonds. Jack Stratton."

"Delmar Reed. Jack Stratton?" He tilted his head and examined Jack's face. "Wait a second, you're the cop from Darrington."

"Yeah."

"You were just on the Vitagliano kidnapping, right? Your picture was all over the news. You got shot, right?"

"Yeah." Jack resisted the urge to touch his side.

Delmar's shoulders went up. "Then why are you saying you're working for Titus?"

Jack paused for a second, then decided to just tell the truth without any spin. "I'm not on the job right now."

"Medical leave?"

Jack shook his head. "I decided to try something else for a little while."

Delmar's lips pressed together and he searched Jack's face. After a minute, he nodded. "Sorry, man."

"It is what it is. Do you know Eddie?"

"I've arrested him so many times I should give him frequent flyer miles. He's a weasel."

"Have you seen him?"

"Not lately, but you're looking in the right place. Grease-E comes down here for…" Delmar trailed off and looked around.

Jack followed his gaze. Da Jewel was gone.

"Damn," Jack said. "I told her I'd give her the fifty to keep an eye out for Grease-E for me."

"Did you give her a phone number?"

"Yeah."

"Don't sweat it. If she sees Grease-E, she'll call."

Jack clicked his tongue. "Why do you think so?"

Delmar smiled knowingly. "'Cause she hates Grease-E more than I do."

14

NOSYKINS

Jack walked up to his apartment door and stopped. *The Beast. I hope she has it locked in her room.* He reached for the knob—and the dog barked furiously before his hand even touched the handle. *Terrific.*

"One second," Replacement called out.

Jack started to open the door.

"Wait!"

"I'd like to come into my own apartment."

"Hold on," Replacement shouted again. "Just one second. All right. Come in."

Jack twisted the knob and gave the door a push. Replacement stood with her feet apart and her hands proudly clamped together in front of herself. The dog sat calmly on its haunches next to her, watching Jack.

Jack smiled. "Is Beast good?" he asked.

"Don't call her that." Replacement frowned. "Nosykins is being very well behaved."

"Nosy… what?" Jack laughed. "I'll stick with Beast. Can I come in yet?"

"No. I want to show you something else first."

"It's been a long day."

"Watch." Replacement moved beside the dog and held up a treat. "Lie down."

The dog lay down. Replacement clapped and tossed her a little cookie.

"Sit."

The dog's claws clicked on the wood floor as she scrambled to sit up.

"Very nice," Jack said.

"Watch this." Replacement beamed. "Stand."

Jack took a small step back as the dog hopped up onto her back legs. *That's the biggest dog I've ever seen.* "Watch your fingers," Jack cautioned as Replacement dropped another cookie into the dog's mouth.

"She's a baby." Replacement rubbed behind the dog's ears. "Sit. Wait," she commanded as she walked forward and put a biscuit on the floor a few feet away. "Ready?" She walked back next to the dog and then ordered, "Get it!"

Although the dog's eyes were fixed on the biscuit, she remained seated.

Jack chuckled.

Replacement frowned. "Go. Go, girl. Get it." Her lips pressed together and she put her hands on her hips. *"Sic 'em!"*

The dog's ears flattened back on its head, its teeth flashed in a snarl, and it lunged—at Jack.

"Stop! Sit!" Jack shouted, leaping back into the hallway with his hands on guard in front of him.

The dog barked ferociously and kept coming.

Replacement managed to grab the dog's collar, but the dog lunged again, pulling Replacement out of the apartment and into the hall.

"Mr. Stratton." The familiar shrill voice of Jack's landlady echoed down the hallway.

"Mrs. Stevens, stay back," Jack warned when he saw her wild red hair appear on the staircase.

The dog spun around and sprinted for the top of the stairs. Jack lunged after it, but Replacement stumbled into him. *"Stop!"* Jack yelled.

Mrs. Stevens was more than halfway up the stairs when the dog reached her. The large woman grabbed the railing with one hand and wrapped the other around the dog's neck.

"How's my baby?" Mrs. Stevens cooed. The dog licked her cheek. "How's my little girl?" She spoke in a voice three octaves higher than normal, and it made Jack cringe.

Jack's mouth dropped open. *Does the Beast only hate me?*

"You're such a good girl." Mrs. Stevens stroked the dog's head as she continued her climb up the steps. "Mr. Stratton, I'd think you'd be a little calmer around a dog."

"Me? That thing was going to eat me and then have you for dessert."

Mrs. Stevens laughed. "My big snookie-wookie wouldn't hurt a fly." She rubbed noses with the dog, and Jack's lip curled.

That's nasty. "Are you all right?" he asked Replacement.

She nodded. "Sorry. It was all my fault. I just wanted her to get the biscuit. I shouldn't say sic—"

Jack's finger shot out and pressed against her lips. "Don't."

"Sorry. Are you hungry? I'll heat up your dinner." Replacement tilted her head and gave him a let-me-make-it-up-to-you smile.

"I'm starving," Jack said.

"I'll let you two eat." Mrs. Stevens ruffled the dog's fur. "Any time you need a dog sitter, just let me know."

"Thank you." Replacement gave a little wave before she scooted back into the apartment with the dog. Jack followed at a safe distance.

"Does Gigantor need to go out?" Jack asked.

"Nope. I just took her." Replacement pulled food out of the refrigerator and turned on the stove. "Sit down and I'll heat up some dinner. Why are you so late?"

"You can use the microwave."

"It doesn't taste as good." She stuck her tongue out.

"That's true, but it's more work for you."

"You're worth it." She smiled.

He gave her a crooked grin back. As he stepped closer to her, he reached out, and his fingertips lightly touched hers. He leaned in and kissed her, stroking from her fingertips, up her arm, and to the back of her neck. She trembled, and then kissed him more forcefully.

Tingles ran down his spine as he felt her relax into him. He pulled her close. As he tilted his head and slid a hand up her back, she stiffened. She leaned back and wrinkled her nose.

"You smell like an old lady." Replacement rubbed her nose. "But… weird."

Jack smelled his own shirt. A strong whiff of Da Jewel's perfume still clung to him. "Let me take a shower."

"Why do you smell like a grandmother?" Replacement raised an eyebrow.

"Work. I was helping that friend of mine and I just got some perfume on me." Jack walked toward the bedroom as he talked. He glanced over his shoulder and saw Replacement standing there with her tongue in her cheek.

She's not stupid. I should just tell her I'm a bounty hunter, but she's going to be ticked I waited to say anything. I can't win. She'd never have let me take the job, but we needed the money.

Jack took his time in the shower, but Replacement never came in. For some reason, that really bothered him. She used to *always* walk in on him before they started dating, but now he couldn't drag her in there.

Jack dressed in some sweats and a white T-shirt, then returned to the living room. The dog was curled up in the corner with her doll, and Replacement was typing on the computer. But as soon as he stepped out of the bedroom, Replacement's hand leapt to the mouse, the screen flashed, and another window covered it. Jack had seen Billy Murphy do the same thing at the police station when he was playing computer poker and someone walked by. He'd quickly switch the screen to hide what he was doing.

Replacement glanced back over her shoulder at Jack. "You startled me."

"Everything okay?"

"I was just—*crud!* Your food." She rushed over to the oven and swore under her breath. "Oh, Jack, I burned it."

"It's fine. I'm not that hungry. I'll just make an English muffin or something."

She groaned and put her hands to her head. "Are you sure? Just give me a minute."

"I can make it."

"I want to. Please?"

"Sure." He flopped down on the computer chair. "Thanks."

Replacement ran around the kitchen to get something for him while Jack leaned back and closed his eyes. "How was your day?" he asked.

When she didn't answer right away, he looked into the kitchen. Replacement exhaled and her eyes rounded. "Sad. I've been looking at Daniel's Facebook. It's just sad." The toaster popped, and she spread some peanut butter on his English muffin.

Jack spun around to face the computer, but Replacement rushed over and half-dragged him out of the chair. "Let me just save what I was working on." She sat down, wiggled the mouse, and closed some windows.

"What's up? Do you not want me to see something?" Jack asked.

She froze for a second, then scoffed. "No. I just didn't want you to close any of the windows that I had open."

Replacement kept looking at the screen, and Jack's frown deepened. "You're sure closing a lot of them. And you got freaked out when I came out of the shower, too."

"You snuck up on me," she said, still without looking at him.

Jack didn't fully believe her, but he let it go. "What did you find out about Daniel?"

"Tons. He seems like a super-sweet guy. He's a lumberjack."

"Usually lumberjack and super-sweet aren't used in a sentence together."

"Well, this guy is. He's twenty-seven. His mom raised him, but she died a few years ago. He doesn't mention any brothers or sisters, so I think he's all alone. He had a snotty girlfriend."

"How did you get all this information?"

"Facebook." She rolled over to give Jack a clear view of the monitor.

A collection of pictures of Daniel appeared on the screen. He stood at about six foot eight, with broad shoulders, curly brown hair, and a lopsided smile. In one picture, Daniel knelt beside the dog at a pond. Daniel had his shirt off, and there was a tattoo on his right breast.

"What's that tattoo?" Jack asked.

"It's one of those old-fashioned ink things and a feather."

"He has a tattoo of an inkwell and a quill?"

Replacement shrugged. "People get some odd tattoos."

"Where does he work?"

"Linskie Lumber."

"Do you want to go there tomorrow?" Jack offered.

"Sounds great. His work should know where he is."

"Did Daniel write anything about his job?"

"Yeah, he wrote about all the guys he works with. It's sorta dumb to write about work, but he had nothing but nice things to say about them. He really likes working there."

Jack looked back at the photos. "Can you print out that photo of him with the tattoo?"

Replacement hit a few buttons, and the printer fired up.

"You said he *had* a girlfriend?" Jack asked.

"He has an ex. They broke up over a month ago. Sandra Hughes. She dumped him."

"He wrote that?" Jack asked.

"No. She did." Replacement pulled up another window. "She dumped him for a new guy and plastered it all over her Facebook."

"Do you have an address for her? After we go to the lumberyard, we should pay her a visit." Jack heard whimpering, and he looked into the kitchen. "Well. There goes my second dinner."

"Oh, no!" Replacement jumped up and rushed over to the dog.

Half the peanut butter English muffin was nowhere to be seen, but the other half was stuck in the fur under the dog's chin. She was trying to knock it off with her paw but was succeeding only in spreading the peanut butter around.

Jack laughed.

"I'm so sorry, Jack." Replacement got a wet dishcloth.

"Don't worry about it. I'm just glad the thief got caught. Getting my English muffin stuck to her head is justice."

"Muffin!" Replacement's face lit up. "That's awesome. I'll call her Muffin."

"Call her Thief."

"No."

"Call her Peanut Butter Head." Jack laughed. "I'll call her Butt Head for short."

"No."

"Are there any other English muffins?" Jack asked.

Replacement wrinkled her nose and shook her head. "I'll make you something else."

"No. I'm good. I'll just head to bed," Jack said.

The dog scarfed up the other half of the muffin and happily wagged her tail as Replacement wiped her fur clean.

In the bedroom, Jack shut the door, peeled off his shirt, and hopped into bed. His stomach growled. He put his arms behind his head and looked at the ceiling. *Great. I'm starving and the dog's full.*

Ten minutes later, there was a faint tap at the door, and Replacement walked into the room with a tray. She had made him a grilled cheese sandwich and poured him a big glass of milk. Jack felt like a little kid as he pulled himself into a sitting position and scooted back on the bed.

His smile dropped when the dog came in carrying her doll and headed for the blanket still in the corner.

Replacement looked from the dog to Jack. "Is it okay if she sleeps in here?"

Jack picked up the sandwich. "I don't know why it wants to. It hates me."

"No she doesn't." She tilted her head and looked at him. "Jack, I'm worried about Daniel."

"We don't know if anything bad happened."

"I'm reading over his Facebook, and I really don't think he'd just leave his dog. Do you know he helped rebuild the Diaz house?"

"That's the family where the father was hurt and they have, like, ten kids?"

"Seven. The father was injured helping at a car accident and then their house caught on fire. Daniel volunteered to rebuild their home. He's all over the website."

"I'm concerned too, but right now all we know is we have a lost dog. I'm hoping Daniel turns up and everything's fine."

"Do you think she just ran away? The leash was stuck on the fence. Maybe she took off and broke the leash. Maybe he's been searching for Muffin?"

Jack took another bite and shook his head. "He hasn't stopped by the shelter or put up flyers. That bothers me. We know he likes the dog, so he'd be looking for her."

Replacement wrung her hands and let out a big sigh.

Jack gave her leg a light squeeze. "Right now, we just don't know. Maybe he doesn't even know she's missing. He could have asked someone else to watch the dog while he was out of town."

"Muffin's in almost every picture with him on Facebook. But he didn't tag any of them. You'd figure he would have written her name somewhere, but I can't find it."

Jack frowned. "Let's see what happens tomorrow." He took a swig of milk.

Replacement laughed. "You have a milk mustache." She leaned forward and wiped his upper lip with her thumb. The tips of her fingers touched his chin. She ran her thumb across his lips again, and they parted. She closed her eyes and then stood up.

Jack reached out for her. "Are you going right to bed?"

Replacement backed toward the door. "No... I still have some research to do."

Jack started to get up. "I'll hang out with you if—"

"No. You're tired. I'm just reading through emails. It'll be boring. 'Night." The door swung shut so fast the dog's head shot up.

The dog and Jack looked at each other.

Yeah, something's wrong with her. Jack lay back and stared at the ceiling. *She hasn't been right since our date night exploded. Something's bugging her. Or some*one *is. It all started after the convenience store.*

Jack rolled over and watched the dog. She lay with her eyes closed and her head on her paws.

It's not looking good for Daniel. If the dog had broken off the leash at the park, you'd figure he'd look for her. That's if he's really a good guy like Replacement thinks.

Jack stared at the ceiling while he waited for sleep to come. He felt his body relax into the bed and he tried to will himself to let go. The dog whimpered. Jack looked into the corner. The dog's leg twitched, and he saw her eyelids move.

She's dreaming. I wonder what dogs dream about?

15

A MINI-VOLCANO

Replacement parked the blue Bug outside the office of Linskie Lumber. The lumberyard consisted of a small, one-story office building with an attached showroom and several open storage barns. Jack sat in the passenger seat and looked back at dog, who had lain down in the back.

"You can't leave the window open," Jack grumbled.

"I have to." Replacement's hands shot out. "One, Muffin needs to breathe. Two, I have to leave her here or I can't go inside and talk to the guy with you."

Which is exactly what I want. Right now, she's a firecracker ready to go off, so her talking to people is not a good idea. Don't grin.

Replacement leaned forward. "Are you smiling? Is that what you want? Do you want to talk to the guy alone?"

"No." Jack leaned away from her blistering gaze. "It's just... not safe to leave the windows of your car open."

"Pfft. Muffin would eat anyone dumb enough to try to steal something."

"That's what I mean. It's unsafe because... what if someone comes by the car and they try to pat the dog? That'd be bad."

"What?" She looked at him as if he had four heads. "Who'd just come over and pat a random giant dog in a car? That's the stupidest—"

"Fine," Jack grumbled, and he got out of the car.

Replacement closed the door and continued to glare. "Would *you* do that? Would you just go over to someone's car and pat a dog?"

"You made your point."

They walked up the small staircase, and Jack held the door open for her. The office was bright and cheery. A middle-aged woman sat behind the only desk in the room, and music played softly from her computer speakers. She stopped typing and turned around in her chair as they walked in.

"Good morning. Can I help you?" she asked.

"Jack Stratton. I'm hoping you can." Jack grinned, and the woman did too. "We found Daniel Branson's dog, and I'm trying to get in touch with him."

"Oh, certainly. Let me look up his phone number."

"Actually, we have his phone number, but we haven't been able to reach him," Jack said. "We're hoping he's here today."

She picked up a pen off her desk and nervously looked over her shoulder. "Well... you see—" Her speakerphone came on.

"Heather, did Bickford pick up the certs for the lot off Ellis Street?" The man's voice popped like a machine gun. "They're supposed to start this afternoon."

She leaned forward and spoke into the speaker. "No, sir."

"Get on the horn right away and make sure he's headed over there."

"I will, sir. Right after I answer this couple's questions."

"Is someone out there with you?" He didn't wait for her to answer but instead kept firing away. "Do you have me on speaker? I've told you—"

Click.

The woman cringed, and the office door behind her flew open. A short man with a pot belly, thinning hair, and a face lined by years of scowling came out.

"Sorry about that," he said, nodding at Jack. "Mike Tate."

"Jack Stratton and Alice Campbell. We're trying to get in touch with Daniel Branson."

Mike exchanged a quick look with the secretary, then put his hands on his hips. He exhaled loudly. "Dan's no longer with the company."

"What?" Replacement stepped forward. "Why? When?"

"It's a personnel issue, so I can't comment." Mike crossed his arms over his big belly.

"Listen—" Replacement began, but Jack interrupted.

"I'm just trying to get in touch with him because we found his lost dog," Jack said. "We went to his apartment and left messages, but we haven't heard back."

Mike pinched the bridge of his nose. "I had to let Dan go."

"When and why?" Jack asked.

"Three days ago. He was a no-call/no-show two days in a row."

"Did anyone get in touch with him?" Jack asked.

The secretary shook her head. "I sent him a certified letter and left two messages."

Now Jack's voice started to rise. "Has anyone spoken with him?"

"Lots of guys just walk," Mike explained. "That's why we have a rule. No-call/no-show, you go."

"How long did he work here?"

Mike turned to the secretary, who held up five fingers. "Five years."

"Does someone work here for five years and not call?" Replacement's hands flew out. "Does someone write on his Facebook wall that he loves his job and not show the next day?"

Mike's wrinkles deepened. "I've still got rules."

Replacement's eyes narrowed. "You can take your rules and—"

Jack stepped in front of Replacement. "So no one has seen him or heard from him, but you haven't gone and checked if he's okay?"

"I just thought he quit," Mike mumbled.

"You're some manager," Replacement spat. She spun around and stormed out the door.

Jack handed the secretary his card. "If you hear from Daniel, please let me know."

She took the card with a trembling hand. "He's okay, right? He was always real sweet."

"I hope so. Is there any other way you can get in touch with him?"

She shook her head, and Mike shrugged.

"Is there someone here he would've talked to if he went away?" Jack asked.

"Glen and Scott were on his crew. They're outside now. He could've talked to them," Mike said.

"Thank you for your time." Jack spun on his heel and headed for the door.

"Hey," Mike called out. "You understand, right? If he walked, what am I supposed to do?"

Jack didn't look at him as he pushed open the door and walked out. He understood rules, but what he couldn't understand was how this man could just blindly follow them.

He spotted Replacement standing next to a truck, speaking to two men. They were both big guys, and one had a leer on his face that made Jack quicken his pace to reach her side. They looked up as he approached.

"Hi, Jack." Replacement gave him a quick wave. "I was trying to ask these guys about Daniel, but they told me to talk to Mike."

"Well, it's good that I just talked to Mike so now they get to talk to me." Jack stuck out his hand. "I just have a couple of questions about Daniel. Are you Glen?"

The taller man looked hesitantly toward the office before answering. "Yeah."

"You know Daniel?"

"He was on our crew."

"Have you seen him in the last few days? We found his dog."

Glen shook his head. "I heard he quit."

The shorter guy, Scott, spoke. "No. He was a no-show. I think he went to Canada."

"Canada?" Replacement made a face.

"He was always going on about going up north," Scott continued. "I figure after last month, he might split."

"What happened last month?" Jack asked.

"It was a real soap opera," Glen said. "His ex's new boyfriend showed up. This little guy started screaming and swearing at Daniel."

"About what?"

"You know. Stay away from my girl type of stuff," Glen said. "It was the new boyfriend marking his territory."

"The guy was really freaking out," Scott added.

"Did it get physical?" Jack asked.

"No, they didn't fight. This guy just got out of his car and began yelling up at Dan," Glen said.

"Did he threaten him?"

"Threaten?" Glen scoffed. "The guy was like a yappy dog. He just yelled a bunch of crap."

"What did Daniel do?" Jack asked.

"Nothing," Scott said. "We were both up in the cherry picker. It's not like the guy could do anything."

"When was this?"

"About a month ago. Maybe a little more." Glen looked at Scott, who nodded.

"Do you know if Daniel has any family?"

"I don't think so. He never talked about any," Glen said.

"Did he talk about quitting?" Jack asked.

"No." Glen shook his head. "I thought he liked it here. I just got back from vacation yesterday, and I was like, huh? I called him a couple of times, but he hasn't called back."

"Did you go over to his place?" Replacement asked.

Glen shook his head. "Not yet. I was going to swing by after work today. He's okay, right?"

"I hope so." Jack handed them cards. "If you hear from him, please give me a call right away."

They both nodded, and then Jack and Replacement headed back to the Bug. Replacement was seething. Jack had barely pulled the door closed when she gunned the gas and the Bug's tires sent dirt and gravel flying. The dog barked, and Jack swore. Replacement gripped the steering wheel and sped up.

Jack grabbed the handle on the ceiling. "You want me to drive?"

"No," she grumbled and flew into a turn.

Jack pressed against the door, and the dog lay down in the back seat.

"Where are we going?" Jack pulled his seat belt on.

"Sandra Hughes. Daniel's ex-girlfriend."

"Why?"

"He may have reached out to her again." Replacement tapped the steering wheel. "She posted on her Facebook something about missing old friends. It could have meant him. Do you have another idea?"

"I know you're upset—"

"I'm beyond upset. I'm really mad." Replacement blew by a stop sign. "You don't get it. He wrote a lot on Facebook about those guys and his work. They were his friends. I mean, come on. They don't go over there? How far is his apartment? They saw him almost every day for five years." She yanked the car into another turn.

"I agree." Jack put one hand on the dash; the other continued to hold the ceiling handle. "Look, we should go back over to the apartment complex. I'll speak to the office and get them to do a wellness check on him."

"Good idea. I'm getting more and more worried about him." Replacement slowed to a stop at a light and banged the steering wheel. "Can you believe his ex-girlfriend? Sandra." The name almost dripped out of her mouth. "She sends her new boyfriend to Daniel's work?"

"You don't know that—"

Her stare cut him off. "I do know that. She wrote it down. All Daniel did was send her some letter. She went off about how he was desperate and couldn't let her get on with her life." The light turned green, and she punched it.

"Where did she write it down?"

"Facebook."

"Can anyone read it? People just write stuff like that for anyone to see?"

"Some people write everything about their lives. Sandra is one of them." Replacement reached back and patted the dog.

"Did he say anything about her?"

"Nope." She popped the word. "He didn't mention her. And you heard the guys. The new boyfriend, Wade, is my size. Daniel would've pounded him."

Jack rolled his eyes.

"Don't make a face." Replacement made a sour one. "You saw how big Daniel is."

"I'm not saying anything about Daniel, but anyone can get their butt kicked no matter how big they are, and that's without bringing weapons into the mix."

"But Daniel's a giant."

"It doesn't matter."

She slowed down, and her lips mashed together. "Who'd try to fight him?"

Jack let go of the handle. "You'd be surprised. Chandler got picked on a few times."

"Chandler?" Her mouth fell open, but she quickly shook her head. "No way."

"He did. Some guys go after the big man. It's like in the Old West and the fastest gun or something. It's a way for guys to make a name for themselves. They pick the biggest guy, and if they win, they get bragging rights. It's like getting a shot at the title without having to work your way up."

"But you said Chandler could fight."

"He never lost. But he tried *not* to fight, and he wasn't in many."

"Then how did he get picked on?"

"You don't have to get in a fight to get picked on. Teasing, name calling, all that crap. Part of it was *because* he didn't fight." Jack turned in his seat to look at her. "Some people see not fighting as weakness. They'd say something to Chandler, and he'd blow it off and try to ignore it. Then they'd get a little bolder and say something else, and they'd keep escalating it. Eventually, the guy would get stupid and throw a punch at him, and then it'd be over. Chandler had his limits." Jack pointed to the right. "There it is."

Replacement cut the wheel at the entrance to an apartment complex. The Bug flew over the speed bump, and Jack's head smashed into the ceiling.

"Damn. Slow down," he grumbled.

She slammed on the brakes, and Jack groaned against the seat belt.

Replacement's voice was flat. "I should get this one."

"You want *me* to stay in the car?"

"Please? This is my case. It's a girl, and if we both go to the door we'll freak her out."

Jack shook his head. "That's not safe. The boyfriend may be there."

"I'll be fine. Besides, I can't take Muffin. Please?"

"I don't think—"

"Please? Her apartment's right there at the top of the stairs. I can see the number from here. I'll be fine."

Jack sighed. "Just don't freak her out."

Replacement rolled her eyes as she got out of the car. "When do I ever freak anyone out?"

Before Jack could argue, the dog scrambled into the driver's seat, pushing Jack against the window.

Perfect. I'm stuck in the car with a wildebeest.

Jack lowered his window and watched Replacement walk up the stairs to a landing. The dog whined. It was a pleasant apartment complex, but Jack's chest tightened at the thought of Replacement knocking on the door. His years of police and military training kicked in, and he cringed when he saw her knock and then step straight back.

She should move to the left. She's standing right in front of the stairs, too. Never put your back to the stairs. I have to start teaching her these things.

The door opened, and a woman in her early twenties stood there with her hand on her hip. She looked annoyed.

That must be Sandra.

Replacement's hand went out for a handshake, but Sandra just stared at it. Jack could see Replacement's body stiffen.

Sandra's medium-length black hair bobbed back and forth as she shook her head. Jack heard her voice rising, but he couldn't make out what she said.

Replacement pointed back to the car, and Sandra leaned forward and scowled. When Jack gave a little wave, her scowl deepened.

Pleasant girl.

Sandra shook her head, and her hands flew around like an angry bird. Her voice got even louder. Jack might not have been able to hear what they were saying, but he knew that the conversation wasn't going well.

Replacement put one foot back, and Jack saw her right hand tighten into a fist.

That's not a good sign. Jack rolled his window down all the way.

This time Sandra shouted loudly enough that he heard her.

"Dated. Past tense. I don't care where he is. Bye-bye." Sandra grabbed Replacement's shoulder roughly.

Jack's hand flew to the door handle, but before he could open the door, the dog lunged over him. Her claws sank into his inner thigh and her thick frame knocked Jack's face into the doorjamb as she leapt through the open car window.

"Get inside!" Jack screamed, leaping out of the car.

The dog's paws came together and her muscles rippled beneath her fur as she sprang halfway up the staircase in one leap. Sandra shrieked, but stood frozen in place. Replacement grabbed the railing.

Two more jumps like that and the dog will be on Sandra's throat.

The dog roared.

Jack reached the bottom step just as the dog jumped to the top of the landing. Sandra screeched and staggered back into her apartment, her hands shaking at the sides of her head.

"Shut the door!" Jack ordered as he raced up the stairs.

The dog's muscles contracted as she readied herself to spring again, and she growled low. Sandra screamed again. Jack reached the top step, but he couldn't grab the dog's collar.

"Shut the door, lady!" he screamed.

The dog stopped suddenly, even before Sandra slammed the door shut.

"Dog." Jack reached for the dog's collar. The animal whipped her head around and snarled at him. He looked at Replacement. "Get the dog and let's get the hell out of here."

"I'm not done," Replacement snapped. She stepped forward and pounded on the door. "I need to know where Daniel is."

"Do you really think there's any chance of her opening the door with the werewolf out here?" Replacement kicked the welcome mat off the landing, then turned and stomped down the stairs.

The dog looked up at Jack, and he shook his head. "Let's go, dog." They followed Replacement back to the car.

Replacement yanked her door open. "Come on."

"Keys." Jack held out his hand.

"No way."

"Keys. You're a mini-volcano heading for Pompeii. Guaranteed the cops are on the way. I'm driving. Let's go."

16

THREE POINTS

As Jack drove down the main street, a police car flew by him.

"Do you think she called?" Replacement folded her arms.

"Without a doubt. You looked like you were going to smack her and feed her to the beast. What *was* that?"

"What was what?"

"You can't just go around screaming at people."

Replacement put her feet up on the dashboard. "I had a good teacher."

Jack drummed the steering wheel. "Look. I have anger issues, but I'm trying. You can't let it get personal."

"It *is* personal." She sighed. "Daniel just seems like such a nice guy, and she's a shrew."

"What happened?"

"I tried to explain that I was just looking for Daniel because we found his dog. She thought I came looking to get back some ring he gave her."

"He gave her a ring? Like an engagement ring?"

She shrugged. "I'm not sure. She got in my face and said it was a gift so she didn't have to give it back. What a jerk."

"Sounds like he's better off without her."

Replacement's arms wrapped around her stomach. "Did you hear her? She doesn't even care that he's missing. I mean, she said she loved him. In her earlier posts, she went on and on about what a great guy he is, but now she doesn't care what happens to him?"

"People are selfish."

"Selfish? They suck." She pulled her knees up to her chest and put her chin on them. "I didn't know he gave her a ring. It had to be an engagement ring." She closed her eyes.

"Love's a funny thing. Looks like he got her wrong."

"She didn't deserve him. You should read her page."

"No thanks."

"Where're we going?" Replacement asked.

Jack's hand tightened on the steering wheel as he felt the invisible, cold bands of dread tighten around his chest. "We still need to swing back over to Daniel's apartment and ask them to do a wellness check."

He considered what they knew. *The relationship was serious if he gave her a ring. The girlfriend dumped him. She posted about her new boyfriend all over Facebook. Daniel got embarrassed at work in front of all his friends. He loved the dog, but he left her tied up to the fence at the dog park. Maybe he left her there so that someone would take care of her after he went home and...*

They rode in silence the rest of the way.

At the apartment complex, Jack parked to the left of the entrance. It was a long, one-story ranch with an office on one side and a small gym on the other.

"I'll go in and get things started, okay?" Jack asked.

The dog whimpered, and Replacement reached back to rub her neck. "I'll take Muffin out and walk her around."

As Jack walked inside, he saw a woman in her late twenties working on a computer. Shoulder-length brown hair, thin build, and a business-casual blue blouse with gray slacks gave her a professional look—but Jack could see the tennis shoes under the desk. Two other desks sat to one side, and pictures of the different apartment layouts were on easels to the other. Besides the woman, the office was empty.

As Jack approached the woman's desk, she looked up from typing and smiled. "Welcome to Archstone." She stood. "I'm Abigail. What can I do for you today?"

Jack shook her outstretched hand. "Jack Stratton. I need to ask for a wellness check on apartment 403. Daniel Branson."

Abigail's brows knit together. "Of course. Are you a relative?"

"Actually, we found his dog. She was lost."

"The poor thing." The woman's head tilted to the side as she looked out the door.

Jack turned to see Replacement getting out of the car. The dog's head was down and her shoulders were slumped.

"We've tried several times to call Mr. Branson, and we also checked with his work. No one there has been able to contact him either."

"I'll call maintenance." She picked up a walkie-talkie from the other side of her computer and spoke into it. "Rob? This is Abigail. Where are you?"

There was a moment's hesitation before a man's voice came over the scratchy speakers. "Building five. There's a leaky air conditioner in 512."

"The Robinsons'? Is it bad or can it wait for a few minutes? I need a health and safety done on 403 as soon as you can."

"Roger. I'll head right over there. I was just putting everything away."

"I'll go meet him," Jack said. "Thanks for all your help."

The woman held the walkie-talkie to her chest. "Can you ask Rob to call me right back?"

"I will. Thank you again." Jack stepped back outside and walked to the apartment.

As he neared the building, he saw a man in his early twenties driving an old golf cart with a ladder strapped to the side. Jack waved as the man parked. "Hi, Rob? I'm here for the wellness check on 403."

Rob got out of the cart and nodded, but when Replacement and the dog came around the corner behind Jack, his eyes narrowed. "Wait a second. Let me see some ID."

"My name's Jack Stratton." He flipped open his wallet for Rob to see his license. "I'm here about Daniel Branson. We found his dog. Abigail just called. She wants you to call her when we're done."

Rob's eyes went wider when he saw Jack's old business card. "You're a cop?"

Jack paused. Replacement came to stand almost next to him. She was struggling to hold on to the dog.

"I was."

"He… retired," Replacement added.

"Abigail didn't say you were on the force." Rob's voice went way up. "I'm fourth on the list to get in the department. I'm just working this job while I wait for a call to go to the training academy."

Jack looked the eager young man up and down and then cleared his throat. "Good job, checking my status. Are you sure you can get us into the apartment, or should I call back down to the central office?"

"I can get you in." Rob held up a huge key ring that had an assortment of keys and fobs. "I've got access to everything here. I'm kind of security too." He walked toward the apartment.

"Do you know Daniel?"

Rob shook his head. "I've seen him. Big, big guy. No complaints or nothing." At the door, he pressed the buzzer. "You don't seem too old."

"Excuse me?"

"To be retired. You look young," Rob said.

"It was a medical retirement," Replacement offered. And then she whispered, "Gunshot."

"Really?" Rob's eyes went wide.

Replacement nodded and gave Jack a wink.

"Do you know if Daniel has a roommate?" Jack asked, ignoring this last exchange.

"I don't think so. That's important, right?" Rob looked at Jack expectantly. "I really only saw him walking the dog. There was a chick—I mean I saw a girl with him once." Rob fumbled with the large key ring, looking for the master key.

When the man had unlocked the door, Jack said, "Let us go in first." He glanced back at Replacement. "Don't either of you touch anything."

"Got it." Rob nodded curtly.

Rob held the apartment door open, and Jack walked inside. He fought the impulse to take out his gun and sweep the room the way he was trained to. Still, he slid to the side of the doorway as he scanned the modest one-bedroom apartment. The living room consisted of a couch, recliner, coffee table, and a large TV surrounded by shelves of DVDs. There was a computer desk with a PC still on in the corner. Jack glanced into the empty kitchen as he moved silently into the apartment.

"Mr. Branson?" Rob called out, and Jack glared. "Sorry," Rob mumbled. "They said we have to announce ourselves if we need to do this."

"That's fine." Jack held up a hand. "It just—"

The dog suddenly strained on its leash and then pulled free from Replacement and darted forward. All three of them followed the dog around the small apartment, but it only took a minute to determine no one was there.

"No one's home," Rob announced.

Jack returned to the living room. "The computer's on."

Replacement walked over to it and looked down. "There's an old drink here." She pointed at the cup on the desk. "I think it was coffee. It's half full."

Jack walked up next to Replacement and whispered, "Don't touch the computer."

She frowned but nodded.

Rob peered around the room. "Are you trying to figure out when he left?"

"Yes." Jack looked at the cup filled with a curdled layer of cream. "No mold. It's not that old."

"What's that mean? Like he's only been gone a few days?"

"At least that's what happens to my coffee," Jack said. "I forgot a cup for a few days and it looked like that, but after a week, you get mold."

"Wow. You were a detective, huh?" Rob looked impressed. "They teach you that stuff?"

"They teach you better than that. That's just a rough observation. I'm sure a CSI team would take measurements—the amount of cream, the temperature in here, and a bunch of different things—and then they could tell you exactly when that cup was poured. I'm just going by the old trick, like putting your hand on the hood of the car to see if—" Jack spun around. "Is his car here?"

Rob's eyes lit up. "He drives a big blue truck."

Jack lowered his voice. "Rob, if you're up to it, I need you to sweep the perimeter of the parking lot and see if the truck is still there."

Before Jack had finished speaking, Rob was heading for the door. "I'm on it."

"I need you to do at least two circuits and look for any vehicles that you don't recognize."

"Yes, sir." Rob stood at attention and gave a quick nod before hurrying out.

The door shut and Replacement asked, "That was good, but why are you getting rid of him?"

"I want to look around without him hovering over my shoulder. Don't touch anything. I'll check that bedroom. Can you look *around* the computer? No touching."

Jack walked down the little hallway to the bedroom. It was a typical single guy's bedroom except for one thing—the bed. Jack tilted his head as he looked at it. *I wonder if Daniel made it. It's, like, seven and a half feet long.*

Jack looked around. Blankets lay pulled back and clothes had been tossed in a corner. The place was slightly messy and a little on the sparse side. He opened the closet. On the top shelf were a box and two closed suitcases.

Single guy. Probably owns only two. He didn't pack.

He stepped into the bathroom and took a quick inventory.

Toothbrush. Shaving cream. Razor. Deodorant. All out. If you were going out of town, you'd take them.

He flipped open the medicine cabinet.

Bingo. Pill keeper. Today's Thursday; last one open is Sunday.

Inside one of the compartments was a little white pill. It had been stamped with some code, but Jack had no idea what type of medicine it was. He returned to Replacement.

"Get anything?"

"Gold mine." Replacement pointed to a desk drawer. "He has a little notebook where he keeps his passwords."

"I said don't touch anything."

"I didn't. I used a pen to open the drawer and the notebook. I saw that on TV."

Jack repressed a smile. "Did you copy the passwords down?"

"No."

Jack exhaled. "I know you have a good memory but—"

She looked back at him. Her green eyes sparkled, and her dimple popped. "I took a picture of them with my phone." She wiggled her butt.

"One point to you."

"That should be worth three."

"Don't get cocky." He pressed his lips into a tight line and returned to the bathroom, where he opened the medicine cabinet and snapped a picture of the stamped pill.

That was definitely worth three points.

The two of them continued to search the apartment, carefully avoiding touching anything. The kitchen was clean. A small stack of mail on the counter looked to be bills, and they were all recent.

Jack's head snapped up when he heard the golf cart approaching. "Time's up. Wrap it up."

"We're good," Replacement said.

The door opened, and Rob marched in. He stood at attention as he addressed Jack. "The tenant's blue Chevy truck is parked in space 404. I did two perimeter sweeps of the parking lot, but I did not see any suspicious vehicles or non-resident cars parked in the visitor spaces."

"Nice job, Rob." Jack took out one of his cards. "I need you to do me another favor. If you see anyone here, or if Daniel comes back, I need you to call me right away."

Rob beamed. "Like a stakeout?"

Jack nodded. "Exactly."

Jack headed for the door, but when Replacement started to follow, the dog whimpered and trotted into the bedroom. A few seconds later, she came back with a rope pull toy flopping in her mouth.

"Ohh…" Replacement gushed as she patted the dog. "She wanted her toy."

Rob looked uncertain. "I'm not sure if the dog should remove anything."

Jack took one look at the dog and shook his head. "I think we should let the dog take its toy. Do you really want to try to take it back?"

The dog growled.

Rob's grin vanished. "Well. I guess it belongs to the dog, so… that's okay." He held the door open and stepped out of the way. When they were all outside, he turned and asked Jack, "Can I use you as a reference for the police academy?"

Jack and Replacement exchanged a look.

"Why don't I do you one better," Jack said. "Email me your information, and I'll see who I can personally talk to."

"Awesome!" Rob's hand shot out and shook Jack's. "I really appreciate it."

"Call me the second you hear anything."

"I will. You can count on me, sir."

17

HOLLY ROAD

Jack drummed the steering wheel as he drove toward downtown.

"Where are we going?" Replacement asked.

"The police station."

"Why? Because of what happened with Sandra?" Replacement's eyes went wide. "Are we turning ourselves in?"

Jack laughed. "No. She doesn't even know who we are, and if anyone asks, I'll just say the dog freaked her out."

"Then why are we going to the police station?"

Jack's jaw clenched, and he lowered his eyes to the road.

Replacement sat up. "You think something happened to him."

"Daniel has no family, so someone has to report him missing—just in case."

Replacement didn't say anything at first. Then she said softly, "He could be okay, right?"

His truck's still at his apartment. No one's heard from him for several days, and he left his dog tied to a fence. "I'm worried." He handed her his phone. "Pull up the last picture I took. Can you look up what kind of pill that is?"

Replacement typed into the phone. After a few minutes she hung her head, and her voice sounded flat. "It's high blood pressure medication. You're supposed to take it every day." She turned her head and looked out the window.

Jack pulled into the visitors' parking lot of the police station and shut the engine off, but his hand lingered on the keys. He stared at the parking lot for police officers across the street. "Last time I parked in the visitors' lot was for my interview."

Replacement leaned over and kissed his cheek. "Can I come in?" She held up a hand. "I promise I'll be good."

Jack lowered the windows for the dog, and they both got out.

As they headed up the steps to the police station, Officer Donald Pugh walked out. Donald was Jack's age and height, but in his summer uniform, the man looked awfully thin. When he saw Jack, he grinned and hurried down the steps.

"Hi, Alice." He gave her an awkward hug and then shook Jack's hand. "How've you been, Jack?" He pushed his hat further up on his sandy-brown hair and put his hands on his hips.

"I've been okay. Are you getting off work or are you heading out?" Jack asked.

"I'm calling it a day. What brings you by?"

Jack exhaled. "I've got to file a missing-person report."

Donald looked from Jack to Replacement and then back again. He cleared his throat and asked, "Who are you filing the report on?"

"His name's Daniel Branson. He's been missing four or five days."

"Are you related?"

Donald straightened up, and his eyes darkened. Jack knew that look. Every cop has had to deliver horrible news. It's never easy, and you try to mask your face when you do it. Right now, Donald wore that mask.

Jack turned to Replacement and tried to keep his expression neutral. "Can you give us a second, Alice?"

Her eyes rounded in concern as she looked back and forth between the two men. Jack reached out and touched her shoulder. Her hand went to her stomach before she turned and walked slowly back to the car.

When she was out of hearing distance, Jack spoke. "What do you know, Donald?"

"A jogger found a body out on Holly."

"Do you have a description?"

"No, but I heard it was bad. Morrison's out there now."

"Thanks for letting me know." Jack started back to his car.

"Jack," Donald called to him, "if you're going out there, you'll want to leave her in the car."

When Jack got back into the Bug, Replacement stared at her hands.

"We need to go out to Holly Road."

Replacement didn't say a word.

***

Through the trees, off in the woods, Jack saw emergency lights. He turned off Holly, down a fire road, and stopped behind Morrison's car. The medical examiner was there, as well as two cruisers and a sedan.

"You need to stay in the car," Jack said.

He was surprised when Replacement nodded.

The fresh smell of pine trees greeted him as soon as he stepped out of the car. It was such an odd mix of dread and pleasant memories that he paused for a moment with his hand on the door.

Just off the road, Undersheriff Robert Morrison was speaking with a patrolman. Morrison, a tall African-American man in his late fifties, nodded when he saw Jack approach. He wore the tan uniform of the sheriff's department without the hat. His curly black hair was short and graying at the temples.

"Undersheriff." Jack came to attention.

"Don't do that, son." Morrison stretched out his hand. "What brings you by?"

Jack stayed at attention. "I'm here because I stopped by the police station in order to file a missing-person report, and I heard that someone reported finding a body."

Morrison put his hand on Jack's shoulder and walked partway around him.

He's keeping my eyes away from the crime scene. It must be bad.

"The missing person," Morrison began. "How do you know him?"

"I don't. A woman found a lost dog and hired Alice to find the owner. The owner's Daniel Branson. He's twenty-seven. He's been missing for four or five days. I did a wellness check at his residence, but he wasn't there. I did find out that he takes medication, but he hasn't taken it since Sunday."

"Do you have a description?"

Jack reached into his pocket and handed Morrison the printout.

"He's a big guy. Six seven, six eight," Jack said.

Morrison rubbed the back of his head and exhaled. He studied Jack's face for only a moment before he turned and motioned for Jack to follow. "Jogger found the body up here."

They walked up a small hill. The woods were almost all pine trees so there was very little underbrush. A twenty-by-twenty-yard section had been surrounded by crime-scene tape, and inside the grid stood the ME, two techs, and a man, looking down. Their bodies obstructed Jack's view.

Jack tipped his chin toward a man about his height who was talking with the medical examiner. He wore a light-gray suit that looked as if it would've cost Jack a week's pay. The man's brown hair was moussed and styled.

"Who's the suit?" Jack asked.

"Ed Castillo. I don't know if you heard, but Joe Davenport retired. Sheriff Collins hired Ed."

Jack thought he detected disapproval in Morrison's voice, but he didn't press the issue. "What do you have?"

"Not much." Morrison stopped. "I need to ask you a favor. I still hear Collins mumbling your name around the office. Let me do all the talking?"

Jack nodded. "I won't say a word."

Castillo noticed Morrison, lifted the police tape, and walked over to them.

"Give me a minute, Jack?" Morrison walked ahead to intercept Castillo.

While Morrison brought Castillo up to speed, Jack watched the crime-scene techs and the ME. Cameras flashed, measurements were taken, and the ME spoke into a voice recorder, but Jack was puzzled by how little they moved.

One tech squatted down in front of what Jack assumed to be the body, but he couldn't see it. The other tech and the ME walked around in a small circle.

Daniel's six eight. How are they walking around a three-foot circle?

Just as Jack was about to shift closer to try to see, Castillo called for the ME. As he and the techs stood up and moved toward Castillo, Jack saw what they had been standing around—a green trash bag, partially torn open. Jack couldn't see what was inside.

Castillo spoke to the ME, nodded, and then turned back to Morrison.

It looks like a regular trash bag, but Donald said they found a body?

Morrison and Castillo spoke briefly, then turned and walked toward Jack. As Castillo approached, he put his notebook in his left hand and stuck the other hand out. "Ed Castillo."

"Jack."

Castillo eyed Jack up and down, then looked down at the picture Jack had given to Morrison. "Jack, Bob gave me the CliffsNotes version. I'd like to talk to you about…" he looked at his notebook, "Daniel Branson. Do you mind coming down to the station for a few minutes?"

Even though it was standard procedure, part of Jack bristled at the request. "That's fine," he muttered. He looked past Castillo to the green bag. "What did you find?"

Jack felt sweat form on his back as he waited for one of them to respond.

"I don't think we'll be able to tell anything until they get him back to the lab," Castillo said. "It's going to be a lot of forensics. You said Daniel Branson was tall?"

"Six eight."

Jack heard the dog bark in the car.

"Do you have the dog with you, Jack?" Morrison asked.

Jack nodded and looked back at the crime scene. He wished he hadn't. A tech lifted up part of the torn bag, and Jack saw the reason the bag was so small—there was only a torso in it.

Mixing with the smell of the pines was the odor of death. Because of his tour in Iraq, Jack was all too familiar with the fragrance.

"Is it just the torso?" Jack asked.

Morrison set his hands on his hips. "Yes. It's lying chest down. They're debating whether to do some processing here or move it to the lab. We're expanding the grid, but there's no sign of the other body parts."

Castillo took Morrison by the arm and walked away from Jack, but he spoke so loudly Jack couldn't help but overhear. "I'd appreciate it, Bob, if you don't say anything to him until I finish talking to him."

Before Morrison could respond, a loud howl split the air and a patrolman started to yell. The dog had somehow gotten out of the car, and it was now racing up the hill with Replacement chasing after it. The patrolman tried to block the dog's way, but she just bounded around him.

Jack sprinted over to grab her, but the dog suddenly stopped on her own. She let out a twisted whimper and started moving from paw to paw. She whimpered again as Replacement ran up.

Replacement stared wide-eyed at Jack. "She started totally freaking out. I tried to get her to calm down but—"

The dog tilted her head back and howled. It was a sound that Jack would never forget. The noise that came out of her throat was the sound of pure grief. She clawed the ground once, turned, and bolted off into the forest.

Replacement looked desperately at Jack, then rushed after her. Jack followed.

It was a frenzied dash. The dog leapt over rocks and darted under bushes, distancing herself from the discovery, and Jack's feet kept slipping in the soft pine needles covering the ground. But then the undergrowth got thicker, forcing all three of them to slow down. Jack growled as a branch raked his face. Replacement bobbed and weaved her way around, over, and under the obstacles in her path so quickly that she actually gained on the dog.

They reached a clearing with thick briars on the opposite side. The dog stopped in the middle of it, tipped back her head again, and howled.

Replacement rushed forward, and the dog spun around. Her ears flattened against her head, and she snapped and barked. Replacement froze, but she didn't back away. She stood firmly with her legs shoulder-width apart and kept an eye on the dog.

Whimpering, the dog turned back around and lay down in the grass.

Replacement started to cry. She walked over to the dog and knelt beside her. She rubbed her neck, but the dog kept her eyes closed.

After a few minutes, Replacement started to stand—but the dog didn't. It just pressed its body closer to her and whimpered.

Replacement turned to Jack. "What should I do?"

"Lady," Jack called softly.

The dog raised her head.

"Why did you call her that?" Replacement's voice was just above a whisper as she reached down and stroked the dog's fur.

"It's her name. Do you remember the woman at the park? When the dog rushed her, I yelled *Lady*. The dog stopped. Same thing at Sandra's."

"Lady?" As Replacement said the name, the dog pushed her muzzle against her leg.

Jack put his arms around Replacement while she continued to pat Lady. He closed his eyes and listened to the soft noises of the woods.

Replacement looked up at him. "She knows."

Jack nodded.

Replacement started to cry again. "Is there any chance it's not him?"

Jack shook his head. "Lady confirmed it."

***

Replacement, Lady, and Jack walked back to the little blue Bug. As Jack put Lady and Replacement in the car, Morrison and Castillo spotted them and came running down.

"What the hell was that?" Castillo grumbled.

Morrison shot him a look, and Castillo's mouth snapped shut.

Jack turned to Morrison. "I need to take them home, and then I'll come down to the station to give you what I found out. My apartment's on the way to the station."

Castillo nodded. "I'll follow you."

Morrison reached in Replacement's window and squeezed her shoulder.

As Jack walked around to the driver's side, he asked, "Have you turned the body over?"

Morrison shook his head.

"When you do, you'll find he has a tattoo on the right side of his chest. It's a quill and inkwell."

18

A WALKING WRECKING BALL

When they returned to the apartment, Lady walked with her head down straight into Jack's bedroom and curled up in the corner. Replacement frowned, then picked up the dog's food and water bowls from the kitchen and started to take them into Jack's bedroom.

Jack cleared his throat. "You should leave them out here."

She looked at him with disappointment in her eyes.

"I don't care about dog food in my bedroom, it's just… if it were me, I'd stay in my bedroom for the rest of my life. If you leave the food and water out in the kitchen, then at least the dog has a reason to come out sometimes."

Replacement set the bowls back down. "I'm going to go lie down in your room."

Lady didn't look up as they entered. Jack pulled the blankets around Replacement and leaned down. "I have to go down to the station for a little while, but I'll be back as soon as I can."

She nodded and pulled the blankets tightly around herself. Jack kissed her forehead. "I'm sorry," he whispered.

***

Half an hour later, Jack was sitting at a metal table bolted to the floor of the interrogation room, while Morrison and Ed Castillo spoke heatedly in the corner. After they finished, Castillo walked over and glared down at Jack. "I've heard all about you."

"Really, Ed? What did you hear about me?" Jack leaned back.

"That you're a walking wrecking ball with a disdain for authority who doesn't follow the rules."

The corner of Jack's mouth curled up. "There's some truth to that. But right now," his face hardened, "that doesn't matter. A man was killed. It's your job to find out who did it, not mine. I'm just giving you what I have. Let's get started."

Castillo turned to Morrison. "I got the heads-up to stay away from him, Bob. I'm writing that in my report. I just started this job and this is my first big case. I'm not flushing my career down the drain because I ticked off the sheriff."

Jack's chair scraped on the floor as he pulled it forward. "My involvement started when the dog was found. Are you ready for my statement?"

Castillo dragged his chair back. He sat down at the table, turned the recorder on, and flipped his notebook open. Morrison sat beside him.

"What's the name of the woman who found the dog?" Castillo asked.

"Mrs. Ida Sawyer. She lives on Acorn. She hired Alice to find the dog's owner."

"Daniel Branson?"

Jack nodded. He ran them both through everything he and Replacement had found out. The broken leash at the park, the lumberyard, Sandra—he didn't leave a detail out. When he finished, Castillo asked him to go over all the facts a second time.

"I have a patrolman over at Branson's apartment now," Castillo said. "You didn't touch anything inside, did you?"

"At the time, we did think we were only doing a wellness check on the owner of a lost dog."

"What about the ex-girlfriend's boyfriend?" Castillo asked. "The coworkers said he threatened him."

"I haven't talked with him."

Castillo glanced at his notebook once more, then thrust out a hand. "Thank you." His lips pinched together. "I'm going to go back over my notes here, and I'll contact you if we have additional questions."

Jack exchanged a look with Morrison, who rose.

"I need to make a million phone calls. Let's get together at three o'clock, okay, Ed?" Morrison said.

"Three? Okay. I need to call the lab." Castillo hurried out of the room.

"Seems like an eager guy," Jack said.

Morrison sighed. "I haven't really worked with him, and if I had to pick a first case, it wouldn't have been this. You know when Collins hears you're involved in this—"

"What Collins thinks doesn't matter. I'm not a cop anymore. Do you have the cause of death?"

Morrison pulled out a pack of gum, popped two sticks in his mouth, and offered Jack a stick, which he accepted. "Multiple stab wounds to the back. Because we only have the torso, there's a lot of speculation at this point. But forensically, they have a lot. We'll get the guy." Morrison tapped the table. "Do you want me to notify animal control? I can have them come and pick up the dog."

Replacement's going to be beyond hurt.

19

I HAVE A PLAN FOR THAT

Jack took a deep breath before opening his apartment door. Inside, he found Replacement typing furiously at the computer. She didn't look up or turn around. The dog was nowhere in sight.

Jack put down the steak he was carrying at the end of the counter and shifted the flowers and chocolate to his other hand. As he walked over to Replacement, he looked over her shoulder at her monitor, which showed a picture of a thin, smiling man in his fifties.

"Hey, I—"

He hadn't realized she was wearing earbuds. When he touched her shoulder, she screamed, jumped up, and swung even before she turned around to look at him. The punch landed right on the tip of his nose, and his eyes flashed, but he managed to hang on to the flowers and chocolate.

Replacement screamed again. Her hands went to her mouth. She gasped, then spun around and shut off the monitor.

"I'm sorry. I'm so sorry." Her hands trembled.

Jack shook his head and blinked rapidly. "You've got a good hook."

"Are you all right?" She held both sides of his face and burst into tears.

"No, no, no." He fired off the words like a machine gun as he tried to lift up her chin. "I'm fine. Fine. Look." He leaned back and showed her the flowers and chocolate.

She cried harder and hugged him.

Mission to cheer her up ends in—failure.

He wrapped his arms around her and rubbed her back.

"I'm so sorry. You scared the crap out of me." She sniffled.

"I thought you were just focused. You don't normally wear headphones when you listen to music."

She looked up and stared at his nose again as she wiped hers. "The music was bothering Lady. Are you okay?" She brushed his cheek.

"I'm fine." Jack grinned crookedly. "Where is Lady?"

Replacement sighed. "She's in the bedroom. She hasn't come out. She won't eat."

Jack winked. "I have a plan for that."

"Are you sure your nose is okay? I'm so sorry."

"Don't worry about it. You hit like a girl."

She shoved him, and he dropped the chocolate.

"Darn it."

"Your fault."

Don't pick it up. Give her something to do to get her mind off crying. Show her the steak.

He hurried over to the kitchen, grabbed the huge steak, and turned around proudly. Her lip trembled again.

Damn. "It's a good thing. It's a good thing." He waved his hands and put on an extra-large smile.

She flew across the room and wrapped her arms around him. He stumbled back a bit from the impact.

"I know. You're such a good man."

Jack shook his head. "I just want to make you happy."

She squeezed him tighter. "Thank you for thinking about Lady."

He kissed the top of her head, turned, and grabbed a pan. "How do you think she likes it? Medium rare?"

Replacement nodded, moved behind him, and clung to his back. As he cooked the steak, she leaned up against him with her head pressed against his back.

"What were you working on?" Jack asked.

She let go and went back to the computer. "I was just looking up some stuff."

"About Daniel?"

She shook her head.

Jack put his hands on the counter. "Who was the guy?"

Replacement's head slumped forward. "It's personal. I don't want to talk about it."

Personal? Jack went back to the stove. He looked down at the steak and flipped it. *Now's not the right time to push her.* "Do you want me to save some of this for you?"

"No thanks. Give it all to Lady."

Jack fanned the smoke from the steak toward the bedroom. "I'm surprised she hasn't come out with all this racket."

"She's super-sad. Did you find out anything at the station?"

"Not really. The guy in the suit—his name's Ed Castillo, Davenport's replacement—he had a little of an 'I'm the new guy–hear me roar' attitude. Communication was pretty much one way."

"You're going to keep looking, right?"

Jack froze. "That's the police's job," he muttered.

Replacement walked back over to him. Her fingers tightened on his shirt, and she gently pulled him to look at her. Her emerald-green eyes searched his. "Daniel was a good man. We need to find who did that to him."

All the excuses went through Jack's mind like a bullet train, but they didn't matter. His jaw set and he felt his hand tighten around the handle of the frying pan. *She's right. Daniel Branson didn't deserve that. No one does. I can't stop now.* "Yeah. We'll find who killed him," he said.

She kissed his cheek.

He turned back to the steak. "Should I cut it up for her?"

She kissed him again.

20

MOUTHWASH

Jack yawned and rolled over. Replacement had gone into her bedroom an hour ago, but he still couldn't sleep. He just lay there and watched the dog. Lady hadn't moved. He'd taken her out once, but she'd behaved like a walking zombie. Now she just lay on the floor with her head on her paws. She hadn't even touched the steak.

How am I going to tell Replacement? She's a beautiful dog, but she's so big—there's no way I can keep her here. It just couldn't work. I'm sure someone will adopt her… Who am I kidding? Who'd take her? She's a moose with fangs. They go for puppies.

Jack's heart sank. He continued to watch the huge dog until his eyes finally closed.

***

IRAQ

The sun had started to set, but the heat was still almost unbearable, and sweat rolled down Jack's back. He leaned against an old, half-broken-down wall, part of the remains of a farmhouse at the edge of the base—a place nicknamed the Pit, even though the ground was as flat as a board. A dilapidated shed stood about twenty yards away. Jack looked at the weather-beaten roof and wondered what kept it from caving in.

Jack dropped his water bottle cap into a hole in the wall and leaned back. They were all supposed to meet here tonight and then head to a volleyball game and barbecue, but so far only Jack, Butcher, two of Butcher's buddies—Dale and Eric—and Joy had arrived.

Jack clenched his jaw. He knew why Joy had come, but he didn't like the way Butcher kept looking at her. Butcher had thanked her when they got back to base. He'd begged her to come and hang out with them before the game, but now that she was here, Jack was quickly getting uncomfortable.

They passed around a bottle of mouthwash. It was an old trick for smuggling booze past security onto an Army base in a dry country—mix vodka and green food coloring in a mouthwash bottle. They'd started pounding it back as soon as they'd gotten back to base and were already slurring their words. Jack turned it down when they offered it to him.

Butcher kept going on and on about how Joy's suggestion to pull an AC-130 as backup had saved all their lives.

He's right. But he's still a creep.

Dale asked Joy about some new communications tool. Joy talked animatedly about it while Jack alternated between keeping an eye out for Chandler and an eye on Butcher and his friends. What had started out as Butcher patting Joy on the back had now escalated.

"Hot damn, we're alive." Butcher whooped at the sky. "And it's all 'cause of you, darlin'." He swayed as he held his cup out toward Joy, then drained it. "Whoo!" he hollered.

She flushed for the umpteenth time that night and held up her hands. "It wasn't just me. If they hadn't listened to—"

"You saved me," Butcher proclaimed in a high, fake, melodramatic voice.

Joy laughed.

Butcher reached out, swept her off her feet, and spun her around. "My hero." He laughed as he pulled her tightly against himself, her feet six inches off the ground. His hands groped slowly down her sides.

"That's enough." She squirmed.

"Just showing my appreciation, girl."

"Let her go," Jack ordered, his voice low and even.

"Screw you, Stratton. I'm just saying thanks." He set her down.

Joy held up a hand. "It's okay, Jack. He's just a little over-happy."

"I'm sorry." Butcher thrust both hands up. "She's right. I'm just over-happy!" he shouted. Dale and Eric cheered.

Jack shook his head as Joy walked with Butcher over to his friends.

I want to get out of here. Where the hell are you, Chandler?

The shadows lengthened. One empty bottle of mouthwash flew over the wall and Butcher pulled another out. Jack watched as Butcher walked over to Dale and Eric and whispered something. Butcher then walked over to Joy, who was leaning against the shed, and placed his hand on the wall over her shoulder.

Jack couldn't hear what he whispered in her ear as he played with her hair, but Joy blushed. Butcher kissed her, and she kissed him back. Butcher grabbed her around the waist and pressed her against the wall, then opened the shed door with one hand. But as he moved toward the opening, Joy started to struggle. Butcher yanked her up, and Jack saw the dark leer on his face.

"Stop—" Joy started to say, but Butcher clamped his mouth over hers.

Jack pushed off the wall and stalked over to the shed. Dale and Eric moved too—to cut Jack off.

"Out of the way," Jack growled.

"Let them party," Dale said.

"She wants to stop." Jack kept walking.

"She's consenting." Eric's lewd smile made Jack's hand twitch into a fist.

"STOP!" Joy screamed.

Butcher pushed her through the door and slammed it shut behind them.

"I didn't hear anythi—" Eric started to say, but Jack's fist slammed into his mouth, and he stumbled backward and fell on his butt.

Jack spun to face Dale, who was slightly taller than him. The soldier pulled back his fist, and Jack's jab snapped out like a whip.

Left eye.

The punch knocked Dale's head back.

Right cheek.

Jack mentally called his shots as Dale stumbled backward with each blow.

Nose. Chin.

The hard right knocked Dale to his knees.

With both men down, Jack stormed to the shed and jerked the door open. Butcher had jammed Joy up against the wall inside. One hand had her arm pinned down and the other groped her breast.

Butcher took one look at Jack and shoved Joy away—hard into the wall. The back of her head smacked into the clay brick, and she groaned.

Jack yanked Butcher forward and punched him in the face. Blood from Butcher's cut lips splattered Joy's uniform as she slid down the wall.

Butcher staggered back, holding his mouth.

Joy's eyes rolled back in her head, and she slumped over onto her side.

Jack reached down for her, but Butcher screamed and rushed him. He tackled Jack around the waist and drove him out the door. Jack's elbow came around in an arc and crashed into Butcher's back. Butcher landed face down in the sand.

Then Eric jumped Jack from behind. He was faster than Jack had thought. Jack tried to twist, but Eric's arms clamped tightly around him. As they both slammed into the ground, Jack pulled his arm free and elbowed Eric in the solar plexus. Eric gasped in pain and sat partway up before Jack's elbow crashed into his face and knocked him back down.

Jack rolled to his side just in time to see Butcher's foot flying toward his face, but too late to do much about it. To minimize the impact, he tried to swing his head in the same direction as the blow, but the heel still caught just above his ear.

Jack's head snapped back, and he fell back to the ground. Dale rushed over and kicked Jack in the stomach. With the wind literally kicked out of him, Jack involuntarily doubled up. Butcher tried to stomp on his head, but his boot hit Jack's shoulder instead. Dale stepped forward and drew his leg back so he could kick again.

Move.

Jack grabbed Dale behind his knee and pulled. Dale's leg went out, and he dropped down to his knees. Jack swung hard for his face, but he felt his knuckles hit the hard bone of Dale's forehead.

Butcher kicked Jack in the back. Pain shot all the way through to his chest. Dale punched Jack hard in the face. Butcher kicked Jack in the back again.

Jack looked up and saw Butcher's bloody lip twisted into a snarl. But the triumphant look turned to one of horror just before a huge black fist slammed into his face and sent him flying.

Dale scrambled to his feet.

Jack rolled to his knees. "Thanks, buddy." He flashed a bloody grin up at Chandler.

Chandler pulled back his fist as he turned to glare at Dale.

Dale held up his hands and backed up. "Not me. Butcher. I had nothing to do with it." Dale grabbed Eric, and they stumbled away.

Jack was sorry to see them go. He knew getting hit by Chandler felt like getting punched in the face by a telephone pole, and part of him wanted to see Dale get his.

"You okay, Jack?" Chandler reached out his hand.

"Great," Jack grumbled as he grabbed Chandler's wrist and staggered to his feet.

"What the hell happened?"

The shed door flew open, and Joy rushed out. She held up her hands, ready to fight, and when she saw Dale and Eric walking away and Butcher groaning on the ground, her shoulders slumped.

Jack moved over to her. "Are you okay?"

"Fine. I just cracked my head."

As he watched her straighten her uniform and fight back the tears, his anger rose. He'd stopped Butcher's physical attack, but that didn't mean she wasn't wounded.

"Let's get you checked out," he said.

"No. I can't. I've been drinking."

"You need to report this." Chandler stepped forward. "You should—"

"No." She held up her hands and took a step back. "Drinking on a dry base? My career would be over."

Butcher scrambled to his feet. His face was covered in blood and sand. "I didn't do anything," he slurred and then spat. "Dale and Eric will back me up." He pointed a shaky index finger at Joy.

Jack surged forward.

***

Jack bolted upright in his bed. He sat there panting, his hands reaching for Butcher, but they grasped in vain at the air in his bedroom. He was drenched with sweat and shaking.

Breathe. Just a dream. Everything... Jack looked up at the ceiling and gulped in air. *Real. It happened, but that was just a dream. I'm just remembering. It's over. Joy's okay. She's back in the States.*

Jack rubbed his mouth, ready to feel his cut lip, but his mouth was fine. The fight had taken place years ago, but the details were fresh and vivid.

He rubbed his face and ground the heels of his hands against his eyes. He swung his legs out of the bed and hung his head. His side throbbed.

In the corner of the darkened room, something scratched at the floor. Jack shook his head and peered into the darkness. Something scratched again. Jack jumped to his feet, his heart pounding in his ears.

It's the dog. Calm down. It's just the dog.

He flicked on the bedside lamp. Lady was whimpering in the corner. Her eyes were closed, but her legs twitched and her body shook. She had kicked her blanket off.

Jack looked down at her. The little whimpers tore at him. He walked over to her with his hand out.

"Shh," he whispered as he squatted and picked up the blanket.

Lady's eyes flipped open, and she lifted her head. She scanned Jack's face for a moment, then put her head back on her paws with another small whimper.

Jack carefully placed the blanket over her and then laid his hand on her head. She scooted forward and pushed her head into his lap. Because he was squatting, she knocked him onto his butt, and he landed with a thud.

"Thanks," Jack muttered as she nuzzled against his stomach.

Lady's fur was softer than he'd expected. He felt the solid muscle underneath as he patted her. Her head was heavy in his lap, but each stroke of her coat seemed to relax them both even more. He put his head back against the wall and listened to the dog's breathing. In a few minutes, they were both asleep.

***

A flash of light caused Jack's eyes to snap open. It took him a minute to realize where he was: sitting on the floor in the corner with the dog. And he was looking at Replacement, who was crouched down with her phone in her hand.

She snapped another picture, and the flash blinded Jack.

His hands went to his eyes, and he angled his head away from her. "Stop. What the hell's wrong with you?"

She knelt beside him and kissed him. "I love you. I love you, Jack." Her face was wet with tears, but her green eyes smiled.

Jack swept his left arm around her waist. He pulled her onto his lap as his right hand slid up her back and pressed her against him. Her old Fairfield High shirt hiked up on her thigh, and his hand moved to her soft skin. He touched her delicately, and she responded by sliding both hands to cradle the back of his head. Her fingers ran through his hair. Softly and tenderly, her lips kissed his, and he felt her mouth slowly open.

Lady licked the side of his face.

"Gross." He pulled his head away from the dog so far that he tipped over and fell on his side.

Lady pressed her head against Replacement's stomach, demanding some attention. Replacement giggled and scratched behind her ears. Lady pushed forward, and Replacement squealed as she fell over, too.

The three of them lay there for a while. Replacement patted Lady, and Jack softly caressed Replacement's hair.

They spent the entire day together—Jack, Replacement, and Lady. They went for two long walks. They watched a movie, and Lady finally devoured the steak. A couple of times Jack thought about going to look for Grease-E, but he knew that Replacement and Lady needed his presence more than they needed the money he could bring in.

And, he realized, he needed them too.

21

THE POET

The following morning, Jack lay in bed, staring at the ceiling. He had only slept off and on during the night. Now he was running through all the information they'd collected about Daniel. A name leapt out at him—*Ray Davis*.

He tossed back the blanket, grabbed a shirt and a pair of shorts, and headed into the living room. Replacement was at the computer, with Lady on the floor beside her. Lady raised her head when he walked in. He kissed the top of Replacement's head and scratched behind Lady's ears.

"You get any sleep?"

Replacement shrugged.

That means none. "What're you looking at?"

"I'm going through some of Daniel's accounts."

"Are you using the accounts and passwords you got from the apartment?"

She nodded. "He only has a few accounts. I'm going through his email right now, starting with the old stuff and working my way forward. Probably should have gone in the other direction, but I wanted context as I went. Anyway, I don't have anything. It's all just friends and e-bills. And poems—he was a poet. He belonged to one site where he posted a lot. Listen to this." She switched windows and started to read:

It's an age-old question, how am I supposed to know?
Should I listen to my heart or do I let you go?
Can love ever fade? Was it never there?
Will you ever come back? Do you even care?
What will happen now? What will come to be?
What will happen to you? What happened to we?
I said that I'd love you forever. I said I'd always be true.
Then how can I say goodbye? Tell me, how can I stop loving you?"

She looked up at Jack, and he noticed her red-rimmed eyes.

"That explains the inkwell tattoo." Jack rubbed her back. "Do you want some coffee?"

"Please."

"Will you look something up for me? There was a murder. It would have been almost two years ago. The victim's name is Ray Davis."

Replacement typed while Jack made the coffee. Before it finished brewing, she called back, "I've got it. He was killed on Birch Grove?"

"That's it."

"Do you think there's some connection?" Replacement spun around in her chair.

Jack spread his hands on the countertop and stretched. "I was thinking about it this morning. Ray's name jumped into my head. His murder was never solved. Statistically, most people get murdered by someone they know. Right now, Daniel has zero enemies. That's what everyone said about Ray. Ray was a big guy too."

He walked over and handed her a cup of coffee.

She took a sip. "Ray was a big guy all right. Six foot eight, I'd say."

Jack took a sip of coffee and frowned. "How do you get that?"

She clicked the mouse. "His Facebook."

The monitor changed to Ray Davis's Facebook page. He was in his late forties, and he was huge. In every picture, the smiling man dwarfed those around him. Replacement's jaw tightened as she looked at the same three kids in many of the pictures.

"Why's his Facebook page still up?" Jack asked.

"A lot of people are doing that now. They keep it there as an 'in memoriam.' Also, the Davis family is asking for help in solving the murder."

Jack's stared at the man on the monitor. One photo was taken during a backyard barbecue. Ray wore a chef's hat and a big apron, and twin boys clung to his legs while he held a little girl on his shoulder. In another photo, Ray and a tall woman posed with brushes in front of a freshly painted doghouse. Ray was smiling at the camera, but the woman was smiling up at Ray. *She loved him. She's a widow now.*

"How do you know about this case?" Replacement asked.

Jack walked over to the window. "Joe Davenport worked the case, but I was the first responder to the scene. I'll never forget that night. Ray's wife…" Jack swirled the coffee in his cup and exhaled slowly. "Ray went to get the mail. It was night, but he was expecting something, and he'd forgotten to check for it. Joe thought it was really odd that he'd go to the mailbox that late, but…" Jack shrugged. "If it were me, I'd have gone out. Anyway, when I got there, she was inconsolable. When Ray didn't come back right away, she went to look for him. She saw a car driving away, but she didn't get a description because they had a stockade fence and she couldn't really see it. She found Ray dead at the edge of the road."

"This article says he was stabbed."

"The same with Daniel. Multiple stab wounds to the back."

"And they were both tall men," Replacement said. "Do you want me to get the report?"

Jack frowned. "If you're asking if I want you to use an unauthorized account to access the police database, no. No, I do not want you to do that."

"No one's going to know if I use one of the service accounts I made."

"They're not going to know because you're not going to do it. Let's see what we can find, and then I'll talk to Morrison."

Replacement huffed, but agreed.

***

Jack stepped out of the shower and threw on some fresh clothes. He and Replacement had spent the rest of the morning looking over articles on the Ray Davis case and taking notes. Then, after lunch, he had finally convinced Replacement to take a nap. To make sure she wasn't disturbed, he'd taken Lady and gone for a run. Now he was showered and clean again.

He stepped into the living room. Replacement's door was still closed. *Good. She needs the rest.* He picked up his phone and checked for notifications.

Titus had sent two texts. The first read: ANY UPDATE ON EDDIE PORTER? CALL ME WHEN YOU BRING HIM IN. The second was just a picture of a clock.

Da Jewel had sent him a text, too. GREASE-E MEETING SNOW WHITE @ 8 @ LA JOLLA — 2NIGHT. U BRING $50. DEBRA

Jack grinned. *Good investment of fifty bucks.*

He sat down at the computer and got on the internet. It took him a minute to find the schedule for the La Jolla strip club. It didn't open until two. He flipped to the *featured dancers* page and clicked on Snow White's picture.

She was in her twenties, with blue eyes and a big smile. She wasn't a homely girl, but she wasn't too attractive either. She had other assets she was trying to show off, however.

When Jack found his eyes wandering around to the other pictures, he closed the page, turned around, and jumped.

Replacement stood in the middle of the living room with a swirling mix of emotions crossing her face. He saw the disappointment and hurt settling in her eyes. It took him a minute to realize what she must have thought he was doing on the computer.

"I wasn't doing what you think." He hitched his thumb back at the monitor.

The color rose to her cheeks. "Jack, I thought… I know… I realize…" Like a clogged motor, she started and then sputtered off.

Jack waved his hands in front of himself. "Not me. I was just looking up the… I mean, I need to see…" His mind raced to explain why he was on a strip club website without confessing he was working as a bounty hunter, but he drew a blank. *Damn. I'm screwed.*

Replacement wrung her hands and spoke slowly. "I figure it's been hard for you… because you're used to having sex… and since we haven't…" She kept getting redder.

"It's not that," Jack tried to assure her.

"No, I understand. But I'm not ready. I've been dealing… If you need to look at—"

"No. No, no, no." He shook his head, and the words were flung from his mouth. "I'm doing some side work, and…" His eyes widened. "It's right near there. It's right where I'm working. Directions. I just needed the address so I could find where I was supposed to be tonight. I couldn't think of anyplace around there except La Jolla—not that I've ever been in there, that is. I needed directions." He gave her his best that-explains-it-all smile.

She exhaled loudly, ran up to him, and then stopped. She blushed again. "I'm sorry I thought you were looking at other stuff."

"Don't. I get why you thought that, but I can assure you I wasn't doing what you thought I was doing."

She nodded. "Where are you going for a job tonight?" She stretched.

"It's nothing. Night security, maybe."

"Security? Would it always be the night shift? We could make that work, too," she quickly added.

"I don't know."

"There's no pressure on you." Replacement reached out for his shirt. "I have another website design I'm doing, and I'm sure we'll start getting some more PI jobs coming in. I just want you to get a job that won't be too strenuous."

Don't make a face. "I'm feeling much better."

"That doesn't matter." Replacement rubbed his side. "The doctor said you need to go slow."

Jack opened his mouth, but she held up a hand.

"That means you don't want to overdo it by getting some crazy job, right?"

Jack swallowed. "Sure."

22

GREASE-E

Jack sat at a window table in the small coffee shop across the street from La Jolla. He scanned every face going into the club.

So far, I'm batting zero. No sign of Grease-E or Da Jewel. No Snow White either, but she may have gone in the back entrance for the dancers.

In his pocket, his phone made the sound of a barking dog, and he got a few odd looks from other diners. He still hadn't changed that barking ringtone Replacement had set up for him what seemed like ages ago.

He checked to see who was calling before picking up. "Hey, Bob. Thanks for returning my call."

"Sorry about the delay," Morrison said. "It's been crazy. Your message sounded urgent."

"Do you remember the Ray Davis case?" Jack asked.

"The murder over in the new subdivision? It's still open. He was a father."

"That's the one."

"I know Castillo's going over old cases, but I'm not sure where he is with that. Do you think there's a connection to the Branson case?"

"Maybe. Ray was a big guy too. Stabbed in the back multiple times. The wife heard the vehicle drive away. Killer sees his victim, drives down a deserted street, and attacks. Same with Daniel."

"How do you figure that? We don't know where Daniel was killed."

"I found the leash on the fence. You saw the size of the dog, and we know that Daniel walked to the dog park, since his truck was still at the apartment. He took the dog for a walk. There was still a cup of coffee at his apartment. He wouldn't just tie the dog to the fence and leave, so something had to have happened there. Either someone walked up, killed him, and dragged him off, or they drove. Daniel must have weighed around two seventy, so I'd say they were driving."

There was a long pause.

"Bob?" Jack asked.

"Sorry. I'm taking notes. That's good work, Jack. I'll pass this on to Castillo and have him pull the Davis file."

"Thanks, Bob."

The weary waitress brought him another refill of coffee. Jack pulled out a few bills, and she shook her head. "Thank you, but you look like you work for your money too." She smiled. "Besides, you've tipped me for the coffee and every refill so far."

Jack shrugged. "You make a good cup of coffee."

She smiled and moved off to another table.

Jack looked at his watch. 9:10 p.m. *I couldn't have missed him.* He looked back across the street and frowned. *Damn. That's the last place I want to go into.*

He pounded down the coffee, put another dollar on the table, and headed across the street. Traffic was light, and only a few people walked down the street.

Bouncer outside. Two hundred twenty pounds. Spring-loaded baton in a case on his left hip.

They exchanged nods as Jack walked past. It was a greeting that meant: stay out of my way and I'll stay out of yours.

Music and multicolored lights assaulted Jack's senses as soon as he opened the door. La Jolla was a throwback strip club that screamed *dated.* Four different carpeted sections surrounded the main stage in a ring, dividing the place like a pie split into four even slices, and each of the areas had a different theme: music, movies, kink, and pink. Not that the patrons cared about the décor. Every eye in the place was focused on the girl on stage, and Jack took full advantage of the distraction to search the men's faces.

Walk like you're heading to the back. Slow. Don't swivel your head too much.

Jack circled around the hall but came up empty. When he stopped for a second, a young waitress tapped him on the shoulder. She was slightly smaller than Replacement and gave him a little wave as she asked, "You want anything?"

From the way she posed the opened-ended question, Jack knew that a lot more than drinks could be included in his answer. He felt his mouth turn into a frown. He struggled to stop it and place his neutral mask back on, but was afraid the look that remained on his face contained pity. The girl's eyes darted to the floor.

"Do you know if Snow White is here yet?"

"They moved her set to nine thirty."

He showed her the picture of Grease-E. "Have you seen him?"

"Not tonight. He comes in a lot, though."

"Thanks."

She smiled and hurried off. Jack decided to go back and wait for Grease-E outside.

As he pushed the exit doors open, the fresh air made him feel as if he'd just escaped a tomb. He breathed deeply. He nodded again as he walked past the bouncer. Then he turned to the left—and stopped dead in his tracks.

Replacement stood in the middle of the sidewalk. Like the neon sign above her shoulder, Jack watched as different emotions flashed across her face. He could tell she was fighting back tears.

I should've told her. "It's not what it looks like." Jack held up his hands.

"You lied to me. I'd have... I mean, if that's what you want, I'll..."

"You've got it wrong. I did lie—but not about that." He took a deep breath before confessing. "I'm working here."

Replacement's mouth dropped open, and she gasped. "You're a stripper?"

Jack stood there, blinking. "What?"

"You work here? Jack, no." She grabbed his shirt. "We don't need money that badly."

"What? No. I mean, right now I'm working—"

"There you are." He recognized the perfume that wafted up behind him before the voice. Da Jewel strutted up to stand next to him and Replacement.

Jack didn't think Replacement's eyes could get any bigger, but as she stared at the older woman with the halter top, seven-inch heels, and micro skirt, he realized he was wrong.

"You're late." Da Jewel held out a hand. "I did your favor. You owe me another fifty."

Jack coughed.

The look on Replacement's face made Jack shudder. "What favor did you do for fifty dollars?" Replacement asked through gritted teeth.

Jack waved his hands and moved his mouth, but the words seemed stuck in his throat.

"Oh, he didn't do nothing with me." Da Jewel smiled at Replacement and shook her head. "He wanted a guy."

Replacement froze.

"Hold on." Jack's hand cut through the air between the women. "Alice, I'm working for Titus as a bounty hunter. I'm trying to find a bail jumper. I didn't want to tell you because you'd think it was dangerous, and the doctor hadn't given me the okay yet. I also wasn't too proud of it. I'm sorry I didn't tell you. I should've right away. I was wrong. Very wrong, and I'm sorry." The confession tumbled out of his mouth, and he had to take a gulp of air at the end.

"So where's my fifty?" Da Jewel tapped her foot.

"Where's Grease-E?" Jack handed her the bill.

"Right there." She pointed at the front door of the strip club as she stuck the money under her wig.

The short man who held the strip club door open deserved his nickname. His long, oily hair was combed straight back, and his face had a slight sheen. But he must have heard Jack say his name, because he was looking right at him. He froze for only a moment before bolting through the door.

Jack said to Replacement, "Stay here," then gave chase. As he yanked the strip club door open, he yelled, "Go to the car!"

The club was almost pitch black now, as the new dancer on stage performed with just a spotlight. Jack jogged toward the back, scanning for Grease-E.

"He ran that way." The waitress from before pointed down a dimly lit corridor.

"What's down there?"

"Bathrooms and private rooms. There's no exit."

"Thanks." Jack frowned as he rushed forward. *Grease-E likes knives.*

He threw open the first door on the right. A naked girl spun around, and three men sitting on the couch looked up. He pulled the door closed and tossed open the next. Empty.

The ladies' room was next on the left, the men's room on the right. He pushed open the men's room door. At the back of the room, he saw two feet disappearing out the little window.

Damn.

One look at the small window and Jack knew he could never make it out that way; he was surprised Grease-E had fit through. He spun around, sprinted over to the dancers' entrance at the back of the club, and flew out into a narrow alley. Two girls leaned up against the wall, cigarettes dangling from their mouths. One pointed down the alleyway, and Jack took off. As he approached the intersection ahead, he tried to remember the layout of the block.

A girl's high-pitched scream echoed off the bricks.

Alice? Was that her? I told her to go back to the car, but...

He flew down the alley, rounded the corner—and only barely stopped himself before stepping on the figure that writhed on the ground.

Replacement stood with her feet planted wide and a little pink Taser clutched in her outstretched hands. Jack looked down at Grease-E, who twitched and moaned on the tar.

"This thing is awesome." Replacement grinned.

Jack started to flip Grease-E over, but the man screamed, "Stop. Stop!"

Grease-E pointed at the Taser barbs, and Jack winced. One had stuck in his face and the other had hit him in the groin. Jack was almost tempted to call an ambulance, but then he saw the knife on the ground.

He pulled a knife on Alice.

Jack grabbed the wires from the Taser. "Don't move," he snarled before yanking them out.

Grease-E screamed.

"Shut up." Jack tossed the wires down and said to Replacement, "Don't touch the barbs. They're sharp, and you don't know where he's been."

Replacement nodded.

Jack flipped Grease-E onto his stomach. "You have any other weapons on you?"

"I need a doctor. This is brutality."

"No. *This* is brutality." Jack knelt on Grease-E's back and cuffed him. "Here's some free advice." He frisked the man. "One. Do you really want to go before a judge and say you pulled a knife on a girl? Two. Do you really want to go into the Bay and let everyone know you got your ass handed to you by a girl with a little pink Taser? Three. You crossed Titus. Do you want me to tell him you need to be shut up?"

Grease-E shook his head.

Jack pulled a crack pipe from Grease-E's pocket. He tossed it on the ground and smashed it.

"Man. Why'd you do that?" Grease-E whined.

Jack yanked him up by his arms. "I'm taking you to jail, genius. Do you want to go with that in your pocket?"

Grease-E just groaned.

Jack looked up at Replacement, who was grinning and hugging the Taser.

"You bought a Taser?" Jack said.

"It works sweet." Her dimples popped. "You should have seen the look on his face. Did you hear him?" She giggled.

Jack shook his head. *I don't know if I'm mad or jealous.* "Point it down," he said.

"Now what do you do with him?" she asked.

Jack pushed Grease-E forward. "I have to take him to the jail and fill out a ton of paperwork."

"Can I come?"

Jack shook his head. "I'm meeting up with Bobbie afterward. I won't be long."

"Bobbie G? I haven't seen him for a while. Please?" she begged.

"Let me think about it." As they neared the street, Jack looked down at the Taser in her hand. "And put that thing away. I'm parked on the right."

"I parked in front of you. Do you want to drop him off, and I'll meet you there?"

"Wait a second…" Jack stopped. "Did you follow me here?"

Replacement's mouth started to open, but then her eyes narrowed. "*You* wait a second. You come home reeking of perfume, I catch you on a strip club website, then you leave your phone on the table and get a text from a Debra talking about meeting her and a stripper named Snow White, and you think I'm not going to check into that? I love you. I trust you. But I'm not going to be an ostrich and stick my head in the sand."

He ran his hand down his face. "You're right. Entirely right. Follow me."

Her face lit up. She tucked the Taser into her pocket and hurried forward.

"Is she your partner?" Grease-E asked.

"Shut up. No."

"No? Why'd she Taser me?"

"Have you looked in the mirror lately?" Jack opened the back door to the Charger and shoved Grease-E in. "This is my car, so behave."

Grease-E glared at him. "It's an old cruiser. You're a wannabe cop?"

Jack got in and closed the door quietly. *Don't let him get to you.*

"How come you couldn't be a real cop?" Grease-E grinned maliciously. "What's next? You gonna work at the mall?"

Replacement tapped Jack's window. "Lady wants to ride with you. Is that okay?"

Jack grinned from ear to ear. "Sure. Put her in the back."

Replacement opened the back door. Grease-E and the huge dog stared at each other for a moment. Lady's ears flattened against her head, and her lips curled back in a snarl.

Grease-E shrieked. Lady barked like crazy.

"Lady, quiet," Jack commanded, and Lady stopped barking. "Easy. Lady, in."

The dog jumped into the back seat, and Grease-E whimpered.

Replacement put both hands on the window and looked wide-eyed at Jack. "Is that safe?"

Jack shrugged. "If Grease-E behaves."

"How do you know Lady won't bite him?" she asked.

Jack leaned closer to her and whispered loudly enough for Grease-E to hear, "I don't."

She gave him the look that two kids share when they steal a cookie. "I'll be right behind you."

"Good girl." Jack reached back and rubbed Lady's head before looking at Grease-E. "Don't move. Don't talk."

Grease-E pressed his lips together and nodded.

23

LITTLE Z

J ack and Replacement walked through the door of Hannigan's, and Jack smiled. It had been years since he'd been here, and the place was just about the same. Hannigan's was a pool hall that served beer—no hard liquor. A dozen tables were scattered across the open floor, but only four games were going on.

Bobbie was playing at a back table. He was alone. He grinned broadly as he strode forward. "Look at you, little Z. You've turned into a beautiful young woman."

Replacement blushed and gave him a big hug. She almost disappeared in his huge arms. "Hi, Bobbie. Long time." She bounced back over to Jack.

"Nice haul this month, Jack," Bobbie said. "Getting Grease-E was some serious icing."

Replacement punched Jack in the arm. "How many does that make this month for Jack?"

Jack knew she was fishing for the answer, and Bobbie fell for it.

"Four." Bobbie grinned.

Jack didn't.

"You're working for Titus too?" Replacement asked.

"Five years. But I'd better be careful or Speedy here is going to put me out of a job." Bobbie held up a hand with two fingers out, and the bartender nodded. "This is on me. They've still got the best drafts."

"I hope one's for you." Jack grabbed a rack and moved to the end of the table.

Replacement rolled her eyes. "I've got the next game." She leaned up and kissed Jack's cheek before whispering, "One beer." She held up her index finger. "Excuse me while I freshen up." She skipped off to the bathroom.

Bobbie chuckled. "You and Z? I figured it had to happen someday."

Jack racked for a game of eight ball. "Little Z?" He hung the rack under the table.

"Z. It's short for Crazy. I mostly call her that." The balls practically exploded as Bobbie broke, but he only dropped one ball.

"Nice break. Why did you say it figures that we're together?"

The bartender brought over the beers. Jack took his and handed the other to Bobbie.

Bobbie lined up a shot. "She told you when she got the nickname, right?" He dropped the two and stood up. "It was when she kicked your ex's ass."

No. Replacement got in a fight with one of my old girlfriends? "She told me," Jack lied, "but I'd love to hear your version. It's always better hearing it from an unbiased observer."

"You were still in Iraq. I was at the movies with Boomer and Antoine, and I saw Michelle and Replacement. Michelle was talking to the supermodel. The blonde with the long hair."

"Kelly," Jack said.

"Yeah. Well, you know Michelle," Bobbie continued. "She wasn't yelling, but the conversation was getting heated, so we went over to keep an eye on her."

"Were they all at the movies together?" Jack slammed the nine into the corner pocket.

"No. Kelly was there with some guy. That's why Michelle was so upset. It's just low class bringing some new guy around your ex-boyfriend's hood, you know?"

Jack's hands tightened around his cue. *I wasn't an ex-boyfriend. Kelly didn't break up with me until after I got home.*

Bobbie chuckled.

"What's funny?" Jack smashed the eleven, and it bounced around the table without dropping.

"Replacement." Bobbie's laugh was deep. "As soon as we arrived, Z just pounced. It was like something out of *National Geographic*. Like a lion. Kelly went flying, and Z just started hammering away. The new boyfriend tried to break it up, and Z beat the snot out of him too. It was funny as hell. The guy's got this poufy hair. You know, all pampered and wavy? Z's pulling it with one hand and pounding him with the other. Uppercuts—like a hockey player. Michelle's trying to get Z to stop, but Z just redlines. You remember how crazy Boomer is?"

Jack nodded. Boomer got his nickname when they were kids because he liked to smash stuff.

"Boomer's *still* scared of her." Bobbie laughed. "He tried to pull Z off the boyfriend, so Z beat on Boomer until he let go of her. Kelly and her boyfriend took off running, and Z was screaming. It was seriously messed up, man."

"What was?" Replacement hopped up on a stool against the wall.

Jack shook his head, and Bobbie caught the gesture. "Nothing. Just talking about Grease-E."

"You're still on this game?" She stuck her tongue out.

Kelly cheated on me. Jack's hand shook, and he scratched the eight in the side.

"I'm up!" Replacement popped around the table and grabbed the balls. "Eight? I break?"

Bobbie grinned. "You gonna call the shots?"

"The only words that'll be heard will be mine," she boasted.

Bobbie laughed.

Jack leaned against the wall. He watched Replacement's face turn serious as she got ready to break. She launched herself forward, and the balls scattered across the table. She dropped three on the break, and her lips didn't twitch into the smile he expected. He thought she'd be hopping up and down, but instead, she became completely focused on planning her upcoming shots.

"Lucky." Bobbie's smile faded. "How's Aunt Haddie?"

"She's always in good spirits." Jack looked down at his empty glass.

"One, cross corner." Replacement drilled the ball into the pocket and raised an eyebrow at Jack. "Only one beer for you, too. You're driving."

"Where'd you learn to play, Z?" Bobbie asked.

"Chandler. He couldn't use English, but he had a great touch."

Bobbie shook his head and laughed again.

"Four in the side. One bank." Replacement dropped the four and the two. "What's so funny?"

Bobbie held the cue. "That was Chandler. He wasn't the best at a lot of stuff, but he was always good at almost everything." He finished his beer, reached over, and picked up another. Jack counted five glasses.

"So why'd you laugh?" Replacement pressed. "Three along the rail."

"My dad. I was thinking about when Jack came to Aunt Haddie's. I was a kid and I'd got jealous of Chandler." He looked down, swirled his cup, and chuckled.

"If it's a story about Jack, I have to hear it." Replacement leaned against the table and grinned.

"When Jack came to live at Aunt Haddie's, he and Chandler were thick as thieves— right away they were, like, tight. I had four sisters and no brothers, so at dinner, I asked my dad if we could get a little white kid to live at *our* house. My dad almost died, he laughed so hard. Him and my mom. She ran out of the room and came back wearing different pants." Bobbie wiped his eyes. "My dad told me later we couldn't. He said Aunt Haddie was special, and she was the only black women he'd ever known that they let get a white kid."

Bobbie laughed again, and Jack joined in. He leaned back and laughed hard. It had been too long since he'd laughed like that.

As they both rubbed their eyes, Replacement called out, "Eight all the way up." Her serious face dropped when the ball did. She giggled and danced in a circle before she rushed up to Bobbie and stuck her tongue out.

"Boy, Aunt Haddie sure taught you to be a good sport." Bobbie shook his head.

Replacement pouted. "Don't be a sore *loser!*" She danced again.

"Come on, Bobbie. I'll give you a ride home," Jack offered.

Replacement kissed Jack's cheek. "I'll meet you back at the apartment?" She grinned. "Sure thing… Z."

Replacement's smile faded.

***

When Jack walked into the apartment, Lady trotted out to him with her doll in her mouth. He rubbed behind her ears for a minute, then she returned to his bedroom.

That sure beats the fangs and barking and almost eating me.

He knocked on Replacement's door. "Did you take Lady out?"

"Yes. 'Night."

I don't think so. He knocked again. "We need to talk."

The silence lasted long enough that Jack felt his frustration click on low.

"Okay." Her voice was so quiet he barely heard it.

He let the door swing open and leaned against the doorframe. Replacement's room was surprisingly neat and spartan: a twin bed, one bureau, and a small desk in the corner. She didn't have a TV. On the bureau was a picture of Aunt Haddie, Chandler, Michelle, and Jack. She sat up in the bed with a blanket pulled tightly around her.

"Little Z?" he asked.

Replacement's eyes widened, and she grinned awkwardly. "Are you gonna freak out?" she asked.

"That depends. Why don't you tell me what happened?"

"Bobbie told you what happened."

Jack nodded. "But I want to hear it from you."

She shook her head.

He turned his hands out.

"I don't want to." Replacement looked down and frowned. "You still talk about her."

"What?" Jack folded his arms. "I've never talked to you about Kelly."

"You have." Replacement exhaled. "In your sleep."

Damn. "You listen to me while I'm talking in my sleep? That ain't fair."

"What am I supposed to do?"

Jack looked around the room. "Don't listen. You know they're nightmares. I'm not, like, dreaming of us in the Bahamas, making out."

She scowled. "I hope not."

"Whatever. Stop eavesdropping on me while I'm sleeping, and tell me what happened."

"I'm not eavesdropping."

Jack leaned back against the doorframe and raised an eyebrow.

"Okay. Maybe I'm eavesdropping a little," she confessed.

"Spill it."

"I was at the movies with Michelle, and she saw Kelly with a guy. You know Michelle. She went up and confronted her. Kelly said she was going to tell you," Replacement looked down, "but it was just after Chandler died. We didn't know how you were doing, and everyone was really worried about you. So Michelle pleaded with Kelly not to tell you right then. All she was asking was for her to give you more time, so you could heal. You had been through so much, but Kelly… she was just mean." Replacement scrunched up her shoulders.

"I think there's more to the story, Z."

Replacement swallowed. "You know how nice Michelle was, and I'd never seen her like that. She basically got on her knees, and that coldhearted witch said, 'He'll have to deal with it.'" She sat up straight, and her body stiffened.

"And…" Jack motioned for her continue.

Replacement's head tilted back and forth and her lips mashed together. "I sorta lost it. I mean, come on. You're in a war zone. You just lost your brother, and she supposedly 'loves you.' Michelle wasn't getting anywhere, and I only meant to scare Kelly, but everything went red, and I went nuts. I remember hitting her, and then the guy grabbed me, so I punched him too." She tossed her hands up. "Sorry." She sat in the middle of the bed with a look on her face that said she was sorry but that she'd do it again without missing a beat.

"Thanks."

Replacement's face scrunched up. "Thanks?"

"Yeah. Thank you."

She tilted her head, and her face contorted even more. "Thanks for telling you, or for punching Kelly?"

Jack laughed. "Telling me. And having my back. I don't agree with you and Michelle not letting me know Kelly was cheating on me, but I see why you girls did it."

Replacement sat there for a moment, taking that in, then said, "So… you're not going to freak out?"

He rubbed the back of his neck and shook his head. "Guess that's what I usually do. Sorry."

"Why not this time?"

He shrugged. *Why not? I thought I was going to marry her; why not go off the rails when I find out she cheated?*

Replacement's eyes smiled.

"What? I haven't said anything," Jack said.

"It's another thing I like about you. You think. You don't just answer."

"I have my reasons. One, I already knew. I knew in Iraq. Not that she cheated, but that she was gone. I could tell in her letters." He closed his eyes. "I didn't really care. I know that sounds cold, and it isn't what I mean. I mean, I was just numb. I was just going through the paces in life. After Chandler, I felt like I died."

"When did you find out?"

"That she cheated? Tonight. But the relationship was over the night I got back from Iraq. We broke up at the airport when she picked me up."

"She told you right then?" Replacement's teeth flashed.

Jack shook his head. "I saw it in her eyes. There was no denying it." He exhaled. "Sorry."

"It just added to it all. All the weirdness. It's hard for a soldier to come back."

"I don't understand."

"I remember getting off the plane. Three days earlier, people had been trying to kill me, and now I was standing in the middle of the airport, surrounded by people who were just…" He waved his hand around. "Living. They didn't have a clue about the hell I saw in the war. Neither did Kelly. When she came walking up to me, I realized, well… nothing here had changed. She was the same, but I was different. I couldn't even talk to her. I was looking right into her eyes, and I knew she didn't know me anymore. I wasn't the same man. So I let her walk away. I guess that's why I'm not so upset. Well, that and…" His voice trailed off.

"What?"

"I have you now."

Replacement moved over in the bed. "Do you want to come in?" she asked.

"No. Not tonight." Jack stood up straight and backed out of the room. "Thanks."

The door clicked shut, and Jack exhaled. His hand stayed on the doorknob. He knew Replacement's heart was going out to him right now. He sensed her desire to protect and comfort him. He wanted to slip over to the bed and lie with her, but…

Not tonight. It needs to be special for her.

24

LIFE'S NOT FAIR

Jack's eyes fluttered open as Replacement crawled into bed next to him. He reached for her. She gasped as he pulled her over him onto the bed and pressed his lips against hers. He felt her relax, and he grinned.

She pulled herself back up and shook her head. "Hold on."

He let his head fall back on the pillow. "Sorry."

She patted his chest. "It's not you. But I came in to tell you there's a news story about a possible link between Daniel's murder and Ray Davis."

"Good. That means Morrison is looking into it." Jack sat up.

"Would Bob tell the news?"

"Sure he would. He's got a real way of working with the media. That's what you want. That's how you get the information out there. Let's hope with the added attention someone remembers something and calls it in." Jack got out of bed and pulled Replacement with him. "I want to go talk to Daniel's ex-girlfriend's new boyfriend, Wade. Did you get anything on them?"

"I ran a background check on both of them. Sandra's got nothing. She got popped on spring break in Daytona for disturbing the peace and drunk and disorderly—that's it. Wade's a real winner. He was arrested once for bad checks and twice for domestic assault, but he walked. He also has three kids in Florida, and there's an open case about failure to pay child support."

"I can't wait to talk to this guy. How long will it take you to get ready?"

Replacement spun around and waved her hands like a magician. "Poof—ready."

Jack kissed her. "Wiseass." He hurried for the shower.

***

The Charger stopped in front of Sandra's apartment. Jack turned to Replacement, and she held up her hand and pledged, "I'll behave."

"You'll stay in the car."

"I'm not staying in the car." She grabbed the door handle. "You already made me leave Lady at home."

"Because last time Lady almost *ate* Sandra. Fine. You can come, but I do all the talking, and you stand behind me."

"Fine." As she pushed her door open, she stopped. "If she goes to call the police, do we run?"

Jack laughed. "She won't be calling the police, because I'm doing the talking."

As they walked up the staircase, Replacement said, "Hey, when you start negotiating with me, do you start as far back as you can?"

"What?"

"I don't think you wanted me to wait in the car. I think you just wanted to do all the talking. But if you'd said to me, 'I do all the talking,' then I'd have said, 'No. I do half.' So what you ask for is more—like you saying I had to stay in the car. Then you agree with me when I say no, and you end up with what you really wanted in the first place."

How'd she figure that out? "No." Jack scoffed and made a face. "You're way overthinking." *I've gotta come up with another technique.*

Jack stopped in front of the door and moved Replacement to the left side, behind him. He lowered his voice and whispered, "Doorknob is on the left, and the door opens in, so you want to stand to the left side in a knock-and-talk."

Replacement giggled. "A what?"

"Seriously?" Jack glowered, and she held up her hands.

"Sorry."

"I'll explain later." He knocked on the door.

A minute later the door opened and a small man stepped out. He wore jeans, cowboy boots, and a white shirt open enough to show gold chains around his neck. He looked at Jack and then out to the parking lot. "You a cop?"

"No. I'm Jack Stratton. I'm here about Daniel Branson."

"I already talked to the cops." He flung his hands out wide.

"Let them come in." Jack heard Sandra's voice from inside.

"They're not cops," Wade called back. "We don't have to let them in."

"Just let them in," Sandra said.

Wade stomped back into the apartment, and Jack and Replacement followed.

The apartment was a one-bedroom with wall-to-wall dark-gray carpeting. The grayish-white walls and the drawn window shades made it feel gloomy.

Sandra was wrapped in a comforter on a couch, with a box of tissues next to her. Her eyes were red and bloodshot. She looked up. "I'm sorry about the other day." She sobbed and blew her nose.

"My condolences for your loss." Jack angled his head. "I need to ask you a few questions."

"You're not the cops." Wade stood near the edge of the couch. "Who are you?"

"Jack Stratton. This is Alice Campbell. We're with Replacement Investigations. We're looking into the murder of Daniel Branson."

"What do you want to know?" Sandra asked.

I need to split them up. I want to ask Sandra about an old boyfriend, but with the jerk of a new boyfriend here she's not going to be too forthcoming. He's a scrawny guy, but I don't want Replacement talking to him alone either.

Jack looked down at the pack of cigarettes on the table, but he didn't see an ashtray. "Wade, I'm just going to ask Sandra a couple of questions, and then I was hoping to talk to you for just a little bit. Do you smoke?"

"Yeah, why?"

"I just thought this whole thing has to be a little stressful, and if you wanted to go for a smoke break, now would be the time." Jack's open hand pointed to the door.

Wade looked at Sandra, who made a face and nodded. He grabbed his cigarettes off the table, touched her foot under the blanket, and said, "I'll be right outside, okay?" Then he hurried out the door.

I've got five minutes. "Sandra, I'm very sorry about Daniel, but I need to ask you some questions about him."

"He was the nicest man." Her sob almost drowned out Replacement's exhale—but not quite.

Jack shot Replacement a quick glare. "I'm sure he was. But being a guy, I know sometimes you don't get along with everyone."

"He got along with everybody. Daniel didn't have a mean bone in his body."

"How about work? Did he ever mention anyone at work he didn't get along with?"

She shook her head. "He never said anything about anyone. Never yelled. Nothing." She sobbed.

"Did he talk about his family?"

"He didn't have any. His mother and father both died."

"Did anyone not get along with him?" Replacement asked.

Sandra stared at her for a minute, then her gaze traveled to the door. "Wade."

"He threatened Daniel at work?" Jack watched her face.

Sandra nodded. "Daniel sent me a letter, and Wade read it. He drove over there, and they yelled at each other."

Jack tilted his head. "They yelled at each other? Did Wade say if Daniel yelled back?"

Her lips contorted, and she started to cry. She shook her head. "Wade made it sound like a huge fight, but… I don't think so. I only know what Wade said, but he exaggerates."

"Lies," Replacement corrected.

Sandra nodded. "Wade said he went over there and told the whole crew to kiss his ass. I think Wade challenged him to a fight. I told Wade before he went over that Daniel wouldn't fight. Daniel's never been in a fight."

"Can you think of anyone else who may have had a problem with Daniel?" Jack asked. "Anyone he's mentioned?"

She shook her head. "No."

"Was he into anything?" Replacement leaned forward so her head was level with Sandra's. "Did he drink or do drugs?"

"No," she cried. "Didn't drink. Didn't smoke. He was just… nice."

The apartment door swung open, and Wade strutted in. "You guys done?"

"What?" Replacement snapped.

Jack put a restraining hand on her arm.

Wade sat in a recliner, and Jack walked over to him. "You spoke with the police?"

"Yeah. A guy named Castillo. He asked me a bunch of stupid questions. I admit I went over to Daniel's work. I needed to put him in his place."

"Is that the only time you spoke with Daniel?"

"Yeah. He wasn't stupid enough to come back around."

"Or maybe he was just respecting her," Replacement growled, nodding toward Sandra.

Sandra sobbed.

"Whatever. That's the only time I ever talked to him. I had nothing to do with it. I've been with her all last week anyway," Wade said.

"Not all the time. What about work?" Jack looked at Sandra.

"He means when I'm not at work," Sandra explained. "We're together then."

"Are you home during the day?" Jack asked Wade.

"Mostly." Wade scratched his chin. "I'm thinking about going back to school." He took out a cigarette.

"You just had a smoke," Sandra said.

"I'm just holding it." Wade's face twisted up. He tapped his foot and then stood. "I didn't have anything to do with anything. You got any other questions?"

"Sit down," Jack growled.

Wade sat.

"One more question. You got a failure-to-appear for your child support case. Why'd Castillo let you walk?"

Wade went pale. "I got that straightened out."

"What? Why would you be paying child support?" Sandra sat up and put her feet on the floor. She looked from Wade to Jack and then to Replacement.

"Ask *him*." Replacement glared at Wade, who stared down at his cigarette pack.

"Thank you for your time." Jack tipped his head and moved for the door.

Replacement paused in the doorway and looked back at Sandra. "You picked the wrong guy for a boyfriend."

When they were back in the car, Jack turned the engine over and shook his head.

"What?" Replacement asked.

"I don't get how it works."

"How what works?"

"Life. Here you get a guy like Ray who looks like he loves his kids, but he gets stabbed to death. And then you get a guy like Wade, three kids, doesn't support them, and doesn't even let his new girlfriend know they exist."

Replacement put her feet up. "And Sandra picked the slimeball."

"Life's not fair." Jack pulled out of the parking lot.

"What do you think?" Replacement asked. "Did Wade have anything to do with Daniel's murder?"

"Wade didn't do it."

"Why are you so sure?"

"He's got no real motive. I know there's the girl, but Wade got what he wanted when he went over to confront Daniel. He wanted to make Daniel look bad and make himself look like a tough guy. He did that."

"I don't think Daniel looked bad."

Jack smiled faintly. "Because you're a smart girl. Fighting doesn't make you a badass; it just makes you an ass. But Wade doesn't think that way. He thinks he won. So there wasn't any real motive. Sandra had already left Daniel for Wade. Now Wade got Daniel to stay away. Why kill him?"

"You saw how she was crying. Maybe Wade thought she still loved Daniel. I'm just playing devil's advocate."

"I don't think the devil needs an advocate, but think about it. How was Sandra *before* she found out Daniel was dead?"

"She didn't care. Daniel was missing, he could have been suicidal, and she didn't bat an eyelash," Replacement spat.

"Sandra got upset *after* she learned Daniel's dead. Before—nothing. She didn't care. So, that and the fact that Wade's a total pansy means he didn't do it."

"Why do you think he's a pansy? Besides the obvious," she added.

"Wade didn't go to Daniel's work until *after* Sandra told him Daniel didn't fight. That's one pansy point. He gets another point for only yelling at a guy when he's in a cherry picker. He gets a third point for going outside while we interviewed his crying girlfriend. The game winner was when I snarled a little, and he sat right back down. That guy's all talk. One hundred percent pansy."

"I thought so too."

They rode along in silence. After a while, Replacement pulled out her phone to check the news. She made a face.

"What's the matter?" Jack asked.

"They interviewed the mayor about Daniel's murder. The mayor called it 'a craven and despicable act.'" Replacement scrolled down. "She goes on to say, 'This gentle giant was cut down by a coward, and the people of Darrington should be assured that everything is being done to bring the murderer to justice.' A reporter for the *Enterprise* asked if the killings of Branson and Davis were connected. She said, 'At this time we don't know, but I want to assure the people that Darrington is a safe place to live.'"

Jack gripped the steering wheel. Black clouds hurried in from the west, and he smelled the storm coming. "Dumb thing to say."

"What?" Replacement looked up.

"You should never comment about the killer unless you want to make him react. She called him a coward. If the killings are linked, and someone is out there targeting people, she just made him very angry."

"She also said it was safe." Replacement tossed her phone on the seat and rolled her window down. "It wasn't safe for them," she muttered, looking up at the darkening sky.

25

WELCOME TO DARRINGTON

A flash filled Jack's bedroom, and a huge crack of thunder shook the windows. A moment later, Lady leaped up on his bed and stepped on him.

Jack groaned in pain. "Lady? Off!" he ordered.

The dog whimpered and flopped down next to him. He glared at her, but one look at her trembling face and he knew he couldn't kick her off the bed now.

"You big baby," he grumbled as he patted her head.

She tucked her face under his arm. They lay like that for several minutes, listening to the storm. Rain pelted the window, and there were several flashes of lightning. But eventually the thunder started to grow fainter.

The bedroom door flew open, and Replacement hurried in.

"Don't tell me you're scared too?" Jack sat up.

"You need to see this." Her face was white, but her voice was strangely even.

Jack looked at the live newsfeed that was playing on her phone. A female reporter was gripping her umbrella tightly, and emergency lights cast strange shadows in the rain. He heard the strain in her voice, but he wasn't paying attention to what she said. There was something familiar about the spot where she stood.

As she moved to the side, both of Jack's hands went to the phone. She was reporting from the town border facing the entrance to Darrington—Westbrook Road. He knew the spot. The police cruisers could make a U-turn right after the huge "Welcome to Darrington" sign. He'd done it hundreds of times on patrol.

But now, in the red and blue flashes of light, he saw something hanging in front of the sign. He wanted to yell at the woman to get the hell out of the way, but he knew she was trying to block the sight from the camera on purpose. Still, he caught enough of the silhouette to see that it was a body.

He handed Replacement the phone, and she dashed out of the room. His years in the Army had taught him to dress fast, and tonight he broke the record. When he entered the living room, Replacement was already at the door.

Jack heard Lady's nails on the wood, and he turned around. She trotted out of the bedroom with her head down, and she looked around nervously. The faint rumble of thunder in the distance caused her whole body to shake.

"Back in bed." Lady spun around and dashed to the bedroom.

Replacement ran out first, and they raced to the Charger. Jack settled into the driver seat as comfortably as a fighter pilot. The adrenaline thrill coursed through his veins, but a knot formed in his stomach.

He tried to relax as they flew down the deserted streets toward the edge of town. Between the rain and slick streets, he had to keep both hands on the wheel and his eyes on the road ahead. As they barreled through neighborhoods, he noticed the darkened houses.

"Power outage. No one has lights," Jack pointed out.

Replacement was still watching the news on her phone, but she tapped over to a different app. "They say widespread power outages in Darrington and the surrounding county."

"Are any other cruisers there yet?"

Replacement tapped back to the news. "I still only see the same lights."

"The place should be swarming."

But as Jack turned onto Westbrook, he saw only one cruiser, a news van, and a half dozen cars.

"Whose cars are those? Where are the cops?" Replacement asked.

"They're probably gawkers. What's he doing? People are walking everywhere." Jack pulled over to the other side of the street.

He and Replacement jogged across the road toward the patrolman who stood outside the lone cruiser, speaking into his radio. A tow truck was parked several car lengths ahead, with its hazard lights on.

"Why aren't additional units here, Officer?" Jack snarled as he walked up. His transformation back into a police officer was so complete that Replacement pulled up short.

The young officer snapped to attention. Jack looked down at the man's nametag. "Billings, where are the other units? Where's Undersheriff Morrison?"

At the mention of Morrison's name, the young cop leaned forward. "We can't reach him. Dispatch can't get the ME either. Over half the town doesn't have power."

"It's a Code N and Morrison's covering for Sheriff Collins. I don't care if you have to have your mother go to his house, get someone over to Morrison's *now*. You have an unsecure murder scene here."

Replacement walked to the front of the cruiser. Sirens down the road caused both men to turn and look. A fire truck was speeding toward them.

Jack turned in frustration toward the officer. "You can get the fire department here and not Morrison? What the hell did you call in?"

"Jack?" Replacement called to him.

The fire truck shut its siren off and started to pull in front of the cruiser, but Replacement stepped in front of it and waved her hands. "Stop. Stop!"

Jack saw the driver of the fire truck looking to the side to see if he was clear of the cruiser; he had failed to notice Replacement.

"*Alice, move!*" Jack screamed.

Replacement begrudgingly jumped out of the way, then pounded her legs with her fists. "Damn it!" she yelled as the fire truck stopped and skidded a few feet in the mud on the side of the road.

"What?" Jack asked.

"I saw something." Replacement thrust her hands out at the mud underneath the truck. "There were tracks. Tire tracks."

"Damn it." Jack spun around toward the crowd. "MOVE BACK, NOW!" His voice boomed over the sirens. "This is an active crime scene and I want everyone back! Fire personnel, gather at the back of the truck. Billings," he called to the patrolman, "start laying a tape. Roadside to at least thirty yards. Everyone else, move back past the news van."

Jack walked forward with his hands out, and everyone backed up—except two women who came striding forward. One was young and short; the other was in her late fifties—the mayor. Both looked as if they had just exited a board meeting. The younger one held an umbrella over the mayor's head.

A female reporter held out a microphone toward the mayor. "Mayor Lewis, can we get a statement?"

The two women didn't break stride. "Later." The mayor's voice was flat.

Mayor Lewis walked straight to Jack. "Officer." She folded her hands in front of her stomach. "Bring me up to speed."

"Madam Mayor," Jack began, "Undersheriff Morrison is in charge and in control of the situation. He's currently en route."

"He'd better get here fast." The woman's pale-blue eyes looked over Jack's shoulder.

Jack turned, and for the first time he saw what he had only glimpsed on Replacement's phone. The flashing emergency lights reflected grotesquely off the dead eyes of a man who hung from the high "Welcome to Darrington" sign. He was dressed in gray work coveralls with a reflective vest. The rope ran from around his neck, over the top of the sign, and was tied around one of the posts.

The tow truck driver.

The man was thin, but very tall. Jack estimated his height at six foot nine.

The mayor turned to her assistant. "It's another tall man. The press is going to have a field day with this. I have to give them a statement."

Replacement exhaled. "Don't tick him off this time."

Mayor Lewis gave her an icy stare. "What did you just say?"

"You called him a coward before. You don't do that to a killer." Replacement returned the glare. "You ticked him off."

The mayor's eyes narrowed, but her face paled. "Are you saying I'm somehow responsible?"

Jack stepped forward. "You're not responsible. Whoever did this is. But you need to be careful about what you say now. Give a neutral, standard response."

"Mayor Lewis, can we get a statement?" The same reporter from before walked up beside her and then turned to face a camera.

The mayor stood up a little straighter, and her eyes locked on the camera. After a moment, she leaned toward Jack. "Officer, I need you to tell them something."

"I'm not—"

"Now." She smiled, but her eyes blazed.

Jack turned to face the camera and swallowed.

Replacement whispered, "If *you* don't say something, I will."

Jack spoke up. "The mayor's office is utilizing all available resources and many different agencies to help solve these crimes. Right now, a special task force is being organized, and we're asking anyone who was driving on Westbrook tonight to contact the police station. Out of respect for the family, we are not releasing information about the identity of the victim at this time. There will be an update at nine a.m. from the mayor's office. Thank you."

The reporter nodded, and the cameraman switched the camera off.

Jack looked across to the small group of gawkers still rubbernecking and pointing. "Wait a second." Jack walked past the reporter and grabbed the cameraman by the elbow. The man was in his forties, and his salt-and-pepper hair poked out of his old, worn baseball cap. "What's your name, sir?" Jack asked.

"Keith."

"I need you to do something, Keith." Jack waited until the man's eyes locked with his. "Keep it low, but I need you to get video of everyone here. People, cars, especially license plates, everything."

Keith looked back to the reporter, who nodded.

Sirens wailed, and two cruisers rushed to the scene. Everyone turned to watch as they pulled over behind the Charger. Jack exhaled when he saw Bob Morrison hurry out.

"Nicely said, Officer...?" The mayor waited for Jack's response.

"Actually," he cleared his throat, "I'm a private investigator."

"We're with Replacement Investigations. Alice Campbell. Proprietor." Replacement extended her hand.

The mayor's hands stayed at her side. "Wait. You're not with the police?" The mayor looked to her assistant, whose mouth hung open.

"Madam Mayor." Morrison hurried toward them. "Jack."

The mayor turned to Morrison. Her eyes flashed and her voice was clipped. "Undersheriff Morrison, do you know this man?"

"I do." Morrison looked at Jack, and the corner of his eye twitched.

"Jack Stratton." Jack extended his hand.

"Stratton?" The mayor frowned. Her assistant whispered something in her ear, and she stiffened. "Jack Stratton," she repeated rather loudly before glaring at Morrison. "You're responsible."

"Excuse me, Madam Mayor, but—" Morrison began to say.

"But nothing." The mayor lowered her voice. Jack was surprised he didn't see her breath, her words were so cold. "If you'd been here, I wouldn't have had this man go on TV representing my office." She turned to Jack. "Your assistance is not necessary."

"Really?" Replacement rolled her eyes. "You might want to rethink that."

"Alice." Jack put his hand on her arm, but she shrugged it off.

"No, Jack. They need us. You've had training in this." She turned back to the mayor. "He also solved the White Rock murders, and he caught the Buckmaster Pond killer."

Morrison cleared his throat. "With all due respect, Madam Mayor—"

The mayor held up a hand and stared at Jack. "Why did you have the cameraman video the crowd?" she asked.

"The man you're looking for is a serial killer. Serial killers fall into three categories, and this one is organized. He normally abducts his victims, kills them in one place, and disposes of them in another place. That puts him in the organized category—although less so tonight, as he had to put the plan for this one together fast. Still, if he's organized, that makes him the kind of killer who comes back and watches the scene. He could be here right now. The police will need video and license plates."

The mayor studied Jack, then turned to Morrison. "Undersheriff Morrison, I expect you'll be needed here for a while. I also expect you to be at my office with a full briefing at seven this morning. There will be a press conference at nine." She eyed Replacement up and down. "I expect the two of you there as well."

Replacement smiled.

Jack didn't.

"Madam Mayor," Morrison began. "This is a police matter, and while I personally have the utmost respect for Mr. Stratton, he doesn't have—"

"Undersheriff." The mayor's terse tone cut him off. She looked back at the sign and the body hanging there. "So far I've seen Mr. Stratton has exactly what I need, and I will not debate my actions with you." The mayor turned to Replacement. "Ms. Campbell. Seven o'clock."

26

A KAWAH BAG

Morrison rubbed the back of his neck and paced. "Dammit, Jack. Half the town doesn't have power, and I have to be in that half. Do you have any idea how mad Sheriff Collins is going to be?"

"Kinda." Jack tried not to make a face. "Didn't your cell go off?"

Morrison huffed. "Of course not. The night a psychopath does this, and I'm caught with my pants down. Collins is going to nail me to the wall." He clicked on his radio. "This is Undersheriff Morrison. I want an ETA on the ME, forensics, the DA, Castillo, and every other division I'm waiting for."

There was a long pause before the dispatcher answered. "ETA on the ME is ten more minutes. Officer Darcey just located Castillo and will be bringing him shortly. Forensics is en route, and the DA just called and is heading your way."

"Do they really need all that?" Replacement whispered to Jack.

He nodded.

"And what was that all about?" Morrison faced Jack and thrust his hand toward the news van. "A special task force?"

"You weren't here." Replacement pointed her finger at him. "Jack was just trying to cover for you."

"Hold up." Jack shot her a look to be quiet. "Bob, the last person I want jammed up is you. We pulled in, and it was only Billings. People were running all over the scene. I was talking to him, and it just happened."

"I know you were trying to cover for me, but think next time. I don't know how I can even bring this up to Collins, let alone what he's going to do." Morrison groaned. "I was sleeping. I was using my cell all day, and it was charging, but when the power went out… Oh, I'm going right under the bus."

Jack looked at Replacement. "You saw something."

"What?" Her eyes went wide.

"Before the fire truck came."

"The tracks." She rushed over to where the fire truck was still parked. "Stupid fire truck." Her hands went to the sides of her head.

"What did you see?" Jack stood beside her and stared at the turned-up mud.

"Tire tracks and footprints."

Morrison frowned. "The rain probably ruined them, but they'd have been nice to have."

Jack scowled and looked under the fire truck. "We won't get anything now. Do you remember anything about them? Was there more than one set of tracks?"

Replacement's brows knitted together as she glared at the mud. She shut her eyes and shook her head. "I didn't even get a good look. I know I saw tire tracks and footprints, but I'd just be guessing on how many or how big they were."

"Good job." Jack patted her shoulder. "Seriously, most people end up making up something so they don't feel stupid. You could have said small footprints, and we'd be looking for a little guy and it would be all wrong and a waste of time. So good job."

Replacement grinned.

Jack looked over the landscaped gravel that covered the area under the sign. "With all the people walking around and all the gravel, getting any footprints is going to be near impossible now. Have we reached out to the man's towing company?"

Morrison nodded. "Joe filled me in by phone on the way over here. He made a couple of calls, including to the towing company. The man's name is Greg Freeman. Twenty-four. The call came in to Pat's Towing at nine."

"Did they get specifics?"

"A male called in for a tow. Said he was driving a light-gray Lexus and the car just died. The caller said it was parked at the 'Welcome to Darrington' sign on Westbrook. I'm putting a BOLO out for the Lexus."

Jack shook his head. "Do it, but I think they'll be pulling over the mayor. She drives a gray Lexus. She ticked him off, so that's probably another dig. Did the towing company get a callback number?"

"Yeah. He left it, and they took it off caller ID too. It came back to a Dixie Barker. We got no answer at that number, but called the Barkers on their home number. Turns out Dixie is a thirteen-year-old girl who lost her phone recently."

Replacement shivered next to Jack. He started to take off his jacket, but she smiled and shook her head. "Yours looks wetter than mine," she chattered. "We'll have to remember to keep raincoats or something in the trunk."

Jack scribbled PERK in the notebook that Morrison had given him.

"What's a PERK?" Replacement asked.

"Personal Emergency Relocation Kit. It's what you want. They call it lots of different things: a go bag, a battle box, or an INCH bag."

"INCH bag?"

"It's an I'm-Never-Coming-Home bag. I'll get you one. I had one in the Impala. I should have gotten one for the Charger."

Replacement grabbed his notebook and wrote: "Get a KAWAH bag."

Jack raised an eyebrow.

Replacement grinned. "Keep-Alice-Warm-and-Happy bag."

Jack chuckled and turned back to Morrison. "It's three a.m. I'm going to take her home and run over what we have."

"I'm good," Replacement protested.

"Your lips are blue. Shut up."

"You'll want access to the computer systems," Morrison said, and Jack saw the slightest dimple start to appear on Replacement's cheek. "I'll call IT and have them email it over."

"Would you mind making the call now, Bob? I want to go over them before I talk to the mayor."

Morrison yawned. "Excuse me. Sure thing. I'll also have Castillo comb through the footage the cameraman took. That was quick thinking on your part." He pulled out his phone and hesitated. "It's good to be working with you again, Jack, but when Collins comes back, I don't know what's going to happen."

"When's that? Where is he?"

"Texas. He's there for two weeks, but he left a week ago. There's no way to get in touch with him. Doctor's orders. His blood pressure had gone through the roof."

"This isn't going to help," Jack said wryly.

27

IT'S EVIL

Replacement peeled off her wet jacket and fumbled with the buttons on her shirt as she headed to her bedroom. Lady trotted behind her. Jack wanted to chase her too, but instead he went into the kitchen.

"I'll put some coffee on," he called out.

When Replacement appeared fifteen minutes later, wrapped in her fluffy bathrobe, she sat down at the computer and cooed as her hands wrapped around the warm coffee mug.

"Thank you." She grinned. "I can finally feel my fingers again."

Jack put his hand over the mouse. "We got the login from IT, but—the report on Davis is difficult to look at. And I don't think you should look at Daniel's report either."

Replacement shook her head. "If we're going to catch this guy, I need to."

Jack took his hand off the mouse.

Replacement scanned the Davis report with Jack looking over her shoulder. "Ray's wife, April, said it was close to ten p.m. when he went outside." Replacement pointed at the monitor. "They were watching a movie, and Ray remembered he hadn't yet checked the mail."

"He was expecting a birthday present for his sons." Jack straightened up. "The police found it still in the mailbox."

"April went outside at ten fifteen and found the body," Replacement said.

A click of the mouse brought up the autopsy photos. Replacement winced. A dozen wounds on Ray's back were numbered and circled.

Replacement began to read. "The blade was thick, approximately six inches long, with a drop point." She looked back at Jack. "What's a drop point?"

"A drop point slopes from the handle to the tip." He tried to use his hands to describe it, but Replacement shook her head. "It's a hunting knife," Jack explained. "The thicker tip is better for cutting and skinning game."

Replacement grimaced and turned back to the screen. "The first wound here," she held her finger over a deep, wide gash high on his back while she continued to read, "cut his spinal cord. These two intersecting wounds came after. These wounds," her fingers moved to three additional places, "would have all been fatal in a short amount of time."

"Does it say how fast he died?" Jack asked.

They both scanned the page, but Replacement found the paragraph first. "They estimated time of death within five minutes of the first wound."

She clicked ahead to the crime scene photos. The first showed Ray Davis on his back near the end of the fence. The second photo was a close-up. His eyes were open and staring straight ahead.

"April said she knelt down beside him," Replacement said. "She could see all the blood and knew he was dead."

"Back up. What about the car?"

Replacement scrolled down and then stopped. "Here's a transcript: 'I called to Ray and then heard a car door close. I couldn't see the car because of the fence but I saw the brake lights glow through the leaves of the maple tree. I thought he might have just been talking to a neighbor so I called out again, but he didn't answer. When I walked to the road, I saw him lying there. I ran over to him and saw all the blood. I thought the car may have hit him, but you could see that he...'" Replacement trailed off.

Jack silently read the rest of Davenport's notes, including where he detailed April breaking down and crying inconsolably. He looked at the close-up of Ray lying in the dirt outside his house and exhaled loudly. *What kind of evil kills a man and leaves him face up in the street?*

Jack took the mouse and clicked back to the page that showed the wounds on Ray's back. "Can you bring up two pictures side by side?" he asked. "The autopsy one and number thirty-four."

Replacement moved the pictures so they were displayed beside each other on the monitor. Photo number thirty-four showed Ray Davis's body in the dirt just off the blacktop from the street. He was on his back, with his arms at his sides and his eyes wide open.

"What do you have, Jack?" Replacement leaned closer.

"Davis is on his back." Jack closed his eyes as he pictured the street.

"Yeah." Replacement pointed to the photograph. "See, he's looking back toward his house."

Jack studied the photo. Davis's head leaned slightly to the side, and his eyes were focused straight ahead.

"No. The killer rolled him over." Jack felt the hair on his neck rise. "One of the first blows severed his spine. I need to ask the ME. I would think he couldn't roll himself over after suffering a wound like that."

"Maybe April rolled him over to try to help him," Replacement said.

"I don't think so. She said it was obvious he was dead. If he was face down, I don't think she'd say that. Plus, look at the blood on his body." Jack pointed to a few different spots.

"There isn't much blood on him," Replacement said. "There's a lot under him."

"Exactly." Jack stood up. "If April had turned him over, he would've been on his stomach for a while and his front would be covered in blood. But if the killer stabbed him and immediately turned him onto his back, there would be a lot less blood."

"Why would the killer roll him over?" Replacement asked.

Jack walked to the window, and his reflection stared back at him. He peered into his own eyes and the darkness beyond. He didn't answer.

"Maybe he's doing it for a power trip?" Replacement offered. "Or to gloat? Why do you think he did it, Jack?"

"The why isn't too important to me." Jack stared at his reflection. "The fact that he watched him die is."

Replacement's expression changed as she realized what happened. She wrapped her arms around herself. "That's horrible." She shuddered.

"It's evil. I need to confirm with the ME, but that would mean the killer stabbed him, then stayed there and watched him die. He didn't leave until April came out and scared him away. That's a long time to stand over a murder victim."

Jack stared off into the darkness while Replacement turned back to the report. After a few minutes, he looked back at the kitchen clock and rubbed his face. "Can you pull the report on Daniel? We're running out of time before the press conference."

The keyboard clicked, and the monitor's screen changed. "There's a list of test results still outstanding on the first page," Replacement said. "It says this report has only the initial crime scene findings."

Jack read down the rows of medical jargon and frowned. "They have a lot of material to test."

"It says the body has been transferred to the state lab. Why?" Replacement asked.

"Standard procedure. They need the results as fast as possible. That probably means Neil Fredrick went to the capital while they ran the tests. Either that or he sent Mei."

"Who is Neil Fredrick?"

"The medical examiner. Mei's his assistant. One of them would've gone with the body."

Replacement reached for the mouse.

Jack touched her arm. "You sure you don't want me to drive?"

"I'm sure."

The first crime scene photo came up. The torso lay on its stomach in a torn-open green trash bag. Replacement recoiled, and Jack quickly grabbed the mouse and closed the window.

"Please. Let me go over this, and then I'll summarize, okay?" He squeezed Replacement's arm.

She nodded and stood up. "Do you want a glass of water?"

"No thanks." Jack reopened the window and clicked to the preliminary report. "The victim was stabbed four times in the upper and mid-back. They haven't determined the weapon but believe a sharp blade was used for dismemberment. Only the torso was recovered. They searched the surrounding area with dogs in a six-man grid."

Jack scrolled to the next page. "The torso had been exposed to the elements and..." He went silent as he read the portions that detailed that animals had eaten part of the corpse. He also jotted down a list of things to ask Mei: what tool was used to dismember the victim, were there any other apparent wounds, could they tell the time of death—his list continued to grow.

Replacement came back over and handed him a glass of water.

"There was a great deal of foreign matter both on the outside and inside of the bag. The bag itself was nondescript with no identification numbers." Jack exhaled. "I need to talk to Morrison and see when the full report will be ready."

Replacement looked at the clock and rubbed his shoulders. "Why don't you go take your shower? I think we could both use a break."

28

THEY'RE NOT SAFE

Jack and Replacement paced while they waited for the others to arrive. The conference room held one long table ringed by a dozen high-backed leather chairs. A projector hung from the ceiling and whiteboards were mounted on three of the walls. The fourth wall was a row of windows that overlooked downtown Darrington.

The door opened, and the mayor's assistant entered with a tray of coffee, muffins, and fruit.

"Thank you." Replacement smiled.

The woman nodded and turned to Jack. "Vicki Young." She extended a slender hand. Vicki wore a dark-blue skirt, matching button-up blouse, and modest heels. Her makeup and shoulder-length brown hair softened the squareness of her face. She was attractive, but no more so than the mayor, Jack noted.

"Jack Stratton." He shook her hand.

"It's a pleasure to meet you in person. Your name has crossed my desk repeatedly for the last few months, and I was curious." She looked him up and down.

"Alice Campbell," Replacement said, opening a bottle of water.

But Vicki's eyes never left Jack. "The mayor will be in shortly. She'll expect a rundown of the facts from you. Undersheriff Morrison has already provided his report, but he's still on the scene. Stick to the facts, and if you present problems, have a solution at hand. The press conference is at nine. She'll want to go over the details beforehand and polish any statements. And she'll expect you to attend the conference as well."

Replacement started to open her mouth, but Vicki continued, "As far as compensation for services rendered, Ms. Campbell and I will be discussing the particulars while you brief Madam Mayor."

"Wait a second," Replacement replied. "Jack and I are a package deal. I'm at the rundown with the mayor too."

"The particulars of your services have to be ironed out beforehand."

"Trust me, she brings a lot to the table." Jack winked at Replacement. "She needs to be there when I brief the mayor."

Vicki's square jaw became more pronounced, but before she spoke, the mayor walked through the door, and Jack snapped to attention.

Mayor Lewis's black suit and steel-gray shirt matched her salt-and-pepper hair. "Getting a contract in place is not negotiable, and time is limited. Shall we start?"

Replacement looked to Jack. "Go," he said, "do what they need you to do. Come back quickly. And you *will* be at the press conference." He said this last with a pointed look at Vicki.

After Replacement grudgingly left the room with the assistant, the mayor walked to the end of the table and sat. When Jack didn't move to sit down as well, she held out a hand toward a chair. Jack preferred standing in general, and he wanted to remain on his feet when giving the briefing, but he reluctantly sat. He'd known from the first time he'd laid eyes on the mayor that she was a woman who didn't beat around the bush.

"A serial killer's targeting tall men in Darrington, Madam Mayor." He waited for a reaction. Nothing. He continued, "There are three victims we are aware of."

"There could be more?" she asked.

Jack nodded. "We have no way of knowing how many. All three known victims received multiple deep lacerations with a thick blade. The ME's report isn't finalized, but the initial autopsy confirmed at least three of the wounds to Branson were fatal and two to Davis. Morrison reported that Greg Freeman was stabbed six times. It's clear the killer is progressing. This last killing was intended to terrorize."

"Do you know why he's killing?"

Jack's eyes locked with the mayor's. "Not yet. I think the motive is secondary."

The mayor's thumb ran along the table. "I find that disconcerting. Why would the reason he's killing be secondary to you?"

"There could be a thousand reasons he's targeting big men, but the motivation for a serial killer's actions typically doesn't come out until after they're caught—or never. Sometimes hate's just hate. You can't explain crazy."

The mayor thought for a second, then leaned back. The door to the conference room flew open, and Vicki and Replacement entered. Replacement's smile conveyed that her discussion had gone well. Jack noticed how Vicki's eyebrow ticked up when she glanced at the mayor.

"I hope I didn't miss much," Replacement said. She walked around the table and sat down next to Jack.

As Vicki leaned in and whispered in the mayor's ear, Jack saw the faint lines in Lewis's forehead deepen. "You opted for a flat fee?" the mayor asked Replacement.

"Think of it as an expensive tryout. I asked for a dollar less than what you'd need to get approval for. That way it's simple and it's between you and me. If Jack solves it quickly, it's more than you wanted to spend. But it's also all-or-nothing: if we don't deliver, you don't pay."

Jack's chest swelled a bit as he looked at her. She crossed her legs and folded her hands.

She belongs at this table.

"Agreed." The mayor nodded at Jack. "Continue."

"The progression and speed are what's worrisome. His targets are the same, but serial killers usually don't operate at this rate. This killer has taken two lives in a week and in multiple locations. He's operating like a hybrid. A spree serial killer."

"That covers the speed. What do you mean by progression?" the mayor asked.

"He made an effort to hide Daniel Branson's body. If that jogger hadn't come across the bag, we might never have found it. But Greg Freeman was lured to the scene and then posed."

"You don't think he lured the others?"

"Branson was a regular at the dog park. Davis was killed outside his own house. The killer met them on their own territory. But this time he wanted to make a point. He took Freeman to the sign, strung him up for maximum shock value. This time, he wanted an audience."

"What're the next steps?"

"Talk to the ME. All of the killings are bad for forensics. Branson was dismembered, and animals—" Jack stopped when Replacement squeezed his leg under the table. He noticed the mayor had gone paler. "With Freeman, the storm complicated everything. Morrison's in contact with the FBI and state."

"Let Morrison handle the interaction with other agencies." The mayor's lips pressed together. "After your past dealings with them, I think that would be best. Am I understood?"

Jack nodded. "There's a long to-do list, but you should concentrate on this press conference. You'll need to do three things: humanize the victims, ask the public for help, and slow down the killer."

"And just how am I supposed to do that?" The mayor's hand smacked the table.

She's got a temper. "Let him know he accomplished his goal. You said people were safe, and he wanted to let them know they're not. You need to let people know he's right— they're *not* safe."

Vicki scoffed. "She can't do that. She'll look weak."

Jack kept his eyes on the mayor. "It's not about politics. You'll look a hell of a lot weaker if this guy gets any madder and keeps killing. We need to get him to cool off. Most serial killers get some satisfaction from the kill, and then they go underground."

"How long do they stop for?"

"It varies. Weeks, months—some go years between kills. We need to do something to get him to back off." He glanced at Vicki. "I'm not talking about creating panic in the street, but just let people know there's a killer out there and that he's dangerous. You tell big guys to be careful. Let them know everything is being done to stop these killings.

"We also need the public's help," Jack continued. "Anyone who was out on Westbrook last night. The killer pulled over near the sign; someone could've seen something. But start with humanizing the victims. If you have pictures, show them. Talk about the families they left behind. Let the killer know they were loved people."

The mayor looked down at her hands, and Jack noticed the slight slump in her shoulders.

"He would've killed again no matter what you said. It wasn't your fault. Right now, you have a job to do, and you need to concentrate on that."

29

LEARN FAST

Replacement sat at the computer with a notebook open, and Lady lay in the corner with her head on her paws. Jack walked over to lean against the half-eaten couch and frowned.

I have to figure out what I'm going to do with Lady.

"The press conference went well," Replacement said. "She kept it short and covered everything you told her."

"Yeah. Morrison has my notes now, too. I pray the murderer cools off."

"You think he will, right?"

Jack shrugged. "I'm not a profiler. I've never worked a serial killing. I was a regular cop."

"But you've taken classes."

"It's totally different. I know you're trying to help, but—"

Replacement smacked the notebook down on the desk, and Lady's head shot up. "Jack Stratton, there are times when your self-doubt really ticks me off."

"We're dealing with people's lives. I screw up, and people die. You've passed me off as this expert and—"

"And what?" She hopped out of the chair and her arms went wide. "What? Morrison's working the case with all the resources the police have at their disposal. It's not all on your shoulders, but you think it is. Look, Jack, whether you like it or not, you keep getting placed to stand in the gap. What do you want to do? Have the mayor pull in someone else? Who's to say if they can solve this any more than you? Even if they worked a hundred cases, I don't care what you say, you're the best person to catch this guy. That's what you do. You stop the bad guys."

"Experience matters."

"Yeah. And you have it. But if you want more—learn fast." Replacement stuck her chin out. Jack stared into her green eyes, and her gold flecks flashed. She sat back at the computer and watched him for a moment. "So, where do we start?"

Jack cracked his neck. "We need to make a to-do list and a profile of this guy."

"We don't have much information."

"We have a lot. What did you find out in the missing person reports?"

"I found three reports for men over six foot six."

"In Darrington?" Jack asked.

"One in Darrington, one lived in Fairfield, and another was from New Hampshire. Hold on." She pressed a few keys, and the reports appeared. "Alan Barnes, Eldin Parish, and Henry Clark. Alan lived in Darrington. He was thirty-eight at the time. Divorced. Lived alone. His ex-wife reported him missing two years ago."

"Detective Davenport looked into it. It's still open," Jack read. "Joe was concerned because Mr. Barnes had recently lost custody of his children, was laid off, and had a substantial amount of debt in his name. His car was recovered on Deer Creek Road, one mile from Deer Creek Bridge."

Replacement gasped. "Did he jump?"

"If someone wanted to kill themselves, I wouldn't think Deer Creek Bridge. It's high, but not high enough. It's definitely not the bridge I'd pick."

"Don't talk like that." Replacement's eyes narrowed, and she turned back to the monitor. "They searched the creek, but no body was found. They didn't locate a note either." She looked back at Jack. "Why would you park a mile away and then jump?"

"You wouldn't. Anyway, that's two similarities for that case," Jack said.

"Two?"

"Height, and the car was found on the side of the road. Daniel, Davis, and Freeman were all killed along the side of the road. What about the next guy?"

"Eldin was from Fairfield. He was twenty-two when reported missing. Had a history of drug abuse. He also had restraining orders against him by his parents. The case is still open, but Detective Lenox in Fairfield thought it was probable Eldin went to Florida to live and wouldn't contact his family."

"How tall is he?"

"Six foot six."

"Anything else on him?"

"Nothing. Detective Lenox interviewed everyone Eldin knew. They all said he was the type of man who could just get up and go."

"Is Lenox still on the force?" Jack asked.

"I'll check. There's also Henry Clark. This one is recent—three months ago. Henry was a photographer. His sister said he was going to Fairfield to take pictures of thatched-roofed barns, and then he was heading to Pennsylvania, New Mexico, or Bolivia." Replacement rolled her eyes. "Well, that narrows it down." Her finger traced along the screen. "Henry skipped out on his hotel bill, and they found some personal items left behind in the room. No camera equipment."

"What about a car?"

"He didn't own one. The sister said he preferred to go by bus."

Jack ran his hands along the sides of his head. "Well, we can't know for sure, but it's certainly possible that all three are victims of our guy. It's a different sort of target—most serial killers kill women, and he's targeting big guys. Six foot six and up."

"How many giants can there be in Darrington?" Replacement asked.

"We should check the census. I also want to call Big and Tall stores. Guys that big need custom clothes."

"Should we try to find a way to warn them?"

"The press conference and the news are the best way. That should at least give the guys a heads-up." Jack rolled his shoulders. "The killer gets these big guys to let their guard down. We'll have to get the ME reports and check for defensive wounds, but I don't think there were any."

"How do we know it's a guy?" Replacement said. "Maybe it's a girl and the guys underestimate how dangerous she is because of that."

"Anything is possible, but we need to look at probable. Statistically, serial killers are men. They also work alone. There are exceptions, so we can't put blinders on, but we need to narrow the field. We're looking for a white male under the age of thirty-four."

"I found the national databases you wanted me to access." Replacement flipped her notebook back. "Two universities are also compiling information. I went through the paperwork, and they should be getting back to me soon."

"The FBI also has one. It's part of ViCAP."

"ViCAP." Replacement's voice rose. "Violent Criminal Apprehension Program?" Jack nodded, and she smiled. "I'm working on my police lingo," she said.

"There's a lot of it. We'll have to go through Morrison on that database, though." Jack smiled wryly.

"Is that it for databases?" Her pen hovered over the notepad.

"No. I want to go back to his first kill."

"Ray Davis?"

Jack shook his head. "We're dealing with a serial killer now. Ray may have been his first human kill, but he may not have been his first kill."

"Human?" Replacement made a face.

"Serial killers usually start on animals when they're in their teens. They work their way up to humans. I want to pull all the records for murdered animals. If he started in this area, we might be able to catch a break there. He may not have grown up here, but it's still worth a shot."

Replacement spun around to the computer. "I've seen that database."

"Get the login that Morrison sent us."

"I don't need it." Replacement grinned.

"Use it. You're not using my old police login, right?"

"Right. They disabled that account when you left the force." She squeezed her shoulders together. "I happened to make a couple of other accounts…"

"There's no reason for you to hack when we have access. So don't hack."

"It's technically not hacking."

"Deranged people do things just for the thrill of it, and since you're not crazy," he raised an eyebrow, "instead of breaking a bunch of laws and risking getting caught, how about you use the account we were given?"

Replacement opened and closed her mouth and pretended to talk while she tilted her head back and forth.

"Funny." Jack headed off to the kitchen and brought back two waters.

The police scanner on the table clicked on, and they both turned to listen. A call came in for a traffic stop downtown. Jack smiled. He'd thought listening to the scanner would bother him, but it didn't. It had the opposite effect.

Some people have those little waterfalls on their desks to relax; I have a police scanner.

Replacement turned back to the keyboard and searched the database. After a couple of minutes, she said, "There're lots of animal murders in here."

Jack nodded. "It's a known precursor pattern, so they started to track it a while back. Can you make up a list of people with prior crimes against animals?"

"I thought serial killers liked lighting fires." Replacement's fingers danced across the keyboard.

"They do. They have a lot of traits in common—and then again, sometimes they have none. Some serial killers end up seeming completely normal."

"Are we looking for any particular types of animal murders?"

Jack looked over at Lady. "We know he's going after big guys, so what if he started with—?"

"Big dogs." Replacement leaned over the keyboard, and her hands became a blur. "They didn't organize the database by size, but they do have weight. There are a lot of codes I don't understand. I may be able to break it out another way."

"You go, geek girl."

***

Half an hour later, Replacement stomped away from the computer in frustration. "Why are all the police databases so half-assed?"

"Do you have any idea how little funding they get? I know the guys at IT. They want a good database, but you need money. You need people to put the data in it."

Replacement held up her hands. "I'm sorry. I'm just frustrated."

Jack kissed her head. "Me too." He walked over to the monitor. "Is there anything you can use?"

Replacement's nose wrinkled. "Who's Gary Shaw?"

"Gary's in animal control. Good guy. A little weird."

"His name's all over the reports," Replacement said.

"Can you get me a number for him?"

"Sure."

Replacement pulled up Gary's number, but as Jack was preparing to call, Replacement held up her phone. "Gary may have to wait. I got a text from Vicki in the mayor's office. They got a call to the tip line. A guy named Chester Pratt reported seeing a dark sedan on Westbrook right before Freeman was killed."

"Did she give an address?"

"He lives over near Herring Run Pond."

"I want to talk to Chester and then Gary." Jack smiled. "Do you want to take a ride?"

30

AS SEEN ON TV

Chester Pratt lived in a small cottage next to Herring Run Pond. The homes that surrounded the postcard-perfect pond were originally summer cottages, but over time the owners had converted them to year-round residences. That meant they had almost no yard and were almost stacked on top of one another. Pratt's house was one of the few with a garage.

Jack parked along the small chain-link fence, and he and Replacement hopped out. As they passed the garage, he noticed an old Impala parked inside. An inch of dust covered it, and fishing rods rested against one side, but he could still make out its blue color.

Jack exhaled. He never saw his Impala again after the accident, and the car in the garage made him want to take it for a ride.

Replacement reached out and squeezed his hand. "Sorry about your car."

Jack rubbed the back of her hand with his thumb. "I love the one you got me. The Charger's my car now."

She grinned as they walked up the steps to a flimsy screen door. Inside the house, a television blared.

Jack rang the doorbell and waited. After a minute, he rang the doorbell again and pounded on the door. He had a good beat going before he heard the TV switch off. The door opened partway, and an elderly man peered out.

"Chester Pratt? Jack Stratton and Alice Campbell. We're here about your call to the tip line."

Chester's face broke into a broad, wrinkled grin. "Jack?" he asked so loudly that Jack leaned away slightly. "You say your name's Jack?"

"Yes, sir," Jack almost yelled, but Chester still angled his ear toward him.

They followed the man into the small living room that must have once been a porch. It held a couch and two chairs, plus a table set with three cups and three sodas.

"You reported seeing something on Westbrook?" Jack asked.

"Why don't you sit on the couch, and I'll sit over here." Chester steadied himself on the furniture as he crossed the room to a worn recliner.

"You were out on Westbrook the other night?" Jack asked again when they were all seated.

Chester's eyes darted to the floor and then back to Jack. "You two want a soda? That's *real* soda." He smiled as he pointed at the can with a gnarled finger. "Not that diet crap."

Jack poured Replacement a drink. "Thank you."

"Candy?" Chester grinned and pushed a bowl of old-fashioned mints Replacement's way.

Jack looked at his reflection in the powered-down TV. He pictured Chester Pratt sitting there doing the same thing: sitting on a couch, all alone, and staring at himself.

"Are you making any progress looking for the Giant Killer?" Chester tried to pour himself a cup of soda, but his hand shook. Replacement smiled and held out her hand. Chester gave her the can, and she poured a drink for him.

"Well, that's why I'm here, sir," Jack said. "I hoped you could help." He stared down at the bubbles in his drink.

There was an inch of dust on that Impala. It hasn't been driven in five years, let alone two days ago in that downpour.

"I can help." Chester sat up straighter, but his knee nervously bounced.

"The tip line operator made a mistake when they took down your message, sir." Jack's lips pressed together.

Chester swallowed. "They did?"

Jack nodded. "They thought you said you were driving on Westbrook, but I saw your car in the garage. That's a 1976 Impala, right?"

"You know your cars," Chester said.

"I had a '78. I was admiring yours, but I noticed it hasn't been out in the rain recently. So I think the operator didn't get your message correct. You weren't driving out on Westbrook the other night, right, Chester?"

Chester's smile faded. He nodded. "They must have got my message wrong." His shoulders slumped.

After a moment of awkward silence, Replacement asked, "Have you been following the case on the news?"

Chester nodded again and looked at the TV.

Jack pulled out his notepad. "Well, can you tell me what you think, sir?"

"What?" Chester angled his ear toward Jack.

"You've been following the case—tell me what you think. Anything about it at all. We could use your opinion." Jack gave Replacement a quick wink.

Chester's smile returned. "Well, I think it's a serial killer." Jack wrote that down. "You're writing that down?" Chester asked, surprised.

Jack nodded.

Chester leaned forward and started to talk. He covered all the known information about the case, from finding Branson's body to the report of Davis being stabbed. He talked about losing power during the storm and waking up and seeing the news reports. Jack took notes, sipped his soda, and listened.

After half an hour, Jack popped another candy in his mouth and stood up. "Thank you very much for all your help, sir."

"You're more than welcome, Jack. Thank you both for coming. I sure hope you catch the guy. That Greg Freeman sure seemed like a nice kid."

Jack stopped. "Did you know him?"

"What?" Chester angled his ear toward Jack.

"Did you know Greg Freeman?" Jack practically shouted.

"Know him? No. But he's on that commercial on Channel 3 all the time."

"What's it for?"

"Pat's Towing. It's the one with the catchy jingle."

"I'll be sure to check it out." Jack waved.

As they walked back to the car, Replacement whispered to Jack, "That was nice of you."

"What was I going to do? Arrest him for calling in a bogus tip because he was lonely? We did learn something."

"What?" Replacement asked.

"The killer didn't need to know Greg Freeman or get a tow before. He could have seen him on TV."

"That's true. Still, you're a good man, Jack Stratton." Replacement gave him a quick hug before she jumped in the car.

31

SKUNK STINK

"Why aren't the animal control offices at the police station?" Replacement asked as they walked up the steps to the two-story brick building. "Animal control in Darrington is contracted out. It's different all over." Jack held open the door, and they walked into the little reception area.

A young girl stood at a printer behind the counter, watching the papers as they printed out. "One second," she called out. After a minute, she glanced over sheepishly. "Sorry. It jams, so you have to watch it."

"I'm just looking for Gary."

"He's around back." She pointed. "Just go out the front and follow the walkway to the right."

"Thanks."

A concrete slab walkway led around the building, but a tall fence blocked the view of the back. Jack stopped at the gate and listened.

"Why do you do that?" Replacement asked.

Jack's eyebrow went up, and he realized that he'd instinctively moved to the right of the gate. "This is what I wanted to tell you at Sandra's apartment," he said. "If you're really determined to do this, you need to listen to a few things to stay safe."

Replacement shrugged. "We're just going to talk to a guy. A guy you already know."

"Okay. But this guy is in animal control. What if behind this fence was a huge rabid dog he just picked up?"

Replacement rolled her eyes. "They wouldn't let it just run around back there."

"How do you know? The girl at the desk might be wrong. Maybe the way to go was out of the building and take a left, and behind this gate is the vicious weasel area."

"There'd be a sign."

"There might not be. Whenever you're going to talk to someone, a knock-and-talk, you don't know who's behind the door. So, if the doorknob is on the left and the door opens in, you want to stand to the left side. Then whoever is opening the door has to move up so you can see them."

"Why do you move to the side?" she asked.

"People shoot through the door."

Replacement's eyes rounded. "They just shoot?"

Jack nodded. "I knew a kid in Iraq…" He stopped talking as he saw the concern sweep across her face. "You just need to be careful."

"It's not me I'm worried about." She moved Jack farther over. "You stay safe."

"Look, I don't want to get you paranoid or freaked out worrying about me." He kissed her head. "Which I find adorable. But you need to be prepared—like a Girl Scout."

He swung the gate open. A white van sat parked in the back driveway. The rear doors were open, and a hose ran inside. The van rocked a bit, and water sprayed out.

"Hey, Gary!" Jack called.

A man with curly red hair stuck his head out of the van, waved, then hopped down. He was dressed in coveralls, and his mouth and nose were covered in a bandana. Carrying the end of the hose, he went over to the water spigot, but before he turned it off, he took off the bandana, leaned over, raised the hose over his head, and rinsed his hair thoroughly.

Jack and Replacement both stopped as the distinct smell of skunk hit them in the face. Gary shook his head like a dog. Replacement laughed, and so did Gary.

"Why hello, Jack," Gary yelled. His teeth flashed in a broad grin. Jack took a step forward and stuck his hand out, but Gary waved him off. "Skunk. Bad."

"I can tell." Jack tried not to wrinkle his nose.

"Let's move upwind of the van." Gary walked toward the fence, and they followed. "What brings you by?"

"Have you heard about the murders?"

Gary's wet curls bounced as he nodded. "Jane was pretty freaked. Her brother is, like, six and a half feet tall or something. Of course, I've got nothing to worry about." He was only a little taller than Replacement. "Do you really think it's a serial killer?"

"That's why I'm here. I was hoping you could help."

Gary's smile got even bigger. Because Gary was animal control, a contracted civilian position in Darrington, some of the police treated him as a menial underling. Jack wasn't one of them.

"You know you can always ask me a favor, Jack." Gary straightened up.

Replacement spoke up. "We were looking through the database on animal deaths to see if we could find a link. I was trying to find a way to see if there's a connection with large dogs."

Gary considered. "We could look. We record the breed, age, weight, and cause of death."

"There were some codes I don't understand. Do you have a reference chart?" Replacement asked.

"Well, you're in luck." He grinned. "I do. Come on in."

They followed Gary inside to a windowless back office that was little more than a large closet with an old desk crammed inside. The minute the door closed, both Replacement and Jack started to cough at the skunk smell that still clung to Gary's clothes.

"Sorry." Gary reopened the door. "Give me five minutes?"

Both Jack and Replacement nodded, and Gary rushed out of the room.

Replacement exhaled. "Wow. That poor guy."

Jack shook his head. "He's always the happiest guy. I think I'd go out of my mind working in here."

She kissed his cheek.

"What was that for?" he asked.

"Because you'd work here if you had to." She wiggled her eyebrows. "I like that in a man."

"The whole hunter-gatherer provider thing, huh?" Jack winked. "You do what you have to do. At least he gets to go outside."

Ten minutes later, Gary came back into the room wearing a fresh pair of coveralls, but Jack still had to work on not making a face from the lingering odor.

"Sorry it took so long," Gary said.

"I'm the guy asking a favor, Gary. Don't apologize. I appreciate it," Jack said.

"Do you have a login?" Gary asked. When Replacement nodded, he held a hand toward the desk chair. "Do you want to sit in the pilot chair? You're probably better at it than I am."

Replacement slid into the chair, and Gary leaned over her shoulder. Jack saw her eyes widen and her mouth clamp closed. *It's true you can't get rid of skunk stink.*

"I can filter the list to dogs and unnatural deaths," Replacement said.

"Good thinking." Gary patted Replacement's shoulder. "Now, you're looking for big dogs? Medium-big, or big-big, or what?"

"Real big. Like the size of a bear." Jack held his hand up chest high.

"Really?" Gary stood up straight.

"No," Replacement huffed. "Just giant breed dogs. Hold on. I'll export everything to a spreadsheet, and then we can check off the big ones."

"That's super-smart," Gary said.

Jack leaned against a filing cabinet while Gary went down the list with Replacement. He'd look at the breed and the weight, and they'd highlight a row if it was a good match. After half an hour, both Gary and Replacement leaned back at the same time.

Jack looked at the screen and frowned. Only a few lines were highlighted.

"I guess we haven't really had much of anything criminal as far as large or giant breed dogs," Gary said. "Just these cases of reported abuse, but it doesn't look like anything came of it."

"When do you notify the police?" Replacement asked.

"Sometimes it's obvious there's a crime, but I'll also notify them if I'm real suspicious or see any possible abuse. Dog fighting, killing, torture—"

Replacement held up a hand. "Got it."

"You can also talk to a guy at the animal shelter." Gary grabbed a pen and piece of paper off the desk. "His name's Ryan Warner."

"Thin build, round glasses, wavy hair?" Jack asked.

"That's him." Gary handed Jack the paper. "Nice guy. Do you know him?"

"Just met him the other day," Jack said.

"Is it okay if I email this spreadsheet to myself?" Replacement asked.

"Sure."

Replacement clicked a couple of buttons and then stood.

"Thanks, Gary." Jack shook his hand as they walked out of the little room. "I'll look over the reports. Can I call you if I have questions?"

"Sure thing. I'd be happy to help." Gary held a different door open than the one they came in. "Let's cut through the office—it'll be faster."

As they walked past the girl who still stood at the printer, Jack asked, "Have you had any recent activity that would raise a flag?"

Gary shook his head. "It's sad, but the ones I see are usually abandoned."

Jack nodded. "Thanks again."

"Are you going to the shelter now?" Gary asked.

"Yes."

"Well, I have a cat that needs to be dropped off there. If you don't mind? It would save me a trip."

"Sure." Replacement grinned. "I like cats."

Gary went into the back and returned with a closed metal box. He held it out to Replacement. "You can just give this to Ryan."

Replacement held the metal box up and inspected the sides. "There are no air holes."

Gary nodded. "That's okay. It's dead."

Replacement almost dropped the box, but Jack caught it. Replacement's mouth contorted into different horrified positions.

"Sorry." Gary turned beet red. "I guess I'm just used to it."

"You can't have them take it over anyway, Gary." The girl looked up from the printer. "I called the shelter this morning and they're still down, so they're not taking any drop-offs."

"Oh. Well, shoot." Gary took the box back. "Thanks anyway. Franklin Animal Shelter is our backup. I'll take it over there later."

Gary waved as Replacement hurried Jack out the door.

32

UNDER THE BUS

The lobby of the animal shelter was empty apart from the beefy young man who waited behind the counter. He had dark-brown hair that needed a wash, a tie-dyed shirt, and a nametag that read "Captain Andy" with a smiling skull sticker on it.

"Hi, is Ryan in?" Jack asked.

"I'll see." Andy turned and yelled into the back. "Ryan? Two people are here to see you."

There's some fine customer service.

"You picking up or looking to adopt?" Andy asked.

"We're just here to see Ryan," Jack said.

"We already have a dog." Replacement smiled.

"What about a cat?" Andy asked.

"That wouldn't be a good idea with our dog," Replacement said.

"You'd be surprised." Andy leaned against the counter. "Sometimes dogs and cats get along really well. We just got in some kittens. I'll go grab——"

Jack put his hand on the counter. "Not today."

Andy opened his mouth, but when he saw Jack's darkening eyes, he closed it.

The double doors swung open, and Ryan walked out. "Jack. Alice." He motioned for them to follow him. "Why don't we talk in my office?"

They followed Ryan down a hallway to an office that was larger than Jack expected. The desk faced the door, and a couch was against the far wall.

"Thanks, Ryan. I had a few questions I wanted to ask you."

"Is it about the Giant Killer?" Ryan motioned for them to sit down on the couch, and he pulled his chair over. "That's what the newspaper is calling him. I watched the mayor's press conference on the Internet, and I saw you."

"It may be," Jack said. "Gary Shaw recommended I speak with you."

"How can I help?"

"Gary said you have a database we'd like to take a look at. Do you keep a record of all the animals that are brought in?"

"We do. Right now, Lacie handles that. But what information are you looking for? I have most of it in this computer up here." Ryan tapped his head.

"We're looking for any patterns of animal abuse or cruelty. Specifically to large dogs."

Ryan tilted his head back. After a moment, he took off his glasses and rubbed his eyes. "I'm sorry. I guess I don't even like to think about it." He brushed back his hair. "I can't remember anything specific about big dogs, but it should be in there. There was one case I remember, but it was neglect. You just want to know about large dogs?"

"The more data, the better," Replacement said. "I'll take everything you have."

"That'd be a job for Lacie." Ryan stood up. "She's out back."

"Do you work closely with animal control?" Jack asked.

"Yes and no. They bring in hurt animals or dead ones for disposal if they aren't too big."

"Too big?"

"Big like a deer or a horse. Our crematorium is too small for that, so they'd have to take them to Willow Farms for burial. Come on, Lacie's out back. We just got in a litter of puppies."

The three of them headed to the back of the animal clinic, where a large fenced-in area was broken up into different pens. Lacie sat next to Carl in his wheelchair, and little yapping puppies surrounded them.

"Hello, again." Carl waved with one hand while he held a fuzzy brown pup with the other.

Lacie hopped up, cradling a yapping puppy. "Hi, Alice. Feel how soft he is." She handed the puppy to Replacement.

"Oh, he's adorable," Replacement gushed as she rubbed the puppy's head.

The puppies stood up on their hind legs, trying to climb on everyone. A few tried to get Carl's shoelaces.

"They're so cute!" Replacement squatted down.

The other puppies swarmed over to her, and their little yaps filled the air. Replacement giggled as they hopped, jumped, and twisted around.

"Hi, Carl." Jack shook the man's hand.

"What brings you by?" Carl asked.

"They're actually hoping Lacie can give them a hand with the database," Ryan said.

"Sure," Lacie replied. "Do you want to look at it now?"

"That'd be great." Replacement reluctantly put down the puppy.

"Hey, Ryan?" Andy called from the door. "The Pekingese is here."

"Be right there," Ryan called back. "Lacie knows where everything is," he said to Jack, then to Lacie he added, "Give them a hand with anything they need, okay?"

"Sure. Come on, Alice."

As everyone started to walk away, Carl cleared his throat. Jack turned around and realized Carl's predicament. *How's he going to corral all the puppies from his wheelchair?*

"I'll only be a few minutes," Ryan called back.

"I can give you a hand," Jack offered.

Stupid. Did I just volunteer to help with puppies?

Lacie grinned. "We'll only be a few minutes. They really need to be out for a little while. Thanks."

Replacement kissed Jack's cheek, and the girls walked away.

"Great," Jack muttered under his breath.

"I take it you're not a dog fan," Carl said.

Jack tilted his head. "Sorry. I'm working on it."

"Here." Carl handed Jack a puppy. "Try puppy therapy. You'd have to have a black heart not to like this little guy."

The puppy squirmed in Jack's arms.

"I take it you *are* a dog fan?" Jack asked.

"You could say that. I want to work with support dogs."

"For the blind?"

"Actually, I want to work with ones for the disabled. They're training service-assistance dogs for people in wheelchairs."

"That's great." Jack thought for a moment. "Do they get things for you?"

"They're perfect if you drop something, but you can train them for other things. They can even pull a wheelchair."

"I bet mine can pull a bus."

Carl laughed. "Lady's a big dog. She'd be great, but she may be too big for most."

"Is that what you do here? Train service dogs?"

"A little. I help where needed."

"Do you work here full time?"

"I'm only part time, but I volunteer the rest."

"That's kind of you."

Carl exhaled and put his hands on the arms of his chair. "Selfish, too. The dogs give me a lot." He winced, then leaned down and picked up the puppy that was gnawing at his shoe. He handed the puppy to Jack, who awkwardly juggled both puppies in his arms.

Carl laughed again.

Jack set the puppies down. "If you don't mind me asking, are you a veteran?"

"No. You?"

"Yeah."

"I was hurt in high school. Wrestling. Not the hitting-the-guy-with-a-chair TV kind, but the Olympic kind. I got swept, and I landed wrong." He shrugged. "Some people have it worse, though. You make the best of it."

"Looks like you are. Training service dogs, that's a good thing."

"I like it, and I get paid to play with puppies." Carl reached down, and the dogs rushed over to him.

A man walked around the corner of the building. He looked to be in his early twenties and walked with a swagger. He tipped his head curtly at Jack, then leaned toward Carl. "Ryan said you might need a hand. Yeah, these beasts look rough."

"I'm fine, Stan." Carl set the puppy down.

Stan laughed. "I'm just giving you crap. Speaking of crap, Ryan wants me to clean all the cages, starting with this one."

"Glad I can't help with that," Carl said.

"Jack?" Replacement was at the door and waved him over.

"That's my exit cue," Jack said. "Nice seeing you again, Carl."

Jack shook both men's hands, then needed an assist from Stan to keep all the puppies from following him while he slipped out.

"How did it go?" Jack asked when he was back inside the shelter.

"Awesome. She gave me the whole database. I can look it over at home. I told her I'd call her tonight. She's pretty cool."

"Great. Let's get out of here." Jack started forward, but Replacement didn't move.

She tugged her ear and smiled up at him. "I was wondering..." Her voice went up, and Jack's eyebrows came down. "Lacie said the puppies are free, and—"

"We have a dog the size of a farm animal in my apartment now." Jack's hands went out.

"Not for us, silly." Replacement shook her head. "You know how Mrs. Stevens is always going on about Lady?"

"No. Absolutely not."

"I'm trying to be nice," Replacement protested.

"Me too. Believe me. You don't want to get a dog and give it to someone as a gift."

"I bet she'd love it." Replacement put her hands on her hips.

"Really?" Jack leaned down. "You figure the guys who work here know about these things, right?"

Replacement shrugged and nodded. "Yeah."

Jack walked back to the door and pulled it open. Carl and Stan were still outside with the puppies.

"Excuse me?" Jack called out. "Do you think it would be a good idea if I picked one of those puppies up for a surprise gift?"

"No," they both shouted back, shaking their heads.

"You never want to do that," Stan warned.

"Just bring the person here as a surprise," Carl suggested.

"Great idea, Carl. Thanks." Jack waved and let the door close. "See?" He held his hands out again.

Replacement glared. "Well, thanks for throwing me under the bus."

"I didn't throw you under the bus. They think it was my idea."

"Yeah, right." She scoffed. "They think it was mine."

Jack shook his head, then pulled the back door open again. "Excuse me, guys? Whose idea do you think it was to give the dog as a present?"

Carl and Stan exchanged a look. "Yours," they both said.

Jack turned to Replacement and smiled. "See? I did not throw you under the bus. They thought it was my idea."

"Sorry," she snapped.

"It was her idea," Jack yelled to the men, then let the door shut. "*Now* I threw you under the bus."

"Jerk." She playfully shoved him.

Jack's phone rang, interrupting them. "Stratton."

"You need to get down to the hospital," Morrison said. "We have a victim who survived an attack."

"On my way."

33

YOU SOUND LIKE MY WIFE

Two ambulances were parked in front of the hospital, along with two police cruisers and Morrison's Crown Vic. As Jack and Replacement walked through the double glass doors, Jack's hands turned clammy. He hated hospitals.

Tossing a stick of gum in his mouth, Morrison hurried over. "I already put out an APB for a white male, mid-twenties, brown hair, five foot seven or eight. Dark T-shirt, blue jeans, and sneakers. First responder got the call an hour ago. The victim is Samuel O'Rourke. He's in surgery now."

"What's his condition?" Jack asked.

"Serious. He got stabbed in the stomach. They said there was a lot of bleeding."

"Stomach?" Jack repeated.

"Not in the back." Morrison popped a second stick of gum in his mouth. "I thought it didn't fit the pattern either, but O'Rourke said he turned around at the last second. He has a slash wound to the chest and a straight-in to the gut. Said he was at Bill's Burger Hut and when he went to throw his trash away, the guy attacked him.

"Officer Pugh got his statement before EMS arrived. He's at the station now, writing up the report. Two officers have the scene secured while forensics works it up. Castillo went to state to talk to the ME there. He's heading back now, so I'm waiting to see if I can talk to O'Rourke."

Morrison's phone rang. He looked at the number, held up his hand to Jack, and took the call.

Jack and Replacement walked over to the nurses' desk. Two women in hospital scrubs were talking behind the counter. As Jack approached, one walked away and the other turned toward him. She was five eight, had short, sandy-brown hair, and was a little on the chubby side. Despite the circles under her eyes, she wore a bright smile.

Jack recognized her but couldn't figure from where. Her nametag read *Tina*, but even her name didn't jog his memory.

"Jack." She walked over to them.

Damn. He felt the color flush to his neck. He gave Replacement a quick please-help-me glance, and she stepped forward.

"Hi, Tina." Replacement waved and smiled. "Alice Campbell—we met at the Boar's Butt."

"Kendra's friend." Jack blurted out the answer like a contestant on a game show. Replacement sighed.

Tina's brows pulled together. "How's your recovery going?"

"Fine. Stronger every day," Jack said.

Replacement squeezed Jack's hand. "Tina was here when they brought you in."

"I assisted in the ER," Tina said. "You had us worried."

"I should say thank you."

"I'm a nurse, and I only assisted."

"I'm glad you did."

"Have you finished physical therapy?" Tina asked.

"All done, and I got a clean bill of health. Alice is taking good care of me."

"I can see that." Tina gave Replacement a wink.

"What can you tell me about Sam O'Rourke?" Jack asked.

She frowned, and Jack held up a hand.

"HIPPA. Don't say anything." Jack smiled thinly. "I understand."

"I can talk to Bob," she offered.

They all looked at Morrison, who stood with his phone pressed against his ear. He held up an index finger and rolled his eyes. After more nodding and explaining, he put his phone away and came over.

"That was Castillo," he said. "Tina, any ETA from O'Rourke's surgery?"

"I saw Doctor Singh come out, so I expect they're wrapping it up. O'Rourke will be out for a while, I'd expect."

Morrison clamped down on his gum and rubbed his eyebrows with his index finger and thumb.

Jack gave a small wave to Tina, and then walked for the door. "Nice seeing you again, Tina."

"Where do you think you two are going?" Morrison asked as his phone rang again.

"I'll come back when O'Rourke wakes up. I'm taking a ride."

"Where are we going?" Replacement asked.

"I want to see the crime scene."

34

BILL'S BURGER HUT

The parking lot of Bill's Burger Hut was surrounded by crime scene tape. Jack and Replacement walked toward the police cruiser, and Jack smiled when he saw Officer Kendra Darcey leaning against the side and speaking to the driver. He considered Kendra a good friend.

Her blond ponytail bounced as she jumped back from the car, and Jack's smile vanished when he realized to whom she was talking. Officer Billy Murphy and Jack had disliked each other from the first time they met. Jack tried to give Murphy the benefit of the doubt and shove those feelings aside, but Murphy didn't. He was the type of guy who if he didn't like you, he let everyone know and did his best to screw you to the wall.

"Stratton," Murphy spat.

Jack just nodded.

"Civilians are supposed to stay behind the police tape." Jack heard the door lock, and the window started to rise. "I'd move you, but I'm off duty." Murphy stepped on the gas and gunned the cruiser out of the parking lot and down the street.

"That's what you get when you breed rats and humans," Jack muttered. He grinned at Kendra.

She tilted her head and laughed. "You're so bad. But he does look like a rat. He's got that coarse brown hair, his eyes are small and close together…"

"You forgot the weasel-like face."

Kendra held up a hand. "Stop it. I still have to work with him, and he's the commissioner's son-in-law. Hi, Alice."

"Hi, Kendra. We just saw Tina," Replacement said.

"At the hospital? Did O'Rourke say anything else? Is he out of surgery?"

"Yes, no, and no," Jack said. "Morrison is still there to see if he can get a statement when O'Rourke wakes up."

"You're working for the mayor's office now?" Kendra asked.

"She worked that out." Jack thumbed his hand at Replacement, who smiled broadly.

"No way." Kendra swatted Jack's shoulder harder than normal. "Sheriff Collins is going to go Chernobyl when he gets back." Her tongue stuck out slightly between her teeth.

"Try to stay out of the blast radius. Did you talk to Donald?"

Kendra frowned. "Donald was real shook up. He doesn't do well with blood, and the guy was bleeding badly. Any word on how he is?"

"Serious condition, but they're already wrapping up surgery. Will you walk us through it?"

Kendra walked them to the back parking lot. O'Rourke's pickup truck was parked ten feet away from a wooden fenced-in area with two green dumpsters. Two technicians in white coveralls were moving around, snapping pictures, while a third leaned over the driver's seat.

"O'Rourke said he was throwing his food away and the guy rushed up behind him. He said he came from there." She pointed to the open field. "The assailant slashed him with a knife, then stabbed him. O'Rourke punched him in the head. The assailant ran for the railroad tracks, and O'Rourke ran for his car."

Jack looked back at the restaurant. "Did anyone see it?"

"Just the aftermath. A lady heard him screaming. Linda Brooks. She had gone through the drive-thru right behind the victim and had then parked out front to eat in the car. She had five kids with her, so when she heard him screaming she didn't go over, but she laid on her car horn and it attracted a lot of attention."

"Did they check the security cameras?" Replacement asked.

Kendra nodded. "The manager is working on it now."

"If it's okay with you, I'm going to go speak with the manager," Jack said.

"Go right ahead."

Jack and Replacement walked up to the double glass doors. The glass shook when Jack pulled on the locked door, and a tall, overweight man in his mid-forties with thinning hair rushed over. His nametag read *Jerry*.

"I'm sorry, but we're closed," Jerry said through the door.

"Hi, Jerry. Jack Stratton. Alice Campbell. We're with the special task force investigating this incident."

"Oh, sorry." He took out a key ring, unlocked the door, and held it open. "Come on in. I saw you on TV. My wife's actually worried about me because I'm so big. I tried to tell her I'm only six two and this maniac is going after guys over six eight or something, but she's a worrywart." He wrung his hands. "Boy, this is going to make her bananas."

"Were you here during the attack?" Jack asked.

"Yes, sir. I was in the office, though. It was pretty slow, but Tommy, he's the drive-thru teller, he came in saying someone was screaming in the parking lot."

"What happened then?"

"I told Tommy to call 911. We have a zero-involvement policy. We always call the police. Then I ran to the drive-thru."

"What did you see?"

"Nothing. The drive-thru faces directly toward the back, but he was off to the side by the dumpsters. I tried looking out the window, but I could only hear someone screaming. Then a diner in the front parking lot began honking. I guess she wanted to attract attention. It worked, because lots of people came. The police were here right away too."

"So you didn't actually see the assault or the assailant?" Jack asked.

"No. I checked with the cook and the cashier and they didn't see anything either. Tommy is the only one who heard anything."

"I'd like to take a look at your security footage," Jack said.

"Sure. Certainly. But—there's one minor problem." He wiped his hands on his pants. "The outside cameras aren't working. They got knocked out in the storm. I told corporate, and they were going to send someone to fix them, but—"

"*None* of the outside cameras are working?" Replacement asked.

"I'm sorry, no." Jerry looked around. "The inside ones are."

"The police are going to need that footage. The techs will want to take a look at the system. They may be able to get something. Please don't touch it," Jack instructed.

"I won't, sir."

"Can we talk with Tommy?" Jack asked.

"Yeah. He's still here. He already spoke with a few policemen, but they said a detective wanted to speak with him too. I'll go get him."

Jerry came back moments later with a teenager whose trembling demeanor made him look even younger.

"Hi, Tommy." Jack stuck his hand out. "I'm Jack, and this is Alice. You were working the drive-thru window when the attack happened?"

"Yes, sir." Tommy's head bobbed up and down and he thrust his hands into his pockets.

"What did you see?"

"Nothing." Tommy shrugged. "I just heard him screaming."

"What did he say?"

Tommy thought for a second. "I couldn't really make out any words. It was more like 'Ahhh.' You know? Like something in a horror movie where there's noise but no words."

"Did you stick your head out the window and look?" Replacement asked.

"I tried." Tommy cast a quick look at the manager.

"I didn't think it was safe for the employees to go outside. I called the police," Jerry said.

Jack rubbed the bridge of his nose. "Do you remember seeing anyone in the drive-thru who seemed nervous or raised any suspicion?"

"No." Tommy dug his hands deeper into his pockets. "I remember the guy who got stabbed. He was in a big pickup."

"Do you remember if anyone drove up behind him who maybe looked out of place?" Jack asked.

"Nope."

"How did the guy seem?" Jack asked.

"I don't know. He seemed okay? I just took his order. I didn't talk with him." Tommy looked at his feet.

"What did he order?" Replacement asked.

Tommy fidgeted. "I don't know."

"You took the order, right?" Replacement continued.

"I took a lot of orders." Tommy finally took his hands out of his pockets. "I don't remember his."

Replacement looked at Jerry. "Can you please look up his order?"

"Certainly. Right this way." Jerry stepped behind the counter and pressed a few buttons. "Do you know his order number?"

"No, but you couldn't have been open long after he ordered," Jack said. "He ate and then was attacked. Let's start with the end and work our way back."

"But we'd still have to know what he ordered in order to know which one is his, right?" Jerry's fingers still hovered over the keys.

"I have an idea," Replacement said. "Just start scrolling back through the orders." She leaned over the register. As the screen scrolled, her green eyes scanned the listing.

"There." She pointed at a huge order. "Five orders of chicken nuggets, five sodas, five fries, a double cheeseburger, and a milkshake."

"He didn't get that." Tommy shook his head. "That was the mom with the screaming kids."

"I know." Replacement rolled her eyes. "But she said she was right behind the victim, so…" She reached out and scrolled to the next order. "He ordered just a regular soda?"

"Is that it?" Jack asked.

"Yeah," Tommy said. "Now I remember. He just wanted a regular soda."

"Some customers do that," Jerry said.

"We're going to take a look out back." Jack stared down at the register. "Don't touch the register or the surveillance systems."

"I won't, sir." Jerry backed away from the register.

Jack and Replacement went back outside and walked toward the truck.

"Don't get too close to the truck," Jack instructed. "I just want to look from back here."

Replacement wrinkled her nose. "Is that from the trash?"

"Summer and trash." Jack looked from the truck to the trash can and then the dumpster. "This doesn't add up."

Replacement nodded. "You're right. I don't get it."

"What don't you get? Tell me what you're thinking."

"I have questions just flying around." Replacement waved her hands next to her head. "Like why would you come to a burger joint and order just a soda? And then why park to drink a soda?"

Jack nodded. "Good. Keep going with what seems off."

"But Kendra and Donald were here, and they didn't see anything off," Replacement protested.

"One, you don't know that. Two, that's not their job right now. Donald needed to get a statement and secure the scene. He did that. Kendra is making sure it stays secure, and she's doing that. Once the detectives get here, they'll ask the same questions we are, but right now that's our job."

"Okay." Replacement exhaled. "Well, then, why would you park next to the super-smelly trash? The whole parking lot back here is empty."

"Where he parked is my biggest question," Jack said. "It's the most secluded spot, but you have a dumpster, then his car, and then over there is the trash can. And look at the inside of the truck."

They were twenty feet away, but with the truck's doors open, they clearly saw inside.

"There's trash on the floor," Replacement said.

"And his drink holder is empty. Why throw out the cup and not the other trash? And if you did want to throw it out, why not open the door and toss it in the dumpster? Instead, he gets out, goes all the way around the truck, and walks twenty feet to the trash can?"

"It makes no sense," Replacement said.

"And what about the attacker? O'Rourke said he came from over there." Jack pointed to the open field.

"Are you really going to start there to attack someone? It's the worst spot." Replacement pointed to the dumpsters. "Why not come at him from there?"

Jack picked up his phone. "Undersheriff Morrison? Has O'Rourke come out of recovery yet?"

"Not yet. Castillo is almost on the scene with you. What have you got?"

Jack ran down everything they found out. The more facts he relayed, the tighter the grip on his phone became. When he finished, there was a long pause.

"We need to keep looking at it like it's legit," Morrison said. "I'll send Castillo to talk to the techs and see what they have. I'll leave the APB up." Morrison sighed. "This one already raised flags because of the change in MO as well as the description of the suspect—no car and a generic description that matches the majority of the male population. I've talked to the operating doctor. The first wound is superficial. Couple of stitches. The stomach wound didn't come near anything vital, but it did go deep. I'm waiting for the background on O'Rourke now."

"Sorry, sir."

"Good work, Jack."

"Undersheriff, we need to quiet this down with the press."

"How am I supposed to do that?"

Jack rubbed the side of his face. "I don't know, but if our killer murdered Freeman because the mayor said it was a cowardly act, what do you think he's going to do now that someone said the Giant Killer failed and ran away?"

There was silence on the other end of the phone.

35

THEY SHOULD BE AFRAID

Jack and Replacement walked up to Vicki's desk at the mayor's office. The dark circles under Vicki's eyes made her seem older than she was. Today she'd gone with her gray wardrobe: gray jacket, gray skirt, and gray shoes. It was a bad choice, because the lack of sleep gave her skin a matching grayish tint.

Replacement set her takeout coffee in front of Vicki. "It's mine, but I haven't taken a drink yet." She smiled thinly. "You look like you need it more than me. It's a regular: cream and two sugars."

Vicki smiled as she took the coffee. "Thank you. I haven't had a second to make any." She held the cup with both hands and took a long sip. "I don't mean this to sound callous, but there is so much going on beyond a serial killer. The mayor is dealing with a water rights issue, two new housing developments, the River Bend Restoration... it's an endless list." She sighed and held the cup in her lap. "And now he attacked another man? Please tell me you have good news."

"I need to speak with the mayor about that attack," Jack said.

Vicki nodded. "I guess I'm so used to seeing things like this solved in an hour on TV." She stood up, snagged her tablet, and moved to the door to the right of her desk. She cracked open the door, peeked in, then turned back to them. "The mayor will see you now." She held the door open.

Mayor Lewis stood up behind her large oak desk as Jack and Replacement entered. She gestured to a table with four chairs in the corner. "Mr. Stratton. Ms. Campbell. Vicki, I'd like you to join us too." She shook their hands as all four of them took seats around the table. "I just got off the phone with the undersheriff."

"I saw him at the hospital. Did O'Rourke come out of recovery?"

"He did." The mayor folded her hands on the desk. "Both he and Detective Castillo spoke with O'Rourke."

"They did? What did he say?" Replacement sat forward in her chair.

The mayor's eyes fixed on Jack. "He's reaffirmed his earlier statements. He insists he was attacked. The undersheriff also informed me that you have suspicions about that."

"I do," Jack said.

The mayor nodded. "Is that what brings you here? It was my expectation there was little my office could do while the investigation proceeds. Do you need my authorization for something?"

"You need to do something Undersheriff Morrison may not want you to do," Jack said. He felt a twinge of guilt for not speaking to Morrison first, but he also knew that if the request came directly from the mayor's office, it would relieve Morrison of accountability.

The mayor raised an eyebrow.

"First, you need to get interviews with the victims' families on the air," Jack said.

Vicki's hand smacked the table. "Putting grieving widows and crying kids on TV is a recipe for disaster." She turned to the mayor.

Mayor Lewis stared coldly at Vicki's hand on the table, and her pale-blue eyes narrowed slightly. Vicki straightened up and put her hands in her lap.

"Why?" Mayor Lewis asked Jack.

"To slow the killer down. O'Rourke's lying. It was a staged attack."

"Morrison is not one hundred percent sure of that."

"He's ninety-nine percent sure of that, but he needs to give the victim the benefit of the doubt and investigate it. You don't."

"How can you be sure that he faked the attack?" the mayor asked.

Jack ran down everything they'd discovered. As he talked, the mayor's expression never changed. She sat there with her eyes locked on his. When he finished, she angled her head slightly. "If he did fake the attack, what do you need from me?"

"You need to announce that your office has no evidence to suggest the crimes are linked. You need to say the Giant Killer's still out there and dangerous. When you had a press conference and called him a coward, he responded by killing Greg Freeman and hanging him from the 'Welcome to Darrington' sign. What do you think he's going to do when he sees reports that say that not only did he fail to kill but he ran away?"

Vicki arched her neck. "You think Mayor Lewis saying he's dangerous will stop him killing?"

"This guy's progressing. We're looking at a serial killer who likes to watch men die and takes his time doing it. Something in the last week has made him snap even more. We need him to cool off. We need to humanize the victims and stroke his ego."

Vicki flicked her hand. "He wants people to be afraid."

"They should be." Jack's voice was even.

"So you want us to get the victims' families on network TV?" Vicki pounded away on her tablet.

"It doesn't have to be network. Local's fine. He watches Channel 3. But we need them to really humanize the deceased."

Vicki looked up, wide-eyed, and the mayor cleared her throat. "How could you possibly know what television station he watches?"

Replacement spoke up. "Greg Freeman was featured on an ad for Pat's Towing Company. I checked. They only played the ad on Channel 3." She squeezed Jack's leg under the table.

"What about Daniel Branson?" Vicki asked. "The police have been unable to locate any family."

Jack thought for a second, but Replacement said, "Linskie Lumber, the secretary there. She may not have much, but she can say something. Daniel was also a poet. We can get some of his poems and have someone read them."

The mayor's fingers tapped the table, and she looked at Jack with as much emotion as a poker player. "The man's a killer. What if he doesn't care? What then?"

"Then more people die."

"What?" Vicki's hand slammed down on the table again, and this time the mayor's glare was withering.

Jack held up a hand. "He's a killer, and he's going to kill again. It'll be someone else's father. Someone else's son. He'll kill unless we stop him, so until then we need to slow him down."

The mayor looked at the table for a few moments. She closed her eyes, straightened her neck, and then spoke clearly and evenly. "Vicki, arrange an interview with Channel 3 news and the victims' families—including the secretary from Linskie Lumber and any fellow employee of Daniel Branson. Have them use his poems, too. Start preparing a statement from our office. In it, we'll do exactly as Mr. Stratton has recommended." She turned to Jack. "I'll contact you with the statement before it's released."

She's got backbone.

Vicki didn't look up as she typed. "And I'll reach out to my contacts in the media and see what they can do to quiet the coverage on O'Rourke."

"I pray this buys you the time you need, Mr. Stratton," the mayor said.

Me too.

36

THAT'S BIG

Replacement scanned the monitor. "The police reports are a little thin," she mumbled, the pen in her mouth bouncing around.

"I called Bob," Jack said. "The ME's reports on Daniel and Freeman should both be ready tomorrow."

He walked over to the window. They were running out of leads. Replacement had gone through the data from Gary and the animal shelter, and she hadn't found any pattern with big dogs. They had gone over the Davis report from every angle. And there had been no new information on any of the missing persons.

Replacement took the pen out of her mouth. "Do you think the mayor's statement helped?"

"I think it should. It's a good thing Vicki has some connections in the media. And O'Rourke has hired a lawyer now. I have to give it to Castillo. Bob said he tore O'Rourke's story apart."

"Why'd O'Rourke do that?" Replacement asked. "I mean, he stabbed himself in the stomach."

"Castillo found out they had layoffs last month at the company O'Rourke worked for. They were going to have another round of layoffs this week. O'Rourke's manager said O'Rourke's name was on the list. Maybe that was the motive. Or maybe he just wanted his fifteen minutes of fame."

"Why's the real killer doing it?" Replacement put her chin in her hands.

"He gets *something* from the kill. It could be the adrenaline rush, or a sense of power, but he gets off on it. I wonder if the method is part of that."

"What?"

"Why's he using a knife? And why let them live for a little while?"

Replacement shuddered. "I hate thinking about it."

"Me too, but I need to get in his head." Jack began pacing. "Let's just say he killed the three missing men. That would mean he took them. Like he took Daniel. He'd have taken Ray, too, if his wife hadn't come out." Jack stopped in the corner and squatted down next to Lady. She raised her head and rubbed her muzzle against his thigh while he scratched behind her ear.

"Maybe he has something against something bigger than him. Or something that scares him," Replacement said. "Maybe he's a little guy."

Jack clicked his tongue. "No. He's a strong guy."

"Why do you say that?"

"Freeman. He had to weigh two eighty, yet the killer moved his body to that sign and hoisted him into the air. The killer's strong. It's only one guy, too. Ray's wife heard only one door close."

"Okay, maybe he's big then. So he's not just killing giants; he's a giant killer." Replacement rubbed the back of her hand with her thumb and looked over at Jack. "Please be careful."

Jack walked over to her and put his hand on her shoulder. "It's not the size of the dog in the fight, it's the size of the fight in the dog."

Replacement put her hand on his. "Do you think the guy could just stop?"

Jack shook his head. "Serial killers don't stop. Something stops them. They get caught, or they die." Jack put both hands behind his head. "Same thing with serial anything. Child molesters are the same way, too. They don't just quit."

Lady got up and trotted over to nudge Replacement's leg. The whole chair moved. Replacement stroked the dog's back.

"Next to you, Lady looks even bigger," Jack said. He smiled, but it quickly faded. "Can you pull up Ray Davis's Facebook page?"

"Sure." Replacement turned back to the computer. "What do you want to see?"

"A picture of Ray and his wife." He scanned the gallery of pictures until it came up. "That one."

"They're painting a doghouse."

"But it's a huge doghouse. I didn't realize how big before, because they're both so tall."

Replacement peered at it. "You're right. That's big."

"Have you seen any pictures with a dog?" Jack asked.

"No, but hang on, let me look at the other family members' pages."

"You can see their pages?"

"I friended them." Her smile thinned out. "I also donated a little money. Ray didn't have much insurance, and April has the kids, and she takes care of Ray's mother, and—"

Jack kissed her head. "That's fine."

Replacement clicked through photos of family members, and then stopped and pointed. "Bingo! Big dog."

"I'll say. Great Dane, right?"

Replacement nodded. "Yep. That's another connection."

"Can you email Castillo and Morrison? We need to look at the three missing persons and see if they had dogs, too."

Her fingers zipped across the keyboard as she typed the email. "Done." She let out an enormous yawn. "I think I'll run some more comparisons on the databases and see if there's some connection I'm just not seeing."

Jack rolled his neck and looked at the clock: 9:40 p.m. They'd been going over the reports all day, and his stomach grumbled loudly. He walked into the kitchen and opened cabinets.

"Are you hungry?" Replacement asked. "I'll make you something."

"I think I'll take a shower first."

"Go take a shower and I'll make you something." She kissed his cheek.

"Okay. You don't have to ask me three times."

As he walked to the bathroom, Lady trotted after him. She followed him right into the bathroom, plopped down, and happily stretched out on the floor. This had become a familiar routine. Every time Jack took a shower, Lady came in and lay down on the floor. She looked as if she loved it.

"You'd think with all that thick fur you'd hate a sauna," Jack said, shaking his head.

He turned on the hot water and got into the shower.

I need to get with Morrison. The ME reports should be done tomorrow. I can swing over there after...

He planned to see his mother at the asylum tomorrow. It was a long ride, and he didn't really have the time, but Dr. Jamison said she was making improvements, and part of that was due to Jack's visits.

I have to go. She's looking forward to it. But should I take Replacement? She's been off lately. Is it the whole dating thing? Money? Jack hung his head. *We're hunting a serial killer, looking at crime scene photos and reports all day, and I'm not sure why she's a little out of sorts? It's probably just that.*

He wanted to stay in the shower for an hour, but finally he shut off the water. Lady whined.

"You can stay in here, you big baby," Jack laughed as he toweled off.

He threw on some sweats and a T-shirt and returned the living room. Replacement was still hunched over the keyboard.

Jack's stomach growled. "I'm going to throw some pasta on," he said. He saw her suddenly closing the windows she had open one by one. "Angel hair or bowtie?"

Replacement put her head in her hands. Jack walked over to her. She started to get up, but he put his large hands on her shoulders and started to rub. She didn't look up. He saw her reflection in the monitor, and her eyes were closed.

"Talk to me," Jack whispered. "I know something's been bothering you." He leaned closer. "If you tell me what it is, I can help."

He smiled. She didn't.

Her eyes squeezed tighter shut. "I'm not feeling well." She reached up and patted his hand. "I'm going to go to bed."

This is bad.

Jack stood back as she got up. "I'll make you up a plate and—"

"No. No thank you. Will you take the dog out?"

"Yeah. Are you sure I can't get you something?"

She shook her head, walked into her bedroom, and closed the door behind her.

37

NIGHT TERRORS

Jack rolled over and looked at the clock: 5:43 a.m. He'd stared at the ceiling all night and still didn't have any answers about the killer—or about Replacement. He'd spent more time thinking about her than him. He couldn't wait for her to get up, but he also dreaded it. He had no idea what to do for her.

Lady's head shot up, and Jack rolled over to look at her. The dog scrambled to her feet and hurried to the bedroom door. A moment later, he heard Replacement scream.

Flying out of bed, Jack ripped open the door. He instinctively scanned the living room as he dashed through it, with Lady at his heels. Replacement screamed again as he barreled through her bedroom door.

She was sitting bolt upright in bed with a look of sheer terror on her face. Her eyes were wide open and her arms were straight down at her sides. Over and over, she screamed.

Jack rushed to her side, but she kept looking straight ahead and shrieking. He put his arms around her and pulled her close. She cried out.

Night terrors.

He remembered Michelle had gotten them when she was little. They were nightmares she couldn't break out of. That was something Jack knew all too well.

"Alice. I'm right here." Jack held on to her.

She shrieked so loudly that Lady stepped back. Jack pulled her closer. Replacement screamed again, and then gasped for air and closed her eyes. Her hands fumbled for him, and she buried her face in his neck.

"Shh," he whispered as he leaned his head against hers. "I'm right here. You're okay."

She whimpered and started to cry. Her hands tightened around him, and then he felt her go rigid. He had already felt the dampness of her sheets, but she must have just then realized what had happened. He stroked her hair, and she shook.

"It's okay," he whispered. "Shh."

"Let me go. I need the shower. Let me go." She pulled a blanket around herself, and Jack slid out of the way.

Replacement ran, crying, into the bathroom. Jack followed after her but stopped at the closed door. As he looked down at Lady, who stood next to him, he knew he had to do something.

Jack grabbed towels, a blanket, and a set of sheets from the hall closet and returned to her bedroom. He stripped the bed, tossed the bedding in the corner, and dried the mattress with the towels. From the kitchen, he gathered up the laundry detergent, an empty spray bottle, and some vinegar. He sprayed the mattress with vinegar, flipped it over, and put fresh sheets and blankets on.

He ran to his own bedroom and pulled on a shirt and shoes. He snagged a handful of quarters from the change jar, then took the bedding down to the little room on the first floor that served as the building's laundromat. After starting the washers, he hurried back up the stairs.

He was standing in the living room, trying to think of what to do next, when he heard the shower shut off. After a few minutes, Replacement walked out of the bathroom with her head down, wrapped in her robe. She clutched it tightly around her body as she fled past him to her room.

Jack let her go, even though he wanted more than anything to grab her and hold her close—to tell her everything was going to be fine. He didn't know why she was hurting, but he was all too familiar with pain that burned so hot it short-circuited your head. The kind of pain that made you lash out at the people you loved. Pain that woke you up in the middle of the night screaming and made you feel worth less than dirt in the morning. He knew what she was going through, and he was helpless to do anything but watch.

At her bedroom door, she stopped. Her hand went to her mouth, and she shook her head. "No. I can't... I can't sleep in there." Her eyes darted around the room to the still torn-up couch. "No," she sobbed. "Stupid dog. Stupid. I have no place. I have no place to sleep."

"My bed. Take my bed." Jack held his arm out toward his room.

She shook her head, her eyes wide and her mouth twisted.

He turned his hands palm out. "I'll sleep out here."

"Just go back to your room. Please."

"Alice, let me help you."

Replacement's hands went to her stomach and she cried, "Help me? You can't help me. You can't fix me. I'm NOT FIXABLE!" Her mouth contorted as she wept. "Get out. Just get out. *GET OUT!*"

Jack backed up to the front door, and Lady followed him. Replacement's hands wrapped around her stomach, and she bent over. Jack took a step forward, but she held her hand up.

"Leave. Please just *leave*," she sobbed.

Jack opened the door and walked backward out of the apartment with Lady. Replacement rushed forward and slammed the door shut behind him. The gust of air blew Jack's hair back.

His head sagged.

Jack had grown up with crazy. His biological mother would fly off the rails, but it was usually because of booze or drugs. And he remembered how he himself was after Chandler died—that was crazy too. Replacement needed him now more than ever. And she'd just shut him out.

"Mr. Stratton?"

Jack didn't open his eyes at Mrs. Stevens's voice. In all the other fights that had taken place in his apartment, she had always run up and threatened to evict him, but now he heard the concern in her voice.

"I'm sorry about the noise, Mrs. Stevens." Jack finally looked up.

Mrs. Stevens slowly walked up to him. "I'm sure she probably just needs some time." She put her hand on his shoulder. "If you'd like, I'll bring her up some breakfast... after she's cooled down a little."

Jack nodded.

"Would you like to come watch some TV? You and Lady are always welcome."

Jack shook his head and stared at the closed door. "We're good. I think I should ask her if she's okay."

Mrs. Stevens's hand squeezed his shoulder. "Sometimes people need a little time. I know you want to do something now, but it may only make it worse. Why don't you take a little drive? I'll be right here, and I'll come up and check on her."

Jack looked at her. "Thank you."

"She'll be fine, Mr. Stratton. Alice is a good girl."

Jack nodded.

38

YOUR CAR'S MOVING

Jack turned off the highway and flexed his hands. They hurt. *I must have had a death grip on the steering wheel.*

The off ramp led to a commercial section outside the cute little postcard town he'd just passed. Here, the homes with manicured lawns gave way to auto shops and supply companies. He slowed down and turned onto a long, curving driveway. The mental hospital was a large brick building that wasn't visible from the road.

It was just after nine, and a few groups of people walked around outside. They were all in pairs.

Patients have to be escorted outside at all times.

Lady whimpered when he parked and lowered the windows.

Jack rubbed her head. "I won't be long."

A wide sidewalk led to granite steps. Jack walked inside and signed in, and an orderly took him to a padded bench in the corner. He waited there for ten minutes before another orderly came through the doors.

"Good morning, Mr. Stratton." The orderly's huge hand shook Jack's.

"Hi, Peter."

Petya Anatoliy stood six foot four and weighed at least two hundred eighty pounds. As always, he was dressed in hospital scrubs and sneakers, and his receding black hair was buzz cut on the lowest setting. Jack couldn't think of a nicer man to watch out for his mother.

"Patty's very excited about this morning. She's been doing much better," Peter reported.

Dr. Jamison had been working wonders with Jack's mother. He'd dialed her medicines way down, and the results were startling. She had put on weight and improved so much that they'd transferred her to the first floor.

"Steven!"

Jack turned at the sound of her voice. His mother was thin and tall. Crystal-clear blue eyes made her simple blue dress pale in comparison. Even her short gray hair looked healthier.

"Steven." As she rushed to hug him, her eyes still darted around the room, and Jack couldn't help but picture a timid bird.

Steven was Jack's birth name—and the name of his father. Jack had confessed to his mother that he'd changed it to Jack, and she'd said she understood, but she still called him Steven.

"Hi, Mom. How are you?" He held on to her a little longer than usual.

She straightened up, and her eyes narrowed slightly before she broke into a smile. "We get to go outside." She pressed her hands together.

Jack nodded. "Peter's going to escort us."

Patty grinned like a little girl as she slipped her arm under Jack's outstretched elbow.

Peter walked a few feet behind them but lingered farther back once they were outside. Patty inhaled deeply and kept turning her face toward the sun. After a few minutes, she took Jack by the hand and walked him over to a bench under an oak tree. He sat next to her and looked down at their hands.

Patty glanced back at Peter, who stood a ways off. "What's wrong, Steven?"

Jack shook his head slightly. He tried to force a smile. "Nothing."

What am I going to say? I'm trying to find a serial killer? My father's death was hard enough on her. Smile and nod, Jack.

Patty chuckled and gazed up into the tree.

"What?" Jack asked.

"You're lying."

The frank statement hit Jack so oddly he laughed. "I'm not."

"Are." She rolled her eyes. "You suck at it. Tell me."

Jack exhaled and looked down at his feet.

They sat there until she leaned over and asked, "Are you going to tell or not?"

He sighed, reached down, and picked up a handful of gravel. "It's nothing." He tossed a rock.

Patty reached down and picked up some gravel too. She flicked her rock out and raised an eyebrow. "Is it Alice?"

Jack still couldn't believe how well Alice and his mother got along. They had talked for over an hour on his last visit.

"Yeah," Jack confessed.

"You fight?"

"Yeah."

"Your fault?"

Jack shrugged. "I don't know."

"Have you asked her?"

Jack nodded. "She doesn't want to talk about it. Something's really bothering her, but she shut me out."

"Then just sit there." Patty tossed a rock.

Jack chuckled. "What's that going to do?" He let the rocks fall out of his hand and watched them hit the ground. He sighed and put his elbows on his knees.

Patty scooted a little closer to him and looked around. "Let her know you're there." She gazed back up into the tree, and her voice was faint as she said, "Steven did that for me."

Jack swallowed. She never spoke about his father. "Really? How?"

"He brought me flowers. No one ever did that before. I gave them back to him. I told him he might not want to give them to me." She chuckled.

Jack waited. Patty kicked the ground with her foot. She squeezed her eyes tightly shut and her lips moved, but she didn't say anything. He reached out and rubbed her back.

"It was nice that he brought them," Jack said.

"I'm not done." She opened one eye to scowl at him, but when she started to speak again, she closed it. "He came to take me to the movies. I told him I wanted to talk. We went to the park near my house. It was cold, so no one was outside but us. I told him all about me. Everything—good and bad." Now she opened her eyes, and they glistened. She exhaled and put both hands on the back of her head. "I figured he'd take off. But he gave me back the flowers." She looked at Jack like a little kid who'd just finished giving a report to the class.

"Thank you for sharing that with me," Jack said.

His mother laughed. "You don't get it, do you?"

"He gave you the flowers back. But…" Jack shrugged, "other than that, he just sat there."

She nodded, crossed her arms, and then stretched them out. "He was there *for me.* That was special."

Patty leaned back against the bench and turned her face to the sun. Jack closed his eyes.

Have I done that? I know I'll always be there for Replacement, but does she *know it? Does she believe it?*

He opened his eyes when Patty touched his leg. "Steven?" Her voice was higher than normal.

Jack sat bolt upright. Patty wasn't looking at him. Her attention was focused on the parking lot.

His mother's hand was trembling. "Your car's moving."

Jack looked at the Charger. Sure enough, it was rocking back and forth. He exhaled when he realized Lady must be making the car move, but when he started to wonder what the dog was doing, his relief turned to panic.

"No. Not my car!" Jack jumped up and raced to the Charger. When he reached it, he saw that Lady was just innocently pacing back and forth between the back doors. It was only because of the size of the dog that the whole car shook.

"Lady…" Jack looked at the sky and sighed. "I thought you were eating my car."

Lady stuck her snout out the window and whimpered.

"A doggie," Patty cried as she came over to stand next to Jack. She clapped her hands and pulled open the door.

"Wait—" Before Jack could hop between the giant dog and his mother, Lady bashed the door straight into him and jumped out.

Patty squatted down, and Lady happily danced around her and licked her face.

"Mom, that's disgusting." Jack reached for Lady's collar.

"No, it's not," Patty protested. "They're kisses. Huh, baby? Good girl." Her speech turned into baby talk as she rubbed noses with the dog, who was ecstatic at all the attention.

Jack looked up as Peter approached.

"Hi, Peter, I know you can't have animals, but just give my mom a second?"

"It's not a problem," Peter said. "They use lots of animals for therapy. Look how happy the dog makes your mother. I was just making sure everything was okay. That's one huge dog." He grinned and rubbed Lady's back himself before walking away again.

Patty sat on the back seat of the Charger with the door open. She rubbed, petted, and scratched Lady until Peter walked back over and pointed to his wrist.

Patty frowned. "Sorry, Lady, I've got to go." She kissed the top of the dog's head.

Jack put Lady back in the car, and Patty let the dog lick her hand through the window for a minute.

"Bye, Lady. Bye, baby." Patty blew kisses at the dog.

Jack took his mother back inside, and she pulled him close and gave him a huge hug. "Just be there," she whispered.

39

KEEP ME ON SPEED DIAL

Jack flew down the highway with his windows open. Lady was sprawled across the back seat, loving life. She stretched out as much as her large frame allowed and let the wind blow her fur. Jack let his head relax onto the headrest.

His phone barked in his pocket, and he scrambled to answer it. "Hello?"

"Good morning, Mr. Stratton." Mrs. Stevens's voice sounded strained.

Damn. "What's wrong?"

"Nothing. Nothing. I took Alice breakfast, but she's still upset. I'm making a pot pie now, and I'll take it up for lunch."

"I'm coming back now, and I can talk to her."

He heard Mrs. Stevens breathing on the other end, but she didn't say anything for a moment. "Well, the pie won't be ready for a few hours, and if you have some additional errands to run…"

"Does she not want to talk to me?"

"I think she's not ready to talk to anyone right now. Give her a little more time."

"Thanks, Mrs. Stevens. I do have some things to take care of. I'll be home later."

Jack hung up the phone and tossed it on the passenger seat.

Put it out of your head. Give her time. Your to-do list is a mile long. Start on it.

He picked up his phone, and twenty minutes later he'd filled the rest of the day with appointments. First, he'd swing by the house of the girl who lost the phone the killer had used to call the tow company. Then he'd give the mayor an update; Vicki had left a message requesting one. Finally, he'd check in with Morrison about the ME's report, which was supposed to come in later today.

As he laid the phone back on the seat, he felt his hand tighten around the steering wheel. All he could think about was Replacement and how she was hurting.

It's going to be a long ride home.

***

Jack parked in front of a two-story white colonial with an enormous back yard. Lady barked.

"Sorry. You have to stay in the car."

She whined.

"I let you out when we got off the highway. Stop complaining."

Lady rubbed her mouth against the headrest, and Jack saw her canines gleam.

"You so much as *think* about taking a bite out of my car after you ate my couch, and I'll start giving you cat food."

He walked briskly up the brick walkway. As he reached up to knock, the door flew open and three teenage girls stared wide-eyed up at him.

"Dixie Barker?" Jack asked, and they giggled.

Two of them looked to the third girl, who had round glasses, a rounder face, and a huge smile. "I'm Dixie," she squeaked.

"Is your mother home? I have a few—"

"Mom!" Dixie yelled down the hallway.

"There's no need to—Hello." A woman in her early forties came down the hall, adjusting her blouse and fanning out her hair. "Can I help you?"

The girls snickered.

"Mrs. Barker?" Jack asked, and the woman nodded. "I'm here to ask Dixie some questions about the cell phone she lost."

"Oh, the police were already here. What was his name?" She tilted her head.

"Detective Castillo," whispered a short girl with braces. She slid over to stand behind Dixie.

"That's right. Castillo. Did you have more questions?"

Jack nodded. "Dixie"—more giggles—"can you tell me where you think you lost your phone?"

Dixie scrunched up her nose. "I think I lost it at the library, but I'm not sure."

All the girls chimed in at that point, listing possible places she might have lost it. Jack couldn't even get them to narrow down where she lost it. The closest he could figure out was the phone had been missing for four days, and she had gone all over town with it.

Jack held up a hand, and the girls stopped chattering. "I take it you didn't have a password on your phone?"

Dixie shook her head.

"Thank you for your time." Jack walked back to his car quickly, eager to get away from the girls who giggled in the doorway.

You'd figure they'd run out of gas after a bit.

***

Jack hated the morgue worse than the hospital. The black-tiled room felt like a crypt. He stood with Bob Morrison and Ed Castillo across from Mei, the ME's assistant. The ME, Neil Fredrick, was still at the capital running tests on material from the Branson crime scene.

"Neil have an ETA yet?" Morrison asked.

"Soon. He thought they'd have something by now, but the condition of the torso and the amount of material has really slowed it down," Mei said.

"Do you want me to call up there, Bob, and see if I can speed things up?" Castillo asked.

"I've spoken to Neil twice today. He's fully aware of the urgency." Morrison looked at Mei. "Okay, Mei, let's hear your report."

Mei walked them over to an examination table and pulled the sheet off a corpse. It was Greg Freeman, laid out on his stomach so the knife wounds on his back were clearly visible. Mei adjusted her rectangular blue-and-pink glasses and glanced at the clipboard in her hand. "He was stabbed nine times with a six-inch knife."

"Nine." Castillo clicked his tongue and jotted a note. "Wasn't that how many giants that guy killed in the children's story? You know, nine in one blow?"

Morrison shook his head. "Seven. It was *The Little Tailor.*"

"A tailor?" Castillo asked.

"It's a fairy tale. The Brothers Grimm," Morrison said. "My dad read it to me."

"Mine too." Mei looked up, and her brows knit together. "That story was in a book called *A Book of Giants.* I remember the cover."

Castillo scribbled.

Morrison cleared his throat. "It was still 'seven in one blow.'" He rubbed his curly black hair at his temples, right where it was graying, then looked at Mei. "Sorry. Please continue."

"The knife used was similar, if not the same, in both the Davis and Freeman killings. A drop-point hunting knife with a six-inch blade." She pushed up her glasses and turned a few pages. "If you look here on page sixteen, I noted the similarities. They're still comparing the wounds, but the blade scraped along the bones in several places and they used that for positive identification."

"They can't link the knife to Branson?" Castillo asked.

"I didn't say that. They're sure it's a similar knife there too, but they need to do more analysis before they draw any conclusions beyond that."

"It'll match," Jack said. "They were all stabbed multiple times in the back. No other areas?"

"No. None of the men had other injuries—besides superficial or post mortem."

"Who had the post mortem injury?" Morrison asked.

Mei flipped through her report. "Davis had additional bruising on his back, most likely caused by the assailant kneeling on his back during the attack. There were minor facial abrasions from the dirt and gravel." She scanned another page. "Freeman had injuries to his neck from hanging, also determined to be post mortem."

"So, none had any defensive wounds." Jack leaned over Mei's shoulder to look at a close-up of Freeman's hands.

Mei turned to a page with three different diagrams. The drawings detailed the pattern and direction of the knife cuts on the victims. "With Branson and Davis, the killer stood almost directly over and stabbed down into their backs. As you can see on diagram 18C, the first knife wound was from an angle almost directly behind Freeman. That angle changes to an almost forty-five-degree angle for nine wounds."

Mei cleared her throat before she continued, "They're still analyzing the fibers and foreign material on Freeman and Davis but so far there's nothing of note. There's a lot of additional material on Branson. Since Branson's torso was found in a trash bag with a great deal of blood on the inside and a number of spots on the outside, a large amount of hair and fibers clung to the bag."

"Did they get the type of bag or manufacturer?" Castillo asked.

Mei flipped pages again. "Page nineteen details the types and locations of the hairs. The trash bag itself is a regular lawn and leaf trash bag. There was no stamp of brand or manufacturer. The blood on the outside was all from Branson, but you'll see there are three different types of hairs: dog hair and two cats. It was the same inside the bag."

"Do you have the breed of dog?" Jack asked. "Daniel had a shepherd, a king shepherd, and Ray Davis had a Great Dane."

"Not yet."

Castillo flipped the pages of his notebook. "Wait a second. I checked those missing persons like you asked." He started to hum as his fingers darted around the page. "Alan Barnes. They had a Saint Bernard. Fat. Two hundred pounder. It wasn't there when he disappeared, though. His wife took it."

Morrison turned to Jack. "So he could be targeting big men with big dogs?"

"We have to consider it," Jack said.

"Freeman didn't have a dog," Castillo pointed out.

"But the guy killed Freeman to make a point," Jack said. "I think he picked him from the TV commercial."

"I can see that," Castillo said. "That commercial really set the poor guy up. Think about it. The attacker knew where and when he was working. The guy called him to kill him like he was ordering a pizza."

Jack pointed at a bruise on Freeman's lower back. "Do you know what caused that?"

Mei looked at the notes. "Blunt force trauma. Given the shape of the bruise it was caused by a knee."

Castillo stepped back. "Killer is stabbing him and kneels on his back. Makes sense. Can you tell anything about how big or small the guy was from that?"

Mei shook her head. "Maybe with more analysis. I asked that too." She smiled sheepishly. "Neil said it depends on the weight, and also if he just knelt down or dropped. He's checking into that."

"What about height from the angle of the knife wounds?" Castillo asked.

Mei shook her head. "Neil is still working that up too. Because almost all of the wounds occurred when the victim was on the ground, determining height of the assailant has been problematic."

"So we don't know anything about the killer physically." Castillo frowned.

"We know he's a strong guy," Jack said. "He's moving all these huge guys around. He has to be strong."

"What if there were two of them? Like the Hillside stranglers," Castillo offered up.

"I think it's one," Jack said. "Ray Davis's wife heard one car door close. That and the fact there are no defensive wounds. The killer's first strike is in the back and takes them by surprise. He sets them at ease. If two people came up to you on the side of the road—"

"You'd be on your guard," Castillo interrupted.

"So we know we're looking for a strong guy. We have your standard profile, but one thing we're missing is height."

Mei cleared her throat. "I was curious that none of the reports contain information regarding shoe impressions."

Castillo tapped his notepad. "We don't have any. In the Davis crime scene, the guy stayed on the tar. The whole area around the 'Welcome to Darrington' sign was eco-landscaped with gravel. And the one place where you'd figure we'd get a hit on a shoe, the fire road, had too many footprints. It's a jogging path, so people are all over it."

Mei nodded. "Currently, that's all we have."

"Thank you, Mei. Let me know as soon as you hear anything." Morrison looked down at his watch. "Castillo and I need to see the mayor. Keep me on speed dial, Jack."

"Yes, sir."

40

DON'T DO IT

Mrs. Stevens opened her door, and Jack's hope fell when he saw her face. "Mr. Stratton." She tipped her head. "I dropped off lunch, and she did open the door a crack and speak to me."

"How did she seem?"

Mrs. Stevens's mouth pulled back into an awkward grimace. "I don't think it's you she's upset about. I thought you had to be the cause at first, but... Alice has had it hard. It might not seem it, but she has a very open and sensitive heart. I'm sure in time she'll come to terms with whatever is bothering her."

Jack exhaled. *She's smiling with her mouth, but not her eyes.* "Thank you for watching out for her, Mrs. Stevens."

"Do you want me to take Lady tonight?"

"No, thanks. Maybe she'll help."

Jack headed upstairs, but when he reached the apartment door, his hand stayed on the doorknob so long Lady whined. At last he walked in, only to find the living room empty and Replacement's bedroom door closed.

He knocked softly on her door. "Alice? We're back."

As he waited, he could feel his skin go cold.

"I'm not feeling well. Please stay out." Her voice was so soft he strained to hear it.

"Alice? Can we talk?"

Lady trotted over to her bowl and began to drink noisily. Anger flashed inside Jack, and he forced himself to let his head rest against the doorjamb. *Lady doesn't know. She's just being a dog. Please, Alice, let me in.*

"Tomorrow. We'll talk about it tomorrow. Please?" Her voice cracked on the last word.

Jack rubbed his neck. *Don't push it. Give her time. She's not crying. Give her time.*

"Sure. Let me know if you need anything."

***

Jack spent the rest of the night looking over the reports while eyeing Replacement's closed door. Several times he intercepted Lady as she headed over to scratch it. He was tempted to let her, but he kept going back to one thought: *Just be there for her.*

At eleven thirty, he was having a hard time keeping his eyes open. He hadn't really slept the night before, and it was taking its toll on him. He hesitated for the umpteenth time outside Replacement's door before finally going to bed. Lady flopped in the corner and Jack lay there, staring into the darkness.

After about fifteen minutes, he heard Replacement's door open. He froze.

Should I go out there? Is she coming to talk to me?

As he lay there motionless, he strained to hear any noise from the living room. He heard the squeak of the computer chair's wheels and then the faint click of keys. He shut his eyes and focused on the sounds, but soon drifted off to sleep.

At some point Lady whined, and Jack's eyes fluttered. He heard a beep and a click from the bathroom, but before he could even think about it, he'd fallen back asleep.

***

The distinct click of the front door closing—and Lady's subsequent bark—caused him to open his eyes for good. Jack threw the blankets back, jumped out of bed, and raced into the living room.

Empty.

Replacement's bedroom door was open. He dashed over to it. Her bed was unmade, and she was gone. He exhaled when he saw the family picture on her bureau and her jacket on the hook.

She's coming back.

He hurried over to the window and saw brake lights at the end of the road. In the light of the street lamp, he saw her little blue Bug drive away.

Damn.

Jack stood there holding the curtain back and looking at the empty street. Muttering, he flopped into the computer chair.

She keeps getting farther and farther away from me. Shutting me out. If she keeps building this wall, she'll eventually never let me in.

Jack put his elbows on the desk and let his head fall into his hands. He must have moved the mouse, because the monitor flickered on. He looked up, and the screen was covered in windows. One of them showed the photograph Replacement was looking at before she punched him in the nose: a picture of a thin, smiling man in his fifties. Jack read the name—Spencer Griffin.

Jack pulled the other windows forward one at a time. One was a map of the west side of Darrington, just past the Pine Creek Golf Club; a circle with a star highlighted 7 Meadow Drive. Another window showed a street view of a split-level garrison house, with the same address highlighted. Yet another window was filled with text. Jack's throat tightened when he saw the words "STATUTE OF LIMITATION FOR SEXUAL BATTERY OF A CHILD."

His hand shook as he reached for the mouse to bring up the window hidden in back. In it, he could only see the green eyes of a little girl, but he'd know Replacement's emerald-green eyes no matter how old she was. He clicked on the bar, and the page shifted to the front.

It's her file.

The words popped off the page as he stared at the picture of the girl with the tear-stained face: "not pursuing the case against Spencer Griffin due to the chain of evidence and the potential trauma to the victim."

She's looking for him.

Jack's hand froze on the mouse. He suddenly remembered hearing a beep last night. He'd been half-asleep and had forgotten about it by the time he'd woken this morning. *That beep when Alice was in the bathroom.*

He spun around. Through the open doorway to his room, he saw a folded piece of paper on his bureau. He rushed over and opened it.

JACK. YOU'RE RIGHT. HE WON'T STOP HURTING CHILDREN. I'M SORRY. ALICE.

In two strides, he slammed the bathroom door open, and he nearly ripped the bottom cabinet's door off its hinges. His fingers flew across the buttons of the little safe tucked behind the towels. It beeped and opened with a click.

She has my gun.

Jack flew into the hallway, grabbed his keys and phone, and raced for the Charger. The stones dug into his bare feet as he sprinted across the gravel parking lot. The Charger bellowed in protest as Jack kept the gas pedal flat to the floor while he started the engine and slammed it into reverse. Gravel pinged off the underbelly as he shot out of the parking lot backward.

He spun the steering wheel, rammed the transmission into drive, and stomped on the gas. Tires smoked, the Charger's engine roared, and the car flew forward. He drove with one hand and fumbled with the phone with the other. Replacement's voicemail clicked on.

"Alice, don't. Don't do it. Please."

7 Meadow Drive. It's the other side of Pine Creek Golf Club.

Car horns blared as he barreled through the intersections. He raced onto Main Street and the trees flew by him in a blur.

"I'll take care of him. Trust me, Alice. Don't you do it. Don't."

Click.

Jack mentally mapped the fastest way there, but each route would take him the long way around the huge golf course.

I can't go around the golf course. It'll take too much time.

The Charger's tires shrieked as he flew onto Old Oaken Bucket. It was a dead end, and his headlights illuminated the chain-link fence at the end of it only a second before the Charger smashed through it. The passenger side of the windshield spider-webbed as the metal flew over the car.

The small lane for golf carts was just wide enough for the Charger, but Jack only stayed on it for a moment. He'd worked security for a golf tournament there and he knew the ninth fairway led straight back to the clubhouse and Meadow Drive.

He struggled to keep the Charger from skidding; driving on the damp grass was like racing on a frozen lake. Sand traps loomed ahead, and he cut the wheel. Momentum carried the car forward despite his best efforts to turn. He locked up the brakes. He heard them kick in, but they did nothing to slow his speed.

He straightened out the wheels and pinned the gas pedal to the floor. In the darkness, he felt the car's tires leave the ground as he raced up and over the slope. He didn't know the course well enough to even guess where he was about to land. He didn't care. He just needed to get to Alice.

As the nose dipped down, he saw grass and tar. Then the tires hit. The impact didn't set off the airbag, but his chest slammed into the seat belt and pain shot through his side. He screamed even as he fought to turn the car, which was barreling toward a huge oak.

He yanked the wheel to the right. The tree passed by and vanished into the darkness.

Exhaling, Jack slumped into the seat belt. His side burned. The fire from his recently healed muscles and tissue reignited, and he groaned.

The darkened clubhouse loomed ahead. Jack got back on the little path and drove straight at another chain-link fence. More of the windshield cracked, but the Charger rammed through.

One right, then Meadow is the first left.

The only headlight still working was kicked up at an angle, and it illuminated the street sign right before he turned. At the end of the dead-end street, he saw the little blue Bug. He flew up behind it, skidded to a stop, and leapt out.

Replacement was seated in the front seat of the Bug. Jack slowly approached the open window. She didn't look up. Her head was down. His gun was in her hand.

"Alice," he whispered. He reached in and took the gun. "I'm here." He opened the door.

She didn't move. He picked her up and slid her over to the passenger seat. As he got in the car, he looked up at the dark house. "Did you go in?"

Please, no.

She nodded.

Dear God…

"Alice." Jack closed his eyes. When he opened them, he knew what he'd do. "Alice, did you touch anything inside?"

She shook her head.

He shut the car door. "Are you sure?" He started the Bug. "Look, I did it. Do you understand? You need to tell them it was me. I found out what happened to you, and I flew into a rage."

"No." Her voice cracked, and tears fell onto the backs of her hands.

"Alice, you have to. I'm taking you home. I need to go fire my gun so I have trace powder on my hands. They already have my bullets in ballistics. If I confess—"

"No." Replacement turned to him and burst into tears. "I didn't kill him. He's not even there."

Jack pulled her close. She clutched his shirt and wept bitterly. He stroked her hair and leaned his head against hers. She gasped and pulled away.

"Take me home," she whispered.

He turned the car around.

"He wasn't there." Replacement shook. "He hasn't been there for a while. There's one of those stupid mail slots. I didn't think they did that anymore…" She leaned her head against the window and didn't say another word.

Jack drove back to the apartment. He made a list of what he needed to do. He ran around the car and gently lifted Replacement out. Cradling her in his arms, he carried her up the stairs to his bed. After he wrapped her in the blankets, he went to the bathroom, put the gun in the safe, and changed the code.

He heard his bed creak. When he turned around, he saw Lady had jumped up on it and was nuzzling up against Replacement. Replacement's whole body shook as she wept.

Jack went to her. He sat on the edge of the bed and stroked her hair for an hour before she drifted off.

When he was sure she was sound asleep, he got up, careful not to disturb her, slipped out the door, and went to Mrs. Stevens's apartment to ask for a ride so he could go back and get the Charger.

41

SOMETHING WORSE

Jack leaned against the bureau and watched Replacement sleep. Her mouth twitched on occasion, as did her feet. Each time, Lady raised her head, watched her for a few moments, and then put her head back down with a satisfied huff.

Be there for her.

Jack hung his head. He felt helpless.

She's right—I can't fix her. But everyone's fixable. She's strong. She can get through this. Please, God, help her.

He looked up to find Replacement staring at him. He started to move forward, and she held up her hand.

"Please." Jack's voice broke. "Please don't shut me out."

Replacement nodded and closed her eyes. Lady nuzzled her back. Replacement pulled the blanket tightly around her and kept her eyes closed as she spoke. "After my family died, they moved me around a lot. But one time it was a salesman and his wife. I was the only kid. They lived in this huge white house. It was like a castle. I had my own room. Everything was pink and purple. That woman would brush my hair."

Jack couldn't help but cringe when she said *that woman*. He heard the bitterness in her voice. Replacement must have called her something else once, but now *that woman* was all she could say.

"They took me on trips, and after a while, I was really happy. But... one night..." Her eyes squeezed even tighter closed. "He molested me. I just broke. I just died inside." She buried her face in the sheets. It was a minute before she spoke again, and when she did, her voice was very quiet. "It went on for a long time."

Jack pushed himself forward, and she opened her eyes and shook her head. His fingers dug into his palms as he forced himself to stop.

"I was so afraid. I would just lie there, and in the morning he pretended like everything was normal. Then one night... I started screaming. He tried to stop me, but I was just hysterical." She looked at Jack. "The woman ran in. She made him leave the room, and then I told her everything." Her lips trembled, and tears ran down her cheeks. "She called me a liar. She"—her voice cracked—she said I made it all up."

Jack hung his head. It was torture for him to stand here helpless and watch her cry.

"That night I ran away and went to the first cop I could find. That's how I ended up at Aunt Haddie's." Her mouth twisted in pain. "Do you remember the other day when we stopped at the mini-market, and the orange juice broke? I saw him in the parking lot. I always thought he'd go to prison forever. How stupid of me. I know better, but I just thought..."

She shook her head. "He didn't even go to prison at all. They said it was because of me. It would have caused me 'too much trauma.' What the hell does that mean?" She pointed at herself. "How much more trauma could it have caused me? And then when you said child molesters don't stop, they're like serial killers, and they just keep doing it—I knew I had to stop him. But the statute of limitations has run out. So I decided to..." Her shoulders slumped, and she began to sob. "I couldn't tell you."

"Why?" The word escaped Jack's lips.

He strained to understand her words through her sobs. "Because you'd kill him. I know you. And you'd have taken the blame and gone to prison if *I* killed him. You were going to, in the car." She covered her eyes. "Why do you love me?"

Jack could hold himself back no longer. He rushed to her side and swept her up in his arms. She wept. He held her until she could cry no more, and then he held her long past that. When her breathing finally deepened and he was sure she was asleep again, he pulled the blanket back up around her and slipped out of the room.

***

Jack dialed the phone number from the old business card.

"Joy Perez."

Six years had passed, but when he heard her voice, he pictured her standing before the Army intelligence briefing. She sounded the same. Although she had left the Army shortly before him, he had heard she was still using her skills to intercept communications—except now she worked for the Department of Justice in their child pornography division.

"Joy? I don't know if you remember me, but I served with you in Iraq. My name—"

"It's been too long, Jack."

"I wish I was calling under better circumstances, but I need to ask you a favor."

He spent the next half hour detailing Replacement's story and Spencer Griffin. He read the data from the reports Replacement had found. Besides an occasional question, the only sound from Joy's end of the phone was her typing notes.

When he finished, there was a long pause. "I consider any case concerning a child as personal," Joy began, "and after what you did for me, Jack..." He heard her inhale and pictured her trying to regain her composure.

"You're the one who saved our lives, Joy. I really appreciate this."

"I'll let you know whatever I find out." There was another pause. "You said she's Chandler's foster sister?"

"Yes."

"Let me see what I can do."

Jack hung up.

Once she called in an AC-130 gunship and brought down hell on earth. I hope she can do it again.

42

MY MOM TOLD ME

Jack punched the code on the safe, but the handle didn't budge. He entered it again, and it still wouldn't open. His hands went to the sides of his head.

That's right; I changed the code because of Replacement.

He tried every combination he could think of, but the handle refused to turn.

Damn it. I was so freaked out last night I can't remember the stupid password.

He tried one more time, then gave up.

When he walked out of the bathroom, Replacement rolled over in the bed to face him. Her green eyes were red-rimmed, but she wasn't crying. She sat up, put her feet on the floor, and looked down.

"Where do I even start apologizing?" she whispered.

Jack squatted down in front of her. He put his hands on either side of her legs and peered up at her. "Don't. You didn't do anything wrong."

"I didn't tell you."

"You weren't ready." Jack smiled. *And you thought I'd kill him.*

She closed her eyes. "If he had been home…"

"He wasn't." Jack brushed back her hair.

She squeezed his arm. "I would have killed him."

He lifted her chin. "But you didn't."

She lay back down and looked toward the window. Jack stroked her hair. "I can't let him hurt anyone else," she said.

Jack took her hand. "He won't. I'm already working on it. I promise you he won't." He felt her tremble.

"Thank you."

He kissed her forehead. "Please just take it easy today. I've got to run some errands. I'll be back as soon as I can. Can I borrow your car?"

"Sure. Why?"

Jack stood up. "I thought I'd try a little softer approach. How threatening is a guy in a little blue Bug?"

He quietly closed the door, took the keys to the Bug, and hurried down the stairs. On the way out, he stopped by Mrs. Stevens's apartment.

"How's Alice?" she asked. Her red hair bobbed back and forth as she nervously wrung her hands.

"Much better. I really can't thank you enough, Mrs. Stevens."

"Don't be silly. She's an angel, and so are you, Mr. Stratton." She grabbed him, pulled him close, and gave him a huge bear hug. He blushed when she kissed his cheek.

He was halfway down the stairs when she called out, "I'll bring a pot pie later."

Jack's smile vanished when he reached the parking lot and saw the Charger. The windshield was spider-webbed. Deep scratches ran along the sides. And the front end…

At least the bumper took the worst of it. A new windshield, a little body work, and a new paint job should be all she needs.

He patted the Charger's hood, then hopped into the Bug.

As Jack zipped down the street in the little car, he slid lower in the seat. Compared to the Charger, this thing felt like a go-cart. He could picture Replacement sitting here, driving. She had so much energy. She would be bouncing around as she listened to her pop music. The car was a perfect match for her, but he couldn't wait to get the Charger fixed.

***

When Jack arrived at the ME's office, Bob Morrison was pacing back and forth outside, talking on his phone. Morrison saw Jack and waved him over. As Jack approached, he caught bits and pieces of the undersheriff's phone conversation: *golf course, fairway, police cruiser.*

Jack cringed.

Morrison put the phone in his pocket and glared at the sky.

"Everything all right, sir?" Jack asked.

"Murphy." Morrison spat the name.

Murphy had been a constant irritant to Jack when he was on the force, and he wouldn't be sorry to see him get his comeuppance, but Jack wasn't the type of man to let anyone, even an enemy, take the fall for him.

"What do you think Billy did now?" Jack asked.

"Someone tore the hell out of the Pine Creek golf course last night," Morrison said. "They drove right across it. Tore up the fairway and a green, and busted the fence in two places. We just got a call from someone reporting they saw a cruiser out there."

Jack scoffed. "A cruiser? Come on. I mean, Murphy's a moron, but he wouldn't be dumb enough to do that. It must have been another really stupid guy."

Morrison waved his hand and popped two sticks of gum in his mouth. "It was him. The witness was Tom Norris. Retired cop. He was on the job a few years back. His house is on the edge of the course, and he said he clearly saw the car. It was just an outline because it was pitch black, but he said he's positive it was a Charger. That's it. Murphy's done."

Jack cleared his throat. "Sir, you can't discipline Murphy."

"I don't want to hear it, Jack." He hiked up his pants and walked toward the building. "It's admirable you're trying to defend him. I know you and he didn't exactly get along."

"That's true, sir, but you really can't discipline Murphy."

Morrison stopped and glared at Jack. "Listen, Jack. I don't care if he's the county commissioner's son-in-law. He took a police cruiser and tore up a private golf course." Morrison's head swiveled back and forth as he looked at the cars in the parking lot. "Where's your car? Did you drive that blue Bug?" His smile faded, and he started to chew his gum faster.

Jack leaned in. "You got an extra piece of gum?"

Morrison handed Jack a stick of gum and rubbed the back of his head with his other hand. "You drive a Charger. All black." He looked up at the sky. "And this morning you're driving a little blue Bug."

He turned to Jack and inhaled deeply.

Jack's hand shot up, and he quickly said, "My mom always told me not to ask questions I didn't want to hear the answer to. I didn't really understand what that meant, but I do now. I think you should listen to my mom and not ask."

Morrison pointed at Jack with a shaking index finger. "You know... *my* mom told me to stay the hell away from kids like you."

Jack's hands went out and his shoulders went up.

"Don't give me that look, Stratton." Morrison groaned. "Great. I've been around you for a week, and I'm already starting to sound like Sheriff Collins. What happened?"

"Sir, seriously, I don't think you want to know."

Morrison's face became even sterner. "You didn't think I should know about those interviews either. The ones on TV with the victims' families."

"I planned to tell you about that afterward."

"Well you didn't. And afterward doesn't do me a lot of good anyway," Morrison snarled.

"Actually, I hope it does." Jack squared his shoulders. "At least it gives you some deniability. No offense, sir, but Collins is still running the show. You're covering. When he comes back, who the hell knows what decisions he will or won't agree with? Right now you can put me straight under the bus." Jack smiled. "Collins will have no problem running me over a few times."

Morrison chuckled. "You know the rock and a hard place I'm stuck between. I won't ask about the golf course, except... should I not look into it?"

Jack shook his head. "Please don't. I'm sure whoever did it will try to pay for the damages—anonymously."

Ed Castillo's convertible swung into the parking lot. "You boys didn't have to wait for me." He laughed.

Morrison didn't.

Castillo's brows knit together. "What?"

Morrison's phone beeped. "It's the mayor," he muttered as he walked away.

Castillo rolled his eyes as he walked over to Jack. "Bobby sure has a bug in his butt this morning. What did I do? Is it because I said *boy*? I heard he's race *sensitive*."

Jack's hand balled into a fist, and he shifted his weight to his back leg. "Ed—"

"Come on. I didn't mean anything. I was—"

"Ed, I'm only going to say this once. You call him Undersheriff or Sir. You call him anything else and I'll smack the crap out of you." Jack got nose to nose with Castillo. "You're new, so I won't break your nose for that comment about race. You don't have a right to know, but if you want to know the truth, Morrison was the stand-up guy in that situation. He's the one who was right, and it's still costing him, but he had the guts to say something. When you get to know what kind of man he is, I hope you have enough backbone to go back to whoever told you that lie and set them straight. I doubt you will, though."

Morrison walked back to them, his phone in his pocket. Castillo kept his eyes focused on the notebook in his hand, and Morrison looked quizzically at Jack.

"Everything fine at the mayor's office?" Jack asked.

"She wants Castillo and me over there after we're done here. I'm sure you'll be getting a call soon."

The three of them walked into the building, Jack next to Morrison and Castillo behind, and headed down to the ME's office. They expected Neil Fredrick to be there, but Mei held the door open for them instead.

"Neil's still at the state, but he sent me the report."

"Mei, please tell me he's got something that'll help." Morrison followed her into a little office.

"I do have a lot of information, Undersheriff. I hope it'll be helpful."

Crime scene and lab photos were laid out on a long table. Next to each photograph was a typed white card.

Mei handed all three men folders with matching reports. "Most of the new information concerns Daniel Branson. The cause of death was a stab wound that punctured his heart. He was stabbed seven times."

"Seven?" Castillo juggled his books and scribbled in his notebook.

If he brings up the fairy tale again, I'm going to smack him.

"Yes." Mei opened her report. "The blood on the trash bag—both inside and out—belonged to Branson. There were three different hairs found: one dog and two cats."

"Can they tell the kind of dog?" Castillo asked.

"A collie," Mei said.

Castillo frowned. "Not a very big dog."

"There still could be a connection there," Morrison said. "Maybe the killer hates big dogs, but he has a small one himself. You said the other hairs were cat?"

Mei read down the list. "Two polydactyls. The cats suffered from hyperdactyly."

All three men looked back at her with blank expressions.

"The cats would have had extra toes. They're more common on the East Coast. Cats typically have eighteen toes, but these cats may have had more."

"How many more?" Castillo asked.

"There's no way of knowing without the actual cats, I'd imagine." Mei tapped the folder.

Castillo took out his phone. "How do you spell that? Poly-whatever?"

Mei spelled it out.

"Did they say how he was dismembered?" Morrison asked.

"Saw. I listed the details on page twenty-two," Mei said. "The torso was then wiped down with bleach."

"Organized killer," Castillo said as he typed something into his phone. "He's trying to hide the trace evidence." He looked at his phone and read from it. "They're Hemingway cats. The author, Ernest Hemingway, was fond of six-toed cats. *Six toes.*" He looked at Morrison meaningfully.

"You're looking at me like I should be following what you're thinking, Ed." Morrison cracked his gum. "But I'm not. You want to connect the dots?"

"Okay." Castillo put down his folder, stepped back, and held up his hands. "Branson was an author, right?"

Jack tilted his head slightly. "He was a poet."

"That's like an author." Castillo waved his hand as if he were shooing away a bug. "Hemingway was an author who liked six-toed cats. Maybe Branson had an author friend who's like a Hemingway wannabe. I mean, how many of these cats can there be around?"

"They're fairly common," Mei said.

Castillo grimaced. "I'm not saying there's a direct connection," he picked his folder up, "but it's something we should keep in mind."

Morrison sighed and rubbed the bridge of his nose. "When we talk to Mayor Lewis, do not bring that theory up."

"At all?"

"At all."

Mei cleared her throat. "There's something else that's very odd about the torso." All three men turned back to her. "The front of the torso was very flat and rigid—hard to the touch. At first they thought it was caused by the body decaying at a particular spot. After further analysis, it would appear the reason would have to be a quick searing, and then the body was left on a flat surface for some length of time."

"Whoa." Castillo held up his hand. "Back up. Searing?"

"Yes."

"As in *cooking*?" Castillo's voice went up.

"Yes. But the report states the torso was only partially seared. It doesn't appear it was exposed to extensive heat for a considerable time due to the depth of the heat effect."

Morrison shook his head. "Do they think someone started *trying* to cook the body?"

Mei shrugged. "I can only relate what's in the report."

"You're doing great, Mei," Jack said. "Was the body burned?"

"No. There was no exposure to direct flame. There is also no evidence of any accelerant being used."

"Are we dealing with another Dahmer?" Castillo asked. "A cannibal?"

"Slow down, Ed." Morrison popped his gum. "Crap. Why else would you start cooking someone?"

"But why'd he stop?" Jack asked.

"Maybe he cooked the other parts first?" Castillo paced. "Maybe that's why we can't find them. In the fairy tales, that's what the giants did, right? They ate people."

Jack turned back to Mei. "Do they have a time frame for the rest of the data, Mei?"

"Soon?" Her lips pressed together.

Morrison cursed under his breath. "Ed, has anything else come up on the tip line?"

Castillo shook his head. "No. I canvassed Davis's, Branson's, and Freeman's neighborhoods. One thing they all have in common is they don't have any enemies. Everyone I talked to says they were the nicest guys in the world." He turned to the back of his notebook and pointed. He had circled the words "Gentle Giant" and made close to a dozen hash marks next to it. "You talk to ten people who knew them, nine will say that. The tenth guy will still say something nice about them."

"All right, well, we'd better go meet the mayor. Mei, can you reach out to Neil and get me everything he has about that searing?"

"There's specific detail on page thirty-four, but it gets somewhat technical—"

Morrison interrupted. "I'd love to get a non-technical explanation as well."

Mei nodded. "I'll go right now and call him, Undersheriff."

"Thank you, Mei." Morrison turned to the others. "Let's all read over these reports and meet back at the station. Is that doable for you, Jack?"

"That's fine, sir."

Morrison tapped the folder. "This may take a while to digest. Tomorrow morning work? Nine?"

Jack and Castillo nodded.

When they got back out to the parking lot, Morrison headed for his car, but Castillo grabbed Jack by his wrist.

"Can I talk to you?" Castillo let go when he saw the expression on Jack's face. "I just wanted to say I'm sorry. It was wrong what I said about Undersheriff Morrison."

Jack searched his eyes. Ed shifted uncomfortably, but held his gaze.

"Accepted. Give Morrison a chance. He's a good man."

The corner of Castillo's mouth turned up, and Jack scowled. Castillo held up a hand and shook his head as he took a step back. "Dial it back, Jack. It's just, I heard a bunch of different stuff about you when I came here, and when you showed up at the Branson crime scene, I said something about you to Morrison." He chuckled and walked away.

"And?" Jack called after him.

Castillo stopped at his car door. "Morrison told me to give you a chance. He said you're a good man."

43

DO YOU THINK I'M TALL?

Jack entered the apartment with his arms loaded with subs, sodas, and snacks for both Replacement and Lady. They both came to greet him, but Replacement stopped halfway across the living room and looked away.

Jack tossed everything down on the counter, walked over to her, and gently wrapped his arms around her waist. He leaned down and waited. Her arms snaked around his neck, and she kissed him.

Lady's barking and whimpering at the counter interrupted them.

"I'd better intercept her before she eats your steak and cheese," Jack joked.

"Mine, Lady." Replacement dashed over to the bags. She pulled out a cup, took off the cover, and made a face. "Ewww… did you forget to order the roll, or did you intentionally put me on low-carb?" She held the cup at an angle.

Jack grinned and grabbed the cup. "It's their new menu item. It's called cup-o-meat-and-extra-cheese-with-bacon." He kissed her again. "But it's not for you." With a quick flick of his wrist followed by a large plop, the contents of the container fell into the empty dog bowl on the floor.

Lady devoured it.

Replacement giggled and clapped. "That's not very economical, but you're the biggest, kindest man I've ever met." She wrapped her arms around him and gave him a big hug.

"Yeah, I'm a softy." He leaned down and kissed the top of her head.

"A gentle giant." She smiled as she unwrapped his sub and opened his straw.

As Replacement said grace, Jack didn't shut his eyes; instead, he looked down at his hands. "Wait a second," he said when she finished. "You think I'm a giant? Do other people think I'm tall?"

"You *are* tall." Replacement jumped up to touch the top of his head. "Anyone would think that—" She took a step back, and her hands balled into fists. "No. No way. *No.*" She stamped her foot.

Jack took a bite of his sub. "Why not? I just don't know if I'm big enough to get his attention."

"What part of no-flipping-way are you having a hard time understanding?"

Jack looked down at his feet. "You know, I could wear boots with a really big heel."

"No! If you think I'm going to let you walk around with a huge target on your back, you're crazier than me."

"Fine, fine." Jack looked over at the computer. "What have you been working on?"

"I'm going over the ME reports. Mei emailed you an electronic copy."

"Did you find anything of interest?"

Replacement walked over to the computer. "I did find something on the animal shelter database. I started looking at the big dog data again. I didn't find any connection to other people, but I did notice a trend, and I graphed it." She pulled up a line chart.

Jack read the bottom axis. "Length of time? Does that mean big dogs got adopted faster?"

"It means big dogs got put to sleep faster. They're supposed to keep them for thirty days, right? Well, sometimes they only kept them a week before they put them down."

"Maybe that's a decision based on economics," Jack said. He saw Replacement's jaw tighten. "I don't agree with it, of course," he added. "I can call Ryan and ask."

Replacement shook her head. "I'll call Lacie. She'll know."

Replacement picked up her phone, and Jack returned to his sub. As he took a huge bite, toasted crumbs fell onto the paper. Replacement started speaking into the phone, but Jack didn't hear her; suddenly, all his focus was on those blackened pieces of bread.

He placed his finger on one of the hard black chunks, and pushed. The piece was pulverized.

Jack's head snapped up so fast that Replacement stopped talking. He forced himself not to shout the question. "Ask Lacie if she's home."

"Are you home?" Replacement listened and then nodded.

"Ask her if we can come over."

Replacement's eyebrows rose, but she asked, then nodded again.

"Tell her we'll be right there."

"We'll be right over. Bye." Replacement hung up. "What was that all about?"

"I think the killer works at the shelter."

"What? How did you… because of the dogs?"

"That's part of it. But I need to ask Lacie some questions. I need to know who has access and see if they have logs."

"I could just ask her. Do you want me to call her back?"

"No, I want to get a read on her." Jack picked up the keys to the Bug. "I can't do that over the phone."

Replacement sighed. "I know. But I'm not up for going anywhere right now."

She's had a rough couple of days. Let her sit this out.

Jack squatted down in front of her. "I've got this. You don't have to go, okay?"

She tipped her head down. "You're just going to go to Lacie's?"

Jack held up his hand. "Just to Lacie's."

"Would you mind, then? I'm just—"

"Shh." He kissed her forehead. "I'll ask my questions and come right back. Hopefully, the place keeps logs, and I'll need you to go through them for me."

Replacement nodded. "She lives at 124 Granite. Come right back."

44

TRUST ME, I KNOW

Lacie lived in a square brick apartment building that had at least six different units—and Jack didn't know which one was hers. As he reached for his phone to call Replacement, one of the apartment doors opened and Lacie looked out. She gave him a big smile and a wave.

"Hi." Jack walked over. "I'm glad you saw me."

"Alice called. She said she forgot to tell you my apartment number, and she wanted to let me know she wasn't feeling well."

I love that girl. "Thanks for seeing me."

The little apartment was about what Jack expected, given Lacie's eclectic wardrobe. A tacky entertainment center took up one whole wall, but an elegant couch and matching recliner faced it. On one wall hung a classic oil painting; on another was a modern art piece made out of discarded bottles, caps, and wires.

"Please excuse the mess." Lacie pushed a pair of sneakers out of the way of the door.

Jack couldn't help but notice how big the shoes were—they were huge. "Yours?" Jack joked.

Lacie laughed. "No. My boyfriend's. We're like you and Alice. Short and tall."

"How tall is he?"

"Six foot six." Lacie sighed. "That's another reason I want you to catch this guy. I worry about Kenny."

"Kenny's your boyfriend?"

"Four years."

Jack heard muffled yapping and scratching. "You have a dog?"

"Dogs. Do you mind if I let them out?"

Don't make a face. "No. Go right ahead."

Lacie gestured to the couch. "Can I get you a drink?"

"I'm all set. Thanks." Jack sat down on the couch as Lacie walked down a little hallway and opened the door.

Four little dogs burst out and headed right for Jack. A dachshund, a Shih Tzu, a toy collie, and the fattest little pug Jack had ever seen flew across the carpet and jumped on the couch. Jack held up his hands as they wiggled and yapped and tried to lick his face.

"Down. Stop. Down." Lacie picked up one dog, but when she set it down, another bounded right back up.

Jack managed to pin two down with one arm and got hold of the third with his other hand. Lacie picked up the fourth, the little pug, and sat in the recliner. When she did, the other three scrambled over to her.

Jack exhaled.

Lacie laughed. "Sorry. They're a handful."

"They'd be a mouthful to my dog." Lacie's eyes bugged out, and Jack added, "Just kidding. I was wondering if you could answer a couple of questions for me."

"Sure."

"How long have you worked at the shelter?"

"Three months. We just moved to Darrington. Kenny got a job at River's Auto. He's a mechanic. We're from Weber originally."

"You work on the computers and help with the billing?"

"I'm actually the assistant manager. They're not big on titles and neither am I."

"That's great. Then you know who has access to the building."

"Everyone."

"I meant, who has access to the building after hours?" Jack asked.

"Everyone." Lacie smiled. "Most of the people are volunteers, and I think everyone knows the alarm code."

"There's only one code?"

Lacie looked uneasy. "I don't want anyone to get in trouble."

"I'm not a cop."

"There's only one code, and everyone shares it."

"That's crazy. What about a key?"

Lacie gave him an over-exaggerated smile. "It's on a hide-a-key attached to the drainpipe next to the door," she confessed.

Jack rubbed his forehead. "Please tell me the medicine for the animals is locked up."

"It is." Lacie straightened up, and the dogs jumped all over her before settling back into their original positions. "It's all locked up in a cabinet, and only Ryan, Faith, and I have a key. I don't think you've met Faith."

"No. How many people volunteer?"

"In a week? Lots. We encourage people, and donors sometimes do it too."

Jack cracked his neck. "Have you ever changed the alarm code?"

"Not to my knowledge. I'd say no. There's another alarm in the main clinic room. That's where the medicine is."

"Good. It doesn't have the same code, right?"

Her sheepish smile answered the question.

"Is that where the crematorium is?"

She nodded. "It's in the back of the room."

"What can you tell me about that?"

Lacie shrugged. "It's broken. The guy should be out this week to fix it. A valve went or something."

"Can anyone use it?"

She petted the little pug. "I don't know if they know how, but there isn't a cage around it or anything. It sits in the far corner."

"When did it break?"

"A week and a half ago."

"When you get stray dogs in, what's the policy for putting them to sleep?"

Lacie pulled the pug closer. "We have limited resources. We try to stick to the thirty-day rule."

"You *try* to stick to it? So if you get a big dog in and you need the space, you may put it down in a week?"

"Oh, no." Lacie shook her head. "We never put them down earlier. I meant sometimes we go *over* the thirty days."

"Or you take them home yourself?" Jack grinned at the four dogs in her lap.

She smiled. "Yeah. It's hard not to."

"What can you tell me about the guys who work there?" Jack sat forward on the couch.

Lacie's shoulders squished together and she smiled awkwardly. "I try to keep things on an entirely professional basis. I mean, the guys are nice, but," she rolled her eyes, "you're going to think I have a high opinion of myself, but it's the opposite. They're the type of guys if you ask them how their weekend was they'll be asking you out. So I just keep it robot-like."

"Have any of them asked you out?"

"All of them." She blew her hair off her forehead. "Doesn't that make me sound conceited?"

"What can you tell me about Andy?"

"Captain Andy?" Lacie laughed. "Annoying. Sort of lazy. He's good with people. I wrote him up for being late a few times. If you're asking if I think any of them is the Giant Killer, if it wasn't such a freaky thought, I'd laugh and say no way."

"You don't think any of them is capable of that? Have any of them shown any anger toward dogs, or anyone for that matter?"

"Everyone gets mad." She bit her lip. "I'd have to say Stan or Ryan has the worst temper."

"Ryan?"

"Believe it or not. But I've never seen anything physical." She held up a hand. "To clarify, we get some sick animals in, and the owner should have brought them to us way earlier. It makes me furious. Think about it: that poor animal is suffering, and the owner does nothing. That makes Ryan nuts."

"On a scale of one to ten, how mad has Ryan gotten?"

"Twelve. It was over a cat. It was so sad, though, and the guy was a jerk, but Ryan went ballistic."

"You mentioned Stan has a temper too? Toward people?"

"He gets mad at everyone, but mostly the dogs. He trains them. We offer obedience classes. I've never seen him hit a dog, but he can go off."

"What about Carl?"

"Carl?" She made a face and chuckled. "I'm sorry. I try not to treat anyone differently, but now I realize I felt bad because there's no way he could be a killer. I guess I shouldn't be so quick to judge. I don't think it's not him just because he's in a wheelchair, but because he's really nice. Horny but nice."

Jack angled his ear toward her. "What?"

Lacie laughed. "Carl's the worst as far as hitting on me. But I guess he's known for that. I felt bad turning him down until I found out he slept with Faith. He goes for the sympathy sex angle, and it works. Right below the waist is still functional, but he uses it as a come-on line. If you want to talk about angry, Faith was ticked when she found out he used the same line with Tammy. But I think she got over it."

"Have you ever seen Carl angry?"

"No. Frustrated when he can't do something, but never angry."

"What does he do there?"

"Pre-screening exams mostly. He gets the dogs on the table and ready for Ryan. He really wants to train service dogs," Lacie said.

"He mentioned that. I told him Lady could pull a bus."

"Lady? Is that what Alice settled on?" Lacie asked.

Jack nodded. "We found out that's her real name. Can you think of any volunteers I haven't met that we should talk about?"

She sighed. "I honestly don't think anyone there could possibly hurt an animal, let alone a human."

Jack cleared his throat. "Alice went through the database you gave her, and she found that a lot of big dogs were put to sleep in under thirty days. Sometimes in just a week." Jack stated the fact bluntly, hoping it would shake her up.

Lacie blinked rapidly. "That can't be."

"Alice is positive. I need to take a look at—"

The sound of a baby crying came from down the hall, and the dogs went crazy. They ran around the room, yapping and jumping on the furniture.

"I'll be right back." Lacie dashed down the hallway. She came back a minute later with a baby held tightly against her chest.

Jack smiled at the curly hair poking out of a blanket. "Is it yours?"

Lacie shook her head. "My girlfriend's. I'm babysitting."

"Sorry. I'll come back."

"It's no problem." Lacie rocked the baby. "Normally she stays asleep. Doesn't even mind all the barking."

"Would it be possible to get a look at the crematorium tomorrow?"

"Sure. But if you need to get over there tonight, I can give you the code."

"Are you sure?" Jack asked.

She looked down at the large sneakers on the floor and then back up at Jack. "Like I said, I want you to catch the guy. The code's three two one seven. You just put in the number. Don't hit the alarm button after, or the police will come." She laughed. "Trust me, I know."

45

BONDED

"You've reached Alice Campbell. Please leave a message, and I'll get back to you."

Jack waited for the beep. "Hey, Alice. I've got a chance to swing over to the animal shelter and check it out. I won't be long. Love you."

She probably has her music cranked. I'll get an earful for not picking her up.

When Jack pulled into the animal shelter, the parking lot was empty. He parked near the ramp and instinctively checked his gun. *Damn.* He didn't have it. It was still locked in the safe.

He walked up the ramp. It was overcast, and the faint light from above the door did little against the gloom. He leaned over the railing and felt down the drainpipe until his hand settled on the square box.

Seriously? He exhaled as he took out the key. *They should just put out a Please Rob Me sign.*

The door swung open, and he moved quickly to the alarm panel and entered the code, careful not to press the flashing red button. The exit lights cast a red glow, but it was enough for him to see.

He headed through the double doors and down the hallway. Here, the corridor was pitch black. He waited a few moments for his eyes to adjust, but he couldn't see the door at the end. As he moved over to the side wall, he let the double doors shut before he flicked on the light. The fluorescents hummed, glowed, and then flicked on.

He walked down the hallway, through another set of double doors into the main clinic room, and turned off the second alarm. Then he turned on the lights and felt the hairs on the back on his neck rise.

The stainless steel all over the room reflected the lights. Two thin grates ran the length of the floor. Jack knew it was used as a surgical room, but it didn't feel like a place where people helped animals. It felt cold. As he looked at the metallic tables, images of dead men lying on them flashed in his head.

Stay focused. You have a job to do. Move.

Jack forced himself forward. In the back of the room, the metal crematorium door gleamed. An out-of-order sign was taped to the front. Jack walked toward it—and heard something.

He froze. All he could hear now was his heart pounding in his chest, but he was sure he'd heard something else. He wasn't sure what, but it had come from the front of the building.

Jack moved silently to the door leading to the front, and peered through the window. Down the hall, someone had turned on the lights in the waiting room.

He exhaled when Carl wheeled into view. Jack pushed the door open and waved. "Hi, Carl."

"Jack?" Carl tipped his head back and squinted. "What's up? Is Ryan here?"

Jack shook his head. "No. It's just me. I was at Lacie's, and she said it was okay for me to come in. I'm glad you're here. I had a question about the equipment, and Lacie thought it would be easier if I looked myself, but I don't have a clue. What brings you by?"

"I was supposed to meet Ryan. Do you need a hand?" Carl put his keys in his lap, then wheeled down the hallway. The door swung shut behind him.

"Great. I just have a couple of questions."

"Are Alice and your dog with you?"

"They're at home." Jack moved aside as Carl wheeled past him into the room.

"Have you been here long?" Carl asked.

"No. I just got here."

"Whoa." Carl zipped over, reached up, and flipped open the cover to the alarm. "This room has an alarm too. Did you shut it off?"

"Don't worry, I already did." Jack pointed across the room at a long metal table. "I just wanted to see one of the tables that you examine the dogs on."

Carl shrugged. "Sure. What questions did you have?" He wheeled over to the table.

As soon as Carl turned his back, Jack entered the code and pressed the alarm button.

"So," Carl twirled his key ring around his finger, "what do you want to know?"

Jack kept looking at Carl as he walked across the room. "How do you get really big dogs on these tables?" Jack asked. "That's a lot of weight to lift."

"There's a pedal underneath." Carl pointed under the table. "It's kinda hard to see."

Jack tilted his head. "It's a poor design. Lacie had to feel around with her foot to find it. You figure they'd put a button on the side."

"It's a pain in the neck." Carl nodded. "They should—" He twirled his keys, and they fell out of his hand and landed on the floor. "Crud." He leaned over and peered down. "Would you mind giving me a hand?"

Jack didn't move. "You do the pre-screening exams by yourself. How do you reach the foot pump under the table?"

Carl's smile faded. "Don't tell me that's what gave me away?"

Jack shook his head. "No, but that was part of it. And you're trying way too hard to get me to walk close to you, bend down, and put my back in the perfect place for you to stab me." Jack smirked.

Carl's hands gripped the armrests of the wheelchair.

"It's all clicking into place now." Jack shifted his weight to his back leg. "Sorry. That's how it usually works. It's like a puzzle. My dad, he's a math teacher. He does jigsaw puzzles upside down so he can't see the picture. He just goes off the shapes. Now that's hard. Kinda like trying to figure out who the killer is from a town full of people. But once you see the picture? Then the pieces start falling into place. Once you know the killer, you connect the dots right away." Jack snapped his fingers.

"You don't have any dots," Carl snarled.

Just keep talking; the police should be on their way. Because of the medicine they keep here, it's a priority response. "I have so many dots now, I could play bingo, Carl. You have the table. That's a dot. I figured out it was the crematorium when I was eating my sub. You know the little burnt crumbs? That got me thinking. What happened?"

"Like I'm gonna confess," Carl scoffed.

"That'd be great, but if you don't want to, the police have enough evidence."

"I don't know what you're talking about."

"Okay then, let me tell you. Alan Barnes, Eldin Parish, and Henry Clark. You cremated them."

Carl's eyes widened. "I don't know those people."

"Sure you do. Alan had that big Saint Bernard, right? You like killing big guys with big dogs. Of course, Eldin and Henry didn't have dogs, but they were big, and you needed to watch them die. You like watching things die, right? It's why you work here."

"You don't know crap." Carl breathed heavily.

"Am I wrong? I don't think so, and I can prove it. Where was I?" Jack exhaled. In the distance, he heard the faint sound of a siren. *Who the hell is responding to a silent alarm with their siren on? Moron.*

Jack raised his voice. "Your crematorium is meant for small animals, not really big men. You send the big animals to the farm, but you can't really do that with a body. So what do you do? You cut them up. At least that's what happened with Daniel. So you cremated part of him, and then you put his torso in. But talk about bad timing—the crematorium broke. Do you know what happened then? The bottom of the crematorium stays hot for a little while, so it seared the flesh."

Carl sat up straighter in his chair and cocked his head toward the back window.

Jack listened, but he couldn't hear the siren anymore. *Hopefully they shut it off and they're pulling up front now.*

"That's how I figured out the where," Jack continued. "I still didn't have the who. Do you want to know when it clicked that it was you? I remembered that you called my dog 'Lady' the last time I was here. When you were playing with the puppies. I never told you her name. That means you spoke with Daniel, and you heard his dog's name before you killed him."

"You've got no proof."

"I've got a lot more. I've got—"

Carl lunged out of the wheelchair. He was huge when he stood up, and Jack saw the flash of metal in his hand. Jack knew it would be a six-inch, drop-point, razor-sharp hunting knife. He processed all these facts as he leapt out of the way and blocked with his right arm.

Jack's right hand connected with Carl's forearm, and he grabbed Carl's wrist. Jack's left hand slammed into Carl's shoulder. The knife spun out of Carl's hand and clattered across the floor. Speed and leverage would be all that was needed for Jack to drive Carl to the floor. The only thing that could stop Jack was the fact that Carl was a giant man whose arms, shoulders, and back had been turned into steel bands by years in a wheelchair.

Carl screamed in rage as he twisted around and grabbed Jack. He flung Jack against a metal cart, and Jack hit the cart with his feet six inches off the floor. Jack's legs shot up, and his head shot down. He tried softening the fall with his hands, but they did little to lessen the impact with the tiled floor. He slid several feet before coming to a stop.

I guess the story of him being a wrestler was true. Jack scrambled to his feet as Carl ran forward. *His legs are fine. Damn.*

Jack's fist shot out, and Carl's head snapped back. Jack danced sideways as Carl swung at his face. Jack zipped left, and a quick one-two combination drew blood from Carl's nose.

"The police are on the way," Jack said.

"NO!" Carl howled in frustration and swung wildly, but Jack easily moved out of range.

He's big and slow. Stay away from him. Jack kept moving.

Carl lifted the big metal cart and flung it at Jack. As the cart spun toward him, Jack darted to the right. He wasn't fast enough. The cart caught him in the side and sent him crashing into the shelves. One of the shelves broke, and everything on it clattered down around him.

"You're too slow." Carl smiled as he reached for Jack.

Jack did what Carl least expected.

Carl had expected Jack to keep moving away from him. After all, most people would. Jack didn't. He went directly at Carl. He twisted his waist and his right forearm swept out, targeting Carl's midsection. The blow hit Carl in the stomach, but Jack kept twisting.

Carl doubled up. Jack's fist shot down and drove into the back of Carl's head. The blow sent Carl face-first into the tiled floor.

Jack staggered sideways, knocking Carl's wheelchair over. Carl moaned and held his stomach. Jack grabbed a pipe from the shelving unit and pulled it free.

"Stay down, Carl," Jack ordered as he tried to catch his breath. "Don't move." He pointed the pipe at him.

"FREEZE!" The double doors smashed open.

About time. That response time sucked.

Jack started to turn around.

"DROP THE WEAPON. DO NOT MOVE."

Murphy.

Jack dropped the pipe and raised his hands. He winced as he felt something in his side pull.

"INTERLOCK YOUR FINGERS BEHIND YOUR HEAD."

"Murphy, you idiot, it's—" Jack started to say.

Carl pointed at Jack and screamed, *"He's going for his gun!"*

Murphy fired his Taser.

Jack screamed as all his muscles seized up. His side burned, and he felt himself pitching face-first onto the floor. His body twitched and his eyes rolled up in his head.

Murphy rushed over and cuffed him.

Jack tried to speak between his clenched teeth. "Watch out."

"Jack?" Murphy clicked the handcuffs closed. "You're attacking a guy in a wheelchair? Why? For drugs?"

Jack groaned. "Moron."

Carl slammed the pipe into Murphy's head. Murphy crumpled and fell on top of Jack. Carl grabbed Murphy's belt and tossed him toward the shelves.

Jack lay on his stomach with his hands cuffed behind his back. He tried to get to his feet, but Carl kicked him in the face. The blow rolled him onto his back, and everything spun and flashed.

He heard Murphy whimpering. Carl grabbed Murphy's zip ties and fastened his left wrist to the shelves. Murphy cried out and went for his gun. Carl grabbed his other wrist. Murphy screamed as he struggled with the much stronger man. Carl punched him in the side of the head with his free hand. Murphy dropped his gun. It clattered against the metal drainage grate in the floor. They both struggled to grab it, but the gun fell through the grate and disappeared from sight.

Carl smashed Murphy in the mouth. "Stupid cop." He grabbed Murphy's right hand and tied it to the shelf. Then he turned to glare down at Jack. "This is all your fault," he screamed before kicking Jack in his side.

Jack groaned and gasped. "How's that work? You're killing people, and it's my fault you're going to jail?"

"Shut up." Carl held the sides of his head with his hands. Suddenly, he ran out the door.

Jack rolled over onto his stomach and spat the blood out of his mouth. "Murphy? Where are the cuff keys?" He pulled his legs up and crawled toward the shelves.

"My pocket," Murphy mumbled.

"Which pocket?" Jack growled.

Murphy shook his head. "Shirt, I think?"

But just then the doors opened again, and Carl stormed back in. He picked the pipe up off the floor and faced Jack.

"The police are on their way," Jack said. He spat more blood out of his mouth and looked at the window on the side wall. It was closed. No one would hear him scream.

Carl shook his head. "I shut the alarm off, and he," Carl pointed to Murphy, "shut the police lights off."

"I pushed the silent alarm. Dispatch sent him. Just because he's a freaking moron who doesn't follow one procedure doesn't mean the other people who *deserve* to wear a uniform won't. Seriously, Carl. You think the police dispatch won't notice he's gone?"

"Shut up. I need to think."

"Carl, look at me. This can all stop. I know you want it to stop. That's why you haven't killed anyone since Freeman. You feel bad—"

"Feel bad? *Feel bad?* I don't feel bad. There has to be some way out of this."

"There is. Give up."

"Shut up." Carl paced. "Tell me. What other evidence do you have?"

"Do you think you're going to undo this?" Jack scoffed.

"Shut up. How? How did you figure it out?"

Keep him talking. They have to come looking for Murphy. Just keep talking.

"I knew you had some feeling in your legs. The puppy bit you, and you winced. The foot pedal under the table. Carl, there's a boatload of facts, and they all point to you. Even your job here gave you away."

"What? How could you know from my job?" Carl rubbed his forehead.

"It's why you got a job here. You kill big dogs. You like watching them die. Why big dogs? Why big guys? I mean, you're a giant yourself... oh."

"Oh, what?"

"You don't like being big; is that it? You like being the helpless guy in the wheelchair. No one asks you to do anything. You get the occasional sympathy sex—"

"Get out of my head!" Carl kicked the cart across the room.

"Just answer this. This I don't know." Jack rolled up on his knees. "The wheelchair angle. Is that just totally fake? Like an insurance scam? I know you use that whole poor-me-I'm-helpless act to get your victims to drop their guard. That's why they came right over, and you could stab them in the back."

"I did get hurt. I'm not a liar," Carl snarled.

No, you're a serial-killing psycho, Jack wanted to say, but he clamped his mouth shut. "You're not a liar. You told me you got hurt. Wrestling, right?"

"I did get hurt. I hurt my back. But you know what? When I was in PT, and people saw me in this chair, they were nice. They stopped asking me for stuff."

"So you stayed in the chair just to keep up appearances?"

"Yes." Carl swung the pipe through the air. "Do you know how people treat you when you're in a wheelchair? It's great." Carl walked forward, bent over, and picked up the knife. "But I guess it's time to move again."

Murphy started to cry. "Don't kill me. Please don't kill me." His legs pushed against the floor, and he shook his head.

"Wait a second, Carl," Jack said. "I have a couple more questions. Just a few. Why do you like to watch? That's why you flipped Davis over, right? So you could look at him? So you could look in his eyes while he died?"

Carl gazed at Jack. He studied his face. "You were a soldier. Have you ever seen it? Have you ever seen someone's light go out?"

Jack nodded. "Too many times."

"Liar!" Carl smashed a shelf with the pipe. "You never *really* saw it. It's like that green flash at sunset. Special sunsets. If you wait until that second right before the sun disappears, you can see the green spark. It's the same with people. But with their eyes. Right before they go, there's this flash."

"Please don't kill me." Murphy sobbed and pulled at his restraints. "Kill *him*," he cried, angling his head toward Jack.

"You piece of garbage," Jack growled. "I hate your guts, Murphy, but you don't hear me offering *you* up to him."

"Who else knows?" Carl now held the knife in one hand and raised the pipe with the other.

"Everyone. Carl, it's so past trying to hide this. Seriously, you have two choices. Run or give up. You run—they catch you. Give up—they help you."

"They can't help me. I need to see it." He shook his head. "You can see it in the big dogs, but it's not as bright. It's different with people. But if you find a big guy who's *bonded* with a big dog... then the flash is really huge." He turned and smiled at Jack. "How tall are you?"

Damn. "I'm, like, five four. I wear heels."

Carl grinned. "You're almost six two, and you've bonded with Lady."

"Bonded with the beast?" Jack laughed. "Me and her? Are you kidding me? You *are* crazy. That dog hates me."

"No she doesn't. She loves you. You're connected now. Now you're special."

Do I roll or try to hop onto my feet? I can still kick, but if he swings the pipe, I'm done.

"I don't have that flash." Jack tried to move back so his toes would grip the tile and he'd have something to push off from. "I'm not special. I have a black heart. It would be like a black flash. Nothing."

"You'll have the flash."

In the window behind Carl, two of the prettiest eyes Jack had ever seen appeared. Large, deep honey-brown eyes blinked at him as Lady stood up on her hind legs and peered into the window. *Lady.*

Jack smiled. Then he inhaled deeply and screamed, *"Lady, sic him!"*

Carl looked back at the window, but it was now empty. Jack waited a second, but nothing happened.

Carl turned back to Jack and laughed. "What do you think I am? Stup—"

Glass and wood sprayed across the room as Lady burst through the window. As soon as her paws touched down, she sprang forward at Carl and her jaw clamped down on his uplifted arm. He shrieked and dropped the knife.

The dog's momentum carried both her and Carl into Jack, knocking him off his knees. But Carl remained standing, and somehow he yanked Lady up into his arms and heaved her hard into the wall. She crashed against the cement and collapsed into a heap.

Screaming, Jack rolled to his feet. Carl grabbed him by the shirt and flung him into the cabinets. Glass broke all around him.

Jack ignored the pain and surged forward—but Carl was already swinging the pipe. He struck low, and the pipe caught Jack in the thigh. Pain shot up Jack's leg, and he dropped to one knee. Carl swung the pipe again. Jack tried to duck and turn with the blow, but the metal glanced off his shoulder and smashed into his head.

Spinning, Jack crashed to the ground. Carl groaned and grabbed the wall for support.

Blood ran down Jack's face from a cut over his left eye. He inched over toward Lady. She lifted her head and tried to stand, but fell back onto the tile, whimpering. Her jaws snapped at the air.

Jack pulled himself onto his left knee and growled at Carl. Everything was blurry, but if he concentrated he could bring the room into focus—and what he saw didn't look good.

Carl had pulled a cleaver from one of the cabinets. And he wasn't smiling now. Now he just looked completely insane.

As Carl came forward, Jack and Lady shifted to face him. Side by side they lay on the floor, their backs pressed against each other. Lady growled, and Jack drove the toe of his left shoe against the wall to prepare for one last lunge.

Carl lifted the cleaver high over his head. His eyes went wide. Saliva ran down his chin and his lips twisted into a crazed grin. The cleaver trembled as he drew himself up to his full height. He towered above Jack and Lady.

Then he shrieked. His whole body convulsed, the cleaver fell from his hands, and he tumbled backward and writhed on the ground.

Replacement stood outside the window with her little pink Taser shaking in her hands. Lady barked.

"What is wrong with you?" Replacement screamed at Jack as she struggled to pull herself through the window. "You go after a serial killer and don't bring me?" She tumbled through the window and landed awkwardly on her feet. "Lady!" She rushed over and hugged the big dog.

Hugs for the dog. Scolding for me. I guess that's fair.

"She's okay," Jack panted. "Call the police. Call the police."

Replacement ran into the hallway and pulled the fire alarm. Lights blared and sirens wailed. Lady howled.

"I heard the call about the alarm on the scanner and came right away."

"Get the handcuff keys before he comes around. They're in Murphy's pocket. Shirt, he thinks."

Just then Carl groaned, and Replacement jumped sideways as Carl rolled onto his knees and forearms.

"Move back!" Jack ordered.

She grabbed a metal tray and slammed it down on the back of Carl's head. He crumpled to the floor and didn't move.

"He hurt my Lady," she growled. "And you," she added. She stormed over to Murphy.

"Don't go too close to his pants pocket, if you know what I mean. It may not be... sanitary." Jack managed to sit up.

Replacement reached into his shirt pocket, gagged, pulled out the keys, and hurried back over to Jack. "Don't get too close to his back pocket either," she whispered.

Jack chuckled and groaned.

Replacement undid the handcuffs and knelt beside Lady. Sirens wailed in the distance. Jack tried to stand, but his right leg wouldn't bear his weight.

Lady whined. Replacement gently talked to her and rubbed her back.

Jack looked at Replacement's foot. One sneaker was missing. "What happened to you?"

Replacement scowled. "I got stuck on the stupid fence."

"POLICE!" It was Kendra Darcey's voice, coming from the front entrance.

"Kendra! Back here!" Jack bellowed.

Kendra burst through the door, and her shotgun swept the room.

"Guy on the ground near the window. Cuff him." Jack's head started to spin again, and he leaned back on his elbow. "Someone needs to cut Murphy free and hose him off."

"Are you okay, Jack?" Kendra asked.

Jack tried to flash a smile, but his cut lip wasn't cooperating. "Don't worry about me. I'm fine. But I need someone to look at my dog."

46

I WANT THEM UNBRIBED

Vicki held the door open for Jack and Replacement as they walked into the mayor's empty office, then she disappeared back into the hall. Jack set his crutches against the table and settled into a high-backed chair. Replacement reached over and squeezed his hand. They waited.

When the door opened again, it was Vicki returning with Mayor Lewis. The mayor shook both their hands.

"You look like hell, Jack."

"Thanks. Where are Morrison and Castillo?"

The mayor and Vicki took seats at the table, and the mayor folded her hands. "Sheriff Collins returned this morning," she replied, "and I think they're trying to sedate him. I thought a separate meeting would be more productive."

Jack chuckled.

"I want to thank you both," the mayor said. Vicki slid an envelope across the table to Replacement. "Payment in full," the mayor explained. "I understand you incurred some additional expenses in apprehending the killer?"

Jack and Replacement exchanged a quick look.

"I was made aware during your investigation you had a brief pursuit of a suspect, and there was some minor damage to the Pine Creek Golf Club."

Did Morrison tell her?

Jack exhaled. "I can explain…"

The mayor's lips pressed together in a tight smile. "That won't be necessary. I've agreed to cover the cost of the repairs. Your vehicle is your own responsibility. In the future, if we're in need of your services again, I trust you'll keep these sorts of incidents to a minimum."

"I will. Thank you." Jack nodded, and winced. "Can I ask another favor?"

The mayor leaned back. "You haven't asked for any favors so far. Trust me. I keep score."

"Undersheriff Morrison. He's a good man, and he did a real good job on this case. So did Castillo. It would go a long way if Sheriff Collins knew that was how you felt as well."

The mayor nodded. "Of course."

Everyone shook hands, but the mayor pulled Replacement aside as they headed for the door. She leaned close and whispered something. Replacement's face lit up.

As they walked out to the car, Jack asked, "What did the mayor whisper back there?"

Replacement grinned. "She said she looks forward to working with us again."

***

Replacement went to bed early, but Jack stayed up and pored over the reports on Spencer Griffin. He had passed the point of frustration a long time ago. The stacks of paper and scribbled notes around him seemed to lead nowhere. He fought back that thought and pushed on.

Everyone makes mistakes. Griffin has to have screwed up somewhere. I just have to find it.

His phone barked, and Lady raised her head and barked too. Jack answered quickly while silently cursing his ringtone.

"It's Jack."

There was a moment of dead silence. "I'm sorry, Jack," Joy said.

Jack exhaled. There was a finality about how she said the words. He knew her news would be bad.

"At first everything was looking good. I found out Griffin was already on our radar and under investigation. We had a proxy company flip six months ago. They were facing gambling charges, but when we hit them with a boatload of other charges relating to child pornography, they rolled. We're still processing the IPs and matching up the records, but he's on them. We had enough to go after a warrant—which was great, because he was investigated twice before, and they never got enough to make anything stick."

She sighed. "Unfortunately, someone screwed up and put a hold on his passport. That's standard procedure, but only *after* you've established his exact whereabouts. In this case, he was in Thailand when we pulled his passport, and it tipped him off. Now he'd be crazy to come back here on his own."

Jack forced himself to not crush the phone. "Are you sure he's in Thailand?"

There was another pause. "Between you and me? One hundred percent."

She broke some rules to find that out.

"Where?"

"Pattaya."

"Can we extradite?"

"No. Not unless someone in the Thai government hands him over." She sighed. "If someone had enough means, they could get officials over there to look the other way. But Griffin has enough funds to retire over there. I tried to get his accounts frozen, but he had already cleared them all out."

"Damn it."

"I think that's what he was planning all along, he just moved up the schedule. He sold a couple of properties last year. He was renting that house in Darrington. I'm so sorry."

"No. I appreciate what you did." Jack struggled for the right words. He kept thinking about Replacement.

"Jack, it's a region in flux. Things change over there. In time… I'll do what I can, and it's possible we can get him back."

"Possible, but not probable. I understand. Thank you, Joy." Jack hung up.

He'll go right on hurting kids. They don't stop.

Jack walked over to the window and looked out in the darkness. *There are monsters out there. One we stopped. One's still out there. Knowing where he is doesn't mean a thing. How am I going to get him back? Who am I kidding? If he bribes someone over there, there's no way.*

Jack went to his bedroom, dug into the back of his sock drawer, pulled out the burner phone, and dialed the one number saved in it. He waited for several rings and was about to hang up when a tired woman's voice answered.

"Officer. I was just thinking about you." Her voice was smooth.

"How've you been, Kiku?"

There was a pause. He didn't know what answer to expect. Kiku was Japanese mafia, and it hadn't been that long ago that the Yakuza had sent her to watch Jack and, if need be, kill him.

"I find speaking of myself to be quite uninteresting. I was dreaming of you. I frequently do, so your call to me was not unexpected."

"I need your help," Jack said. "Where are you?"

"The world is a very small place, Officer. I am only moments from anywhere."

"Do you have any contacts in Thailand? You or… your organization."

"Let's keep this between friends and leave it as a matter between you and me. What is it you are looking for?"

"Thailand doesn't have an extradition agreement with the States. I need someone brought back here."

"Why?"

Jack's jaw clenched. "They broke the law. They're wanted. I'm told if you have enough money, you can bribe someone to let you stay in Thailand."

"That is true."

"Well, I want them unbribed. Do you have any contacts?" Jack asked.

"What was the crime?"

Jack exhaled.

Kiku laughed. It wasn't derisive, and he pictured her canines flashing as she tossed back her head. "Trust, Officer. After all we have been through, I would think you would trust me. Especially since it is you requesting this favor."

"I do trust you." Jack walked over to the window. "He hurt Alice."

Even over the phone, he heard her teeth grind. "Is she all right?"

"Yes. Well, no. It happened years ago, but she expected him to go to prison. He didn't."

"The number of people I consider friends, I can count on one hand. You and Alice are a majority of that number. What specifics can you provide?"

Jack went back to computer, reopened the files Replacement had created on Griffin, and sent Kiku everything: pictures, links, all of it.

"Kiku, don't take this the wrong way." Jack cracked his neck. "I want him to come back to the United States."

"I understand, Officer."

"Seriously, Kiku. Extradited. Let me know what all this will cost, and I'll cover it." *How, I have no idea.*

"Always the white knight." Her voice was smooth. "As I said, you are my dear friend, Officer. I would never think of taking money to help you in any way. But I do promise I will return Spencer Griffin to the United States."

"Thank you."

Jack hung up the phone and stared into the blackness.

If anyone can take down a monster, it's Kiku.

47

IF SHE'S LADY...

The following evening, Jack limped into the living room and stopped in his tracks. The lights were all off except for two candles that flickered on a little table in the middle of the living room. Replacement was in the kitchen serving up pasta, and when she looked up at him, she looked so nervous he expected her to bolt. He hurried over to her and, despite her protests, wrapped his arms around her waist and kissed her.

After a minute she stopped struggling, and he felt her relax. After another minute, she moaned softly and really started to kiss him back. He pulled away, and she exhaled.

"Now," he whispered, "we're not going to even think about going further tonight. Agreed?"

She sighed. "Are you sure?"

"Completely." He grinned.

"Thank you."

"That's why you love me." He smiled and limped over to the table.

Replacement looked into the bedroom and frowned. "Is Lady still at Mrs. Stevens's? Do you mind if I go get her?"

"Um…" Jack smiled awkwardly. "She's not there."

Replacement turned back to the pasta. "Where is she?"

Jack exhaled. "I had Mrs. Stevens take her over to the shelter and—"

A sob burst from Replacement's throat, and she covered her mouth. She spun around, tears forming in her eyes.

"No, no, no." Jack got back up.

Replacement waved her hands. "I'm sorry. I understand. The apartment's too small. I just—"

"No. I didn't—" A knock on the door cut him off. "Trust me. Please," Jack pleaded as he hobbled over and opened the door.

Lady burst in and ran straight to Replacement. She was freshly washed and brushed, and had a huge pink bow on her new collar.

Replacement sobbed even louder now, and she wrapped her arms around the dog's neck.

"They said she's fit as a fiddle," Mrs. Stevens announced as she stepped into the apartment. "Oh, you're getting ready for a romantic evening." She blushed and grinned as she looked at the candles. "Would you like me to take Lady for the night? It's no trouble."

"No, she can stay." Replacement wiped her eyes and stood up.

"Thank you for taking her." Jack hugged Mrs. Stevens, and she turned even redder.

"Well, you two kids have fun tonight." She smiled as she stepped outside. "But not too much fun." She wagged a finger at Jack.

As Jack shut the door behind her, Replacement ran over, grabbed him, and kissed him again. "Thank you. Thank you."

"I didn't do anything."

"You're the best man. Now sit."

"Do you need a hand?" He headed for the table.

"Nope. I made angel hair. It's all ready." She picked up two plates heaped with spaghetti and meatballs and walked over to the table. She set Jack's down, but as she sat down with her own plate, it slipped from her hand and landed face down on the floor. "Oh, no!"

Replacement stared at the mess on the floor. Her lip trembled.

But Jack just smiled. "Come on, Lady," he said cheerfully. "Alice made you a special supper too, and you're joining us." He slid his chair over right next to Replacement's and picked the plate up off the pile of spaghetti. Lady eagerly chomped away.

Replacement put her hands on the back of her own neck. Jack reached out and pulled the remaining plate of spaghetti over in front of them, then put an arm around Replacement and pulled her close. "This idea was very romantic. Side by side, sharing a plate of spaghetti? And a plate for Lady, too. What could be better?" He kissed her cheek. She blushed and then grinned.

Replacement bowed her head, and Jack did too. After a minute, Jack opened one eye. Tears rolled down Replacement's cheeks, but she had a huge smile on her lips.

"Amen," she whispered.

"What was that?" Jack laughed. "Silent grace?"

"It was between God and me." She kissed his cheek again.

"You're not going to tell me?"

"Nope." She grinned and ate a big forkful of pasta.

They ate in silence. Replacement kept one hand entwined with Jack's. After a few minutes, Lady raised her head. Flecks of pasta and sauce clung to her muzzle.

"That's not very ladylike, Lady." Replacement laughed, then wiped the dog's mouth with a napkin.

Lady whimpered.

Jack looked down at the last big meatball on their plate. Lady's honey-brown eyes rounded as she looked up at Jack.

"Are you all set with meatballs?" Jack asked Replacement.

"I'm fine."

Jack picked up the plate and pushed the meatball off it onto the floor. It plopped down just under Lady's nose.

Lady raised her head and looked at Jack.

"Go ahead," Jack said.

Lady gobbled the meatball while Replacement clapped. Jack smiled, leaned over, and kissed Replacement's cheek.

He sat back, and Lady put her paws in his lap and licked the side of his face. "Gross."

Replacement laughed. "Hey," she cried, "this is just like that movie. The one with the dogs. Wait a minute! If she's Lady..."

"Don't say it." Jack's eyes narrowed.

"You're Tramp!"

48

I NEVER PROMISED

Kiku Inuzuka was early; she wanted to park in front of the large, garish hotel before he got there. Several other cabs made their way through the traffic, but she wasn't concerned he would take another. She'd arranged everything previously.

She was very familiar with the city of Pattaya. Thailand was a beautiful country, but this part of the city was a cancer. Pattaya was world-renowned for its sex trade. In the darkening shadows of nightfall, the street came to life with people who had traveled here from around the globe, seeking to fulfill their perversions. Like bugs attracted to the flickering lights, they appeared from the shadows and then disappeared into the hotels and brothels that lined both sides of the road.

An older Thai man jogged up to the cab as she pulled up to the curb. His mouth fell open when Kiku opened the door and slid out. Her black hair was pulled back in a bun. The flowery dress she had selected to blend in now clung to her hips and accentuated her breasts due to the humidity. She wanted to downplay her body and assume the role of a simple taxicab driver, but the weather had made that impossible. Another look at the man who stood before her, nearly drooling, confirmed that.

She handed him the commensurate bribe, plus a bonus. When he looked up questioningly, she answered in Thai, "The extra is for you to go. Now."

The snarl that started to form on his face vanished as soon as his eyes met hers. He turned and hurried back to his chair and an electric fan near the base of the stairs.

Kiku leaned back against the cab and waited. Many of the men moving down the sidewalk started to move closer to her as they approached, ogling her up and down, but when they drew near, they all changed trajectory and kept their distance.

Kiku frowned and glanced back at her reflection in the cab windows. With her high cheekbones and creamy white skin, she could be a model. She wondered why the men all moved away, but she found the answer in her own eyes. Her reflection glared back at her with a coldness that scared even her. She could almost hear Jack make some sarcastic wisecrack about her terrifying everyone.

She didn't want to frighten the man she was waiting for—at least, not immediately—so she forced a smile on her face. Her canines flashed, long, white, and pointy. The dark reflection now added a cold indifference to her wolfish appearance, and the result was truly terrifying.

She pressed her lips together and put on the mask of a naïve, unintelligent Asian girl with wide eyes.

Bow and say thank you a lot. Act submissive and stupid, and this fool will go along, Kiku instructed herself before glaring murderously at her reflection.

Spencer Griffin appeared at the top of the stairs and started down. The thin man's smugness made her fingers twitch. She switched to the demure smile and let her eyes flit to the ground and then back to him.

A smile spread across his face as he came over. She opened the back door. He got into the cab. She closed his door and then slid behind the wheel.

"White Blossom," Griffin said.

Kiku nodded twice. "Very good. Very good."

She let her eyes flit once to the rearview mirror before she pulled out into traffic. They weaved back and forth down the busy street. Griffin constantly fidgeted in his seat and looked around. Kiku fought back the bile that rose in her throat. He looked like someone eagerly awaiting a surprise present, barely able to contain the anticipation. She tried to drive from her mind the images of the terrified child Griffin hoped to prey on.

"Traffic bad," Kiku said haltingly and pointed ahead. "Go round?" She pulled herself up in her seat and pretended to look over the cars in front of them.

"Fine." Griffin exhaled. "Just get me there."

"Very good. Very good." Kiku nodded three times before she took the next right.

The cab weaved its way through side streets barely wide enough for two cars. Darkness hung over this section of the city, and Griffin's expectant grin quickly faded. After a few more turns, he sat forward on his seat.

"I don't care about the traffic. Just get us back to the main road," he groused, but she heard the fear in his voice.

Kiku didn't answer. She saw her destination ahead. The old man she had paid off waited beside the open garage door.

"Did you hear me?" Griffin grabbed the headrest and pulled himself forward. "Go back to the main road, you stupid bi—"

The ridge of Kiku's hand slammed into Griffin's windpipe. His eyes bugged out and his mouth dropped open. He fell back in the seat, clutching his throat and gagging.

Kiku nodded at the old man as she drove into the garage, and he pulled the door closed after her. Tossing the cab into park, she got out, opened the back door, and dragged Griffin out by his hair.

He feebly swung at her, and in one motion she snapped his arm. He shrieked. She smashed him to the ground and frisked him.

"I have money. I give you money," Griffin begged as Kiku dragged him over to a chair.

"Do not speak." Kiku grabbed zip ties and fastened him to the chair.

"I'll pay you—"

Kiku's elbow broke his jaw.

She finished tying him up. Her heels clicked on the cement as she walked back to the cab, reached through the passenger window, and pulled out a folder. Griffin started to cry when she stopped in front of him. Kiku held up a photograph of a little girl with green eyes and flecks of gold.

Griffin shook uncontrollably.

Kiku crouched down and stared directly into his eyes. "I promised a dear friend I would send you back to the United States."

Griffin's eyes darted around the room and then back to her. Her words seemed to sink in, and he sobbed. He tilted his head back and sighed. Then, despite his jaw, he nodded his head and let out a little chuckle.

Kiku put the photo away and stood. She looked down at Griffin and pulled out a pistol. "I never promised you would be breathing."

THE END

THE DETECTIVE JACK STRATTON
MYSTERY-THRILLER SERIES

The Detective Jack Stratton Mystery-Thriller Series, authored by *Wall Street Journal* bestselling writer Christopher Greyson, has over 5,000 five-star reviews and over one million readers and counting. If you'd love to read another page-turning thriller with mystery, humor, and a dash of romance, pick up the next book in the highly acclaimed series today.

AND THEN SHE WAS GONE

A hometown hero with a heart of gold, Jack Stratton was raised in a whorehouse by his prostitute mother. Jack seemed destined to become another statistic, but now his life has taken a turn for the better. Determined to escape his past, he's headed for a career in law enforcement. When his foster mother asks him to look into a girl's disappearance, Jack quickly gets drawn into a baffling mystery. As Jack digs deeper, everyone becomes a suspect—including himself. Caught between the criminals and the cops, can Jack discover the truth in time to save the girl? Or will he become the next victim?

GIRL JACKED

Guilt has driven a wedge between Jack and the family he loves. When Jack, now a police officer, hears the news that his foster sister Michelle is missing, it cuts straight to his core. The police think she just took off, but Jack knows Michelle would never leave her loved ones behind—like he did. Forced to confront the demons from his past, Jack must take action, find Michelle, and bring her home... or die trying.

JACK KNIFED

Constant nightmares have forced Jack to seek answers about his rough childhood and the dark secrets hidden there. The mystery surrounding Jack's birth father leads Jack to investigate the twenty-seven-year-old murder case in Hope Falls.

JACKS ARE WILD

When Jack's sexy old flame disappears, no one thinks it's suspicious except Jack and one unbalanced witness. Jack feels in his gut that something is wrong. He knows that Marisa has a past, and if it ever caught up with her—it would be deadly. The trail leads him into all sorts of trouble—landing him smack in the middle of an all-out mob war between the Italian Mafia and the Japanese Yakuza.

JACK AND THE GIANT KILLER

Rogue hero Jack Stratton is back in another action-packed, thrilling adventure. While recovering from a gunshot wound, Jack gets a seemingly harmless private investigation job—locate the owner of a lost dog—Jack begrudgingly assists. Little does he know it will place him directly in the crosshairs of a merciless serial killer.

DATA JACK

In this digital age of hackers, spyware, and cyber terrorism—data is more valuable than gold. Thieves plan to steal the keys to the digital kingdom and with this much money at stake, they'll kill for it. Can Jack and Alice (aka Replacement) stop the pack of ruthless criminals before they can *Data Jack?*

JACK OF HEARTS

When his mother and the members of her neighborhood book club ask him to catch the "Orange Blossom Cove Bandit," a small-time thief who's stealing garden gnomes and peace of mind from their quiet retirement community, how can Jack refuse? The peculiar mystery proves to be more than it appears, and things take a deadly turn. Now, Jack finds it's up to him to stop a crazed killer, save his parents, and win the hand of the girl he loves—but if he survives, will it be Jack who ends up with a broken heart?

JACK FROST

Jack has a new assignment: to investigate the suspicious death of a soundman on the hit TV show *Planet Survival.* Jack goes undercover as a security agent where the show is filming on nearby Mount Minuit. Soon trapped on the treacherous peak by a blizzard, a mysterious killer continues to stalk the cast and crew of *Planet Survival.* What started out as a game is now a deadly competition for survival. As the temperature drops and the body count rises, what will get them first? The mountain or the killer?

Hear your favorite characters come to life
in audio versions of the
Detective Jack Stratton Mystery-Thriller Series!
Audio Books now available on Audible!

Novels featuring Jack Stratton in order:
AND THEN SHE WAS GONE
GIRL JACKED
JACK KNIFED
JACKS ARE WILD
JACK AND THE GIANT KILLER
DATA JACK
JACK OF HEARTS
JACK FROST

Psychological Thriller
THE GIRL WHO LIVED

Ten years ago, four people were brutally murdered. One girl lived. As the anniversary of the murders approaches, Faith Winters is released from the psychiatric hospital and yanked back to the last spot on earth she wants to be—her hometown where the slayings took place. Wracked by the lingering echoes of survivor's guilt, Faith spirals into a black hole of alcoholism and wanton self-destruction. Finding no solace at the bottom of a bottle, Faith decides to track down her sister's killer—and then discovers that she's the one being hunted.

Epic Fantasy
PURE OF HEART

Orphaned and alone, rogue-teen Dean Walker has learned how to take care of himself on the rough city streets. Unjustly wanted by the police, he takes refuge within the shadows of the city. When Dean stumbles upon an old man being mugged, he tries to help—only to discover that the victim is anything but helpless and far more than he appears. Together with three friends, he sets out on an epic quest where only the pure of heart will prevail.

ACKNOWLEDGMENTS

I would like to thank all the wonderful readers out there. It is you who make the literary world what it is today—a place of dreams filled with tales of adventure! To all of you who have taken Jack and Replacement under your wings and spread the word via social media and who have taken the time to go back and write a great review, I say THANK YOU! Your efforts keep the characters alive and give me the encouragement and time to keep writing. I can't thank YOU enough.

Word of mouth is crucial for any author to succeed. If you enjoyed the series, please consider leaving a review at Amazon, even if it is only a line or two; it would make all the difference and I would appreciate it very much.

I would also like to thank my wife. She's the best wife, mother, and partner in crime any man could have. She is an invaluable content editor and I could not do this without her! My thanks also go out to: my two awesome kids, my dear mother, my family, my fantastic editors—David Gatewood of Lone Trout Editing, Faith Williams of The Atwater Group, and Karen Lawson and Janet Hitchcock of The Proof is in the Reading. My fabulous proofreader—Charlie Wilson of Landmark Editorial. My fabulous consultant Dianne Jones, Kay Bloomberg, the unbelievably helpful beta readers, including Megan Mason and Michael Muir, and the two best kids in the world.

ABOUT THE AUTHOR

My name is Christopher Greyson, and I am a storyteller.

Since I was a little boy, I have dreamt of what mystery was around the next corner, or what quest lay over the hill. If I couldn't find an adventure, one usually found me, and now I weave those tales into my stories. I am blessed to have written the bestselling Detective Jack Stratton Mystery-Thriller Series. The collection includes *And Then She Was GONE, Girl Jacked, Jack Knifed, Jacks Are Wild, Jack and the Giant Killer, Data Jack, Jack of Hearts, Jack Frost,* with *Jack of Diamonds* due later this year. I have also penned the bestselling psychological thriller, *The Girl Who Lived* and a special collection of mysteries, *The Adventures of Finn and Annie.*

My background is an eclectic mix of degrees in theatre, communications, and computer science. Currently I reside in Massachusetts with my lovely wife and two fantastic children. My wife, Katherine Greyson, who is my chief content editor, is an author of her own romance series, *Everyone Keeps Secrets.*

My love for tales of mystery and adventure began with my grandfather, a decorated World War I hero. I will never forget being introduced to his friend, a WWI pilot who flew across the skies at the same time as the feared, legendary Red Baron. My love of reading and storytelling eventually led me to write *Pure of Heart*, a young adult fantasy that I released in 2014.

I love to hear from my readers. Please visit ChristopherGreyson.com, where you can become a preferred reader and enjoy additional FREE *Adventures of Finn and Annie,* advanced notifications of book releases and more! Thank you for reading my novels. I hope my stories have brightened your day.

Sincerely,